P9-CLP-189

Hanging
by a
Thread

KAREN TEMPLETON

spent her twentysomething years in New York City. Before that, she grew up in Baltimore, then attended North Carolina School of the Arts as a theater major. A RITA® Award-nominated author of seventeen novels, she now lives with her husband, a pair of eccentric cats and four of their five sons in Albuquerque, where she spends an inordinate amount of time picking up stray socks and mourning the loss of long, aimless walks in the rain. Visit her Web site at www.karentempleton.com.

Karen
Templeton

Hanging
by a
Thread

**RED
DRESS
I N K**™

First edition November 2004

HANGING BY A THREAD

A Red Dress Ink novel

ISBN 0-373-25076-2

www.RedDressInk.com

Printed in U.S.A.

This book is dedicated to anyone who's struggling
with seemingly impossible decisions, and to anyone who's
made a few that have come back to haunt you.
I trust Ellie's story will give you hope.
Or if not hope, at least a good laugh.

And to all the folks on the richmondhillny.com message
board...thanks for actually believing I was a writer and not
some weirdo stalker, and double thanks for answering what
I'm sure were some really eye-rolling questions.

chapter 1

Through a jungle of eyelashes, eyes the color of overcooked broccoli assess the image in front of them. Which would be me, a short, pudgy woman in (mostly) men's clothes, clutching a size eight (regular) Versace suit. Scrambled data is transmitted to Judgment Central while a bloodred, polyurethane smile assures me the saleswoman's only reason for living is to serve me. Whatever galaxy I'm from.

"Would you—" eyes dart from me to suit back to me "—like to try this on?"

An understandable reaction, since we both know I've got a better chance of finding Hugh Jackman in my bed than shoving my butt into this skirt.

I lean forward conspiratorially. "It's for my sister," I whisper. "For her birthday. A surprise."

The smile doesn't falter—she's been trained well—but I can't quite read her expression. I'm guessing either pity for my apparently having been dredged from the stagnant end of the gene pool, or—more likely—seething envy that I'm not *her* sister. Not that I would actually buy my own sister an eight-hundred-dollar anything, but still.

"Oh." Smile falters a little. "All right. Will that be a charge?" A discreetly tasteful vision in taupe and charcoal, she leads me to the register, her movement all that keeps her from blending completely into her cave-hued surroundings. Why is it that half the sales floors in this city these days make me want to go spelunking instead of shopping?

"No. Cash," I say, clumping cheerfully behind in my iridescent magenta Jimmy Choo knockoff platform pumps. When we get to the counter, I dig in my grandmother's '70s vintage LV bag for my wallet, from which I coolly extract nine one-hundred-dollar bills and hand them over. I grin, brazenly flashing the dimples.

She cautiously takes the money, as if whatever's tainting it might somehow implicate her, mumbles, "Er, just a minute," then vanishes. To check that it's not counterfeit, maybe. While I'm waiting, my gaze wanders around the sales floor, checking out both the flaccid, shapeless offerings on display and the equally shapeless women—all of whom put together wouldn't make a decent size 6—circling, considering. The air hums with awe and expectancy. Their breathing quickens, their skin flushes: tops, skirts, dresses are plucked from racks, clutched to nonexistent bosoms, ushered into hushed waiting rooms for a hurried, frenzied tryst. For some, there will be an "Oh, God, *yes!*" (perhaps more than once, if they chose well), the heady rush of fulfillment, transient and illusory though it may be. For others (most, in fact), the encounter will prove a letdown—what seemed so alluring, so enticing at first glance fails to meet unrealistic expectations.

But true lust is never fully sated, and hope inevitably supplants disappointment. Which means that soon—the next day, maybe the day after that—the cruising, the searching, the trysts will begin anew.

Thank God, is all I have to say. Otherwise, schnooks like me would starve to death.

My unwitting partner in crime returns, her smile a little less anxious. Apparently I've passed the test. Or at least my money has.

"Would you…like that gift-wrapped?"

"Just a box, thanks."

My conscience twinges, faintly, as I watch her lovingly swathe the suit in at least three trees' worth of tissue paper, laying it tenderly in a box imprinted with the store's logo, as if preparing a loved one for burial. The irony touches me. Minutes later, I'm hoofing it back downtown in a taxi, the suit ignorantly, trustingly huddled against my hip.

The taxi reeks of some oppressively expensive perfume, making my contact lenses pucker, making me almost miss the days when cabs smelled comfortingly of stale cigarettes. Opening the window is not an option, however, since Reykjavik is warmer than it is in Manhattan right now. It's that first week after New Year's, when the city, bereft of holiday decorations, looks like an ugly naked man left shivering in an exam room. I take advantage of a traffic snarl at 50th and Broadway to fish my cell phone out of my purse and call home, half watching swarms of tourists trying to decide whether or not to cross against the light. They're so cute I can't stand it.

"Mama!"

I'm immediately sucked back through time and space, not just to Richmond Hill, Queens, but into another dimension entirely. Instead of feeling connected, I feel oddly *dis*connected, that the woman in this taxi is not the person my daughter hears on the other end of the line. In the background, I hear Mr. Rogers reassuring his tiny viewers about something or other (my throat catches—how could Mr. Rogers *die?*). Guilt spurts through me again, sharper this time; I push the box slightly away, spurning it and everything it connotes, as if Fred Rogers is looking down from Heaven and sorrowfully shaking his head at me.

"Hey, Twink," I say to the little girl who dramatically altered the course of my life half a decade ago. "Whatcha doing?"

You would think I would know by now not to ask leading questions of loquacious, detail-obsessed five-year-olds.

"I got hungry so I fixed myself a peanut butter sandwich," Starr says, "but the bread was totally icky so I had cheese and crackers instead, and a pickle, and then I had to pee, and then you called so now I'm talking to you. Oh, and I saw *the* cutest puppy on TV—" a subject she's managed to wedge into every conversation over the past three months "—and Leo said he'd take me for a walk later, if it's warm enough, and you would not *believe* the loud fight those people behind us had this morning—"

I elbow my way through a comma and say, "That's nice, honey…can I talk to Leo for a sec?"

I hear breathing. Then: "So can we?"

"Can we what?"

Breathing turns into a small, pithy, much-practiced sigh. "Get a puppy."

Considering I want a puppy about as much as I want a lobotomy, I say, "We'll see," because I'm in a taxi and this is using up my free minutes and while I basically know more about nuclear physics than I do about mothering, I do know what kind of reaction "No, we can't" will bring. And I have neither the minutes nor the strength to deal with the ramifications of "no" today.

Of course, the little breather on the other end of the line is a poignant reminder of the ramifications of "yes," but there you are.

"Put Leo on," I say again. Breathing stops, followed by a clunk, followed by heavier, masculine breathing.

"Yes, I'm still alive," are the first words out of my grandfather's mouth.

"Just checking," I say, playing along. Sharing the joke. Except my father's father had a quadruple bypass a few years ago. So the joke's not so funny, maybe. I can hear, immortalized through the magic of reruns, King Friday pontificating about something or other. My grandfather is not immortal, however; there will be no reruns of his life, except in my memory. An unreliable medium, as I well know.

"Just checking?" He chuckles. "Three times, you've called today."

"I worry," I say, sounding like every woman stretching back to Eve. Whose *real* reaction to Adam's nakedness was probably, "For God's sake, put something on, already! You want to catch your death?"

"You shouldn't worry," my grandfather says. "It can kill you."

Black humor is a big thing in my family. A survival tactic, ironically enough. "I'll take that chance."

Another chuckle; I listen carefully for any sign the man might momentarily drop dead. Never mind he's been healthy as a horse since the operation. But at seventy-eight, he's already bucking the family odds. I mean, one glance at my family medical history and the insurance examiner got this look on her face like she half expected me to keel over in front of her.

With good reason. Not only does our family exhibit a propensity for dying young, but without warning. Well, except for my mother. But other than that, it's hale and hearty one minute, gone the next, *boom.* My mother, at forty, from ovarian cancer. My father at fifty-one, massive heart attack. Grandmother, sixty-three, stroke. Assorted aunts, uncles, third cousins— *boom, boom, boom.* Okay, and one *splat,* but Uncle Archie always had been the black sheep in the family.

"Well," my grandfather says, amused, "nothing's changed since lunchtime, I'm fine, the baby's fine, everybody's fine. Except maybe you."

By the way, my graduation present was a burial plot. What can I tell you, the Levines tend to be practical people.

I change the subject. "You fix the Gomezes' leaky faucet?"

My grandfather owns a pair of duplexes. We all live in one, he rents out the two apartments in the other. Sure, they bring in extra cash, but speaking as somebody who finds changing a lightbulb a pain in the butt, I keep thinking he should just sell the place, give over the responsibility to someone else.

"This morning," he says. "Think maybe I'll switch out their refrigerator, too."

"What's wrong with their fridge? It can't be more than, what? Ten years old?"

"It's too small. Especially with the new baby coming."

Which would make their third. Sometimes, I'm surprised Leo even bothers to collect the rent. These aren't tenants, they're family. Not that I don't like the Gomezes—or the Nguyens, in the upstairs apartment—don't get me wrong. Mr. Gomez paints his own apartment, just asks Leo for the paint; and Mrs. Nguyen's window boxes in the summer are the envy of the neighborhood, regular forests of petunias. Besides, the Gomez kids give Starr somebody to play with, on those odd occasions when she's in the mood for other children. It's just…oh, hell, I don't know. I just think he should be free by now, you know?

"Don't worry," he says. "I can sell the old one, it'll be okay."

My brain's slipped a cog. "Old what?"

"Refrigerator."

"Oh." The taxi driver blats his horn, scaring the crap out of me. Nothing moves, however. "Starr says maybe you'll take her for a walk later?"

"I thought maybe. We've been cooped up in this house too long. It's up in the mid-twenties, I'll make sure she's warm, don't worry."

But this time, even as I smile, I realize the knot in my gut isn't anxiety (for once), it's something closer to envy. My grandfather will dress my daughter in her leggings and heavy, puffy coat and mittens and that silly fake fur hat he gave her for Christmas—she will look adorable, very Beatrix Potter— just as he did me when I was her age, and take her on the same walk, up and down the funny little elevated Richmond Hill sidewalks, show her the same things, tell her the same stories. Will she listen as I did? Will she be as enthralled with Leo Levine as I was at her age?

As I still am?

"And I think you should get her that dog," he says, and the sentimental bubble I'd been floating in goes *pfft*. "We could go to the pound on Saturday, let her pick. Something small."

I shudder. "Small dogs are yippy. And neurotic."

"A big dog, then."

"Like either of us wants to pick up a big dog's poop. Anyway, I probably have to work on Saturday," I add, which is the truth.

"Again?"

"You know Market Week's coming up. Nikky needs me."

"Your daughter needs you, too," he says quietly. "So do I, for that matter."

I get this funny, tight feeling in my chest. "Oh, come on— you two do just fine without me."

"That's not the point." I can hear the smile in his voice. "When you're not around, it's like…like ice cream without the chocolate sauce. Nothing wrong with plain ice cream, plain ice cream is fine. But with chocolate sauce, ah…then it's a *party*."

I laugh, which jostles loose the funny feeling, just a little. "Great. Now I'm gonna crave an ice-cream sundae for the rest of the day."

"So. You won't work on Saturday?"

My smile fades. "I'm sorry. I have to."

"What kind of life is this, that you can't spend the whole weekend with your daughter?"

"It's *my* life," I say softly, because what else can I say? "The one where I have to work to support my kid, you know? Like you and Dad did your kids?"

"That was different," he says, with a deep sadness, like a man watching helplessly from the riverbank as floodwaters wash away everything he's known and accepted as real, solid, indestructible.

"Yes, it was." Up ahead, traffic finally jars loose. I skid across the slick seat like a pinball as the cabby swerves into what he perceives to be an opening in the next lane. "We'll talk later," I say, adding, "I'll try to be home by six," before clapping my phone shut and stowing it back in my bag, shoving that part of my existence right in there with it.

I swear, sometimes I feel like Batman, living two lives. Except I'd look totally stupid in that outfit.

We shoot through Times Square and on down Seventh Avenue like a front-runner in the Daytona 500. Something like three seconds later, the taxi screeches to a halt in front of the building that houses Nicole Katz's showroom and offices, way up in the thirtieth floor penthouse.

The cabby nods his thanks at the hefty tip—I'm very generous with other people's money—and I haul myself and the poor unsuspecting garment out of the cab. I can feel the cabby's eyes glued to my backside as I dodge passersby to get to the revolving door. Considering the amount of clothes I have on, the guy must have some imagination, is all I have to say. Considering how long it's been since I've had anything even remotely resembling sex, I'm not even tempted to take offense.

Thirty stories and a major head rush later, the elevator opens directly onto reception. Chinoiserie for days, lots of black lacquer and reds and yellows, don't ask. I'm sure it was cutting edge in 1978. Sprawled across the wall over the reception desk like a row of stoned Bob Fosse dancers, ridiculously large, gleaming gold letters spell out:

Nicole Katz, Ltd.

Valerie, our receptionist since Christmas, is too deeply engrossed in what I assume is a personal phone call (frown line snuggled neatly between her dark brows, liberal use of "Ohmigod!") to acknowledge my return as I pass the desk. Whatever. She's twenty-one. Engaged. Working at Nicole Katz is not exactly her life's goal. A year from now, she will be remembered only as what's-her-name, that brunette receptionist we had a while back, name started with a *V,* maybe? And she will undoubtedly remember me as the short, chunky chick who wore all those strange hats and weird clothes.

Our relationship is based on mutual dismissability.

I yank open one side of the double glass door and walk into the showroom. Which, I observe on a sigh, has been visited in my absence by a small but potent explosive device. Rumpled, discarded samples and fabric swatches obliterate every pseudo-Chinese surface; Joy and leftover cigarette smoke duke it out for air rights. Nikky's personal handiwork, would be my guess. The devastation is even more grotesque in the harsh winter daylight blaring through the wall-to-wall windows overlooking the Hudson.

The woman is a total nutcase, but she's a successful nutcase.

"Where is it, where is it?" I hear the instant the door shooshes closed, cutting off Valerie's next "Ohmig—" Before I can answer, Jock, the draper, lunges at me, snatching the box from my hands with only a glancing leer at my wool-swathed chest. "You got a size 8, right?"

Having done this at least a dozen times in the past year, I do know the drill. "Yes, Jock," I say, yanking off my hat and shrugging out of my father's camel topcoat, then one of his Pierre Cardin suit jackets (both altered to fit me), wedging the lot into the mirrored closet next to the showroom doors. I tug down the hem of one of my mother's Villager sweaters, circa 1968. The dusty rose one with the ivory and blue design across the yoke. Starr has already informed me she wants it when she gets big. We'll see.

My desperately-needs-a-trim layered hair crackles like a miniature electrical storm around my head. My Telly Monster imitation. This does not stop Jock from grabbing me, plastering his (not exactly impressive) crotch against my hip and planting a big, sloppy kiss on my cheek. Then he's off to do what a draper's gotta do. I hope, for his sake, he got more out of our little encounter than I did.

Oh, Giaccomo Andretti's basically harmless, his lothario complex notwithstanding. He's just a bit doughy and married for my taste. And his view of his skills as a draper is a tad skewed. Jock sees himself as a world-class pattern maker. That he hasn't draped an original pattern since Dinkins was mayor is beside the point.

Not that the Versace will be recognizable once its progeny have Nikky's label in them. She's not stupid. The lapel will be wider or narrower or ditched altogether; the skirt will be longer or shorter or slit up the back if this one's slit up the sides; the fabric will be a print if this one's a solid or solid if this one's a stripe, silk instead of linen, a fine wool instead of gabardine.

In other words, this so-called "designer" doesn't have an original idea rattling around underneath her Bucks County Matron silver pageboy. Her "classic" fit is derived from, quite simply, other designers' slopers.

Yep. By three o'clock this afternoon, Jock will have carefully dissected the Versace and traced the pattern from it. By noon tomorrow, Olympia, Jock's best seamstress, will have so carefully reconstructed it no one will ever know it was apart. And by the next morning, I will have returned said suit to the salesgirl, with the sorrowful explanation my sister didn't like it, after all.

And for this I spent four years at FIT.

Divested of my contraband goods, I hie myself to what passes for my office this week—a banquet table crammed into a corner of the bookkeeper's office. Apparently my boss can't quite figure out what I do or where to put me. She only knows she can't do without me. Or so she says. Which is fine by me. Making myself indispensable is what I do best.

And yes, I've asked for an office. Repeatedly. Nikky keeps saying, "You're absolutely right, darling, I've simply got to do something about that…." and then she promptly forgets about it.

Before you ask, "And you're here why?" two words: *Benefits package.*

A stack of new orders awaits me. In Nikky's completely indecipherable handwriting. Of course, even if the woman weren't writing in some ancient Indo-European dialect, since she routinely leaves out things like, oh, sizes and colors…

At least, these seem to be mostly reorders. So in theory, if I look up the stores' original orders, I should be able to figure it out.

In theory.

Long red nails a blur at her calculator, Angelique, the bookkeeper du jour, doesn't even glance over. "Thought you'd like that," she says in her Jamaican accent. Nikki is nothing if not an equal-opportunity employer. In the past three months, we've had one Italian, one Chinese, and two Jewish bookkeepers of various genders and sexual orientations. And now Angelique, who I give two more weeks, tops. Especially as her crankiness indicators have been rising quite nicely over the past few days. It takes a special person to work here. Sane people need not apply.

"Nikky said to tell you Harry needs these ASAP so he can figure out the cutting schedules and get them to the subs."

The subcontractors. Better known as the sweatshops that

permeate the relentlessly drab real estate over on 10th and 11th Avenues, filled with seamstresses who speak a dozen different languages, none of which happen to be English. Skirts that retail for two- four- eight-hundred bucks, cut out by the dozens by powersaws on fifty-foot long cutting tables, stitched together by industrial sewing machines that sound like 747 engines, for which the sub gets a few bucks a skirt. Which is not what the seamstresses get, believe me. But hey—Nikky can say her products are American-made.

Of course, I can't sit at my ersatz desk because my chair is piled with samples dumped there by God-knows-who. So I gather them up—from the current fall line, we're all sick to death of them—and haul them back to the showroom, thinking maybe I should straighten out the showroom before Sally, Nikki's saleswoman, sees it.

"*Je*-sus!"

Too late.

I shoulder my way through the swinging door, my arms full, to be greeted by large, horrified blue eyes. Sally Baines is the epitome of elegant, with her softly waved, ash-blond hair and her restrained makeup. Today our lovely, slim, fiftyish Sally is tastefully attired, as usual, in Nikki's (cough) designs—a creamy silk blouse tucked into a challis skirt in navy and dark green and cranberry paisley, a matching shawl draped artfully over her shoulders and caught with a gold and pearl pin.

"An hour, I was gone." The words are softly spoken, precisely English-accented. "If that. How can she do this much damage in one bloody *hour?*"

This is a rhetorical question.

"Come on," I say, hefting the samples in my arms up onto the rack, then turning to the nearest mangled heap. "I'll help."

I hear the ghosts of anyone who's ever lived with me laughing their heads off. Okay, so I'm not exactly known as the Queen of Tidy.

Just as Sally and I are cleaning up the last of the debris, in this case lipstick-marked coffee cups and full ashtrays, Nikki sweeps in through the doors, swathed in Autumn Haze mink and looking as fresh as three-day-old kuchen. She scans the now-clean room (I'm brought to mind of those insurance commercials where the destruction is undone by running the film backwards), then beams at us as much as the Botox will allow.

"You two are absolute angels," she says, sweeping over to me to give me a one-armed hug. "*Angels.* I would have straightened up myself later, you know that—"

Sally and I avoid looking at each other.

"—but I got stuck at lunch with my attorney and time just got away from me. Did you get the suit? Is Harold here? Did my daughter call?"

"Yes, I don't think so, and not that I know of," I said, wondering why she doesn't ask Vanessa or Virginia or whatever the hell her name is, since, um, she's the one paid to answer the phone?

Harold, by the way, is Nikky's husband. You'll undoubtedly meet him later. Lucky you.

Nikky goes on about whatever it is Nikky goes on about for another thirty seconds or so, then sweeps into the back to assuredly wreak more havoc, leaving a zillion startled molecules in her wake. Ten seconds later, the yelling starts.

So Harold *is* here. He has a teensy office, way in the back (where all good bogeymen live) just large enough for him to run his own business from. And what business might that be, you ask? Okay…picture some Lower East Side bargain emporium, racks and racks of sleazy little tops for $5.99. Those are Harold's. He actually hires a—picture quotation marks drawn in the air—*designer* to crank out these things, which are then produced someplace where monsoons and leeches are taken seriously. We all try to ignore him, but unfortunately he periodically emerges from his lair, snarling and snapping, to fight with his wife and piss me—and everybody else—off. An occupation in which he is apparently presently engaged.

Sally bequeaths me a sympathetic glance as I haul in a breath, close my eyes and reenter the Twilight Zone. However, I think as I return to my cubbyhole and begin logging all those orders onto the computer so I can print out the cutting list so Harry, our production manager, can order fabric and send specs over to the subs, compared to some jobs I could name, this one is downright cushy. There is that medical plan, for one thing. And I tell myself, as I often do, that one must endure a certain amount of indignity on the way to the top, if for no other reason than to be able to enjoy inflicting similar indignities on those underneath you when you get there.

It's all part of some divine plan. Or at least, part of *my* plan. After five agonizing years on salesfloors and in buyer's offices, Seventh Avenue is a major, major step. "Assistant to name designer," the ad had said.

Yeah, well, she has a name all right. But then, so do we all.

Actually, Nicole isn't her real name. My guess is Rivkah Katz didn't quite project the image she was looking for. Not much call for babushkas in the Hamptons. But for all her hard work (cough), for all her stuff isn't cheap (as opposed to her husband's stuff, which redefines the word), you won't find Nicole Katz Designs in Bendel's or Barney's or Bloomie's. You won't find Gwyneth or Renee or Julia sporting her togs. Anna Wintour isn't wetting her pants to get a sneak peek at her fall line.

You will, however, find her clothes tucked away in Better Sportswear in Macy's or L&T or Dayton's, in boutiques catering to well-off women of a certain age. You might catch the broad-stroked sketches splashed across a full page in the *Times* twice a year, showcasing her pretty silk blouses and fine wool skirts; a cashmere twinset; a suit, suspiciously familiar. Pricey enough to be taken seriously by many, but not pricey enough to be taken seriously by those who—supposedly—count. No doubt about it, Nikky Katz is solidly second tier. But she'll never be first tier, never have her clothes mentioned in the same breath as Prada or Klein (either one) or Versace.

The thing is, though, she's in a damn good position for someone whose talent is limited to sticking with the tried-and-true. And for knowing which designs to knock off. Hey—the woman's raking it in hand over fist, producing a stable product that continues to sell by dint of its *not* being subject to the whims of the rich, bored twenty-somethings that fuel the upper echelons of the fashion industry. Her customers depend on her to give them what works, and in twenty years, she hadn't disappointed them yet.

All in all, not a bad gig. Especially as she's all but invisible, way up here in her snug little niche, her customers clinging to her like bees to a hive. Neither the big designers nor the young and hungry newbies want her market share. Ergo, in one of the most fatuous, unpredictable, unstable industries in the world, Nikky Katz's business is as solid and safe as Fort Knox.

Which is why she's my idol.

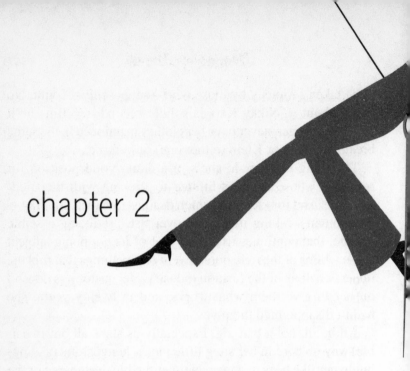

chapter 2

Now before you say, "You are one totally sick puppy," hear me out.

God knows, I don't emulate the woman personally. But you better believe I admire her success. And I count myself blessed for the chance to suck every bit of knowledge about the biz out of her. Because while I may be totally over the moon about fashion, I can't design my way out of a paper bag any more than she can. And I figure, hey, if Nikky Katz can make it, then there's hope for me.

Granted, I've known how to sew since I was five. I can make up anything from a pattern, and I'm a magician at alterations, if I say so myself. I can rework and adapt with the best of 'em. But let me tell you, I've got more filled sketchbooks than you can possibly imagine crammed in my closet at home, without a single creative, original, hot idea among them. In fact, my design teachers at FIT kindly suggested I switch to merchandising, because I was wasting their time and my money otherwise.

So, yep, forget the designing. Somebody else can design…and I'll do the marketing. Because that, I *am* good at. Yeah, I know, most people would consider drawing the pretty pictures and playing with the fabrics the "fun stuff." But see, it's the whole philosophy of fashion that fascinates me so much: whatever it is that drives people—women, primarily—to wear what they wear. How we *costume* ourselves, choosing each article of clothing, each accessory, to telegraph to the world who we are. Or who we think we are. Or, in many cases, who we'd like to be. Even the most casually donned attire says something, if nothing other than that the wearer doesn't give a damn.

For me, the rush doesn't come from designing a garment, but from figuring out why it appeals. I mean, that scene back at the store? Honey, watching all those women get worked up got *me* worked up. Like fashion porn. And I got a real early start—not to mention all the cute shoes I wanted—hanging out at my family's shoe store in Queens when I was a kid. I learned early on that the relationship between a woman and what she chooses to put on her body is a sacred thing. And I knew I had to be part of it, even if I was woefully untalented.

So. Working for Nikky Katz is my dream job, for the moment. And until she figures out what to do with me, I get to do a little bit of everything. I can deal with a little yelling, a little craziness, now and then if it helps me reach my goal….

The phone rings on Angelique's desk. She answers it, says, "It's for you."

One day maybe I'll have my own desk with my own extension.

One day maybe I'll be able to get a phone call without my heart clogging my throat.

But it's nothing scary, only Tina, my best friend since she, her mother and two older sisters moved across the street from us when I was five. Tina's married to my other best friend, Luke Scardinare. His family—he's one of six brothers—and mine have lived next door to each other my whole life. Luke used to make my life miserable on a regular basis and I'd kill with my bare hands anybody who even thinks about badmouthing him. Which is the same way I feel about Tina, even though she didn't make my life miserable on a regular basis.

I realize she's asking if we can meet up at Pinky's, a bar a couple blocks from where I live. "I need to talk," she says, her voice giving nothing away, which is unusual for Tina because usually her voice gives *everything* away. Twelve years ago she says to me, "Does this lipstick make me look slutty?" and I instantly knew she and Luke had done it for the first time.

"Sure, okay. What's up?"

"I'll tell you when I see you. Seven okay?"

"Eight, eight-fifteen would be better." Her Queens accent calls to mine, buried deep beneath the Manhattan persona I apply like makeup every morning. "I gotta read to Starr at seven."

"Couldn't you skip it, just this once?"

Tina and Luke don't have kids, even though they've been married for five years already. They don't talk about it, and I don't pry, but I know Luke's mother, Frances, wonders. Tina's mother is blessedly no longer close enough to inflict direct damage. Although my guess is Tina and her sisters will be mopping up the fallout from their childhood for some time. On the outside, Tina's your typical smartmouthed Outerborough Broad; on the inside, thanks to Dear Old Mom, she's a tangled mass of insecurities.

"No, I can't skip it, I promised her this morning."

There's a tiny pause, like when a reporter halfway around the world doesn't answer the New York anchor's question right away. "Okay, fine," she says on a sigh, and hangs up. I'm tempted to feel guilty, until I realize if it was that important I would have heard it in her voice. Or she would have been sobbing and incoherent, like she was that time Luke and she broke up their senior year. Of course, they were back together before the weekend was out, although not before Tina had gone through three boxes of tissues and two pans of brownies. Not a fun weekend. Well, except for the brownies, which she shared.

Before I have a chance to cancel my guilt trip, I get another call. Angelique hands it over. Judging from her expression, I'm guessing she's finding this an interesting way to break the afternoon's tedium.

It's Luke this time. "You gonna be home tonight? I need to talk."

Gee—you don't suppose these two calls are related, do you? And why, out of the approximately eight million relatives these two have between them, do they pick me to help them sort through whatever it is this time?

Because they always have, that's why. Because they know they can trust me.

I'm quiet for too long, I guess, because Luke says, "Shit— Tina already called you, huh?"

And the cornerstone of my trustworthiness? An ironclad policy of not lying. Unless I absolutely have to. "Uh…yeah. She did."

That gets another "Shit" and a very heavy sigh. Then: "She say anything?"

"No."

"You sure?"

"Yeah, I'm sure," I say, thinking even admitting her wanting to talk is probably a confidence violation. However, telling him we're meeting up at Pinky's definitely is. I can't help it, I've always been protective of Tina. Probably more than is good for her, I know, but I can't help it. Although my wanting to shield her from life's doo-doo is nothing compared to how Luke treats her. The term "spun glass" comes to mind.

"Hey," I say. "What's going on?"

"Gotta go, I'll talk to you later."

And *he* hangs up.

Luke and Tina. My very own reality show. With extra cheese.

"He sounds sexy," Angelique says after I hand back the phone.

Sexy? Luke? Yeah, I suppose. In that heavy-lidded Italian thug kind of way. Not that Luke's a thug, but put him in tight jeans and a T-shirt, dangle a cigarette from his lips, put lifts in his shoes, and you got it.

"Married friend."

"How married?"

"Very. Five years. To the woman who called earlier, in fact. They're nuts about each other, have been since ninth grade."

"Huh." Some keys click. "Bet that voice sounds even better in the dark."

She may have a point. However, as I've been listening to Luke since we were communicating in monosyllables and grabbing our Gerber teething biscuits out of each other's hands, I can't say as his voice has made much of an impression on me. Okay, maybe once or twice, in a weak, deluded moment, but not for a long time.

A very long time.

"He's a plumber," I say, don't ask me why. "Well, plumbing contractor. Works for his father."

"Hey. Plumbers make good money. And they'll never be out of work."

This is true. "But he's married," I repeat, realizing this is the first real conversation Angelique and I have ever had. And possibly the last, if I win the how-long's-she-gonna-last pool. "To my best friend."

After more paper shuffling and clicking, Angelique says, "So. You have a boyfriend?"

I don't have the time or energy to deal with a puppy, what on earth would I do with a boyfriend? This, however, doesn't stop images from springing to mind. Involving things one might do with boyfriends and various appendages attached thereto. I quickly, if regretfully, push the images away.

"Not at the moment. My old one broke and I never got around to replacing him." I then add, tempted to look around furtively and lower my voice, "I have a daughter, though."

Her dark eyes light up. "Me, too! How old is yours?"

"Five going on forty. Her birthday was a couple of days ago."

"You got a picture?"

Do I have a picture, is the woman nuts? Like CIA operatives in a clandestine meeting, we drag out our wallets and compare children. I compliment Angelique on hers, already a knockout at seven. But let's be honest here, Starr is going through what I hope to hell is an awkward phase. God knows, nobody's going to mistake me for Catherine Zeta-Jones— even at her most pregnant—but my baby's skinny, she's near-sighted (like her mama), she's got all this frizzy black hair (like her Great-Gran Judith)…poor thing looks like a myopic johnny mop.

"She looks very…sweet," Angelique says at last.

Sweet is not the word I'd choose to describe Starr, but my heart cramps anyway because I'm crazy in love with her. Even if she totally freaks me out at times. "Thanks," I say softly.

It's kinda nice, being able to talk about my kid at work. Not something I ever thought about when I was *really* single. I mean, please—is "single mother" an oxymoron or what? "Single" implies "alone," and God knows, the one thing you're not once you've got a kid is alone. Anyway, it's not as if nobody knows about Starr, it's just that women who aren't mothers aren't real interested in hearing about your kids. Not that I blame them. If you're not living it, it's kinda hard to understand the excitement generated by that first dump in the toilet. Still. It gets old, pretending your children basically don't exist while you're at work. As if they're houseplants or something. Because, you know, we couldn't *possibly* be a hundred percent focused on our work if we're also worrying about our kids. Never mind that some of us can actually do two things at once. And do them well, to boot.

Nikky suddenly bursts into the office, a frantic expression overriding the Botox. "Ellie! Darling! Come quick! You have to help me!"

Exclamation points whiz past my ears. "Sure, I'll be there in a sec, right after I get this cutting list done—"

"No! This can't wait! The Volare rep just called and said the company's discontinued the floral print! Which means I have to pick a substitute! And I've got stores expecting those sundresses in six weeks!"

Even I can see there's no turning off the panic button until the crisis has been resolved. Now, you might ask (understandably enough) why the woman can't just pick a substitute fabric and be done with it. Well, there are several reasons, number one being—as you may have noticed—Nikky's brain shuts down in a crisis. Two, since several hundred thousand dollars' worth of orders are riding on this particular item, the substitute fabric has to be chosen very carefully. And three—and this is something almost no one else knows—Nikky is color-blind.

Yes, it's very rare in women. And she only has trouble distinguishing greens, which is why you'll never see any green items in her line. But she wanted a bold rose print for this particular model, and roses have leaves, and leaves are green (at least, they were in this print), so she had to rely on someone else to "see" the green for her and make sure it wasn't some ugly baby poop color or something. But I'd really like to get home on time tonight, which means I could do without the handholding routine. However, if I don't help her, Harold will get involved, and God knows—

"Problem, Nik?"

—nobody wants that.

Nikky schools her features before turning to her husband. "Nothing, just a little detail I need to work out with Ellie."

Droopy-lidded eyes give me the once-over; it's like being scrutinized by a jowly Kermit. Sparse strands of no-color hair cling to his liver-spotted scalp like drowning men to a life raft; underneath a white dress shirt and pleated suit pants quivers a large, amorphous body. I practically have to pin my finger to my lip to keep it from curling.

"It's that goddamn Volare, isn't it? I heard on the extension—"

A real jewel, this guy.

"—they pull a fast one on you, what?"

"They didn't pull a 'fast one,' Harold," Nikky says wearily, "they just discontinued the fabric for one of the items, it's no big deal—"

"Goddammit, Nikky, what the hell's the matter with you? I *told* you to dump those shysters, didn't I? Right? Didn't I tell you that, after the last time they pulled this shit? How many times you gonna let those sons of bitches do this to you before you find the balls to take your business elsewhere?"

"Oh, get over it, Harold!" Nikky crosses her arms and meets his gaze dead-on. When push comes to shove, she can stand up to him, I'll give her that. But at what price? "I'm not going to destroy a twenty-year relationship simply because they canceled a fabric on me!"

"Why do you let these sons of bitches screw you to the wall over and over, Nikky? Why? I mean, Jesus—when're you gonna stop acting like a woman and start acting like a businessperson?"

Silently, she stares him down for several seconds, then turns to me. "Come on, Ellie—"

"You stay right there," Harold orders, jabbing a finger first at me, then his wife. "You're gonna get on that phone, and you're gonna tell those sons of bitches they will honor that order or that's the last one you'll ever place with them! Or better yet, maybe I'll let Myron give 'em a goose, let 'em know they can't get away with this shit—"

"You even *think* about calling the lawyer and you're a dead man! This isn't your business, Harold Katz, it's mine! And I will run it as I see fit!"

"Right into the ground, the way you're going! And since I sank every dime I had into this harebrained scheme of yours, I'll stick my nose in whenever I damn well like!"

By this point, I half expect to see the hair raised on the back of her neck. Mine sure as hell is. And you should see Angelique's eyes.

"And since I paid you back—three-fold—since then," Nikky says, barely above a snarl, "butt the hell out." Her gaze deliberately shifts to mine. "Ellie?"

I rise and follow, managing not to go "Ew, ew, ew" when I have to brush past the man. Who watches us, his little amphibianesque eyes burning a hole in the back of my head, before I eventually hear his footsteps retreat to his office.

How—*why*—the woman puts up with the man is beyond me.

Especially as I notice, when we reach her office, how shiny her eyes are.

I never know whether I should say anything or not, whether she'd welcome my sympathy or spurn it. Pride's an unpredictable thing. But while Nikky might be addle-brained and totally disorganized, at heart she's not a bad person. Medical plan or no, I wouldn't still be here after a year if she was. And nobody deserves to be talked to like that. Ever. Well, except Harold. Or your average despotic dictator.

Then she pulls the substitute swatches out of the FedEx envelope with shaking hands, and my conscience shoves me from behind.

"Nikky, I—"

But she shakes her head, cutting me off.

"I don't…" She clears her throat, then smoothes her hand over the polished cotton. The roses are similar to the original, if a bit smaller and redder. But the green is this yucky olive that brings to mind things nasty and distasteful. "I don't think this one's too bad, what do you think?"

"I think…" Oh, hell. "I think you should call the rep and tell him you're holding them to the original contract. Or you'll sue."

Nikky's head jerks up, the ends of her silver hair brushing her silk-clad shoulders. In her own, paralyzed way, she looks as flabbergasted as I feel.

"You agree with Harold?"

Since I'd always figured I'd have a better chance of agreeing with Rush Limbaugh than Harold Katz, you can image what this revelation is doing to my insides. "I think he…has a point. Even if I do have issues with how he makes his points."

That gets a short, airy laugh. "You don't have to be so diplomatic."

"Yes, I do. I need this job."

Another laugh, this one with a little more substance to it. Nikky sinks into her chair, a high-backed swivel number in a gorgeous flame stitch fabric. She twists the cap off a bottle of designer water, then digs a pill box out of her purse. Hell, if I had to live with Harold, I'd probably be scarfing down whatever the la-la drug of choice is these days like M&M's.

She takes another swallow of water and replaces the cap. "Why?" she says, all smiles. Wow. Must be good stuff. "Why do you agree with Harold?"

"Because—" I pick up the substitute swatch. "Because this is total crap compared with the original. Because something tells me they *are* pulling a fast one. I mean, think about it—

why should they yank the pattern when you've got how many hundreds of yards on order? Unless—"

"Unless a bigger designer saw it and pulled rank. So they're only *telling* me it's no longer available. I have figured that out."

She doesn't seem particularly surprised. Or disturbed. I, however, am both. Her lips curved at my obvious distress, she gestures for me to sit, then takes a cigarette case from her desk; five seconds later she's calmly blowing smoke away from me. "Darling, in the scheme of things, six hundred yards is nothing. Especially if another house comes along and orders twice, maybe even ten times that. I don't know...." A stream of smoke cuts through the air. "I can't really blame the supplier for wanting to make the other guy happy, right?"

"But you've been a loyal customer for twenty years...."

"Because they're willing to work with me and my smaller orders." She leans forward. "Sure, there are other fabric houses I'd rather use. You think they'd give me the time of day?" The cigarette smoke stream jumps as she sinks back against the chair. Frowning, she brushes an ash off her left breast, then looks at me. "I've got more clout than some, less than others." A shrug. "You learn to compromise. Pick your battles. Contrary to what Harold thinks, pitching a fit isn't going to endear me to them. Or keep me in business."

"So you just...back down?"

"I prefer to call it playing smart. However..." Her fingers brush the fabric, then shove it away, as though it's toxic. "I may be second best, but I'm not stupid enough to pick something that's gonna make *my* dress look like the knockoff—"

Somehow, I manage to keep a straight face.

"—so we start over." Squinting, she crams the cigarette back in her mouth and says around it, gesturing toward the teetering piles on the long table over against the far wall, "Hand me the Volare book, wouldja? Let's see what we can come up with."

I do, but as I root through the rubble, I have to ask, "But isn't it a little late to switch fabric on the stores now?"

"Like they care. You find it yet?"

I have, miraculously enough. I hand it to Nikky, who thunks it onto a six-inch pile of jumbled papers. Where they'd come from, I have no idea, since I'd just straightened up yesterday. "So," Nikky says, the cigarette dangling from her lips, pool-shark fashion, "We chuck the roses altogether and go with…" She flips through the book. "A plaid, maybe? Or something completely different, like…" With a grin, she turns the book around, yanking the cigarette out of her mouth with a flourish. "Hats. These are cute, right? Is there any green in it?"

I shake my head. She grins.

"Yeah, hats. It's brilliant." With a wink, she grabs her phone and punches a single digit. Ten seconds later she's going, "Lenny! Nikky. How are you? Good, good… Listen. Here's the deal. Forget the roses…yeah, yeah, I don't like this sample you sent over, it's very Target, you know what I mean? So instead, send me swatches of…" She randomly flips through the book, rattling off a dozen numbers. Then, as if she couldn't be bothered, "And this cotton with the hats…number 2376, just for the hell of it. They all available? You're sure? Great. And I can have the swatches tomorrow?" She gives me a thumbs-up. "You're a doll, Len. Take it easy, now."

She hangs up, stubs out her cigarette, and smiles at me.

"I don't get it," I say.

A low laugh rumbles from her throat. "I know everybody thinks I'm a ditz. Including you, you're just nicer about it than most. But let me tell you something…" Again, she leans forward, and I see in her eyes exactly why she is where she is. "People let their guard down if they think you're stupid. Then *they're* the ones who do the stupid stuff, you know what I mean? Lenny has no idea which of these I'm really interested in. And by the time I clue him in, it'll be too late for anybody else to get one up on me again. And I think I like the hats better, anyway."

I think she's kidding herself. But hey, not my business.

"Anyway, so when the swatch comes, you'll scan it and send it to the buyers, tell them the other fabric came in flawed and this is what we're switching to, and that'll be that—"

Her eyes lift over my head, to her office doorway. The hair on the back of my arms bristles.

"Problem solved?" Harold asks.

"Yes, Harold," she says, then adds, "By the way, Marilyn left a message on my voice mail, said seven was fine, she'd meet us at the restaurant."

"How'd she sound?"

"Who can tell over voice mail?" Nikky says with a shrug. But her mouth thins in concern. "In a rush, though. As usual."

"She gets that from you, you know. Never knowing when to stop."

That's okay, folks, don't mind me.

"Mar's a big girl, Harold. She doesn't need Daddy clucking over her like some Jewish mother."

"Yeah, well, maybe if the Jewish mother she's got was doing her job, I wouldn't have to," he says, then walks away.

I get up, making noises about getting back to my work so I can leave on time tonight—

"He would die if I left him," Nikky says softly.

"Um…what?"

"I know what you're thinking. That you can't understand why I put up with his crap. Well, I put up with his crap because he needs me. And what can I tell you, it feels good to be needed."

Okay, fine, I can buy that. To a point. Otherwise, how could I constantly deal with Tina and Luke's string of crises? Why would I be *here,* for God's sake? But there's a difference between being needed and getting off on self-flagellation. And before I realize it's coming, I hear myself say, "But the way you let him yell at you—"

"That's right. I *let* him yell at me. Because I make the money and I bought the house in Bucks County and I'm paying for our daughter to go to NYU and yelling at me is the only way he can still feel like the protector."

Right. A protector who constantly tears down the person he's supposed to be protecting? I'm sorry, but this is seriously not working for me.

"Oh, ditch the outraged expression, Ellie," Nikky says with a gravelly laugh. "It's all…posturing. He's never laid a finger on me. And he did put everything he had in this business when I started out. Everything. If I live to be a hundred, I will always owe him for that." Then she looks at me, hard, like a teacher awaiting my response on an oral exam.

"So…you're happy?"

Her laugh startles me. "God, you're so young," she says, and probably would have said more if her phone hadn't rung just then. Grateful for the interruption, I scurry out of her office and back to my cubby-of-the-week, wondering how fast I can get my work done, wondering what's up with Tina and Luke, wondering why a woman like Nikky Katz would be so willing to settle for…whatever it is she's settling for.

And thanking my lucky stars I'm not like that.

chapter 3

The bad news is, it takes me nearly an hour to make the trek on the A train from midtown Manhattan to Richmond Hill. The good news is, our house is only a few blocks from the subway stop. And it's at the end of the line, so if I pass out—which has happened more than once—the conductor usually gives me a poke to make sure I get off.

Except for a few months, I have lived my entire life in this neighborhood. I don't hate it, exactly, but the place is like quicksand. The harder you fight to get out, the more it sucks you back in. I've watched too many of my friends from high school settle into virtually the same lives as their parents had, even if they moved to another neighborhood, to Ozone Park or Forest Hills or Jamaica. Not that there's anything wrong with that, as long as you're sure that's what you want.

I don't.

And yet my entire body betrays me, sighing with relief the

minute I set foot on Lefferts Boulevard. For good or ill, this is home, has been my entire life, and there's something to be said for leaving the stresses of the city behind on the train. I can almost hear them, banging and howling as the train pulls away on the elevated tracks overhead.

I breathe in the bitterly cold, damp air as I clomp along, my toes freezing in these damn shoes (you will rarely find me in flats—without heels, I look like I'm standing in a hole). Pushing out a crystallized sigh, I pass the duplexes that were pretty much all single family homes when I was a kid, now almost all turned into apartments. Cooking smells accost me as I walk, cruelly taunting my empty stomach—East Indian, Caribbean, Asian stir-fries, the occasional whiff of something solidly middle European. We live near the end of the block, our pair of semidetached houses the same baby blue with white trim as they have been ever since I can remember. Twin front yards flank identical stoops, each just about big enough for ten blades of grass and a tub of marigolds or impatiens in the summer, although the Nyugens installed a small, gurgling fountain on their side last summer. We have a garage, in which resides a 1979 Buick LeSabre that my grandfather drives maybe three times a year, that I drive when there's absolutely no way I can avoid it.

After my grandfather returned from the Korean War, when my father was six, he used a VA loan to buy the half that Leo, Starr and I live in now. When the Goodmans next door decided to move to Jersey in '73, Nana and Leo bought the other side for my parents and sister, who was then a year old. The rationale was, since my father and grandfather were now partners in the shoe store over on Atlantic Avenue, why not live close to each other, too? I've often wondered how my mother felt about this arrangement, especially as she and my grandmother did not get along. Of course, my grandmother never got along particularly well with anybody, save for maybe my sister.

I pass Mrs. Patel's, across the street and a couple houses

down from mine, trying to remember when she first put up the plastic flamingo. Junior High, I think. Brightly illuminated by a pair of spotlights, he leans rakishly in her speck of a yard, still dressed in his Santa Claus hat.

The windows in both of our houses are lit up; a muted salsa beat throbs from the Gomez apartment, from what had been our living room when I still lived there. My gaze shifts to the other side, where I live now with my daughter and grandfather. And out of nowhere the thought comes, *What if you never leave this house? What if you end up marking every season for the rest of your life by whatever outfit Mrs. Patel's flamingo is wearing?*

My blood runs cold. Home is all well and good, but your *childhood* home is someplace you're supposed to be able to come back and visit, not rot in—

"Hey, you! You forget where you live or what?"

That's Frances. Scardinare. Luke's mother. Figures she'd get home the same time as me. Not that I don't love Frances, but sometimes there just isn't room in your head for anybody else.

But I smile anyway. Between Mrs. Patel's spotlights and these damn halogens, the street's lit up practically like it's daytime. "Just trying to figure out if I've got the energy to haul my butt up these stairs, that's all."

"I know what you mean." Frances passes her own stoop, her long, thin arms weighted down with several grocery bags. Let me tell you, when I hit my late fifties? I should look half as good as Frances does. Not that I will, considering she's a good head taller than I am and has all this incredible bone structure. And *legs.* Even after six kids, she's still a size ten. Without dieting. And since she started earning her own money selling real estate a couple years ago, she dresses well. Has her hair done at Reggio's once a month, too, this really flattering, layered style that sets off her big eyes and high cheekbones. And somehow, it stays looking good between cuts. Me, my hair already looks like it's growing out by the time I've tipped the shampoo girl.

Still clutching the bags, Frances holds out one arm for a hug, her wide mouth splayed in a huge grin. My heart does a little skip: when my mother died and my grandmother didn't seem any too hot on the idea of filling the gap in my life, Frances did, like a mother cat taking on an extra kitten. The woman scares the snot out of me, but I would not have survived my teenage years without her. Or at least, I doubt anyone else would have.

She lets go, a frigid breeze toying with her dark hair. "Did you hear? Petie and Heather are finally getting married!"

Pete's—nobody, but nobody besides Frances can get away with calling him "Petie"—the brother after Luke, a year younger. Heather Abruzzo was three years behind me, I think, but her older sister Joanne used to hang out with Tina and me from time to time when we were teenagers. "No! When?"

"June, when else—?"

My front door pops open; with an affronted, "Geez, *finally!*" my daughter shoots out of the house and down the steps to the icy sidewalk, fusing to my hip. I hug her back, noticing she's in her nightgown and Elmo slippers.

"Get back inside, you'll catch your death!"

Through her glasses, reproachful, and slightly pitying, brown eyes roll up to meet mine. "You don't catch colds from the cold. You catch 'em from *germs.*"

I do know this, actually. But it's unnerving hearing it from someone who's still short enough to ride the bus for free.

"Maybe so." I scoop her up into my arms—it's like picking up a dust bunny, she's so light—and kiss her on her cold, freckled little nose. I want to eat her up, even as the thought that we're stuck with each other forever still gives me pause. "But you could get frostbite," I say, "and that would be a lot worse, 'cause then your toes'd fall off."

That gets a considering look. I can tell she doesn't quite believe it, but is this really a chance she wants to take?

"Go back inside, Twink," I say, putting her down, feeling like a fraud, wondering if I'd feel less like one if she'd been planned. If I could tell her the truth about her father. If I *knew* the truth about her father. "I'll be up in just a minute, I promise."

"Swear?"

"Swear."

She trudges back up the stairs, a tiny, shivering figure in flowery flannel, only to turn and threaten me: If I'm not inside by the time the big hand's moved to the next number, she's coming to get me.

After the door closes, Frances laughs. Then she says, "You're getting home kind of late, aren't you?"

"It's not seven yet," I say, but she gives me this reproving stare, her mouth all screwed up, then sighs.

"You work too hard."

"And you don't?"

"My kids are grown. Or nearly." Her five oldest sons are out of the house; the youngest, Jason, is seventeen and probably wishes he was. "It doesn't matter if I'm not there to cook their dinner." I laugh, and she rolls her huge, almost black eyes. "Okay, so maybe I never did cook their dinner, but at least I was there. And speaking of dinner—" she shifts her bags to one hand, flexing the fingers on the other "—we're going up to Salerno's, you and Leo and the baby should come with us. Our treat."

Frances and Jimmy are always like this, wanting to take us to dinner, their treat. Of course, my grandfather is just as bad, which gets to be a major headache when he and Jimmy start fighting over the bill.

"Starr's already in her jammies."

"So she'll get dressed again. It's barely seven. What's the big deal?"

"Leo did brisket."

"Which is always better the next day, right? So come on, you look like you could do with a night out. And if you're there, we might even be able to enjoy our meal without looking at Jason's sulky face all night."

An understatement if ever there was one. My needing a night out, I mean, although I know what she means about Jason's sulking, too. Poor kid. Adolescence has hit him harder than all his brothers combined. Not that the Scardinare testosterone surges didn't terrorize the neighborhood for several years—there was an eight- or ten-year period when there were at least four teenagers in the house at any given time—but I guess it's harder on Jason, being the baby and not having his older brothers around all that much. He's like a walking David Lynch movie—very dark, very weird, with lots of incomprehensible erotic undertones. If I hadn't baby-sat for him when he was little, he'd probably creep me out.

To further complicate things, I think he has a crush on me. He's over here constantly when I'm not at work, following me around, his big moony eyes peering out at me through his straggly black bangs, like prisoners who've lost all hope. Think Nicholas Cage in *Moonstruck,* then multiply by ten. And like Cher, I want to smack the poor kid and yell "Snap out of it!"

But I don't have the heart.

Then I remember, with a sickening thud, the main reason, or reasons, I can't leave the house tonight: Tina. Whom I'm supposed to meet in a little over an hour.

"Mama!" Starr's shrill little voice darts out from the doorway. Her hands are on her hips. "The big hand's moved past *two* numbers! That's *ten minutes!*"

"Another time," I say to Frances.

She sighs and shakes her head, then turns toward her house, shouting, "Dinner, here, Sunday, Heather wants to show off her ring," over her shoulder as she goes.

And I head up the stairs, wondering how somebody with no discernible personal life can have so many demands on her time.

* * *

An hour later, I'm by the front door, slipping my father's coat over an outfit more appropriate to Pinky's—Levi's, slouch boots (with heels that could double as shishkebob skewers), a dark red vintage mohair sweater I found on eBay for ten bucks. I don't know why I prefer older clothes to new, other than the obvious fact that I can't afford to buy new. Nor do I know anybody who can. I mean, I read *Vogue* and think, *chyeah,* right. Not that I don't think some of the stuff is seriously hot, but Jesus. Even if I weren't a foot too short to wear any of it, by the time I could afford it, I'd be so old I'd look like a freak in it, anyway. I mean, two grand for a fringed skirt shorter than something I'd let my five-year-old wear? Please. And let's not go anywhere near the six- or eight- or fifteen-hundred-dollar handbags. You're supposed to be afraid that somebody might steal what's *in* your purse, not the purse itself. Or am I missing something here?

So I wear old, cheap and/or free stuff. Mind you, having never harbored a secret desire to look like a bag lady, it's old, *good-looking* cheap and/or free stuff. I do have, if I say so myself, a certain flair. For the ridiculous, perhaps, but at least nobody can accuse me of looking like everybody else.

Or around here, like *anybody* else. Sorry, but I don't do big hair.

*Any*way…by the time I read Starr the next chapter of *Through the Looking Glass*—interrupted a billion times by her pointing out words she recognized—and did two thorough monster sweeps of her room (there's a big hairy purple one with a snotty nose and "sticky-outty" teeth who's been a real pain in the butt lately) and tucked her in, it's too late to eat, and my stomach is pitching five fits.

My grandfather, who's been vacuuming the downstairs rooms, glances up from winding the cord into a precise figure eight, over and over, around the upright's handles. It drives me nuts when I use the machine after he does. I keep telling him, it takes twice as long to do it this way, why not just loop it around the handles and be done with it? All that matters is that it's up and out of the way, right? But he insists it's neater the way he does it, that's the trouble with the world these days, nobody takes the time to do anything carefully.

"You're going out?" he says, hauling the Eureka out of the room.

"Yeah." I cram an angora beret over my hair, yelling out, "Just to Pinky's for a bit. Tina asked me to meet her there."

Leo returns, plopping down into his favorite armchair and picking up the Nintendo controller. A second later, one of the Mario Brothers games blooms on the TV screen. The game system's a hand-me-down from some Scardinare brother or other. Leo plays for hours, insisting it keeps his reflexes fine-tuned. "What's up with her?"

"Couldn't tell ya."

He pauses the game to give me a more considering look, although I can't really see his eyes through the sofa lamp's glare off his glasses. But I can sure feel it. You have to understand, my grandfather is by no means some shriveled, sunken little old man. Still more than six feet tall, with a ramrod posture he expects everyone around him to emulate, even seated he's an imposing figure. Age-loosened skin drapes gracefully around features too broad, too crude, to be called handsome, as though the sculptor had been in too much of a hurry to do much more than get the basics down. If he chose to be mean, he would be frightening. As it is, no mugger in his right mind would dare mess with him. Ironic considering that nobody's a softer touch than Leo. I don't dare take him into Manhattan—he'd be broke before he'd been off the train ten minutes, giving everything away to every panhandler he saw.

"Did you eat?"

"When I get back, I promise." I cross the thickly-piled Ori-

ental—in mostly blues and dark reds, to match the overstuffed
Ethan Allen furniture my grandmother bought the year before
she died—bending down to give him a kiss on his scratchy
cheek. Heat purrs soothingly through the registers; the house
smells like brisket and freshly washed clothes (there's a bas-
ketful on the sofa, waiting for me to fold) and my grandfather's
spicy aftershave, and all I want to do is crash in my bedroom
with a slab of meat large enough to feed Cleveland and watch
one of my Jimmy Stewart movies. But instead I'm dragging
my hungry, exhausted carcass back out into the bitter cold, because my friend needs me. Because I know Tina would do the
same for me.

And has, I think as I hike to the bar, braced against the wind.

I mean, there was that time a couple years ago when we all
came down with the flu—I'm talking near-death experience
here, not your run-of-the-mill chills and fever crap—when
Tina, despite an aversion to illness bordering on the obsessive,
basically moved in, force-feeding the lot of us Lipton's chicken
noodle soup and ginger ale for two days and disposing of
mountains of tissues like the Department of Sanitation clearing the streets after a blizzard.

Or going back even further, to when we were fourteen and
had lied to our families about going to Angie Mason's for a
sleepover. Instead we went to this party at Ryan O'Donnell's
(remind me to *never* believe anything my teenage child tells
me, ever), where I, being basically stupid and having zip tolerance for alcohol, got so drunk I wanted to die. And Tina, who
even then could hold her booze like a three-hundred pound
sailor, and who also knew if I went home in that condition, I
would die, hauled me into the john and forced me to puke,
made coffee in Ryan's kitchen, sat there with me while I drank
it, and got me home, shaky but sober, by curfew.

She was also there, at her insistence, when I told Dad and
Leo I was going to have a baby.

I push open the heavy wooden door to Pinky's; hops-saturated steam heat rushes out to greet me like long-lost relatives, defrosting my contacts. Like most neighborhood bars, the decor runs primarily to neon beer signs, dark wood and linoleum. At eight on a weeknight, the place is nearly empty—two or three guys at the bar, staring morosely at the rows of bottles lined up in front of the mirror; a couple talking softly at one of the small tables in the center of the floor. As Madonna yodels from the not exactly au courant jukebox, I take off my hat and gloves, shoving them in my coat pockets as I blink, willing my eyes to adjust to the dim, albeit smoke-free these days, light.

"Hey, Ellie, how's it goin'?"

My gaze sidles over to Jose, wiping down the bar. A year or so older than me, Jose's been the night bartender here for the past couple of years. He's got this whole pit bull thing going. Solid, you know? Not necessarily looking for a fight but up for one should the occasion present itself. In the summer, when he's wearing a T-shirt, the tattoos are nothing if not impressive. The man on the stool closest to me bestirs himself long enough to give me the once-over. I give him a withering look, then pop out the dimples for Jose.

"Pretty good," I say, then ask about his wife and kids—they're doin' okay, thanks, he says—then I ask if he's seen Tina.

"Yeah, she came in a while ago. In the back. She looks like shit."

Hey. If you're looking for diplomacy, steer clear of Pinky's.

I spot her in the booth farthest in the back, waving, so I grab a bowl of pretzels off the bar and head in her direction. Except the woman sitting at the table turns out to be Lisa Lamar, who sat next to me in half my classes all through high school and who will be forever after known as not only the first girl in our class to give a boy a blow job, but to pass on her newfound knowledge to a select few of us the following day. An act which solidified my standing in the ranks of the "cool" girls, which means I owe Lisa my life.

So of course we have to do the thirty-second catch-up routine. Only thirty seconds stretches into a good two minutes while she introduces me to her date, some guy named Phil whose unibrow compensates for the receding hairline, then fills me in on Shelly Hurlburt's parents' divorce after thirty-six years, could I believe it? (actually, I could) and asks me if I know whatever happened to Melody McFadden's cousin Sukie, who was supposed to marry that baseball player, whats-his-name (I don't, but I tell her I'll ask around, one of the Scar-dinare daughters-in-law probably knows). Then after noisy hugs and both of us swearing we've got to get together, soon, I continue back to Tina.

Jose's assessment was, unfortunately, not an exaggeration. Even in the murky light, she looks like holy hell.

While neither of us is, or was, a raving beauty—at least not without a lot of help—Tina's always had a knack for making the most of what she has. No taller than I am, and in no danger of being mistaken for an anorexic, either (we were known in high school as the Boobsey Twins), her eyes might be set too far apart and her nose could use a little work, but with enough lip gloss and a Wonderbra, who cares? And she's the only woman I know who can actually get away with that cut-with-a-weedwhacker-hairstyle—it hides a narrow scar over her right ear from where her mother threw a bottle at her when she was six—albeit with dark brown hair instead of blond. But tonight we're talking Liza Minelli, The Dissipated Years.

"I know, I know, I look like crap," she mutters as I slide into the booth. As usual, she's wearing black, a heavy knit turtle-neck that hugs her breasts. If I know her—and I do—the ass-cupping black jeans and hooker boots are right there, too. And in the corner, I see a hint of fake leopard. Mind you, none of this stuff is cheap. It's just that Tina never really caught on to the concept of *subtle*. "I'm two screwdrivers ahead of you, so catch up."

At least the girl's getting her Vitamin C. However, since I haven't eaten, and since that experience at Ryan O'Donnell's left me bitter and disillusioned, I opt for a Coke. She makes a face and slugs back half her drink. I don't like this. See, there are two Tinas, Okay Tina and Total Mess Tina. For most of our childhood, she was Total Mess Tina, mainly characterized by the absolute conviction that she somehow provoked and/or deserved her mother's relentless physical and mental abuse. The girl had the self-confidence of a blind flea. Okay Tina only came out from time to time, like when I was puking up my intestines. It took Luke and me—with the help of various family members—years to send Total Mess Tina into remission. After all our work, relapse is not an option.

But I keep these thoughts to myself. For now.

"So I take it Luke doesn't know you're here?"

She laughs, but it's not a pretty sound. "What, do I look like somebody with a death wish?" She finishes off her drink and gestures toward Jose for another. "Jesus, it's cold tonight. You sure you don't want something with a little more zing to it?"

My mother alarm goes off. "Tell me you didn't drive over here."

"What are you, the DUI police?"

I decide to leave it for now. But if she's not walking steadily when we leave, no way is she getting behind the wheel. "So what'd you tell Luke?"

"He thinks I'm grocery shopping."

I stuff about fifty little pretzels into my mouth at once, then say around them, "You don't think he'll get suspicious when you get home with no groceries?" Not to mention the fact that she's gonna smell like, well, somebody who's been hanging out in a bar.

"Like I'm not gonna pick up some things before I go home,

geez, Ellie. Besides—" she picks up a little white box off the seat beside her "—I made a swing by Oxford's and picked up a couple of those Napoleons he likes so much." At my crest-fallen look, she smiles and produces a second box, which she shoves across the table. "And éclairs for you."

I clutch the box to my bosom, inhaling its bakery smell. "I owe you."

"Yeah, well, I'm gonna hold you to that."

Jose brings us her drink and my Coke; she picks it up, her wedding rings a flashing blur. Her first engagement ring was so small you had to take it on faith there was a diamond in it. But Luke does pretty well now, I gather. So for their fifth anniversary last year, they upgraded to two carats. Looks real good with the long maroon nails.

I set the box on the seat beside me so I won't be tempted to rip into it before I get home, then get down to business. "So. What's going on?"

That gets another long look, then Tina hauls a purse the size of Staten Island onto her lap; before I know it, she's lit up a cigarette. Which is now a huge no-no in New York bars.

"What the hell are you doing?" I growl across the table. Tina spews out a stream of smoke and holds the cigarette under the table, giving me a look like a she-wolf whose pups have been threatened.

"There's like nobody here, okay? God, quit being such a priss." Then, after another quick, surreptitious pull, she says, with no emotion whatsoever, "I'm pregnant."

We stare at each for a heartbeat or two. But the instant her cigarette bobs to the surface, I lunge across the table and grab it, dumping it into her drink.

"Bitch," she mutters, calmly lighting up again. Tina's got these pale blue eyes, like ice. And right now, the look she's giving me is fast-freezing my blood. Which doesn't prevent me from going for the second cigarette, but her hand ducks under the table before I can get it. "Chill, for God's sake. It's not like I'm keeping it."

My gaze jerks to hers. "You're not serious."

"You bet your ass I'm serious."

This is too many shocks on an empty stomach. "But Luke…" I lean over, whispering. "You know how much he's always wanted a kid—"

"And you know how much I don't. And swear to God, if you tell him, I'll never speak to you again."

My eyes burn, and only partly from the smoke. I hate this. Hate secrets. Especially ones that put me in the position of having to lie to somebody. "So why are you telling me this?" I sound whiny and I don't care. "Why are you making me an accessory?"

"Because I need you to go with me when I…you know."

"Me?"

"Yeah, you, who else? What, I'm gonna ask my *mother?* Luke's mother? One of my sisters? Who else can I trust, huh?"

I feel sick. Who knew being trustworthy could be such a liability?

Tina puffs some more, then says, "God knows how this happened. We always use protection. *Always.*" I look at her with what I expect is a chagrined expression; I was on the Pill when Starr happened, too, which she knows. Tina sighs. "Sorry. I forgot."

And because I am doomed to be the sympathetic one, I realize just how much this is tearing her apart. Criminy, she's shaking like somebody coming off a three-day bender.

"Yo, Tina," Jose shouts from the bar. "Put out the cigarette, babe, you wanna get my butt in a sling here?"

She blows out a breath and dumps the second butt in her drink, then goes for my pretzels.

"How far along are you?"

Her shoulders hitch. "Three weeks. More or less."

"Then maybe you should give yourself a few days to think about this. I mean, right now you're just in shock."

"No shit. But the last thing I want to do is *think* about it."

I know what she means. Oh, boy, do I know what she means. Because thinking about it opens the door to making it real. Makes it harder to not start thinking in terms of "baby."

"And they say it's easier the earlier you have it done," she goes on. "I'm not waiting."

Arguing with her right now would be pointless. But if she won't go without me, maybe I can put her off for a couple days, buy some time for her to think this through. Yes, it's all about choices, but my guess is panic's short-circuiting her synapses right now. And when you're freaked is not the time to make a decision that's going to impact the rest of your life. Especially when there's somebody else involved, I think with a sharp stab of pain.

"Tina, honey…you didn't always feel this way. About not wanting kids."

"Yes, I did," she says flatly. "I just thought—hoped—I'd get over it, you know? For Luke's sake? But I see all my sisters with their kids…and I can't do it, Ellie. I'll fuck the kid up, I know I will, just like my mother fucked us up."

Her assessment of her mother's relationship with her three daughters is, unfortunately, not an exaggeration. Renee Bertucci was a real piece of work. I have no idea why she put her girls down all the time, why she seemed to think it a sign of weakness to show them any affection. But I do know Tina didn't spend so much time at my house, or Luke's, just because of us, but because our mothers spoiled rotten everyone who set foot across their thresholds.

Which apparently Tina, in her near-hysteria, is forgetting.

I know I have to tread carefully through the minefield of Tina's fragile psyche. One wrong step and she's gonna blow.

So I point out that she'd had plenty of examples of good mothering, then add, "And maybe you should give yourself some credit for learning from your mother's mistakes."

Her eyes flood. "Then I'll probably make other ones, ones I won't even know I'm making until it's too late. And what if what they say is true, that our mothering instinct's in our genes?"

"But sweetie—your sisters are doing okay, right?"

"They're older. They got out before Mom got really bad." She looks down at her shaking hands, then back up at me. "I'm not like you, the way you are with Starr."

My laugh clearly startles her, even as my stomach does another flip. "You don't actually think I know what I'm doing? Believe me, I've lost plenty of sleep wondering if I'm going to screw *her* up. But honey...this isn't all about you. You know that—"

"Yeah, but see, here's the thing, Luke's totally okay with not having kids. We already discussed it. He says what we have, just by ourselves, is fine."

Nobody knows more than I what Luke would say, or do, to protect Tina. But I can't let this go.

"That's not what he said to me," I say gently, and her eyes flash to mine.

"Oh, yeah? And when was that? When we first got married? Before that, when we were just kids? I'm his freakin' *wife*, Ellie. I think maybe what he tells me carries a little more weight that something he might have said to you ten years ago."

"I'm not talking ten years ago. I'm talking last month at his parents', when J.J. and Julie came in from Jersey with the new baby."

Confusion knots her brows. "Where was I?"

"I dunno, in the bathroom, maybe? Anyway, Luke came into the kitchen, holding the baby. Said the only thing that could make it better was if the baby was his."

Her fingers tighten around the glass; she lifts it, remembers the butts floating in there like dead fish, clunks it back down. "I don't believe you."

"You can ask Frances. She was there."

We stare at each other for several seconds, then she awkwardly skootches out of the booth, grabbing her coat and punching her arms through the sleeves. "I always thought I could count on you," she says, her words trembling. "Just goes to show how much I knew."

She throws money down on the table, then grabs the bakery box with Luke's Napoleons and storms out. Without even a hint of a stagger.

I ache with that dull pain that comes from being torn between wishing you could turn back the clock and acceptance that you can't. I slide out of the booth, slip my coat back on and settle up with Jose. For a second or two, I consider leaving the éclairs—they seem tainted now, somehow—then reason prevails and I return to the booth to retrieve them. I cram on my hat and button up, almost looking forward to the slap of frigid air in my face.

On autopilot, I start back home, huddled against the cold, my own thoughts not much less screwy than Tina's are right now, I don't imagine. I'm shattered that there's no way I can be objective about this, whether I understand—in theory—her dilemma or not. In fact, it stuns me, how much I'm against her having an abortion. Because doing it behind her husband's back…how is that right? But if she tells him…

I know Luke. There's no way he'd ever make Tina have that baby if she really didn't want it. But it would kill him, I know it would, if she didn't.

Hunger, cold and confusion have joined forces in an attack at the base of my skull. I quicken my pace as if I can outrun this irritable, judgmental, hypocritical person trying to take over my body. All I want right now is my grandfather's house and my brisket and my kid and, if I hurry, *Will and Grace*—

A hand snakes out of the darkness and grabs my wrist, spinning me around as I let out a scream loud enough to reach Yonkers.

chapter 4

"Jesus, Ellie!" Luke winces, letting me go. "You trying to deafen me or what?"

"What did you expect, skulking in the shadows like that! I nearly peed my pants—!" My eyes go wide. "Were you *following* me?"

"No, numbskull, I was following my wife—"

"Who is out there, please?" heralds a delicate, musical voice from several houses away. We glance up to see a tiny silhouette standing on her top step, haloed by a yellowish light. "Ellie Levine? Is that you?"

"Yeah, Mrs. Patel," I say, moving closer so she can see me, shielding my eyes from flamingo spotlights. "It's me. And Luke."

"Luke? My goodness, you two gave me a fright!"

"Sorry, Mrs. P.," Luke calls out. "I just startled her, I guess. It's okay."

The woman shuffles back inside her front door as Luke grabs my arms and crosses the street, making me hotfoot it beside him. Like all the Scardinares, Luke's not particularly tall—maybe five-eight—but he's built like Fort Knox and he's got a grip like iron. Especially when he's pissed. Which is my guess, at the moment.

"Where're we going?"

"Back to your place. I'm freezing my ass off out here. What's in the box?"

"Tina brought me éclairs. You're getting Napoleons. Which she expects you to be home for when she gets there," I point out. The cold has exponentially expanded the Coke in my bladder, my urgent need to pee distracting me from the potentially disastrous track this conversation could take if I'm not careful. Not that I have any intention of blabbing her secret, but Luke has been able to see inside my brain before we were potty trained.

Maybe I shouldn't think about potties right now.

"So if you knew where we were," I say, "why didn't you just come inside?"

He snorts. "Like she'd be real happy to know I followed her, for one thing. And like it would've done any good, for another. I figure I've got a much better chance worming the truth out of you—hey!"

I may be short, but these thunder thighs come in handy for sudden stops.

"And if that's what you really think, buster—" I say, peering up at him from underneath the slouched beret, my arms crossed—sorta, this coat is kind of bulky "—you can just haul your butt right back home."

He gives me one of his sullen, hooded looks, shakes his head and turns back around, continuing down the block. I wrap my scarf more tightly around my neck and trudge after him. When we get to my steps, he stops, his breath puffing in front of his face.

"Can I come in?"

"I told you, I'm not—"

His gaze slams into mine, knocking my breath on its butt.

"And maybe I just need to talk, okay? To somebody who might actually listen. But who won't go nuts on me, either."

I'm starving, PMSing and my best friend has just dumped a secret on me I have no idea what to do with. He's assuming a lot here.

"Fine," I say, pushing past him and on up the stairs, wondering just how long I'd hold up in an interrogation type situation.

Guess I'm about to find out.

Funny. Luke and I talk probably two or three times a week, but I'm just now realizing we haven't been alone together since before he and Tina got married. Not really a conscious decision, I don't think, as just something we naturally fell into, considering the situation. No sense giving tongues a reason to wag and all that. So it's been a long time since Luke's been in my kitchen without Tina being there, too. The last time being…gee, I guess not too long after I realized I was pregnant.

I open the fridge to get the brisket; he reaches around me to get a bottle of grape juice, his arm grazing my shoulder. I smell the cold on him, his aftershave, the residue scent from his leather jacket, which he's draped across the back of the kitchen chair just like he has for the past ten years. He smells like a man, not the hot, sweaty boy who used to pin me down and tickle me mercilessly when we were kids.

We separate, him to find a glass, me to thunk the foil covered pan onto the counter. I slice brisket as he pours—*glug, glug, glug*—while Mario boops and beeps from the living room. My grandfather didn't seem particularly surprised to see Luke, but I'm sure I'll get the third degree later.

I steal a glance at Luke as I plop three slices of brisket on a plate. He's wearing a thermal Henley and snug jeans, worn

Adidas, muscles I still can't quite believe are there (he was pathetically scrawny as a kid). He keeps his dark hair short these days, hugging his scalp. I get the impression he thinks it makes him look tougher. Maybe it does, I don't know. The planes of his face do seem sharper, though. Although the long, black lashes kinda kill the effect.

Intense, dark eyes meet mine; one brow lifts. Heat rising in my face, I duck back into the fridge for leftover peas, noodles, thinking I can't remember the last time I had a man in my kitchen. Had a man *standing* in my kitchen. That *there was* a man standing in my...oh, never mind.

I don't get out much, can you tell?

Silence blankets the room, more pungent than the aroma of rewarmed brisket. Luke sips his juice, watching me, as I remove my delayed dinner from the microwave, carry it to the table in the pumpkin-orange kitchen I keep threatening to repaint, one of these days. I hear Luke's glass clunk onto the counter, our unspoken thoughts stretching between us like tightropes neither of us dares to cross.

"You're uncomfortable," he says softly.

"A little, maybe."

"Me, too."

I carefully cut my meat, fork in a bite, chew, swallow. I'm too hungry to not eat, even though I don't really want to. This weird, three-way friendship between him and Tina and me is based, if nothing else, on our being able to trust each other implicitly. That confidences are inviolate. We only have one rule—that the only secrets we keep from each other are those that would do more harm than good to reveal.

A rule I find I like less and less as time goes on.

"So you're really not gonna tell me what she said."

I get up to get a glass of milk. "I'm really not."

"Okay, then how's about I tell you how things look from my perspective, and you can just nod if I'm getting warm." I return to the table with my milk, which I nearly spill when he says, "She wants out of the marriage, doesn't she?"

"What? No! Ohmigod, Luke—" I crash into my chair. "Where on earth is this coming from—?"

Leo ambles into the kitchen, gives me a hard look. "You okay? I thought I heard you scream."

"That was hardly a scream, Leo, sheesh." But he's already spotted the Oxford box. "What's in there?"

"Éclairs. Take one."

He undoes the box, grinning at me and winking at Luke. "Then make myself scarce, right?"

"That'll do."

Chuckling, he gets a plate down from the cupboard, lifts out one of the éclairs. He nods his head in my direction but says to Luke, "You think she looks run-down?"

"Leo, for God's sake—"

"Yeah," Luke says, eyeing me. "I do."

"See…" My grandfather licks his fingers as he looks at me. "He agrees with me, you're working too hard."

This would be an opportune moment to point out I probably wouldn't look so run down if everybody would a) give me a chance to get dinner at dinnertime and b) leave me the hell alone and stop looking to me as their own private Ann Landers or whichever one it is that's still alive. But I'm too damned tired to go there.

While Pops takes foreeeeever to get a glass of milk, he and Luke talk about his work, local politics, some firehouse that had to be gutted because rats had taken it over, the Knicks. I eat and silently seethe, two things I'm extremely good at. After about five thousand years, my grandfather finally carts éclair and milk back out into the living room and I realize I have no idea how to get the conversation going again. Or even if I want to.

I get up to put my plate in the dishwasher; Luke says, "He's right, you look beat. And I'm slime for bein' so caught up in my own crap I didn't stop and think how tired you might be—"

"Oh, please. When have any of us ever been too tired to help each other?"

He gets a funny look on his face. "You sure?"

"No. And if you expect advice, fuggedaboutit." I dig an éclair out of the box, not bothering with a plate. "But I can listen. And I really want to know why you think Tina wants out."

The muscles tense in his face. "Because things have been strange between us for a while now."

"How long?"

"I dunno. Months. A year, maybe."

I nearly choke. A *year?* How did I miss that?

"Yeah," he says. "I don't understand it, either, we always got along so good. I mean, you and me, we always fought, got on each other's nerves, right?" Our gazes bounce off each other before he looks away. "But not Tina and me. I mean, the way she'd look at me…like I was her hero, y'know?"

Yeah. I know. Because he was. Because he was the big strong protector and she'd been the damsel in distress for as long as any of us could remember. But it worked both ways, because Tina's wide-eyed worship fed Luke's ego like no other. Nobody had ever needed him the way Tina did, and nobody had ever made her feel as safe as Luke did. In other words, they were the perfect match.

"But now," he continues, "I dunno, it's like we don't even have anything to say to each other anymore. I come home, we eat dinner, we watch TV, we go to bed. We have sex—occasionally—but I'm not sure why we're bothering, to tell you the truth." His eyes lift to mine, dark with hurt and confusion. "I'm scared for her, El, that she's gonna fall apart again, like she did that one time in high school. I'm not stupid, I know something's bothering her. But why won't she talk to me?"

In silence, I finish off the éclair, wishing there were about six more. Both because I need something to keep my mouth occupied and because my mood's just swung dangerously close to self-destructive. I don't know whether it's because I'm tired, or my hormones are being punks, or what, but once again, my reaction surprises me.

It's not that I don't feel for him, or Tina, because I do. My closest friends are both hurting, for godssake. Who else are they gonna come to if not me? Because that's the way it's always been. Except for one time, when I found out I was pregnant with Starr, I've always been the one the other two turned to to fix things between *them.* And up until this moment, I was fine with that, maybe because their needing me made me feel a real part of something. But now...

Now I realize just how long I've actually only been on the outside looking in, living vicariously through somebody else's relationship.

How screwed up is that?

So now, even as my mouth performs its appointed task as Duenna to the Deluded, my brain is desperately trying to scratch out of the kennel I've kept it in for the past twenty-something years. While I've been doing all this repair work for their lives, my own has fallen to rack and ruin.

What the hell does any of this have to do with me? I want to scream.

But I keep all this under wraps because Luke looks so miserable.

"No comment?" he says.

Great. If I plead the Fifth, he'll take that as a confirmation of his suspicions. If I reassure him Tina never said anything about their marriage being on the rocks, either he'll think I'm lying or he'll start wondering what she did want to talk to me about. Talk about your no-win situation. While all this is rumbling around in my head, however, Luke says, "I just wish I knew what was going on, if she's afraid to talk to me because of what she went through as a kid, if she can't stand the thought of the marriage failing…"

He yanks out a chair and drops into it, apparently out of steam. But I can tell, it's not Tina who's afraid of the marriage failing. I get a flash of their wedding day, both of them grinning like idiots, Tina as pretty as I've ever seen her in a dress I knocked off from a picture of some six-thousand-dollar number in *Modern Bride.* With the exception of two or three brief separations, they'd been going together for nearly nine years by that point. They were so comfortable together, finishing each other's sentences like an old married couple. Like Luke, I don't get it.

"Hey," I say lamely. "Everybody goes through rough patches."

His expression breaks my heart, because he knows this is more than a rough patch. Then he suddenly glances over my shoulder, the worry etched in his brow evaporating in an instant. "Hey, Twink! Your mom said you were asleep."

My daughter's already in his lap, her skinny arms wrapped around his neck. Next to Leo and me, Luke's her favorite person in the world. And I think I often slip to second place. Maybe third. Not that she doesn't have positive male role models coming out of her ears—my grandfather, the legion of Scardinare males. Even Mickey Gomez, one of the tenants, who's been teaching her Spanish. But her relationship with Luke has always been special, a relationship that's worked both ways. Oh, yeah, Luke's taken his "uncle" duties very seriously, even from before Starr was born.

I let her have her éclair, which I cut into bite-size pieces so most of the chocolate and custard lands in her mouth instead of on her face, thinking saccharine thoughts about not being able to imagine my life without her. Trust me, I don't always feel this way, so I'm going with the moment because it makes me feel good about myself. Like I deserve her.

Luke listens carefully as she prattles on about her day, her yawns getting bigger and bigger as her eyelids droop lower and lower. Finally, chuckling, he stands, Starr clinging to him like a little sedated monkey, and carries her upstairs to put her back to bed. I don't follow, because I know seeing him with her is only going to get my thoughts churning again about his being denied the one thing he really wants.

But you know, nobody forced him to marry Tina. And she's right: he did know going in she didn't want kids.

His decision, I tell myself. His consequences to deal with.

"Man, she's getting so big," he says when he comes back downstairs.

"Yep. Give 'em food and water and damned if they don't grow."

He smiles, a sad tilt of his lips. "It's late," he says, lifting his jacket from the back of the chair. "I should go."

This time, I don't stop him. We walk out to the front door; Leo's gone up to his room, so no eagle ears are listening (I assume) as we stand in the foyer.

"I saw your mother earlier," I say. "Pete and Heather are finally getting married, huh?"

Another smile, this time a weary one. "Yeah. At least there's some good news, right?"

I grab his arms, my impetuousness clearly surprising him. Not to mention me. I get another whiff of his scent, and something inside me goes, *Huh?*

"You and Tina need to talk. Tonight," I add, ignoring both his scent and the *Huh?*-ing. "You gotta get all this out in the open, tell her exactly what you've told me." It's a long shot, but maybe if Luke opens up, Tina will too, absolving me of a responsibility I realize I do not want. "I'm not a marriage counselor, a shrink or a priest, and I'm tired of getting caught in the middle."

He gives me a hard look and says softly, "Then maybe you shouldn't've put yourself there," and walks out the door.

What the hell…?

My cell rings, faintly. It takes me five rings to locate it, still in my purse on the kitchen counter.

"Hi," Tina says in a voice I haven't heard her use since she was about six.

"Uh…hi?"

I hear a whoosh of cigarette smoke. "Luke's there, isn't he?"

"Not anymore. And no, I didn't say anything."

"What? Oh…I didn't think you would." Surprise peers out from between her words, as though it never crossed her mind that I might. I can't decide if I'm touched or ticked.

"Teen—you two have got to hash this out. By yourselves." I give her a second or two to absorb this. "And I think you know that."

When she next speaks, I can barely hear her. "God, Ellie…I'm so scared."

"I know you are, sweetie," I say, as gently as I know how. "Which is why you have to talk to Luke. Trust him, okay? You know he loves you."

I do not like the silence that greets this observation. So I prod her for the answer I want. "Right?"

"Yeah," she says at last. "I guess."

"Tina?"

"What?"

"Promise me you won't do anything until you've talked to him?"

There's another long pause, during which I can hear smoke being spewed.

"Promise?" I prompt.

"Okay, okay, fine."

"I mean, I know it's your body and all that, but—"

"Jesus, I get it, already!" I expect her to hang up, but instead I hear, "Luke's the best thing that's ever happened to me, you know? The thought of letting him down…it makes me sick."

I don't know what to say to this. Then she says:

"You really think I'd make an okay mother?"

Like I know what kind of mother she'd make. But I inject a bright note into my voice and say, "Hey. If I can do this, anybody can—"

"Crap, I hear Luke's key in the door, I gotta go. I'll call you tomorrow, 'kay?"

I click off my phone and toss it back in my purse, thinking, man, I am so glad I'm not in her shoes right now.

Especially since I'm not sure I'm doing such a hot job staying balanced in my own.

"So what's up with Luke and Tina?"

Frances's low, furtive voice ploughs into me when I emerge from her downstairs bathroom the following Sunday. Thank God I already peed. But I look Luke's mother straight in the eye and say with remarkable aplomb, "I have no idea what you're talking about."

Like that works. Knowing nobody will hear my screams for mercy over the din of Scardinares yakking away in the dining room—half the Italians left in Richmond Hill are in this house right now—Frances drags me into her home office and shuts the door, leaning against it for good measure. Underneath artfully tousled hair, bittersweet chocolate eyes bore into mine. A look I know is responsible for hundreds, if not thousands, of impassioned promises over the years to never do again whatever it was that provoked the look to begin with.

"I know Tina," she says with the exasperated affection of a woman who loves more than understands her daughter-in-law. And who, like everybody else, wanted nothing more than to see Tina finally get a fair shake, to really be happy. She's hugging herself over a velour tunic free of any signs of having even been in a kitchen today. That would be because Jimmy Sr., not Frances, does all the major cooking. He says it relaxes him.

Frankly, I think it was that or starve to death. "Since when does she miss the first viewing of an engagement ring?"

I tell myself that since I'm not her child, I am impervious to The Look. "Maybe one of them's not feeling well?"

"So they'd call." Her eyes narrow; my resistance dissolves like an ice cube in a frying pan. "You know something, I can tell you do. Luke's always talked to you more than anybody else, ever since you were kids."

You remember what I said about not lying if I can possibly help it? This isn't due to an overabundance of moral fiber on my part, it's because I totally suck at it. My mouth goes dry; my cheeks flame. Then I realize that, since I haven't heard from either Luke or Tina since the other night, anyway, whatever information I might be able to dispense is already outdated. Right?

"Sorry, Frances. I honest to God have no idea what's going on."

"Which I suppose is why your cheeks are the color of Jimmy's marinara sauce."

"It's hot in here?"

The question mark at the end probably wasn't very bright. But before she can move in for the kill, somebody knocks on the door. It's Jason, looking particularly fetching tonight in several layers of shredded black T-shirts, torn jeans, and rampant despondency. He looks at me, his mouth struggling with the effort to smile. Kinda like my belly the one time I tried Pilates.

"Starr's wonderin' where you were," he says to me, then turns to his mother. "And Luke called. Said he was sorry they couldn't make it, but Tina's not feeling good."

"Oh?" Frances perks up like a hound catching a scent; Jason ducks her attempt to brush his hair out of his eyes. "He say what was wrong?"

"Uh-uh."

"He want me to call back?"

"Dunno."

"Oh, for God's sake," Frances says, but I'm already out of the room to go find my daughter, so my butt is safe.

Until the next day, when Luke calls me at work.

"El! Guess what? I'm freakin' gonna be a *father!*"

chapter 5

The joy in his voice is indescribable. As is my reaction. Although let's go with stunned senseless, for the moment. I mean, yes, I'm relieved she's changed her mind. I guess. But at the same time, I'm getting disturbing images of trucks heading straight for brick walls.

Behind me—I'm taking the call in the middle of the workroom—Nikky and Jock are screaming at each other in different languages.

"Wow!" I force out. "That's wonderful! Congratulations!"

"Isn't it great? I mean, I had to do some fast talking to convince Teen it's gonna be okay, but she'll come around, I know she will. And maybe this'll get things back on track for her and me, you know?"

I swallow past a knot in my throat. "What did your mother say?"

"I haven't told her yet, Tina says she doesn't want to tell anybody until she's really sure. Something about getting past the first trimester. But how could I not tell you, huh? Anyway, gotta run, we'll see you later. Dinner to celebrate, you and Starr, our place, maybe this weekend?"

"Sure," I say, but he's gone.

Well. This is great. Really. Luke's gonna have Tina *and* a baby. Just the way it's supposed to be. What he wanted. What I'd helped him get.

Well, send in the big fat hairy clowns, why not.

Behind me, Harold sticks his nose into the argument; the noise level is deafening. And heading my way.

"Where the hell do you get off," Harold is now screaming in my face, "accepting that return from Marshall Field's?"

You know, I am so not in the mood for taking the brunt of somebody else's screw-up right now.

"Since the order clearly states the delivery date was three weeks ago," I say with the sort of calm I imagine someone resigned to their imminent death must feel, "I didn't see as I had much choice. I couldn't exactly send it back, could I?"

Harold's face turns an interesting shade of aubergine. And the finger comes up, close enough to my nose to make me cross-eyed. "Then I suggest you get on the goddamn phone, young lady, and do some fast talking and get them to take it back! We can't afford to lose that order!"

The first words that come to mind are, *"So why didn't somebody make sure they got the frickin' order on time?"*

"Harold," Nikky says as she comes up behind him. "Leave Ellie alone. It's not her fault—"

He whirls on her. "That's right, it's not. It's yours, for being so goddamn disorganized you can't even make sure your goddamn orders are delivered on time!"

She doesn't say a word. Nor does her expression change. But not even three layers of makeup are sufficient to mask the color exploding in her cheeks.

Swear to God, I want to wrap my hands around the man's blubbery neck and choke him until his froglike little eyes pop out of his head.

"Nikky?" I say, "I'll call the buyer, see what I can do. Maybe if we give them a small discount—?"

"Like hell!" Harold bellows.

"Hey!" I bellow right back, because frankly, I don't care if Harold Katz thinks I'm the biggest bitch on wheels. "You wanna give me a little leverage here, or you want the whole order to land in an outlet mall in Jersey?"

The aubergine begins to fade to a dusty magenta. "Do what you can," he finally says. "Just don't start out talking discounts, you got that?"

He turns on his heel and storms off. I'm tempted to salute behind his back, but Nikky's still standing there, looking at me as though I've either lost my mind or deserve a medal, I can't quite tell. Then it occurs to me that, to add insult to injury, Harold didn't suggest *Nikky* call the buyer. That he trusts some schleppy little assistant with about as much clout as a worm more than he does his wife, who happens to own the business.

"You wanna call 'em?" I say.

She seems to think this over for a minute. "I take it you're not asking me because you don't want to make the call."

"Truthfully, I'm not sure that anybody should be making this call. But I don't mind doing it. If that's what *you* want."

Her Lancômed lips twitch into a smile. "Start off with ten percent, on top of the standard seven/ten EOM." The usual seven percent discount for bills paid by the tenth of the month following delivery. "And then pray the damn stuff sells so it doesn't boomerang back to us, anyway."

Then she, too, turns and walks away, basically trusting me to fix things. Not that I mind—or care—but, excuse me? What's happening here? Is this really the same woman who only a few days ago played hardball with that fabric vendor, who shrugged off her husband's bad-mouthing as nothing more than a mild annoyance?

Suddenly, I want to curl up in a ball and cry. Or go to sleep for a very long time. And I have no idea why. Aside from the fact that all the yelling has made my head hurt. But that, for the moment at least, seems to be over. Nikky, Harold and Jock have all spun off in different directions; all I can hear now is the hum of the heaters, the stop-and-start whirr of the sewing machines, the sporadic ringing of the phone and Jock's totally irritating Easy Listening FM station.

I'll make that phone call in a few minutes, when I'm not feeling quite so shell-shocked. Instead, I wander back out into the showroom, which, once again, is a wreck. So I start cleaning it up, my thoughts more jumbled than the samples covering every piece of furniture.

Luke's going to be a father, which he's always wanted. Tina's going to have the baby, which absolves me from having to keep a secret that was going to make me sick to keep. And who knows, maybe they can work things out, get their marriage back on track.

So why do I feel like shit?

Actually, I think I know. But going there would be on the same level as the dumb-as-dirt Gothic novel heroine who goes down into the cellar, by herself, at night, in her nightgown, because she hears a strange noise.

I pick up a wool crepe dress with a loose waist. The fabric is gorgeous, but I've never liked the neckline. Or where the waist falls. What's the point of making loose-fitting clothes if they just make a heavy woman look fatter?

You could do better, a voice whispers, startling me.

"Ellie, *cara,* have you seen the pleated linen skirt?"

I look up. Jock's leaning against the door frame, one hand in the pocket of pleated black trousers, a lock of black hair casually slung across his forehead, just a hint of chest hair curling over the dip of his black, V-neck cashmere sweater. He has these weird light eyes, somewhere between gray and green, that surrounded by his olive skin seem to laser right through me.

"The 1140?" I say.

He smiles. "I have no idea what the number is. Do we have more than one pleated linen skirt?"

"No, actually," I say, riffling through the pile on a padded bench until I unearth it. Needless to say, it's a total mess. Which means I'll have to press it, *blech.*

"Yes, yes, that's it," Jock says, crossing the room to take it from me, his aftershave arriving five minutes before he does. "*Cara?* Are you all right?"

My head whips around at the genuine concern in his voice. "I'm fine. Why?"

To my shock, he tucks a finger under my chin, his eyebrows dipping. "You are lying. I see worry in your eyes."

I turn away from his touch, which I neither need nor want. Or rather, I don't need or want Jock's touch. Because I'm suddenly and profoundly aware that I wouldn't mind *somebody's* touch. You know, a little masculine tenderness? Some guy who wants to take care of *me,* for a change? Not that I need to be taken care of, but it would be nice to have someone who wanted to.

Does that make sense? Or does it just make me a dopey, prefeminist throwback? And do I really care?

"I'm tired, that's all," I say, realizing I'm perilously close to tears and really, really pissed with myself that I am. A linen blouse slips to the floor when I try to hang it up; Jock retrieves it, deliberately grazing my hand with his when he gives it back. It's everything I can do not to roll my eyes.

"That Mr. Harold," he says gently, "he is a son of a bitch."

Tempting as it is to agree with him, discretion isn't exactly one of Jock's strong suits. And playing people against each other is. So I mutter something noncommittal and will him to go away.

He doesn't.

"Ellie…you are so young to be taking on other people's burdens," he says, so naturally I turn to say, "What are you talking abou—?" which Jock somehow interprets as an invitation to kiss me.

I guess I kinda poke him with the hanger because the next thing I know he's yelling "Ow!" and holding his palm over his eye.

"Oh, God, I'm sorry, I didn't mean to hurt you! But I don't fool around with married men, Jock. Ever."

"It was just a little kiss," he says, pouting. He slowly lowers his hand, as though he's afraid his eyeball might fall out.

"Something tells me your wife might not see it that way."

"She would not have to know."

"I would know. You would know. Whether she knew or not is immaterial." When he frowns, I explain, "It wouldn't matter. Whether she knew or not. Because we did."

"Ah. You have, how do you say? Principles?"

"One or two I keep tucked away for special occasions."

A rueful expression crosses his face. "I apologize, then. It was just that I thought—"

When he hesitates, I prompt (because I'm clearly insane), "You thought what?"

"I see a very pretty young woman who has not been kissed in a long time, so I think maybe I should do something about that."

Gotta hand it to the guy. If he was aiming to stun me silly, he accomplished his mission.

"You know, maybe I should've wrapped this hanger around your *neck* instead," I say, jamming it into the blouse's sleeves and clanging it onto the nearest rack. "Even if it had been a long time since I'd been kissed—which you would know how?—where do you get off thinking it's up to you to do something about that?"

Jock chuckles. God, what an annoying little man. "Ah, there is the passion I suspect lies beneath that beautiful skin of yours." He leans closer and winks. "The passion I feel in your soft lips."

And then he walks away, rumpled skirt in hand.

Leaving the words "beautiful," "passion" and "soft lips" hovering in the air in his wake.

Is my life a joke or what?

I take several deep breaths, reassure my poor bedraggled hormones it was just a false alarm, to go back to sleep, and manage to get through the next several hours without anyone trying to either bully or seduce me. Later that afternoon, I'm checking in several bolts of a gorgeous silk/linen blend that just arrived when Nikky—who's been gone most of the afternoon—pops up beside me.

"Were you able to make that phone call, darling?"

"To Fields'? Yep. All taken care of. I've already relabeled everything for UPS. Second Day Air." When a pained look crosses her face, I add, "It was that or nothing, Nikky."

She nods. I fully expect her to leave. But as I rip through the plastic wrapping to inspect the next bolt of cloth, she says, "Is everything okay?"

Geez, am I wearing a sign on my forehead or something? I blink up into what passes for Nikky's worried expression. I mean, I think she really wants to be empathetic. It's not her fault she's missing that gene.

"Yes, everything's fine."

"Oh. Well, then…Marilyn and I were wondering if you could do us a huge favor."

Marilyn's the daughter. Who must've come in the back way, unless I can now add blind to befuddled and depressed. While I can tolerate doing favors for Nikky—since she pays my salary and doesn't treat me like pigeon poop—the idea of doing a favor for her daughter—who doesn't and does—isn't sitting well, just at the moment. However, resisting would require more energy than I have. So I abandon the bolts of fabric and follow Nikky back to her office.

And there she is, the dear.

"Hi, Marilyn," I say brightly. "How's it going?"

Suspicious, dull blue eyes peer out at me from the safety of an equally dull, lethargic pageboy. A silvery gleam catches my eye—a stethoscope, nestled against a flat, broadcloth-covered chest all but hidden by a blah-colored trenchcoat. "Vintage" Burberry, as *Vogue* would say. Otherwise known as "old."

Her chapped, bare lips purse, the word "Fine" squeezing through like a desiccated turd.

This epitome of charm and elegance is a first-year resident at Lenox Hill. I've yet to see her when she hasn't looked like a snarly, starving dog who dares you to take its bone away. However, since I'm a nice person—mostly—I offer her a smile. It is not returned. I do not take this slight personally, since I've never seen Marilyn be nice to anybody. Somehow, I doubt she's in medicine due to an overwhelming desire to ease the suffering of her fellow man.

I catch the expression on Nikky's face when she glances at her daughter, though, and I can't help but ache for her, a little. It's that did-*I*-do-this-to-you? look. It's a look I hope to God nobody ever sees in my eyes. A look I'm petrified somebody will, someday.

Do all mothers live in mortal fear of screwing up? I think of Tina, her terror at the thought of being a parent; of Frances, the worry lines permanently etched between her eyebrows, bracketing her mouth, lines that deepen to gullies whenever her kids pull a number on her. Whenever Jason enters her line of sight.

My heart begins to race as all the 4:00 a.m. ghoulies make

a rare daytime appearance, that Starr will be irrevocably damaged because I work / am single / leave her with her grandfather / leave her with Jason / leave her with Frances / won't get her a dog / let her eat junk food / eat too much junk food myself / wear my father's clothes / give her too much freedom / don't give her enough freedom.

And that's just in the first thirty seconds. You want the full list, leave a number and I'll get back to you.

"Ellie, angel," Nikky says, draping an arm around my shoulder and shaking me out of my brooding. Is it my imagination, or does the glower intensify from across the room? "We just bought Marilyn *the* most adorable one-bedroom in the West Village—"

Hey. When Nikky Katz atones for her guilt, she doesn't mess around.

"—and I actually found a decorator who says she can get it in shape—you wouldn't *believe* the wallpaper in the bedroom— before Mar's roommate gets married at the end of the month. Anyway, the poor baby's just swamped, has to go straight back to the hospital, and God knows I can't get away, so…"

A manila folder, clippings crammed inside like refugees in a fishing boat, appears in front of me. "I was wondering if you'd mind whizzing down there and giving these to the decorator? They're ideas I pulled from magazines to give her an idea of what we're looking for."

Mildly curious, I glance over at Marilyn to see if there's any reaction, but she's gone into zombie mode, staring out at the ice floes meandering down the Hudson. I'm tempted to toss something at her, just to make sure she's still alive.

"The decorator's supposed to be there around four or so, taking measurements and such." This is said while I'm being led toward the door. "Oh! Before I forget—would you tell her to send her bills here? And to invoice the company, not me personally?"

Every bookkeeper since I've been here has had a cow about Nikky's taking her daughter's personal expenses as business deductions. And God knows how she pulls it off. But then, it's not my problem, is it?

Nikky rattles off the address to me, then asks me twice if I've got it—yes, Nikky, I can remember a two-digit house number and apartment 2-B—but just before I step out of the office, some perverse impulse makes me turn back and say to Marilyn, "I bet you're excited, huh, getting your own place?"

The question seems to startle her. "I guess," she says, the words dragging from her lips. "Not that I've seen the apartment. But I imagine it's perfect. After all—" Like twin lizards, her eyes dart to Nikky. "It must be, if Mom picked it out."

Okay, I'll just leave now, shall I?

I mull over that little scene during the subway ride. Can you imagine what holidays must be like for the Katzes? There's an older brother, I hear, but I've never seen him. He escaped years ago. To Chicago, I think. Smart man.

Twenty minutes later, I find the building, a charming four-story redbrick on West 10th. A very pretty block, even in the dead of winter, the kind filmmakers use for romantic comedies set in New York. Oh, yeah, this place has Meg Ryan written all over it. I ring the bell for 2-B; a lively, slightly breathless female voice answers and buzzes me in. The apartment is on the second floor, the door slightly ajar. I hear children's voices, wonder if I've made a mistake.

I step inside, only to stumble backwards as egg yolk-yellow walls jump out and yell *SURPRISE!*

God, the place is—or at least, will be—gorgeous. Honeyed wooden floors blurrily reflect the brick-and-marble fireplace at one end; through the pair of virtually transparent floor-to-ceiling windows, I can see a small terrace. "Hello?" I call out, my voice echoing tentatively inside the large, bare living room.

A pair of toddlers streak out of what I guess is the bedroom, startling me. The one girl, long-legged with curly dark hair, chases a smaller blonde, their laughter shrill and infectious in the still, empty room.

"Hillary! Melissa!" Dragging a metal tape measure behind her, a tall, bony, very pregnant woman in a stretchy black jumpsuit suddenly appears, her expression slightly harried underneath an explosion of dark curls. "Sorry," she mutters with an apologetic smile, then tries to glare at the two little girls. "Hey, you two. Cool it."

Naturally, they just laugh all the harder and take off again, their sneakered feet beating a syncopated rhythm against the bare floorboards as they race each other up and down, up and down, the length of the room. The woman rolls her eyes, then smiles in a whatcha-gonna-do? grin. "Baby-sitter crisis, sorry." She extends her hand. "I'm Ginger Petrocelli. You must be Marilyn?"

"No, Ellie. Levine. Her mother's assistant. Marilyn couldn't make it."

Ginger's brows lift slightly, then she grins. "God, that is a *great* hat," she says, eyeing my red wool cloche. "Where'd you get it?"

"It was my grandmother's," I say, once again scanning the living room. "Is this place a knockout or what?"

The woman laughs. "That's one word for it." Over in the far corner, the little girls collapse on the floor in a fit of giggles. "At least they're not trying to kill each other," Ginger mumbles under her breath, then nods toward the folder clutched to my chest. "Is that for me?"

"What? Oh, yeah." I hand it to her. "I tried to organize it a bit on the way over, but I'm not sure how much good I did."

Halfheartedly shushing the children, Ginger starts flipping through the torn-out magazine pages. A plain gold band gleams on her left hand. And from out of nowhere, I feel this...prick of envy.

This is very weird, especially since I don't tend to think much about my marital status, much less obsess about it. Maybe because I already have a kid, I don't know. Not that I haven't gone out occasionally since Starr's birth. Fix-ups happen. But honestly, it got to be more trouble than it was worth. You dress up, you go out, you're on your best behavior. So what do you really learn about the other person, other than whether or not he's got good table manners? Then there's the whole will-or-won't-he-call-me-or should-I-call-him? trauma, which usually is more about your own ego than whether or not you really want to see him again—

"Well, if nothing else," Ginger says beside me, scrutinizing one of the clippings, "she's got good taste."

"That would be her mother. I don't think Marilyn has any taste—"

We're interrupted by the tiny brunette who looks just like Ginger, all done up in mauve Baby Gap.

"Gotta go potty."

"I thought you just went."

"Gotta go 'gain."

"Sounds familiar," I say, following them back through the equally large, airy bedroom to the bathroom. Yeow—Nikky wasn't kidding about the wallpaper in here. Sunflowers. The size of garbage can lids. On a lime-green background.

"You have kids?" I hear from the bathroom.

"One." I look away, but now reverse-image sunflowers are seared onto my retinas. "A five-year-old girl. With the smallest bladder in the metropolitan area."

Ginger emerges, the little girl shooting past her and back out to the living room, where the giggling starts up again. "I doubt that. Right now, that honor goes to me."

I like this woman, I realize. Her neuroses seem to lie within the normal range. For New York, at least. Since that's a rare thing in my life, I'm reluctant to leave just yet.

"When's your baby due?"

"In six weeks. Might as well be six years."

"Are the girls fraternal twins?"

"They're not even related," she says, smiling. "The dark-haired one's actually my half sister. My mother's testimony to yes, you can get pregnant after you think you've gone through menopause. And little blondie's my husband's." Her voice softens when she says this, except then she mutters "Shit" under her breath and glances at her watch. "I've got another appointment on the upper East Side in twenty minutes. Girls, get your coats and let's get cracking! God, I hope I even can get a taxi at this hour!"

We all troop down the stairs, the girls jumping from step to step. I tell her about billing Nikky's business, she nods and digs a card out of her purse.

"I don't really need—"

"You never know," Ginger says with a shrug. "And when you're just starting out on your own, believe me, you give business cards to *everybody.*"

I glance at the spiffy logo on the card as we all thread through the door and down the steps. *GPW Designs,* it says, with an address in Brooklyn.

"What's the W for?" We hang a right and head toward Sixth Avenue; Ginger laughs.

"Wojowodski. My husband's name." Hanging on to one kid with each hand, she tosses me a grin. "What can I say, I've got bad name karma."

"Is he worth it?"

"Most days, yeah."

I get that funny feeling in the pit of my stomach again, decide to change the subject. "So—you're in business for yourself?…Oh, here, let me do that," I offer when I realize Ginger's going to try to hail a taxi while hanging on to her briefcase and two wiggly little girls.

"Thanks." She moves them all back nearer the curb as I step out into the street. "I just hung out my shingle a few months ago."

"How do you like it?" I say over my shoulder as cab after cab whizzes by. "Being on your own?"

Her silence makes me turn. She seems to be considering how to answer my question, as a sudden breeze whips her curls into a froth around her face.

"It's scary as all get-out," she says at last. "Knowing I could lose my shirt. That I now have to pay for my own health insurance. It's a real shock after working for big firms. Taking the safe road. Oh, God…bless you," she says as a taxi pulls up in front of me and she herds her charges toward it. After she gets them in, she turns to me, our gazes level since I'm now standing on the curb. Her brown eyes are huge and unnervingly imploring, as if she's been sent to warn me of something. And I can tell she's as perplexed about why she's answering my question as I am about why I asked it to begin with.

"But you know what?" she says. "I've never been happier. And I knew the longer I waited, the harder it would be to take the plunge."

"Mom-*mee!*" the blonde calls out. "I'm cold!"

With a smile and a "Thanks again," she gets in, slams shut the door, and they go shooting off up Sixth Avenue.

Huh.

I turn south to walk the few blocks to Washington Square and the subway, yanking my cell from my purse. I call home, tell Leo I'll be there in about forty-five minutes, then punch in Tina's number. Of course, I get her machine, since she works until six, at a lumber supplier in Long Island City. I toss the phone back into my purse and find my mind wandering, back to that dress. The one with the dropped waist, in the showroom. How to change it to make it work for, I don't know, somebody like me.

With the exception of my sister, the women in my family,

on both sides, tend to be short and bosomy. My hunch is that Starr will follow in this genetic tradition, even though she's got spaghetti strand appendages now. So did I at her age. Imagine my shock when I awoke one morning to find these bizarre protuberances jutting out from my chest.

At twelve, I was already a D-cup. They should make it a rule, when you get breasts that early, that you have to put them away for later. Like the pearl necklace my great-grandmother gave me for my sixth birthday that I wasn't allowed to wear until I was deemed mature enough to handle the responsibility.

I'm okay with them now, though. My breasts, I mean. The necklace, sad to say, vanished in the back seat crevice of Donny Volcek's father's Taurus on prom night. The good news, though, is that a Taurus's interior is definitely roomier than it appears from the outside.

As I was saying. I came to terms with my short, bosomy self some time ago. That's not to say I don't have body issues from time to time. Like whenever I go bra shopping. Or try to find a pair of jeans that even remotely go where my curves do. You know what I'm talking about, right?

Men don't have these problems. All a guy has to do is yank on a T-shirt or a sweatshirt or something and he's done. No wires to pinch, no straps to slip, no overflow ooching over the sides or between the zipper that refuses to close unless you lie flat on your back and give up breathing. Okay, so men have the tie thing to deal with, but please. How many men wear ties these days? At least on a full-time basis. When you're a D-cup, you damn sight wear a bra every single day or by the time you're sixty you have to kick your ta-tas out of your way when you walk. This is not something a man has to face.

Not too often, anyway.

I fall in with the herd resolutely filing down the stairs to the subway entrance, wishing I had something to anesthetize me for the long subway ride.

Wishing that adorable little apartment were mine.

What is it with me tonight? First my reaction to Ginger's wedding ring, now the apartment. I am not—normally—a covetous person, wanting things that belong to someone else. Especially things I couldn't afford in my wildest dreams.

I swipe my Metrocard and meld into the pack on the platform, while way, way back in my brain, something blips, very faintly, very quickly. Hardly enough to register, really. But it was there, I can't deny it, like not being able to deny that, yes, that was a rat skittering across your path:

Resentment. That if I hadn't had Starr, maybe things would be different.

As I said, the feeling is fleeting, like the shudder from seeing that rat. But that it surfaces at all gnaws at me. Just like that rat.

And now that I've beaten that metaphor to death…

A gush of heavy, stale air and an increasingly loud series of mechanical groans and whines heralds the train's arrival. Doors open, bodies get off, bodies get on, doors close. I find a seat, amazingly enough, settling in and forcing myself to think about all the things I have to be grateful for. One of my mother's tricks, whenever either one of us was tempted to feel sorry for ourselves.

We used it a lot, there at the end.

But there were days when thoughts of losing her crowded my brain to the point where trying to find something positive about my life seemed as insurmountable as my being able to come up with a cure in time to save her.

"So start small," she'd whisper in the North Carolina accent nearly twenty years in Queens hadn't been able to budge, her smile strained against skin so fragile-looking I was half afraid it would tear.

"I got an A on my math test," I'd say. Or, "Nancy DiMunzio wasn't at school today." Or, "My zit's all gone." Or, depending on whether or not this was one of her good days, "Jennifer and I actually got through breakfast without biting each other's heads off."

If she had the energy, she'd chuckle, then add something of her own to the list. That she'd had me was always part of it, a thought that tightens my throat even fifteen years later. In any case, we'd go back and forth, and before I knew it I'd filled a whole loose-leaf page.

So tonight, I shut my eyes, shutting out the whispers of discontent, and start small. *I've got a seat on the train,* I think.

The man next to me doesn't smell like a distillery.

My daughter makes me laugh.

I'm not having my period.

I open my eyes and fish a tiny sketchbook out of my purse, flipping through a few ideas I had for altering some of my grandmother's dresses. I jot down what I've already listed, then add to it. By the time I get home, I've got more than fifty items. Crazy.

Leo's in the kitchen, basting a chicken. The house smells like Heaven. I mentally add this to my list.

"Where's Starr?"

"Gomezes'. You got a phone call."

My stomach jumps, which doesn't stop me from trying to pinch off a piece of chicken skin. "Who from?"

"Heather Abruzzo, I wrote it down. Didn't you used to hang out with some girl named Abruzzo?"

"Heather's older sister. Joanne."

"Joanne, now I remember. Cut that out!" He smacks at my hand, but the prize is already mine. "It's not done yet."

"What'd she want?" I say around the sizzling hot, succulent piece of garlic-and-pepper seasoned chicken skin.

"Something about her wedding dress. I think maybe she wants you to make it?"

Uh-boy.

chapter 6

A week later, my living room is wall-to-wall big hair and Queensspeak. It seems that not only does Heather want me to do *her* dress, she wants me to come up with something that will work for twelve—at last count—bridesmaids, ranging in size from a 4 Petite to a Woman's 24.

I tried to talk her out of it, I really did. Not that (now that I'm used to the idea) I'd mind making Heather's dress—with her curvy figure and those deep blue eyes and all that dark hair, she's going to be a knockout in white. But a dozen brides-maids? I think not. Besides, I pointed out, by the time she buys the fabric and pays me for my time—her sister and I weren't *that* close, for pity's sake—she'd do just as well, if not better, buying from Kleinfeld's.

"Right. Like I'm gonna find dresses that'll work for ev-erybody at Kleinfeld's," she said over the phone when I called back. "And everybody still talks about that dress you made for

Tina, and that was five years ago. God, that was one fucking *gorgeous* wedding gown."

Hard to resist a compliment of that magnitude. Of course, she would bring up Tina, who remains amazingly elusive for somebody I used to talk to no less than three times a day.

Anyway, not wanting to appear rude—and needing time for the head-swelling to subside from her praise—I told Heather we'd talk about it. The plan was, since I've yet to meet a newly engaged woman who doesn't go "just looking" for bridal gowns within a week of getting the ring, that she'd find the gown of her dreams before she and I got together, and my involvement would become a nonissue.

Next thing I know, she shows up at my house armed with twenty bridal magazines, her sister Joanne (who's been married for four years and has three kids), her mother Sheila (who looks like an older, drier version of her daughters), her best friend Tiffany (there's one in every bunch) and the worst case of wedding lust I have ever seen. And I've seen some pretty bad cases over the years, believe me.

So. Here we *all* are, in my teensy living room. It's like Fran Drescher night in Vegas. The clashing cheap perfumes alone are enough to knock me over, let alone the noise of—let me count—sixteen women all yakking at once. Unfortunately, Heather's dress hasn't yet "found" her, as she puts it. So she's enlisted the help of the entire wedding party. Which, by the time she included her sister, her sisters-in-law-to-be, three cousins she couldn't get out of including and five of her closest friends, swelled to the monstrous proportions you see here. Except for Tina, who's supposed to be here but isn't.

The crowd is beginning to make hungry noises; grateful for the excuse to escape for a few minutes, I hustle out to the kitchen where Leo and Starr are hiding out, playing checkers.

"Quick. I need mass quantities of food, here."

"I just bought chips and cookies," Leo says, not bothering to look up from the board. "In the cupboard."

I grab bowls and plates, rip open bags and dump out treats, stealing a Chips Ahoy for myself. Also not looking up, Starr says, "What're they gonna drink?"

Good question. I open the fridge to half a bottle of probably flat root beer, a carton of Tropicana, a jug of ice water and a gallon of two-percent milk.

"I could go to the store, pick up a few things," Leo says.

"Two twelve-packs of Diet Coke," I say without missing a beat. "From the refrigerator case so they're already cold."

From the coatrack by the back door, my grandfather grabs his parka, hands Starr her puffy coat. "You know," he says as he opens the door, letting in a blast of frigid air, "that could be you one day, planning *your* wedding in our living room."

I find this a highly unlikely possibility, but this is not the time for a reality check. So all I say is, "Believe me, if I ever even *think* of having twelve bridesmaids, you have permission to shoot me."

I cart bowls of goodies back out, barely having time to set them on the coffee table and jump out of the way before the pack attacks. I do notice, however, that Heather's begun to slip into the Fried Bride stage. Her lipstick's gone, her hair is sagging and she's got that desperate, panicked look in her eyes. "This one's not bad," she says for at least the hundredth time. And for the hundredth time, she is pelted by a barrage of objections.

"Oh, no, that's way too plain, honey—"

"It'll squash your tits—"

"You can't be serious. Long sleeves in June?"

"All those bows? What? You wanna look like you're six?"

"Don't take this the wrong way, baby, but that's made for somebody with a much smaller ass."

A word of advice—choosing a wedding dress by committee is a seriously bad idea.

She looks up at me, tears glittering in her eyes.

"Why don't you give it a rest for a moment?" I say.

"Yeah," Joanne says, brushing cookie crumbs off her front. "Maybe we should talk about the bridesmaids' dresses?"

Panic streaks across Heather's face. "We can't do that! Tina's not here!"

Oh, yeah, like this poor woman needs one more opinion. "Heather?" I sit down beside her, put my arm around her shoulder and hand her a cookie. "You can do this, honey." She takes the cookie and nibbles on it, but her brow is a mass of wrinkles. "Now, do you—*you*," I repeat, "have any ideas?"

"Well…not really. Except I know I want something the girls can wear again."

Naturally, that brings a chorus of "Yeah, that's right," along with the sporadic fire of bridesmaid-dresses-from-hell stories. However, unless she's planning on putting the girls in halter tops and suede miniskirts, ain't gonna happen. Like "Just relax, this won't hurt a bit," the concept of recyclable bridesmaids' dresses is a myth.

"That's a great idea," I say, because, really, who wants to know it's gonna hurt, right? "What colors do you have in mind?"

"Colors?"

Oh, boy.

A sane, solvent person would gently extricate herself right now. Since I am neither—and since Sheila Abruzzo has already given me a hefty check up front—I smile and start tossing out suggestions. By the time Leo gets back with the Diet Cokes—at which point we get a rerun of the swarming locust action—we've narrowed the choices down to yellow, magenta, lavender, dark green, mint-green, pearl-gray, or some shade of blue.

"You know what?" I heft a *Modern Bride* off the teetering stack at her feet and lay it on her lap. "Maybe once you find your dress, the color scheme will come to you…."

My attention is snagged by Leo's *psst*-ing me from the kitchen. I excuse myself, threading my way through the sea of lush Mediterranean womanhood.

"What?" I say when I get there.

"It's Tina."

"That's weird, I didn't even hear the phone ring—"

"Not on the phone. Here. In the kitchen."

She's sitting at the table, the green tinge to her skin clashing horribly with her mustard-colored sweater, letting Starr try on her necklace. Tina's always been really sweet to my daughter, but her affection has always seemed…cautious, somehow. As if she's afraid to let loose.

"C'mon, Twinkle," Leo says, "Time to get jammies on."

"Aw…"

"Now."

With a huge sigh, Starr hands Tina back her necklace and troops off after her great-grandfather.

"God, she's getting so big," Tina says. "Who's she look like?"

"Judith," I say, referring to my father's mother. "Isn't it obvious?"

"Yeah, you're right, I don't know why I didn't notice it before."

The conversation comes to a dead halt; I try kicking it back to life by saying, "Uh…Tina? Aren't you supposed to be in *there?*"

"Would you be, if you had a choice?"

Point taken. I sit down beside her. "So how come you didn't return my calls?"

"Sorry. I just wasn't feeling real sociable, that's all."

I take her hand and say gently, "Luke's so happy about the baby."

Her lips stretch into a thin smile. "I know. But please, El, not a word to anybody else. In case, you know, something happens."

"Nothing's going to happen, honey."

She nods, not looking at me. Then, on a sigh, she glances toward the door. "So is it a total zoo in there?"

"Total. And you've been missed."

I'm not sure she's heard me, her attention focused on the sporadic explosions of laughter from my living room. Suddenly, her gaze meets mine.

"I'd forgotten, how crazy and fun it all was. How happy I was. How I thought…" Tina shakes her head, removes her hand from mine. "Pete and Heather are so good together, you know?"

"So are you and Luke," I say through a thick throat. "And you damn well know that—"

The kitchen chair nearly topples over, she gets up so fast. "I'm sorry, I thought maybe, once I got here, I'd feel better, I'd be able to do this. But…I don't know, maybe it's hormones or something." She's slipped her coat back on, the same faux leopard job she had on the other night. "I'll call you, I promise," she says, then vanishes out the back door.

The woman is going to drive me nuts.

But then, I think as I rejoin the madness in my living room, I apparently don't have far to go. Elissa, Heather's size 24 cousin, corners me with a plea to steer Heather away from choosing a sleeveless attendant's dress; I say I'll do what I can, only to find myself nose-to-chest with the only redhead in the bunch besides me, some friend of Heather's I only know by sight, making an impassioned case against magenta.

And suddenly, don't ask me why, I'm up for the challenge. Of course, four months from now may be a totally different story, but at the moment, I actually think this might be kind of fun. If nothing else, I'll be too busy to worry about things I can't control.

Dressing these chicks for the biggest day in Heather Abruzzo's life—now *that,* I can control.

Across the room, Heather lets out a shriek, clamping her

hand to her chest like she's just been shot. "Ohmigod! Oh-migod! I found it!"

After I elbow my way back over, kohl-smudged eyes lift to mine, shimmering with a mixture of hope and dread. Hands shaking, she holds out the picture, as if offering up her first-born. Sixteen sets of eyes fasten on my face as I take the open magazine from her. Sixteen sets of bosoms collectively hitch with bated breath.

The girl has chosen well, I must say. We're talking enough tulle to outfit an entire "Swan Lake" corps de ballet, but the beading is minimal, there's no lace, and—with a few adaptations to camouflage the, shall we say, weaker aspects of Heather's figure—the pattern's a piece of cake.

"I can do this," I say at last, and a roar of joy goes up from the crowd.

Power's a heady thing, you know?

I may have to resort to a tranquilizer dart to get my daughter to sleep tonight. Since I put her to bed an hour ago, she's been back up three times. Like one of those trick birthday candles you can't blow out. By this time I'm in bed myself, although I never have been able to go to sleep as long as she's awake. Unfortunately, the little monkey knows this.

Floorboards creak behind me. "Mama?"

I keep my eyes shut, breathing so deeply I nearly hyper-ventilate.

"Ma-*ma!*" Starr climbs up onto the bed and flings herself over my shoulder, her hair tickling my face. "I *know* you're awake!" I grunt when she scrambles over me, bony little el-bows and knees landing where they will as she turns on the bedside lamp. Great. Now I'm bruised *and* blinded.

"Honest to God, Starr!" I shield my eyes, blinking in the glare. "Did you get into the Diet Cokes?"

She vigorously shakes her head. "I just can't sleep. Guess I'm overwrought."

Her word of the week, ever since she heard somebody say it on some TV show. Last week's was *evocative*. I kid you not. Can you imagine what she'd be like if I'd started shoving flashcards in her face when she was six weeks old?

"C'n I look at this?"

I yelp as a fifty-pound something whaps me in the arm. "What?" I peer at the weapon, which turns out to be an abandoned *Martha Stewart Weddings*. Starr knows she doesn't have carte blanche to look at everything that comes into the house, not since the day she walked in with one of my Nora Roberts books and asked, "Mama, what's *he cupped her* mean?"

That freethinking, I'm not.

"Yes, that's fine," I say, entertaining a sanguine hope that she'll haul her find back to her room. Instead, I nearly bite my tongue when she yanks my extra pillow out from underneath my head and wads it up against the headboard.

"Uh, Starr? You're doing this in here because...?"

"'Cause there's no monster in here." Damn. I have *really* got to get rid of that thing. She pushes her glasses farther up onto the bridge of her tiny nose. "Oh, this is a pretty dress."

This from the kid who screamed bloody murder when I tried to get her to wear a dress to somebody's wedding last year. I squint at the picture, giving in to the inevitable. Never again will I take for granted the luxury of going to sleep when I'm tired. "Yes, it is," I say on a yawn.

She skootches closer to me, smelling like watermelon shampoo. "It looks like fun, getting married."

"It can be, I suppose."

"Will I get married when I grow up?"

"Maybe. That's not something anybody can predict."

After a minute or so critiquing a spread on wedding cakes

that cost more than my first year of college, she says, "Why's Tina so sad?"

Not what I was expecting. But then, that pretty much describes my life these days. "She's got a lot on her mind right now."

"Like what?"

"Grown-up stuff, Twink. Nothing that would make sense to you."

"Mama. I'm *not* a baby, geez."

I stifle a chuckle. This kid was *never* a baby. A memory surfaces from several weeks before her fourth birthday, of Starr with her head in her hands, moaning, "Why am I still *three?*"

"I know you're not, sweetie pie. But you're not a grown-up, either. And I am—" maybe if I say it with enough conviction, I'll believe it "—so I get to make the decisions about what you need, or don't need, to know."

"That is *so* lame."

"And you *so* have to deal with it."

She slams shut the magazine, her sharp little eyes meeting my bleary ones.

"You weren't married to my daddy, were you?"

I have long since given up trying to figure out my daughter's thought progressions. Fortunately, I'm too pooped to flinch. "No, baby. I wasn't."

"How come?"

You know, I always swore I'd never put her off, never dismiss her questions. But for some reason, I'd always pictured her being older and me being awake. And that I'd have answers that actually made sense. To at least one of us. Why is life so freaking *messy?*

I pull her into my arms. "Would you be really mad at me if I told you I can't answer your question right now, but I promise I will one day?"

"Why can't you tell me now?"

Why couldn't I have had a kid content to ask me why the sky's blue? Or, since we live in New York, snot-colored?

"Because, baby, I just can't."

"Like you can't about Tina?"

"Kinda, yeah."

"Well, that just blows," she says, and I'm sorry, I can't help it. I burst out laughing.

Starr's bottom lip starts to tremble. "It's not funny."

I hug her harder, trying to tamp down the chuckles. Underneath that so-cool-I-rule exterior is a very sensitive little girl. "I know it's not, honey. And I'm not laughing at you. But honestly—where did you hear that?"

"Jason. He says it all the time. He says some other stuff, too, but he told me I can't say those words, 'cause you'd burn his butt."

I crack up all over again.

Of course, the next time I see Jason, he is *so* dead.

"Ohmigod! Ellie Levine!"

Ten days have passed. I'm standing in a crush of bodies at a new deli close to work—I'd given my old one the heave-ho the day I saw a cockroach the size of the Hindenburg taking a stroll through the potato salad—when I hear the voice. I crane my neck, but even in four-inch heels all I see are chests and arms.

"Ellie! It's me! Mari!"

My mouth drops open. Ohmigod, is right. Mariposa Estevez, my best friend from college. We fall into each other's arms—much to the annoyance of the hundred or so people in our immediate vicinity—as I wonder how I managed to lose touch with somebody I thought would always be close.

Of course, then I remember. Daniel. Who happened at a time in my life when I hadn't yet figured out there's a difference between installing a man as the center of my universe and letting everybody else spin right out of my orbit.

"Girl," Mari says with a huge smile. "You are looking *good!*"

She is nothing if not kind.

The tall, thin product of a French mother and a black Cuban father, the woman in front of me, the woman fully aware that every straight man in the place is gawking at her, the woman radiating some out-of-this-world perfume she probably didn't rub on her wrists from a magazine strip, is unbelievably gorgeous. Skin a perfect golden milky color, huge dark gold eyes, God-given below-the-shoulder ringlets, full lips shimmering in some right-this-minute burgundy that would make me look like my great-aunt Esther three weeks *after* her funeral. She is wearing a coat that, swear to God, looks like it's made out of rags, thigh high black leather boots with five inch spike heels that scream dominatrix (but classy), a striped miniskirt and a tiny, olive-green cashmere sweater that on anyone else would look like moldy cheese.

"So are you!" I say, thinking, Why is it so hard to hate nice people?

"Numbah fawty-three!" booms from behind the counter.

I check my number. Seventy-five.

"I can't believe we lost track of each other!" she says, beaming. "How are you doing? *What* are you doing?"

"Seventh Avenue," I hedge. "You?"

Mari rattles off a major designer name. As in, not just first tier, but on the right hand of God. "But I'm thinking of moving on. It's all about keeping your options open, you know? Listen, I'm running like three years behind here—" she grins "—but we have *got* to get together for drinks...shit, hold on..."

She pivots to the man behind her and says at the top of her voice, "You got some kinda affliction that makes you grab women's butts or what? And don't even think about giving me some sorry-assed story about how crowded it is in here. You don't see me with my hand on your balls, do you?" Then, muttering "Jerk," she turns back to me, fishing for something in her pocketbook. Gucci. *This* year's. The girl is doing well. "Are you uptown or down?"

"Oh, um, actually…neither. But here's my cell…" I pretend to rummage through my purse. "Damn. I must've left my card case at work."

"Not a problem." She pulls out a second card, scribbles my cell number on it. "I've gotta couple evenings free next week. Will that work for you?"

"Uh, sure."

"I'll call you, I swear!" she says, slithering through the crowd, undoubtedly leaving a plethora of hard-ons in her wake.

"Sixty-fowah?" I hear. "Sixty-five? Yo, sixty-five?"

My bag rings. My arms squeezed so close to my ribs I'm about to suffocate in my cleavage, I somehow get my phone from my purse, while number sixty-six—presumably—and one of the guys behind the counter are having a major set-to about exactly how fresh the tuna salad is. Guy sounds like nothing's gonna do it for him short of the fish swimming up the Hudson that morning, then taking a taxi over from the 42nd Street pier.

"Hey," comes the faint, pitiful voice through the phone after I say hello. "It's me."

I now understand what they mean by "her heart leaped into her throat."

"Tina?" I press the phone harder to my ear, stuffing my index finger in the other one. "I can't hear you very well— where are you?"

"Home," I barely hear as "Seventy-five!" booms right in front of me. Jesus. How'd it get to be my number so fast? I wave my hand; a round-faced, white-shirted man beckons to me with a gruff, "Okay, sweetheart, what'll it be?"

"Hang on," I say into the phone, then: "Liverwurst on whole wheat, mayo on the side, lettuce, pickle." Back into the phone: "We've got a crappy connection, I can't hear you—"

"We just ran outta whole wheat, you wan' white, rye or pumpernickel?"

It's not even noon, for God's sake, how can they be out of whole wheat already? "Rye. No seeds—"

"Oh, God, Ellie—I'm so sorry…"

"About…what?"

"I couldn't go through with it." By now, she's sobbing. "I just got too scared."

My stomach drops. "What are you talking about?"

"What do you think?" I can hear her now, boy. Hell, half the people on either side of me can hear her now. "I got rid of the baby! I went by myself, and just…did it."

"Here ya go, sweetheart," the deli man says, handing me a white bag emblazoned with hieroglyphics over the glass case. "Pay at the register. Number eighty-t'ree!"

Ten people surge in front of me, shoving me into the minuscule air pocket left in their wake. I tell Tina to hang on a sec as I peer inside the bag, noting a suspiciously dark image through the butcher paper and nothing that even remotely resembles a container of mayo. Which means either there isn't any or it's slathered on the bread thicker than Anna Nicole's makeup.

Just a mite too preoccupied to assert my usual snarky self, however, I elbow my way through the hordes and over to the register, grabbing a Dasani, a bag of chips and a Hershey's bar to round out my meal. Juggling the bag, my purse, my now-extracted wallet and the phone, which is too damn small to wedge between my shoulder and my ear, I finally say, "You went alone?"

"Yeah, it was okay, I took a taxi home after."

The dark-haired hottie on the register gives me a total that could feed a family of six in his country of origin for a week; I swipe my Visa and say, quietly, "You okay?"

The silence on the other end slices right through to my soul. "You're not mad?"

Frankly, I don't what I am. And God knows, I don't know what to say. I do know, however, that she didn't call just to give me the news.

I sign the slip and say, "I'll be there in forty-five minutes."

I told Gretta, our new bookkeeper—Angelique did indeed throw in the towel, the end of last week—I had a family emergency and to tell Nikky to call me on my cell if she needed to get in touch with me. So far, she hasn't. Which actually might break the tension as Tina and I sit here on her king-size bed in her aqua-and-peach pseudo-Southwest style bedroom, watching Ricki Lake and sharing my mayonnaise-drenched liverwurst on pumpernickel. I gave her my whole chocolate bar, though. I think she needs it more than I do.

More than anything, I want to ask her what she's planning to tell Luke. Who stopped by last night to show me the itty-bitty pair of athletic shoes he found. The day before that, a toy elephant nearly as large as a real one. Well, a baby one, anyway.

The people at the clinic told Tina since she had it done so early, she should be basically okay by this evening, just to take it easy for a day or so.

But there's "okay" and then there's "okay." I've finally sorted out my feelings at least enough to know that I'm feeling sick about the whole thing, but I can't tell what's going on inside Tina's head. Which, as I said, is totally unlike her, since at any given moment her emotions hover a good foot outside her body. Rather than really talking, she's instead providing running commentary about the bozos on today's show. Something about fat girls who slimmed down and then slept with men who hadn't given them the time of day when they were heavy. Without bothering to reveal their true identities, of course.

"Jesus," Tina says, finishing off the chocolate bar and licking her fingers while I find myself wondering how, exactly, they get these losers to come on the show to begin with? I mean, didn't these guys kinda wonder what's up when they get the call from the Ricki Lake people? "You really have to wonder why the women thought these turkeys were so hot to begin with, don't you? I mean, is this mullets-on-parade or what?"

And unfortunately, they weren't all on the men.

"Holy shit!" Tina lands a sideways punch on my upper arm. "Is that Emily Laker? It is! Ohmigod, I don't believe it!"

"Where?" I say, squinting at the TV and rubbing my arm.

"The blonde, all the way over on the right! In that blue leather miniskirt!"

"You're nuts, that's not Emily—"

"The hell it's not! Look, look—see? She's still got that scar on her upper lip from when Rosario Cruz punched her in the face in the ninth grade!"

I swing my legs off the bed to go get a closer look, only to let out a gasp. "Ohmigod—you're right! Then…wait a minute, you don't think…"

"And here's the boy who wouldn't give you the time of day back in Richmond Hill High…Andy Fratelli!"

Tina and I shriek with laughter as Big Bad Andy Fratelli saunters on stage. There's a not-so-little pooch underneath his T-shirt, and his forehead stretches a little farther back than it used to (which in his case isn't a totally bad thing), but his grin is just as clueless as ever. Until Emily—who easily weighed three hundred pounds in high school and who now has the slut look *nailed*—reveals her true identity. I swear, I can see Andy's balls shrink from here.

"Guess he missed the scar, huh?" Tina says, nearly choking because she's laughing so hard.

"Like he was looking at her *face!*"

We both dissolve, our giggles escalating into howls as Emily reads poor, dumb Andy up one side and down the other. Until I realize Tina's laughter has turned into uncontrollable sobs.

I stab the power button on the remote and crawl onto the bed beside her, taking her in my arms. She's incoherent and in-consolable by now, keening a nonstop litany of "Ifuckedup, Ifuckedup, Ifuckedup…" My insides cramp; I don't know what to say. I wish I could somehow take her tangled confusion and regret and recriminations and straighten it all out for her. I wish I had some answers. *Any* answers. All I know right now is that she's in pain. She doesn't get another chance to change her mind.

She can't go get the baby back.

"I want Luke," she says, her face wet against my sweater. "I can't stand this, I've got to tell him."

I freeze. *Now* she wants to tell him?

"Please," she says, her watery, black-rimmed eyes beseech-ing, "you've got to call him, tell him to come home—"

"I don't think that's a good idea," I say. "Not until you're a little calmer. Besides, he'll be home soon, anyway—"

"No, I've got to do it now, before I change my mind, before I chicken out." A tsunami of remorse floods the room. "He'll be furious, he'll hate me, I know it, but I can't face him with this on my conscience."

The urge to vanish is nearly overwhelming.

Especially when I hear the clunk of the front door deadbolt.

chapter 7

If I'd had a drop of sense, I'd be long gone. But something—guilt?—keeps me glued to the edge of Tina's sofa while Luke and she talk in their bedroom. At this point, I'm not so much afraid that he'll be angry—that's a given—as I am that he'll never forgive either one of us.

Except then I remember that I didn't know she was going to do this. Yes, I knew she was thinking about it, but as far as I knew, she'd changed her mind.

And maybe she had. Because Tina's my friend, because I don't want to give in to the insidious doubt gnawing at my stomach lining, I refuse to believe she'd planned it this way all along. That, rather than dealing with my less than supportive reaction to her original plan, she lied to me. And to her husband.

After what seems like hours, I finally hear the bedroom door open, then click softly shut. My heart pounds as I hear

Luke's rubber-soled footfalls on the wooden floor as he comes down the hall. I look up, swallowing nonexistent spit, my insides caving at his wrecked expression.

"Is…is she okay?" I tentatively prod, as you might a snake to see if it's really dead. As opposed to getting the hell out of there.

His gaze drifts out the window, one hand cupping the back of his neck. "I guess. Or she will be, eventually. I told her to try and get some sleep." Dark, perplexed eyes meet mine, and I think, *okay…here it comes.* "What I don't get is why she called you instead of me."

Oh, God. This must be one of those low simmer mads, that he's too angry to even let it out. I swallow again. "I guess…it's just one of those woman things, you know? Maybe…she felt better having me be with her first. But I swear," I quickly added, "I hadn't been here an hour before she started asking for you. In fact, I was about to call you when you walked in."

"Yeah. She told me." He sinks into a chair at right angles to the sofa, but there's nothing relaxed about his pose. "Now I understand why she didn't want to tell anyone. In case this happened. I mean, I know it's not unusual, especially with a first baby, but you just don't expect it to happen to you, you know?"

Something's not right here. "Especially with a first baby?"

"Yeah. J.J.'s and Vinnie's wives had miscarriages with their first, too."

What?

I only hope Luke takes my sudden fit of trembling for being as upset as he obviously is.

Holy crap. I glance back down the hall, barely able to control the impulse to march into Tina's bedroom and smack the daylights out of her. Maybe she hadn't planned on aborting the baby after telling me she'd changed her mind, or maybe she had. I don't know, and frankly, I don't want to. Any more than I want to know whether her lying to Luke was a spur-of-the-moment thing, either. I do know the only thing keeping me from spitting out the truth right now is that it would only hurt Luke even more than he is already.

As for Tina…right now, I don't give a damn whether she's hurt or not. Whatever sympathy I felt for her—for her fears, for her confusion—has just gone right down the tubes.

She could have lied to me, too, dammit. She could have told me she'd miscarried, and I wouldn't have been the wiser. But no, she had to confess to *somebody,* didn't she? And who better than good old Ellie? Ellie the Trustworthy, Ellie the Reliable…Ellie the Chump. After all, why should I mind sharing her burden of guilt any more than I shared my liverwurst sandwich earlier?

How is it I get to know *all* the secrets, but each of them only gets to know half? How is this a good thing?

"Ellie? You okay?"

When I force myself to look at him, I realize that as heartbroken as he is at the moment, his pain will heal, eventually.

I'm not so sure about mine.

I manage a smile. "Yeah. More or less." We get up at the same time; he gives me a hug. Or maybe I give him one, I'm not sure. In any case, it's awkward and stiff and we break apart quickly. I grab my coat and purse off the couch and sidle toward his front door. "Okay, well, since you're here now…I might as well get going. I mean, I've got work to do and stuff…."

"Oh, yeah, sure." In two strides, he's around me and to the door, opening it for me. "Teen will probably call you later, though."

I nod, not sure what to say, then step out into the hall.

"Hey," he says softly. "Hold on a sec."

My nerves twitching with the need to flee, I force myself to turn back; his gaze barely touches mine before he averts it, rubbing his palm against the outside of his thigh like he used to when he got nervous as a little kid. When he looks back up, my throat clenches at the raw vulnerability in his eyes, a look

I've only seen a handful of times before. A look, I now realize, I doubt few other people ever see.

"Okay, this is gonna sound sappy, but...you know, Tina and
I really lucked out, having you for a friend. And, well, I just
wanted you to know that. How important you are to us. Both
of us," he adds, just to avoid any misunderstandings.

I'm not sure what to say to that. Or even how to react, even
though I don't doubt he means it. And on some level, I'm
touched. But it's like making that perfect swing at the ball a
millisecond after it crosses the plate: What's the point?

"Thanks," I say. "But...maybe now's a good time for the
two of you to wean yourselves from me." As his eyes widen,
I add, "Or maybe I'm the one who needs to do the weaning, I
don't know—"

"What the hell are you talking about? You think we
shouldn't be friends anymore?"

I can feel my eyes burning, but I've had plenty of practice
holding back tears. "Remember what I said the other night,
about feeling like I'm always in the middle? You even made
some comment about me putting myself there. Remember
that? Well, you were right. That's exactly what I've done. And
frankly, constantly being squeezed between the two of you's
getting just a little uncomfortable."

Then, partly because I don't know what else to say and
partly because the eye-stinging's just gotten a lot worse, I
scoot down the hall, trying to shut out Luke yelling, "Ellie!
Ellie, *dammit*—what the hell's going on with you?"

Would that I knew.

Starr's already been asleep for a good hour or so when
Tina calls.

"I'm so sorry," she whispers in a broken voice. "I'm so
fucking sorry."

My own eyes burn. I'm still angry and confused, but I'm

calmer. Somewhat. I don't get why she's done this. But after all these years, dammit, her pain is, and always will be, mine.

"Where's Luke?"

"He went out, I don't know where. His parents', maybe?"

I check the window. "No, his car's not out front."

"You sure?"

"Yeah."

I can hear her sniffling, then blowing her nose.

"Teen? Why didn't you tell Luke the truth?"

"I meant to, I swear to God. Then Luke came in and…oh, El—" She breaks down, her words nearly unintelligible. "If you c-could've seen the look on his face, how broken up he was…it was horrible. A-and I opened my mouth, and…"

"Lied."

"Oh, God! It was like somebody else had put the words in my mouth!" She blows her nose again. "El? Why aren't you saying anything?"

"What do you want me to say?"

"That you understand?"

"But I don't, Tina. *I'm* sorry. I wish to hell I did. But I just…don't."

"Don't hate me, El," Tina says in a tiny voice. "Please. I don't have anybody else I can talk to, nobody understands me the way you do."

There's that word again. *Understand.* I think, obliquely, that maybe even more than love or food or shelter or sex, what the human animal craves most is for another human being to understand him. To absolve him of that which he doesn't understand himself, someone to sort through the fragments of another person's psyche and say, "See—this is why you act and think the way you do, it's not your fault, you're a good person who's been screwed over." The old *I'm okay, you're okay* approach to relationships.

And the thing is, Tina *is* a good person. And she *has* been screwed over. And in many ways, I know I'll never have a better friend.

"I don't hate you," I say, finally, wearily. "But maybe that's why it hurts so much, why *I* can't understand how somebody can put a friend in the position you just put me in."

Silence.

"I'm sorry," she says at last, and hangs up.

Weeks pass. Life trudges on. It's late February now, still bitterly cold and damp, that time of year when you've decided Mother Nature is a nasty old witch and spring will never come. Everything is relentlessly gray—buildings, sky, the ever-present slush that only seems to accumulate where I need to cross the street, my mood. Even my clothes. This morning, for instance, I opened my drawer to pull out a sweater, and all the bright colors immediately set my teeth on edge, like those annoyingly upbeat door-to-door salesmen determined to sell me something I don't want, never have wanted, and never will want. I grabbed a putty-colored turtleneck and slammed shut the drawer, muttering to myself.

You know, I think as I snatch a few minutes at Nikky's computer (she's off getting sandblasted or something) to enter the latest batch of orders, it's as if everybody's moving forward except me. At least, it seems that way. All around me, people are getting on with their careers, getting married...getting laid, if nothing else. Yet here I am, with no social life outside of going next door for dinner with the Scardinares once a month, making other people's wedding dresses, wading through other people's traumas. And who am I fooling about this job? Hell, after the Tina debacle (I haven't heard from either Luke or Tina since then, which has been a lot harder than I thought), I couldn't even use my work as an excuse to avoid my life. *What* work? I don't even have my own desk, for God's sake. And what have I learned, really, in the time I've been here? I mean, please, like I didn't already know how to hang a bias-cut skirt.

For someone with a family history of premature demise, this is not good. Unlike the majority of the population, I can't count on *later*. If I don't get a move on, *later's* gonna turn into *never*.

So, chica—*what're you gonna do about it?*

Of course, that's the tricky part to all this. I haven't got a clue.

Sure you do.

No. I don't—

Great. I'm having arguments with myself.

Whatever, the unidentified voice horns in. *So when you gonna stop and figure out who the hell you are and what you want?*

Uh…now?

Now would be good.

This leads to several seconds of intense nail-tapping on the desk while the computer hums complacently in front of me. I shut my eyes and think, *Okay, what's the first thing that comes to mind?* praying the answer doesn't involve either joining some religious group or, worse, a singles club. Oddly—and thankfully—enough, the thought *Call Mari* blips on the old mental radar screen.

Hmm. Of course, it's been more than a month and she hasn't called *me*. Not that I expected her to. One, because she's obviously one of those people who is getting on with her life, and two, because I can't see any reason why she'd really want to resurrect our friendship after all this time. Yeah, we had a great time in school, but that was then, this is now, and I'm a wuss when it comes to making overtures like that.

Which could account for—the light dawns—why I'm here and she's working for The Right Hand of God.

I get up, march myself into the bookkeeper's office (Corey, now—Gretta lasted four days) and retrieve my purse from the bottom drawer of his desk. The guy's like, ten. I'm talking right off the assembly line—no nicks, no scratches, no dings. And he reeks of Victoria Secret's *Very Sexy*. Which on Corey just comes across as *Very Desperate*.

"Hey, Ellie," he says, grinning up at me as I wait out the brief dizzy spell from standing up too fast. "Wanna do lunch later?"

This makes the third time he's asked this week. And it's only Tuesday.

"Busy, sorry," I say, my voice trailing in my wake as I hot-foot it out of there. Once in the john, I dig Mari's card out of my purse. I have no idea what, if anything, this will lead to. I have no idea of anything, least of all what I'm doing. But the fact is—pause for heart palpitations—I'm *doing*. Taking action. Moving forward. Putting myself *out there*.

She answers on the first ring, sounding truly like a person who has the world at her feet.

"Ellie! Thank God you finally called me! Girl, I have been trying and trying to get you, but you must've given me a wrong number or something, 'cause the dude I finally got didn't have a clue who I was talking about!" She laughs; I'm thinking, I gave her the wrong number? I'm meticulous about numbers, always have been. But when we double-check the number, yep. I'd transposed two digits. So now I can add avoidance dyslexia to my list of sins.

"So when can we get together?" she says.

Oh, God. I'm gonna throw up. But I say, "What's good for you?"

I hear the faint punching of Palm Pilot keys. "Thursday? Meet me here after work, we'll play it by ear from there?"

This means not getting home until after Starr's in bed. Everything inside me whines *You can't do this.*

Everything except the single brain cell that says—out loud— "Sounds good."

* * *

"Of course, you should go out." My grandfather practically slams down the dinner plate in front of me. Pot roast, potatoes, stewed tomatoes. Across the kitchen table, Starr is giving me her you-can't-be serious face, but I can't tell if it's meant for my announcement or dinner. "It's not right, a young woman like you never doing anything with her friends. Never going on a *date.*"

Ah, yes. The Ellie Doesn't Date issue. There being no Jewish mothers currently in residence, my grandfather, bless his heart, has assumed the role, matchmaking apparently being a cultural, rather than a gender-specific, calling. But at least I've yet to find some strange guy sitting on our sofa when I get home from work, or get phone calls that start, "Hi, you don't know me, but…" All that may change, however, if I reach thirty without a ring on my finger.

I fork in a hunk of pot roast. "When would I have time to date?"

"If you're going out with this Mari person, you could go out on a date."

"Not the same thing. I hate dating, you know that."

"That's because you keep dating shlubs. Or did, when you used to date."

Can't argue there. "The problem is," I say, watching Starr poking her fork over and over into her stewed tomatoes, making them ooze, "there's no way to find out if they're shlubs until you've gone out with them. By then, there's nothing to do except suffer through the rest of the evening."

Leo glances up, cutting his meat. "I worry about you, being alone."

"Alone? When am I ever alone?"

"You know what I mean, don't be fresh."

"Hey—it's been a long time since I ventured out from under my rock. Give my eyes a chance to adjust before turning the light on full-blast."

He grunts. Starr emits a particularly soulful sigh.

"What is it, sweetie?" I say. As if I don't know.

"These," she says, wrinkling her nose at the mangled to-matoes. "They're dis-*gust*-ing."

An appropriate enough label for something that now looks like fresh roadkill. "Then don't eat them."

"What is this, don't eat them?" my grandfather says. "The baby needs her vitamin C. And A. Tomatoes are loaded with A."

"I'm not a baby—!"

"I know, sweetie. And she takes a multivitamin every morning, Leo."

"That's not the same as getting your nutrients from your food. And it sets a bad precedent, letting her pick over her food like that. She'll grow up with one of those eating disorders."

I decide against pointing out that the two have nothing to do with each other. Unfortunately for the rest of us, Leo eats everything. Always has. His rebellion against his mother's kosher kitchen, would be my guess.

"Honestly, Leo—so she doesn't like stewed tomatoes. Big deal."

"How does she know if she's never tasted them?"

I sigh. We can end this now, or we can drag it out to its painful, and inevitable, conclusion. Knowing full well what Starr's reaction is likely to be, I turn to her and gently say, "You could take one bite, just to taste—"

"That's not fair!" Betrayal screams in her eyes. "You can't change your mind like that!"

Never mind that *she* does at the drop of a hat.

"One bite. Or no dessert."

Starr actually squawks, then rams her arms over her chest, her face crumbling into a mutinous glare. We may be here for a while.

I turn to my grandfather. "You *sure* you're up for dealing with…things for another few hours on Thursday?"

Leo chuckles. "Like I haven't seen that look before." He touches my hand, a rare show of physical affection. "You need to spread your wings, sweetheart. I sometimes think it's not right, this life you lead. Not married, not really single… In limbo."

Naturally, hearing my own thoughts echoed immediately prompts me to refute them. "I'm hardly in limbo. Not with Starr—"

"Who will grow up and leave and start her own life, and here you'll be. Left behind. Wondering what happened to all those years you let slide by."

I take a bite of potato, but I can feel my face redden. "That's ridiculous."

"It's true. And I see it in your face, that you know it's true. But you deny what you feel. What you want." While I sit there, gawking at the man, he reaches for a roll, starts to butter it. "How much time we waste," he says, more to himself than to me, "lying to ourselves, ignoring the truth—"

Somebody knocks on the back door, making me jump. I get up to answer it, keeping one wary eye on my grandfather, only to jump again when I see the stocky form standing outside. For a second, I think—hope?—it's Luke, only to immediately realize, no, of course not, it's only Jason,

Imploring, puppy dog eyes latch onto mine when I open the door, as, for the second time that day, a tsunami of cologne bowls me over. From underneath the rim of his black beanie, bits of gold shimmer in his eyebrow, both earlobes. The kid forms a shallow, upright *S* as he stands there, his hands stuffed into the front pocket of his hoodie.

"C'n I hang here for a while? My folks are, like, driving me insane."

"Of course you can, Jason," Leo booms behind me, getting up from the table. "We've got chocolate cake for dessert, would you like some?"

"Sure, whatever." He shuffles in and over to the table, where Starr's still giving the tomatoes the evil eye.

"Stewed tomatoes?" he says. "Dude. Those are the *bomb*."

My daughter shoots him a look as if he's totally lost it, but damned if she doesn't shove a bite of tomatoes in her mouth. Granted, she's making faces as she chews like she's been poisoned, but eventually, and with a grimace worthy of a woman birthing a twelve-pound baby, she swallows. After a melodramatic shudder, she grabs her milk glass and gulps down half the contents.

"That was," she announces, "the *worst* experience of my entire life."

Jason turns to me, beaming at his accomplishment. And looking like he's expecting something in return. Something I cannot, and will not, give him.

Some princess I am. I don't even get frogs. Just tadpoles.

An hour later, I'm down in the basement, pinning pieces of muslin onto Beatrice, my dress form, padded out to match Heather's measurements. Leo and Starr are upstairs, reading together. Jason is here with me, following every move I make like a moony cat.

I know I should just send the kid home, but I can't. Yeah, yeah, I'm a pushover, we've already established that. And I know I'm going to eventually ask him what's wrong. Because something definitely is, more than his usual "life sucks" mood.

Now he's shifted his attention from me to stare at the bulletin board I've set up against one paneled wall, on which I've pinned both the photo from the mag and a few of my own sketches to flesh out what I can't see. My grandparents did the whole rumpus room thing with the basement when my dad was a kid, so it's very *Leave it to Beaver* down here. All we need is a cocker spaniel to complete the look. The Ping-Pong table even converted quite nicely into a cutting table.

"You're, like, really good," he says.

My mouth's full of pins—yeah, I know, bad habit—so all I can do is mumble, "Shusta cuppy," which he somehow understands.

"Like hell, dude. This is way cooler than the dress in the magazine."

You think maybe this is how Stephen Cojocaru started out?

We're both silent for several seconds; Jason's jamming out to some punk rock he put on the CD player earlier. I'd prefer Alanis Morrisette, myself, but he's the guest. Then he says, "You think Heather and Pete'll work out?"

"I s'pose they've got as good a shot as anybody," I say around what's left of the pins. "They've been together a long time."

"Yeah, well, so were Luke and Tina."

My eyes shoot to the side of his face; I ditch the rest of the pins before they end up in my throat. "What are you talking about?"

"I overhead Mom on the phone this afternoon, talking to Luke. I couldn't help listening in, she was kinda loud. Anyway, they must've split up." He frowns, the light dawning oh-so-slowly. "You didn't know?"

"No. I…we haven't been in touch for a while." My chest tight, I take a pull from the can of Diet Coke beside me, then twist the form around, pretending to stare at the back. "Are you sure you didn't misunderstand?"

"I overhead Mom talking to Pop later. She was, like, in total shock, goin' on about how totally random this was."

Somehow, I doubt Frances said "totally random." But I say, "I don't know, Jase. Maybe they're just taking a little time apart or something."

"That's what Dad said, but Mom said they'd already filed the papers."

I sink onto the stool by the form, the wind knocked out of me. I mean, yeah, they were having problems, *serious* problems, but they've been on the outs before, and they've always patched things up. So I just figured...

What? That Luke was making it all up, about their growing apart? That I'd just imagined the fear in Tina's eyes? A fear that first made her decide to go through with a pregnancy she didn't want, only to turn around and terminate it, then lie to both Luke and me about what had happened?

And why am I taking this so personally? Why do I feel as if, somehow, *my* life's just been torn apart?

"Ellie?"

I look over into Jason's worried eyes.

"I'm sorry, El. I thought you knew. I didn't mean to dump all that on you."

"No, it's okay. That you told me. I'm glad you did, actually."

"I figured maybe I'd better, since I heard Mom say something about seeing if you could talk some sense into them."

Heart attack time. "Tell me you made that part up."

"Uh, no. What, you don't want to see them back together?"

"What I want has nothing to do with this. With them. What on earth does Frances think *I* can do?"

"Dunno. I guess she thinks because you guys have been friends so long..." He shrugs. "I dunno."

"Well, I do." I stand up, spinning Bea around to jab pins in her left boob. "It's Luke's and Tina's problem to work out, or not, as they see fit."

"But I thought—"

"You thought what?"

"Geez, Ellie—it's always been the three of you, as long as I can remember. You can't walk away now."

I know he doesn't understand. And Frances isn't going to like this, either. But…"Things change, Jase," I say gently. "We've changed. Tina, your brother, me. We're not the same people we were, so our relationship can't remain the same, either."

He stares at me for a moment, then lets out, "That just blows."

No shit.

chapter 8

On Thursday evening, Mari—looking teeth-grindingly gorgeous in faux fox, three inches of lace skirt and these totally hot royal blue Fendi pumps with bows and chains and things—suggests a club not too far from her work. In my vintage (and yes, *I* mean vintage, not leftover) pink cashmere sweater complete with the de rigeur dive bomber boobs, paired with one of my grandmother's old wool pencil skirts that actually makes me look more than two feet tall, I'm not sure I'm dressed for clubbing. At least, not in this decade. More like Woolworth's counter, Brooklyn, 1962. Half a Rita Hayworth.

Aside from my attire, however, I'm even less sure I'm in the *mood* for clubbing. Not that this is saying much, since I've never been real big on the whole bar scene. Partly because, after a single glass of wine, I've been known to haul my sorry self onto the nearest elevated surface and belt out showtunes like some down-on-her-luck drag queen. I swear, lab rats have a higher tolerance for alcohol than I do.

But aside from that, I'm just the teensiest bit distracted right now, between Jason's revelation two nights ago about Luke and Tina, and Frances's begging me—he was right about that, too—to see what I could do. Since I wasn't about to go into the whole *mishegoss* about why I hadn't talked to either her son or daughter-in-law for all these weeks, I mumbled something vague and inconclusive and let it go at that.

However. Since Leo threatened to lock me out of the house unless I went out, here I am, trying to play grown-up. Yeah, I hear things about what's hot and not in the city, but since it's not like I ever actually get to any of these places, my recommendations are usually based on a three-line blurb in a copy of *New York Magazine* some tourist left behind in the subway or a snippet of conversation gleaned over somebody's tinkling in the stall next to me.

"I've never been here before," Mari says, handing her jacket to the coat-check person—and I'm not being PC, I honest to God can't tell—and peering into the bar beyond. "Have you?"

"Nope. New to me, too," I say, suddenly missing Tina—missing *Pinky's*, for godssake—with an intensity that borders on painful.

Hmm, Mari's looking at my chest. Since I doubt it's because she suddenly has a yen for me, I take a gander at myself, wondering if I've got egg salad on my boob or something. "What?" I say, yanking down my sweater to get a better look.

"Girl, only you could pull off that look."

"What look?"

She laughs. "The one that's got all the guys checking you out."

"Uh…" We move toward the back, her like a gazelle, me like that little chubby dude in *The Lion King,* not the one with Nathan Lane's voice, the other one. The warthog, that's it. Mind you, I don't usually go through changes about my appearance. Among other warthogs, I can definitely hold my own. Next to a gazelle, however...

"That's not me they're checking out," I say, "that's you."

"Honey," Mari says with a hand flap, "this city's got chicks like me comin' out their ears." No argument there. You can't walk three feet in Manhattan without tripping over something tall and stunning. "But you've got your own thing going. Voluptuous and feminine and *real*." At my flummoxed expression, she says, "Why do you think implants are such big business?"

"Not for hips, it isn't."

Mari rolls her great big, gorgeous eyes and grabs me by the shoulders, twisting me around so I can see in the smoky mirror behind us, then says in a low voice that only I can hear, "Trust me, Ellie—*that's* what nine out of ten of the straight guys in this place are gonna have wet dreams about tonight."

Assuming there are nine straight men in here. Although...maybe that guy over there is giving me the eye. And like I said, I've never thought of myself as a dog—or a warthog, actually—but while short, chunky quasi-Jewish girls are a dime a dozen in the greater metropolitan areas, they're not exactly the gold standard for what constitutes beautiful in these here parts. Keeping one's self-confidence highly polished isn't always easy.

Then the guy over at the bar grins, lifting his glass in a toast. Wow. Maybe there's something to this getting-out-more thing after all. So I do a little chin-lifting and boob-thrusting and Mari winks at me, all those succulent curls swishing over her regal, bony—but in a nice way—shoulders. Having shed the dead animal wannabe, she's wearing this slinky, shimmery bronzy halter top that shows off her adorable little breasts, nipples and all. On Mari, this is okay, since she's got tits that stay put when she removes her bra, unlike those of us for whom the effect is more like a pair of grain sacks plummeting several stories.

We head into the back, settling in at a cozy little table. It's early yet, only sixish, so the place isn't exactly hopping. "Damn," Mari says, getting right back up. "I'll be back. Whoever came up with the idea of drinking eight glasses of water a day should be taken out and shot."

I sit back, feigning "cool." But I can't exactly say I'm comfortable. Just being in one of these places brings back memories. Way too many memories, and not just of my impromptu musical performances. All that thinly veiled desperation, thicker even than the cigarette smoke (then), the manic laughter. *Whoo-hoo,* everyone seemed to be saying. *Look at me, having fun! Interacting! So drunk I can't feel my feet anymore, but hey, I'm sure I'm having a blast!*

Why do so many people think they can't enjoy themselves unless they've got enough alcohol in their system to warrant a HIGHLY FLAMMABLE! sticker on their forehead?

That was Daniel's pickup line, actually. So a note to any guys who might be reading this: If you can read a woman's body language enough to echo her thoughts, you're in.

It was a breath-sucking June night, the humidity a good ten percent higher than your average Central American rain forest. I'd just graduated and landed an assistant buyer's job in Saks's junior department. Mari and some blond, anorexic chick whose name I've mercifully consigned to oblivion decreed this a cause for celebration. Unlike moi, who, being acutely aware that I was still stuck in Richmond Hill for the foreseeable future—since assistant buyers earn less than street cleaners and the prospect of a four-way share in an apartment barely large enough for one person and a goldfish didn't exactly ring my chimes—was not in much of a celebratory mood. However, they were having none of my Eeyoria, and finally strongarmed me into going with them to some dive in the Village with all the ambiance of an internal combustion engine.

"ISN'T THIS GREAT?" Nameless Anorexic Chick shouted over eardrum-splitting music. Before I could answer, how-

ever, we were sucked into the sea of gyrating bodies like socks into a washing machine's agitator. Seconds later, bruised and sweaty and alone, I was spit out at the other end.

I should have left then, I know that now. But for some reason—probably the thought of fighting my way back out through all those icky bodies—I stayed. I figured, fine, I'd stick it out for a half hour, until I'd finished my wine or began to suffocate from the smoke, whichever came first. I wasn't too concerned about anybody hitting on me. For one thing, nobody ever did. For another, the noise level reduced communication to about the level of what must have transpired when the Dutch bought Manhattan off the Algonquins for twenty-four bucks worth of tchotchkes.

However, precisely at the twenty-nine minute and thirty-second mark, what looked like a quartet of Jersey City accountants appeared on what I suddenly realized was a stage. So I decided to stick around for a second, see what they were up to.

What they were up to, was jazz.

Now, I'm a total sucker for jazz. The old stuff, especially, from my grandfather's collection—Billie Holiday, Thelonius Monk, Dave Brubeck, Duke Ellington. Ella. For years, I thought jazz was *supposed* to sound scratchy. But I knew good stuff when I heard it. And for a bunch of nerds, these guys were pretty damn good.

Okay, so maybe I don't have much room to talk, lookswise, but I reserve the right to define my eye-candy. These guys were more like eye-spinach. At least, three of them were. Because suddenly the tobacco fumes parted, and I got my first really good look at the piano player.

Lust sprang awake inside me like somebody'd dumped a pail of water on it. Was it my imagination, or were Piano Guys's eyes…yes! Yes, they were! He was looking right *at me!* And he was smiling in that "Yeah, *you"* way! My heart beating wildly in my chest, I smiled back—

"Could I buy you a drink?"

What?

After a second or two, during which I processed the fact that Piano Guy hadn't somehow managed to speak to me via telepathy, I whipped around, my eyes flashing (well, I'm sure they were), intent on killing the bozo rude enough to snap me out of the first decent fantasy I'd had since junior high. Because let's be realistic, here: generally speaking, the only time men like Piano Guy notice me is when there's nobody else on the subway platform and they've left their watch at home. This was truly One of Those Moments, a moment now shot to hell by…by some dude with frizzy black hair and a beard in serious need of a hedge trimmer.

Although (even in hindsight I have to admit this), he had kind of a nice smile. What little I saw of it, anyway, before my glower sent it skittering away.

"Sorry," he said, looking crestfallen. "I didn't think you were with anybody."

And I thought, Jesus, somebody worse at this bar thing than I am. Then I thought, See? I can't even attract the guys with the decent pickup lines. Or even the bad pickup lines, for that matter.

It didn't help that he continued to sit there, looking crestfallen, while my brief flirtation with bitchiness went bye-bye. Granted, the Urban Jewish Mountain Man look doesn't normally do it for me, but from what I could tell, the only thing obnoxious about him was his hair.

Then I remembered Piano Man's smile for me and thought, *What am I thinking?* The Black Forest or a possible lifetime of jazz on command?

While I was pondering this dilemma, the music stopped and suddenly Piano Man was right there beside me, ordering a round, smiling at me, and I tilted my head in what I prayed was a provocative slant and purred, "That was really great."

"Thanks," he said, which was as far as the conversation got because then some blonde with legs longer than the Mississippi sidled up to him, shoved her tits through his ribs and whispered something in his ear that made him laugh. And kiss her.

To this day, I have no idea if they knew each other or not. But then, what difference would it have made?

Anyway, so there I sat, my fantasy lying in limp tatters at my feet, and Hedge Face gave me the HIGHLY FLAMMA-BLE! sticker on their forehead line, and I laughed and he smiled. And suddenly, the Black Forest didn't look so bad after all. "I'm Daniel," he said, holding out his hand. Which was warm and dry when he wrapped it around mine.

"Ellie," I said.

Then he said, "I know I wasn't the front runner, but I'd still like to buy you a drink."

And like a damn fool, I said, "Make it a Diet Coke and you're on."

Mari returns at last from the ladies' room and we order, an apple martini for her, a wine spritzer for me. I realize that's only a half step removed from a Shirley Temple, but morphing into Bernadette Peters isn't on my agenda this evening. For the next twenty minutes, we play catch-up. Sorta. I don't need wine in my system to realize how totally uninteresting my so-called professional life is, especially compared with hers. I can't evade the topic completely, however. And Mari easily picks up on the subtext.

The noise level has increased considerably as more people file in after work. But I can still easily hear her gentle, "I don't get it. You were so incredibly focused in school. How the hell did you end up working for Nicole Katz? You were meant for more, El."

"You don't know that—"

"The hell I don't." She takes a sip from the antifreeze-colored martini served in a glass as big as her head. "So what happened?"

After a suitable pause, I say, "I had a kid."

Mari's eyes get huge. Then her entire face lights up. "No shit? When?"

"Five years ago."

"That was practically right out of FIT!"

"Yep."

Even in the dim, bar-ry light, I can see her trying to digest this information. After the muscles in her face relax, she says, "Boy or girl?"

"A girl. Starr."

"A little girl! But that's fantastic!" Her smile fades when the rest of what I haven't said clicks in. "Oh. No daddy in the picture?"

"Nope." I tilt my glass, realize it's empty. Realize, too, that I have just the slightest buzz going. My shrug is blasé. Worldly. "Just one of those things."

"That's cool. It's not like it's any big deal, being a single parent these days. Not that I mean it's no big deal what you're doing," she quickly adds. "Just that it's practically become the norm."

"You wanna take a crack at it?"

"No damn way," she says on a laugh. Then she gets this pensive look. "Look, I'm gonna say something here, and you can tell me to go to hell if you want, okay? But you never struck me as the type to use having a kid as an excuse to check out."

"I hardly call what I'm doing 'checking out.'"

"That's because you're not sittin' on this side of the table."

"Okay, so maybe I've been a little...cautious about my career the past few years."

"Girl, you're working for Nicole Katz. That's not cautious. That's suicidal."

"It's not that bad—"

"I know three people who worked there before you. It's that bad." She leans forward. "And it's not gonna get better. Is it?"

I stuff a whole handful of peanuts in my mouth, mumbling, "The medical's terrific," around them.

"Ain't gonna do you any good if the job kills you—"

We're interrupted when the guy who'd raised a toast to me earlier tries to pick me up. Or at least, pick up my breasts, since he seems to address most of his remarks to them. A shame, too, since he's relatively good-looking, well dressed and doesn't seem too sloshed. A little WASP-y for my tastes, although that's not a real big issue for me. However...

"Thanks, really. But I have to get home to my five-year-old daughter."

Man takes off like he saw a flea in my hair.

Mari is giving me one of her are-you-sure-you're-for-real? expressions. One she used to give me with unnerving regularity when we were in school together.

"What?"

"Why the hell did you tell the guy you had a kid?"

"Because I do?"

"Girl, you have a lot to learn."

Although I don't take offense, I'm beginning to understand why Mari and I lost touch. She's great, and I love her, but when you get right down to it, we simply don't operate by the same set of rules. Not that I knew I was operating from more than anything but sheer dumb luck, but there you have it.

"Hey. If a guy can't deal with my kid..." I grandly wave my hand. "Fuck 'im."

Hoo, boy, that spritzer packs a punch. God, I need food. Something that once mooed would be good.

Mari lets loose with a laugh that, had we been anyplace other than Manhattan, would have turned every head in the place.

"I always did like your style."

"S'got nothing to do with style. S'gotta do with being true to myself. Or something."

Mari studies me for a second, then says, "Like you're being true to yourself about your crappy job."

"S'not crappy. Like I said, the medical's great."

"Like Nicole Katz is the only house in town that gives decent medical."

I wish I had a cigarette. Which is bizarre since I don't smoke. But the moment just screams for the heroine taking a dramatic pull on her ciggy, quirking one brow, then hissing out the smoke around the word, "Meaning?"

The effect isn't quite the same with a pretzel.

Mari does more of that pensive-looking thing for a minute, then leans forward and says, "Meaning…can you fax your résumé to me tomorrow?"

Every other morning of my child's life, I can give her a bowl of Lucky Charms and a cup of orange juice, and she's good for an least an hour in front of the TV. Except for this morning, when my fate hangs in the balance and for some inexplicable reason my mascara refuses to fatten my eyelashes. I'm standing at the bathroom sink, glaring at my reflection, when Starr clomps in, wearing these adorable red cowboy boots Tina gave her for her birthday and clutching the bowl of cereal I gave her not five minutes ago.

"These are yucky."

I look at her in the mirror, nearly putting my eye out with the damn mascara wand. "What're you talking about? That's been your favorite cereal for two years."

"What can I tell you? Things change."

I skip past the *And I have three boxes of this crap in my cupboard why?* thought and say, because I have exactly fourteen minutes in which to talk to Leo before I have to leave for work and I have the eyelashes of a gnat, "Fine. So whaddya want instead?"

"Dunno."

I give up on the mascara and toss it in my makeup bag, then *vroom* out of the bathroom, Starr clomping right behind me as I trot down the stairs. "Another kind of cereal?"

"Like what?"

"Corn flakes? Raisin Bran? Wheaties?"

"Yuck."

I am operating on roughly three hours sleep. Not because I got home all that late, but because, once the two-and-a-half molecules of alcohol in my system burned off, the full ramification of Mari's offer sank in. And with it, a rampant case of panic-induced insomnia.

You know the adage, Be careful what you wish for?

Now in the kitchen, I whip open the freezer. "How about some Eggos?" I try. "A toaster pastry? Eggs?"

"Uh-uh."

"French toast sticks?"

"No."

"Pop-Tart?"

"No way."

I look down at her, standing there in her Clifford jammies (yes, with the boots), her frizzy hair stuffed behind her little bat ears, her eyes so damn serious behind her glasses, and my exasperation stumbles. "C'mon, kid, help me out here."

Her mouth wiggles from side to side. "Sorry. Guess my tummy doesn't know what it wants this morning."

Okay. That's it.

"Then how about…" I slam shut the freezer and swoop down on her, her giggles turning into squeals as I haul her into my arms. "Some yummy frog tongues? Lizard toes? No? Then how about spider bellies in a lightly seasoned cream-of-grub sauce?"

By now she's laughing so hard she can hardly get out, "Mama! That's disgusting!"

Leo wanders into the kitchen, showered and dressed and in his Reeboks. My grandfather has this thing about never wearing slippers during the day, that putting on shoes tells your feet to be ready to roll at a moment's notice.

"I heard," he says. "So I'll give her something later. No big deal."

I hitch Starr higher on my hip—the damn boots must weigh twenty pounds—and say, "But breakfast is supposed to be my job." He waves away my protest; I smack a kiss on the top of my daughter's head and whisper in her ear, "Why don't you go on out into the living room and watch TV?"

"Don't wanna."

"Just for a few minutes, okay?"

"Why?"

Leo is frowning at me. Could it be he hears the subtle I'm-gonna-freak note in my voice? I can't talk to him with her here. And the minute I say, "I need to talk to Leo," I'm dead. She'll *never* leave.

I set her down on the floor again, saying, "You're missing *Sesame Street.*"

"That's not on yet, remember?"

My grandfather cups Starr's head and says, "Go watch TV, and I'll make you pancakes later."

With a brilliant smile, off she goes.

"You do know that's the only thing I left off the menu," I say.

"That's because you don't make pancakes."

This is true. And what's also true is that I now have eleven minutes left to talk to him.

"So how was your night out?" Leo says, pouring me a cup of coffee, then spooning in three sugars and a good-size dollop of half-and-half. "You got in after I was asleep, you must've had a good time."

"Yeah, it was fine." I sit at the table, taking the coffee from him and downing half the cup in one gulp. When I come up for air, I say, "But something came out of it I didn't expect."

"Oh?" Armed with his own cup of joe, Leo sits catty-corner from me. "Like what?"

"Like...a possible new job."

His eyes never leave my face. "A better job than the one you have?"

O-kay, hold on to your hat. "Much better. As in, not even in the same galaxy better. See, Mari's taking another position in the company—" I've already told him who she works for "—which leaves hers vacant and she thinks I'd be perfect for it so she wants me to fax her my résumé today before the ad goes into the paper on Sunday."

My heart is pounding so hard it hurts.

"But this is wonderful!" Leo frowns. "Isn't it?"

"Yes! I mean, it could be..."

"But...?"

"It involves some traveling. Okay, a lot of traveling. Visiting department stores around the country to make sure the house's boutiques are up-to-date and in good shape, or establishing them in new stores."

"I see." He gets up, plops two pieces of rye bread in the toaster. "The pay is good?"

"Did you hear what I said? I'd have to be away—"

"I heard what you said. Well?"

"The pay is fantastic. And the benefits..." I bite my lip.

"So what's the problem?"

"What do you mean, what's the problem? It's about this child I have? The one you already think I'm shortchanging because I have to occasionally work on the weekends?"

"Oh."

That's it? I'm proposing something that would radically alter all our lives and all he says is "Oh"?

We sit in silence for several seconds until the toaster pops up, making me jump. Leo plunks the toast on a plastic plate, then carts it over to the table with the margarine tub he's already gotten out of the fridge. Only after he's carefully smothered both pieces of toast does he say, "So maybe I should look at things from a different perspective."

I frown. "You're confusing me."

A half smile tilts his mouth. "The prerogative of an old man." He takes a bite. "So what are you asking me? You want my permission? My blessing? What?"

"I don't know."

"So let me ask *you* something…how badly do you want this?"

I try lifting my mug to my lips, but my hand's shaking too much. "As badly as Starr wants a dog. And if this had been five years ago—"

"What?"

"I would've killed for this opportunity."

"And now?"

"And now…I'm not exactly a free agent, am I?"

"Meaning you don't think I can handle Starr while you're away."

"It's not a matter of whether or not you *can* handle her. But I don't think it's fair to ask you to, not more than you already are."

"Why not?"

I glance behind me, then lean forward, "She doesn't drive you batty?"

That gets a chuckle. "Only once or twice a day. Nothing compared with what you used to do."

I snort.

"Look, trust me—if it got to be too much, taking care of her, I'd tell you."

I don't believe this for a minute, but I say, "You swear?"

"On your parents' graves," he says quietly. "As for looking after her while you're away—" he shrugs "—she's in bed by eight, anyway, and you're rarely home before seven. I think I can manage the extra hour."

"Which means I'd be giving up the little time we have together now." I blow out a sigh. "Not exactly putting her first."

"There's more than one way to put your child first."

"Yeah, well, *being there* is kinda right up at the top of the list."

"So is doing something that makes you happy, that gives her an example to follow when she grows up."

Oh. Hmm. Still…

On a groan, I plunk my elbows on the table and ram my hands through my hair. Lucky for me the shaggy look is hot right now. Leo reaches over and lays a hand on my head, just like he'd done with Starr a few minutes ago.

"You'll have an interview, right?"

I nod.

"Then maybe you should find out more about what the job entails before you give yourself an ulcer over it. Who knows? Maybe on some of these trips, Starr and I could come with you. Maybe we can hire someone to help, if you're afraid I'll fall apart from watching one quiet five-year-old. Maybe you should trust a little more, that this opportunity has come to you for a reason." He grins. "Maybe you'll meet a nice man on one of these trips."

I should've known.

I glance at the clock and let out a gasp. Calling out to Starr that I'm leaving, I grab my bag and coat off the back door coat tree, shrugging into it as my daughter comes barreling into the kitchen for our morning goodbyes. A dozen hugs and kisses later, I'm hotfooting it to the subway, sweating under my coat even though the temperature's barely above freezing. Instead of feeling settled about things after the conversation with my grandfather, I'm feeling more conflicted than ever. Which is dumb. Come on, guys—there are only two choices here: either I go for this job, or I don't. So why isn't it obvious, which choice I should make?

Then I start shivering hard enough to generate power for Buffalo. Not because I'm cold, though, but because I realize just how much I want this.

This could be it, my ticket out of Queens, out of the stultifying existence I'd let myself believe was my only option. With that salary, Starr and I could eventually move to Manhattan. Maybe in the summer, after Heather's wedding. I'd always thought the Village, but maybe the Upper West Side would be good, too. And it's true, she and Leo could go with me sometimes, and she could stay with him in Richmond Hill when they couldn't.

This really could work out, you know?

I mean, if I even get the job. That's not exactly a given.

Still, I'm grinning like an idiot as I trudge up the stairs to the elevated platform, realizing I haven't felt so happy, so this-is-*right,* since the midwife laid Starr in my arms for the first time.

Me, working for one of the most important fashion houses in the world.

Ohmigod, ohmigod, ohmi-freakin'-*god.*

chapter 9

Making sure nobody sees me, I fax Mari my résumé the minute I get to work. Five minutes later, the phone rings.

"This needs work," she says. "Let me see what I can do. I'll fax you back in, hmm, twenty minutes?"

Shit. This means I have to find some reason to hang around so nobody else sees the fax. My heart can't take this. And what does she mean by "needs work"?

"Uh, sure, okay."

For the next twenty minutes, I'm a nervous wreck. Nikky's not in yet, thank God—she never comes in before ten, so I'm safe there—but her darling husband is circling the place like a vulture.

"Ellie!" Harold booms. "Run down to the coffee shop and get me…"

A loud roaring sound floods my ears. Since when does he send me to get his morning coffee? Whatever happened to calling *down* and having the little guy bring the coffee *up?* Do bogeymen have some sort of sixth sense about things, that he knows what I'm up to? I look at the clock. Sixteen minutes before Mari's going to fax me back. Of course, then it occurs to me, duh—I can call her and have her hold off until the coast is clear. Which I do, the minute I get out on the street.

"Okay," she says, "but don't make me wait too long. Apparently somebody else here recommended his boyfriend, so we have to move *fast.*"

Ten minutes later, I deposit Harold's decaf, Danish and change on his desk, then scamper back to Nikky's office and the fax machine. I call Mari.

"Okay, now."

A minute later, the fax comes through.

It's twice as long as the one I sent her. And what's amazing is that, somehow, nothing on this new and improved version of my working life is actually a lie. It's just…

Freaking fantastic, is what this is.

I call her back. "Honey," I say, "if I liked girls, you would get so lucky tonight."

She laughs. "It's all in the spin you put on things. Anyway, so you're cool with me taking this to my boss?"

My heart starts that hammering thing again.

"Absolutely."

Five minutes later, she calls back.

"Eight o'clock, Monday morning, *chica.* You're first on the list."

Ladies and gentlemen, we have liftoff.

Sunday afternoon, I'm down in the basement stitching together the muslin mock-up of Heather's bridal gown bodice. To keep from totally obsessing over the upcoming interview— as opposed to only mildly obsessing, which is a given—I've spent the weekend either schmoozing with my kid or ditzing with this pattern. At some point—like, yesterday—I'm going to have to start thinking about what to do with these fricking bridesmaids, too. Good thing I thrive on stress, is all I've got to say.

Over the whirr of my Pfaff, I hear the door at the top of the stairs squeak open, followed by footsteps thunking down the cement steps. Figuring it's Jason, I don't even bother looking up. So Luke's softly spoken, "Hey, El," three feet in front of me—I was intently focused on a particularly bitchy curved seam—scares the crap out of me.

It takes me a second to realize I've stitched the side of my finger to the mock-up.

"Shit!" Luke says as he notices the blood ooching from my finger and all over the creamy muslin. "Are you okay?"

Calmly—it's not as if I've never done this before—I manually crank the wheel to raise the needle and dislodge it from my mangled digit. It's just a nick, really, but now I have to wear a Band-Aid for the next few days. Damn.

"Yeah, yeah, I'm fine." I grab a scrap of muslin from the wastebasket beside the machine and wrap it around my finger. "No, it's okay, I've got it—"

"Shut up and let me see. Christ, I didn't mean to scare you—"

"You didn't, I swear, really, it's no big deal...."

But he's got my hand in his, folding back the muslin to look at my finger. It hurts more than I want to let on. And I'm not just talking about the finger.

I remove my hand from his grasp, muttering, "Thanks."

The problem with celibacy is that it doesn't take much to remind you what a sucky deal it is. You can go for months—or, in my case, months and months and months—convincing yourself you don't miss a man's touch. And then *ka-bam!* Fooled ya!

Luke drops my hand and backs away slightly, his own

stuffed in his leather jacket's pockets. "You need to keep pressure on it until the bleeding stops."

Oh, yeah. I know all about keeping a wound tightly under wraps so it doesn't start bleeding again.

"After all the times I mopped up after you when we were kids," I say, wondering why he's here, afraid to find out why he's here, "you're giving me instruction on how to stop bleeding?"

He grins. Sorta. "You know, you were the only girl I ever knew who didn't turn green at the sight of blood."

"Probably because I saw enough of my own."

I swear, I think I was fourteen before I didn't have scabs on my knees. Between being a klutz and my determination that anything the Scardinares could do, so could I, I was always banged up and bruised. My father used to joke that half his pay went toward keeping us supplied in bandages and Bactine. My mother used to despair of me, wondering aloud how one of her daughters could be such a priss (that would be my sister Jennifer, who'd have a conniption if she got a mosquito bite) while the other one was constantly walking along the tops of fences or climbing trees or sliding into our sandlot third base face-first.

I'm still diving into shit headlong. And I've got the scars to prove it.

"Leo let me in," Luke says unnecessarily. "Where's my girl?"

My chest twinges. "Taking a nap. We took her for a long walk this morning and wore her out."

"Didn't think that was possible," he says with a grin.

I smile back. "Neither did I." Then I take a big breath and do that diving thing. Face-first. "I'm so sorry. About you and Tina."

The grin fades as he nods, then walks over to this beat-up, olive-green couch we put down here when my grandmother got the new stuff. He sinks into one corner, his hands splayed on his thighs. He's still wearing his wedding ring, which I find both reassuring and unsettling. Especially as I'm getting this real bad feeling about where this conversation is headed.

"I take it Mom told you?"

"Jason, actually. He overheard Frances talking to you."

Another nod. I carefully lift the muslin; the bleeding's nearly stopped, but I wrap the finger up again for good measure. Other than the chair by the machine or the lone, hard stool, the couch is the only place to sit. So I plant my wounded self on the other side, my foot tucked up under my butt, and wait.

His fingers drum the arm of the couch for several seconds before he looks at me. "You know how I said things've been weird between her and me for a while? Well, a couple weeks after the miscarriage, she told me—" He takes a deep breath while my heart stops. "She told me there'd been someone else."

For a good five seconds, I don't breathe. Then I finally whisper, "What did you say?"

"That there's—"

"Never mind, I heard you. Ohmigod, Luke…are you sure?"

"She said it's nobody I know, some guy out in LIC. Close to where she works."

"And the baby…?"

"She said it wasn't mine." He looks at me, desperately searching my eyes for…what? "You didn't know?"

"I swear to God, she never said a word." Probably because she hadn't made up that part of the script yet. And that's just what this feels like, a bad scene from a third-rate soap. I half expect to hear the ominous, minor chord before we cut away to a detergent commercial.

"Under the circumstances," he says, "I figured it was better to let her go."

Straight into an institution, I barely manage to keep from saying.

I mean, I suppose it could be true, but I honest to God don't think Tina's capable of keeping something like that under wraps. In the past year, wouldn't I have picked up on *some-*

thing? Well, other than the very real possibility that my best girlfriend's a pathological liar. *Aiyiyi.*

"So, that's what's happening in my neck of the woods." He reaches over and gently slaps my knee. "What's doin' with you?"

"Uh…I don't think you came over here to talk about me."

"Actually, that's where you're wrong. I've been sittin' in my new, empty, apartment every night, feeling like shit, and it occurred to me I'm never going to get over this if I don't get out and do something about it. So here I am." He folds his arms across his chest. "Talk to me."

"Luke, you've got some heavy-duty issues to deal with here—"

"That's what I'm doing. Dealing. By asking you about your life." He tries a smile. "So work with me here, okay?"

It's a little hard to stick to my vow to stay out of it when I want to throttle Tina to within an inch of her life. And as soon as I get three minutes to call my own, I may well do just that.

In any case, since he asked, I tell Luke about the job possibility.

His expression doesn't give anything away. But then, that's Luke for you. "Sounds great," he finally says. "Getting to travel all over the place like that. It's what you always wanted."

"Is it?"

"Whaddya mean, *is it?*" His mouth pulls into a grin. "When we were kids, it was all you talked about, about how you couldn't wait to get out of Richmond Hill. Frankly, I expected you to be long gone by now."

Did I really talk that much about wanting to leave? I know I *thought* about it, but I honestly didn't think I'd voiced my dreams aloud all that much.

"So how come you don't sound more excited?"

"Dunno. Didn't seem right, under the circumstances."

"Because of my situation, you mean?"

"Yeah."

"That's nuts, El. What's goin' on with me has nothing to do with you." Again, his hand lands on my knee. And this time, he doesn't remove it right away. "I'm happy for you, babe. This is what you want, you should go for it."

"It's not that easy. I mean, I *do* want this. But I'm worried about leaving Starr so much. About Leo."

"Eh, they'll be fine." He finally takes back his hand, leaving an odd little tingling sensation on my kneecap. "And Mom and I'll check up on them, you know that." Then he gets this wistful expression. I so do not need wistful right now. "I'll miss you, though."

Rapidly steering both of us away from an area of the woods I have no wish to explore, I playfully slap *his* knee. "I don't even have the job yet, doofus. And besides, we just went a month without talking to each other, right?"

"And it was hell," he said. Too fast. With his eyes locked in mine.

I have gone way too long without love/sex/a boyfriend for eye-locking with somebody I know better than I know myself. Misinterpretations happen. They have before, they could again. Except this time, I can see the land mine; ergo, I can avoid it.

"So why'd you stay away?"

Or I can walk right up to it to get a closer look. *Sheesh.*

He gets quiet for a moment, but his eyes never leave mine. And deep, deep in the pit of my stomach, I get this…feeling. Sort of a combination of dread and excitement. Of course, that could just be the anxiety about tomorrow's interview. Yes, let's go with that, shall we?

"Because I decided you were right," he says at last. "That Tina and I needed to hash things out without anybody else gettin' in the way. I mean, Jesus. She'd run to you, I'd run to you… What the hell was wrong with us, that we couldn't sit down and talk to each other? No wonder we fell apart."

My stomach torques. I lean my elbow on the back of the

sofa, casually sifting my hand through my hair until it occurs to me that might look like I was trying to be seductive or something. "So…when did she tell you? About…the guy?"

"Last week sometime. It was so weird, the way we were having this conversation and suddenly it just…popped out."

"God. That must've been horrible."

"I've had better days, believe me. I mean, I keep replaying the scene over and over in my head, like I think that one of these times, the end'll be different." He swallows so hard I'm afraid he's gonna choke. "I don't get it. Did she think I was gonna give her a hard time? That I'd try to make her stay against her will?"

"I don't know, honey," I say, then add, "Funny how you think you know somebody so well, and then…" I shrug, at a loss for words.

"Yeah. I know. Well…" He stands. "You're in the middle of something, I don't wanna keep you…" But he walks over to the bulletin board, surveying the photo and sketch. And I realize, the moment's passed. He's not going to bring up the subject I thought/feared/half hoped he would. And God knows, neither am I. Not when he's still reeling from this whole business with Tina.

But the reprieve is only temporary, I know that.

He nods toward the board. "This for Heather?"

"Uh-huh," I say, getting up as well. "What do you think?"

That actually gets a laugh. "It's a white dress, what's to think? I just go to these things for the food." Then he turns to me. "This new job—it sounds like a good deal."

"It could be. It's just…scary." I let out a sigh. "I'm nearly thirty. And a mother. So why do I still feel like a little girl sometimes?"

"Aw, honey…" He drapes a solid, leather-scented arm around my shoulders and gives me a quick hug, but he doesn't say anything. After planting a glancing kiss off my hair, he starts up the stairs. Halfway, he stop and leans over the banister. "I brought the Twink a new game for the Nintendo. It's on your TV."

"Great. Thanks."

He bangs his hand twice on the banister, then continues up the stairs.

I pick up the bodice to rip out the last seam so I can replace the bloodied panel—Heather might not find it amusing—but after a few frustrated minutes, I give up.

Leo's in the living room in his recliner, watching football.

"Going to Tina's," I yell out as I pass. "Taking the car."

"Make sure you put gas in it, don't leave me with an empty tank."

"Got it," I say, shutting the door behind me.

Tina's not home when I get there, but I figure I'll give her an hour, what the hell. If she's not back by then, I'll leave, taking it as a sign that I'm not meant to beat the living daylights out of her.

Not that I really intend to beat the living daylights out of her. I cart spiders outside and let them loose, for God's sake. But you know what I mean.

I'm sitting on the floor in her hallway, reading a Dean Koontz, when the elevator door opens and out she pops. I have never actually seen somebody turn white as a sheet before.

"Ellie!" Nervous smile. "What are you—?"

"Honey, you got some heavy duty 'splainin' to do."

Underneath her leather jacket, her breasts heave with the force of her sigh. "I take it you've talked to Luke?"

I get to my feet, trying to massage some feeling back into my butt. Bad-ass Queens broads, the pair of us, in our leather jackets, tight jeans, two-story tall boots. "How'd you guess?"

On another exhalation, she opens her door and gestures for

me to go in. The door barely snicks shut behind her before I light into her.

"You were *cheating* on him?"

Amazingly enough, she gets even paler. At this rate, she's going to turn invisible. But instead of answering right away, she dumps her jacket on the sofa and goes into her kitchen, an open-to-the-living-area jobber. "Wanna beer?"

"No, I don't want a beer. I want some answers. Some straight answers, this time."

Tina pulls a can of Pabst from the fridge and pops off the tab, knocking back five or six gulps like a guy. "It wasn't something I planned, okay?"

"Are you out of your *mind?*"

After another swallow of beer, her mouth tilts into a sad, ugly smile. "Was there ever any doubt?" Then: "So...what did Luke tell you, exactly?"

"That you said there was some guy in Long Island City. And that the baby wasn't his?"

A second passed, then she nods.

Am I the only one here having a hard time making the pieces fit?

"Let me get this straight. You had a problem with telling me you were carrying another man's baby, but you didn't with telling me you wanted to abort your *husband's* kid?"

This time, when she lifts the beer can, her hand trembles. "It seemed like the lesser of two evils, what can I tell you?"

"The truth might be nice."

Her eyes shoot to mine. "I *am* telling you the truth!"

"And I'm supposed to know this how? For crying out loud, Tina—every time I turn around, the story's changed! Why the hell weren't you up front with me to begin with?"

"Because I was scared shitless, okay? I didn't know what to do. I couldn't *think...*"

"Oh, Tina..." I collapse onto one of her dinette chairs, a

throne-size upholstered swivel number on casters. "You could have had the baby. Luke probably wouldn't even have known it wasn't his."

After a second, she says, "The father's, um, a redhead. If the kid'd come out with red hair, he would've known. Besides, how honest is *that?*"

Oh, brother.

"Is the affair over?"

"Yes. Oh, God, yes. It didn't even last that long, you know? A few weeks, maybe."

Gotta admit, she'd be damn good on the witness stand. Of course, she'd burn in Hell later, if you believe in that sort of thing, but Tina's never been much for planning ahead. "Then why did you let Luke think otherwise?"

She looks confused for a second, then seems to recoup. "Because it was the only way I could think of to get him to let me go."

So Luke hadn't been imagining her pulling away. Still…"Dammit, Tina…if you wanted out, why didn't you just tell him that?"

"Because that wouldn't've been enough, don't you see?" The wall-to-wall carpet sucks up the sound of her heels as she swings around the counter to sit across from me. "He'd've wanted to talk, or go to marriage counseling. He wouldn't've accepted it, just like that. You know how protective he's always been about me, how he'd always make excuses for the crazy stuff I did. I had to do something drastic, or he would've seen our breaking up as somehow *his* fault. That he'd somehow failed me. And after everything he's done for me, I just couldn't do that to him." Her mouth twists. "And I didn't want him to feel sorry for me anymore."

This might sound totally off the wall, but I see a glimmer of understanding here I've never seen before. Tina's never been stupid, and she obviously needs to talk to somebody with some major degrees up on their wall, but she's always had a knack for not seeing what didn't suit her purpose. I'm not sure even Luke gets just how much his feelings for Tina are based in large part on his compassion for what she'd been through, but I sure as hell didn't think Tina had an inkling that's what was going on.

What *I* didn't get, however, until this moment was just how crappy a foundation that makes for a real relationship. I mean, I'd simply accepted it for what it was. The fact of their being together superseded the reasons behind it, I guess. Which is what comes, I suppose, from making these decisions without understanding *why* you're making them. Just as I'd accepted my relationship with Daniel without taking two minutes to analyze why I thought I loved him. Had I done that, my life might've turned out very differently.

Had I thought through a lot of things, my life might have turned out very differently.

"Then why didn't you tell him you had an abortion?" I ask.

She looks down at her nails, then tucks them into her fist. The iridescent rose polish is badly chipped, which only goes to show what a bad state she's in. I don't think I've seen Tina with a neglected manicure since she was seven.

"I don't know," she says quietly. "I guess because I just couldn't bring myself to admit I'd gotten rid of his baby."

"I thought you said it wasn't his baby."

"But I'd told him it was! Dammit, you're confusing me!" Tears glitter in her eyes. "I know I've made a huge mess of things, okay? And I know both of you will probably hate me, but that just proves my point, doesn't it?"

"What point?"

"That I don't belong with him. He doesn't deserve me. He deserves *you*. But as long as he was tied to me, he was never gonna see that."

For the second time that afternoon, I feel as though someone's clunked me over the head with a brick. Even as we speak, cartoon birdies are tweeting over my head.

"You don't believe me?" she says.

The only thing I believe right now is that I've been somehow catapulted into an alternative dimension where the language is the same, but the words all have different definitions.

I get up from the table. "Now I know you've lost it."

"Not about this, El!" She rises as well, scooting around to block my exit. "You have every right to think I'm off my nut, that everything I say is circumspect—"

Wow. I didn't even know she knew that word.

"—but just think about it, okay?" She rams her hand through her already windblown hair, her eyes enormous. "Whenever he's needed somebody to talk to, who does he go to, huh? You, that's who. Not me. Me, he just screwed—"

"You, he *married,* lughead—"

"—I mean, I tried to pretend it was okay, him picking me over you, that maybe one day he'd love me for real, you know? But it never happened. His dick might've been in bed with me, but the rest of him belonged to you. So I'm removing myself from the picture. And by making him hate me, you'll look even better."

Suddenly, shock and confusion give way—once again—to anger. Or maybe it's indignation, I can't quite tell.

"Christ, Tina. I don't know what's worse, listening to you blow off Luke's feelings for you, or the fact that you think you can just…just hand him over like a coat you've grown tired of! *Here, Ellie, go ahead and take it, the lining's a little worn, but you should still be able to get some use out of it!*"

"*No!* God, Ellie—that's not what I meant at all—!"

My phone shrills in my purse. Since I don't know what else to say, anyway, I fumble for it, wiping tears from my eyes as I answer it.

"Ellie?" Frances says softly. "Honey, where are you?"

Too shaken to puzzle out why she's calling me, I say, "I just went out for a little while, to get some air—" I grip the phone so hard it nearly slips out of my hand. "What is it? Ohmigod, something's wrong. Is Starr—?"

"Starr's fine, baby. She's with me." She pauses. "It's your grandfather. You need to come home right away."

chapter 10

The paramedics did what they could, but Leo was already gone. Starr had found him, dialed 9-1-1, then called Frances, who came right over and took charge.

Christ. What kind of mother lets her child find dead people in her living room? I should've been there, would've been there, if not for Tina's insanity. Or if I'd followed my own advice about staying out of it. I'm apparently much more upset about this than Starr is, though.

"Leo just went to sleep, that's all," she said when I finally stopped holding her so tightly she said she couldn't breathe. "And he looked happy."

A fact which Frances corroborated. And the paramedics, who assured me he'd gone in his sleep, he hadn't felt anything. I suppose I'll have to take their word for it. And after all, that's what we all wish for at the end, isn't it? Just go to sleep and not wake up. No pain, no fear, no knowledge, really.

There won't be a funeral, or sitting shiva, or anything even remotely a service to mark his passing. He was adamant about that. For one thing, Leo hadn't been a practicing Jew since he was a kid, although he went through the motions on High Holidays for my grandmother's sake. For another, after the funerals for my mother, my father, my grandmother, he swore he'd come back and haunt me if I put anybody else through hell like that. Or wasted the money. I'd never known my grandfather to be stingy in his life, but spending money on a big, fancy box that was just going to be put in the ground, never mind a boatload of food he wouldn't even get to eat was, in his opinion, downright idiotic. And if God, or anybody else, had a problem with that, tough. If there was an afterlife, He could take it up with Leo then. If there wasn't, it was all moot, anyway.

He'd made arrangements with a local funeral home some time ago, so all I had to do was make a phone call last night. Easier than making a dentist's appointment, he'd said when he'd told me. So the undertaker's already taken him away. The cremation will be tomorrow morning, and I can get the ashes anytime after that. I have no idea what I'm going to do with them. Leo had made noises about going out to Shea Stadium and dumping them, but can I really do that?

I can't understand why I'm not crying. Funny how I've been dreading this for years, but now that it's happened…

Why can't I feel anything?

Of course, it hasn't even been twenty-four hours. The grief will come in its own good time, I suppose. It always does.

Not surprisingly, I totally spaced the interview. Mari was very sympathetic when she called, wondering where I was, saying she'd try to convince them to hold off making a decision until I could get in for an interview. I had just enough presence of mind to tell her not to bother. I mean, what's the point? I can't leave Starr now. And even after we've all adjusted, it's not as if I have anyone I can leave her with, is it?

Mari said she totally understood, asked if there was anything she could do (I said no), to take care and she'd call me in a few weeks. I doubt she will, but whether she does or doesn't is hardly a top priority in my thoughts right now.

Nikky, too, did the I'm-so-sorry-dear-take-all-the-time-you-need number. Although I could hear her suck in her breath when I said it would be at least a week before I'd be able to sort things out. Because of my daughter and all.

"Well, dear…I'm sure you'll do the best you can."

That's the plan, yep.

I knew Leo had left a will, but when I couldn't find it, I called the number listed under "lawyer" in his address book. Somebody named Stanley Goldfine. Stan—that's what he told me to call him—asked me if I wanted him to messenger me a copy or come to his office, which wasn't too far away. I opted for the office, figuring if I had any questions, he'd be right there, but that he send copies to anyone else mentioned in the will as he saw fit. I made an appointment for later this afternoon, called the few remaining relatives who would be even remotely interested in Leo's passing, then steeled myself to call my sister out in Oyster Bay. I got her machine; since I didn't think she'd exactly be broken up over the news, I left a message. I didn't say anything about the will, since I honestly didn't know at that point if she was even in it. Knowing Jennifer, however, I imagine she'll contact *me* about it soon enough.

I asked Starr if she'd be okay with the Gomezes for an hour or so—it's slowly dawning on me that, at least for the time being, I'm a landlord, criminy—threw on a turtleneck and two heavy sweaters (one my grandfather's, one my dad's) over a pair of jeans, slapped on enough makeup so I wouldn't frighten any small children I might encounter, finger-fluffed my un-washed hair, and set off for the lawyer's.

Which is where I am now.

Stanley Goldfine is one of those men you look at and think, gee, I bet he wasn't bad-looking when he was younger, except then you realize he's not old enough that you should be thinking this. Not a sharp edge anywhere on the man. Rogaine-fuzz blurring a rapidly retreating hairline, behind which lurks wavy, suspiciously dark hair. A beer keg where the six-pack abs should be. Still, he's got kind blue eyes behind his tortoise-shell wirerims, a soothing voice and a very sweet smile. In other words, a chicken soup kinda guy—dependable, comforting, good for you.

I can't remember the last time I had chicken soup.

Anyway. Stan shows me into his office (pleasantly, but not ostentatiously furnished, in neutral colors) dispenses the standard condolences, then motions for me to have a seat. Since I'd never heard my grandfather mention him, I ask him if he knew Leo well.

"No, not really," Stan says, settling in behind his desk. "He just contacted me to draw up the will a few years ago, then once again after your father's passing."

He prattles on about this and that, nothing that needs my full attention, while I process that his gray suit is a few years old, I'm guessing, American-made, good quality but not top-of-the-line. And slightly ill-fitting—a little pulling at the shoulders, the sleeves a trifle too long—as though they didn't have his exact size at Men's Wearhouse so he took the closest thing, then couldn't be bothered with alterations. I glance at his left hand, and…yep. Just as I thought. Indentation, but no ring. The telltale mark of the recently divorced.

I think of Luke and my chest cramps.

"Do you want me to read it to you, or read it yourself?"

What? Oh, right. The will. Which I'm about to read because my grandfather just died. Yesterday. I feel this emotional…heave. Like when you know you have to throw up but you're not quite ready to let it go, yet. So I should be thinking about that, not about this guy's ill-fitting clothes—and the fact that it's taking everything I have not to ask if he'd like me to rework those armseyes, take up those cuffs—or Luke, or anything not directly related to why I'm here. God, I'm a horrible person. Then again, maybe this is some sort of defense mechanism, shielding me from reality until I can think about it without becoming hysterical.

I look across the desk at this benign little man and say, "I think I'd rather read it myself, if that's okay."

"Sure, sure, not a problem. Actually, tell you what…" Stan gets up, jiggling some loose change in his pocket. "My coffeemaker bit the dust this morning, so how about I just pop out for coffee, give you a little time to yourself? Nothing worse than having someone hang over your shoulder. Can I get you anything?"

Well, heck, since he's offering. "A hot chocolate, maybe?"

"One hot chocolate, coming up. I'll be back in two shakes. Oh—there's a pad and pen right there, so you can jot down any notes you might have."

After he's gone, I smile a little. Who on earth says "two shakes" anymore? I settle back in the chair and start to read, peripherally aware of the soft drone of the receptionist talking on the phone on the other side of the closed door, the clanking of the radiator under the window, that undeniable hum in your own head you can only hear when you're in a quiet room. I've always wondered what that was. Your own energy, maybe, like an engine on idle?

The first part of the will's straightforward enough. Since my name's been on Leo's bank and money market accounts, that all passes to me, anyway. For what it's worth: the last time I saw any statements, he wasn't exactly rolling in it, although he was never in danger of going bankrupt. Then we come to a few small bequests to a distant relative or two I'd never met. Jennifer and I are equal beneficiaries of a modest life insur-

ance policy, which I already knew, and I get all the furniture—
such as it is—in the house, which I didn't. He and my grandmother had already set up a trust fund for Starr, which he'd
continued to contribute to; that'll come due when she's eighteen.

Then we get to the good stuff. A pair of good stuffs, actually.

First, he left the rental house to me, the other one in trust
for Starr. But she can't sell hers until she turns twenty-one, and
I can't sell mine as long as either of the current tenants wants
to stay. Then, before I can fully absorb the implications of that
bit of news, I see a codicil, added a couple years ago, that
leaves all the funds in another, heretofore unknown money
market account, to one Sonja Koepke.

The door opens behind me. "Well, then," Stan says, "how
are we doing?"

I look up. "I'm not sure. Who's Sonja Koepke?"

A tidy little frown settles between his brows as he removes
the hot chocolate from a white paper bag and sets it in front of
me. "I was hoping you could tell me."

I frown back. "My grandfather didn't tell you?"

"No. Although…" The lawyer finally sits, rooting in the bag
for his coffee, which he lifts out so carefully I find myself holding my breath. He shoots me an apologetic look. "I periodi-
cally go through my clients' files, to make sure they're
up-to-date, see if they want to add or change anything to their
wills, and I realized I still didn't have Ms. Koepke's address
or phone number. Which your grandfather had told me he'd
get to me some time ago." He shakes his head. "I was going
to call him this week, as it happens."

I decide this is a good time to take a sip of the hot chocolate,
which instantaneously smelts my tastebuds.

I jump; so does Stan. "Ms. Levine! Are you okay?"

Unable to speak, I pantomime this whole it's okay/it was just
the hot chocolate/sit, sit schtick.

He hesitates, then carefully lowers himself back into his seat. Stanley Goldfine, I decide, is a very careful man. "Are you sure you're all right? Your eyes are red."

I nod vigorously and croak out, "I'm fine, please go on."

"Anyway, do you know anybody who might know who she is?"

The searing pain has finally subsided, leaving in its wake a scorched wasteland where my tongue used to be. "I'll ask around," I manage. "Then there's this part…"

I point to the bit about the houses; Stan cranes his head to see where I'm looking, then turns to that page in his own copy. He reads as he pries the lid off his coffee, squinting slightly, like he won't admit he needs glasses.

"Ah, yes. Thought you'd wonder about that." He takes a sip of his coffee, then peers at me. "You're not happy with it?"

"I'm not anything," I answer truthfully. "I guess I figured he'd split them between me and my sister, if anything. Not me and my daughter."

Something you could almost call a smile twitches at the lawyer's mouth. "I may be speaking out of turn, but I don't think your sister was ever part of that equation." Then he leans forward. "Your grandfather wanted to make sure you and your daughter always had a home, though. And you can sell the rental house, as long as his conditions are met."

I smirk. "I don't see either the Nguyens or the Gomezes leaving anytime soon. Not with the deal my grandfather gave them."

Ten year leases at five percent increases per year, on rents that are below market to begin with—leases he only offered after both families had lived there for a year and proved to him they cared about the property as much as he did. Those two apartments were the best-kept secrets in Queens, let me tell you. No way were either of those families going to leave.

As Stan drones on about property values and how the houses probably weren't in danger of devaluing by the time Starr might be ready to sell hers—in sixteen years—reality is beginning to entwine its nasty little tentacles through my brain. My grandfather's "ensuring" Starr and I had a place to live translates to the simple fact that, unless I miraculously land some phenomenally well-paying job, we're stuck in Queens for God only knows how long. Hell, we're stuck in that *house* for God only knows how long. And on the face of it, I know Leo meant well. He only wanted to protect us. All of us, including the rental families. Except…except I can't help feeling what he was really saying was that he didn't trust me. That, if he'd left both houses to me free and clear and I'd sold them, that I'd somehow…I don't know. Blow it, I suppose. That I wouldn't be smart enough, or judicious enough, to know how to handle the money.

And you know what the really sad thing about all this is? That I can't for sure say that he wasn't right. I mean, I haven't exactly proven so far that I have a clue how to function in the real world, have I? What have I got to show for my twenty-eight years? A résumé consisting of a string of (let's face it) shit jobs and an unplanned pregnancy, that's what.

"Ms. Levine?" The lawyer's gently spoken words rattle me out of my maudlin musings, which is when I realize I'm crying. Damn. He's holding out a tissue across the desk, which I take and loudly blow my nose. "It's just now hitting, isn't it?" he says kindly.

"Yeah," I say, wiping my eyes. "You could say that."

There are flowers on my doorstep when I get home. Many, many flowers. I cannot deal with them right now. If ever. I'm not sure what I can deal with, frankly, but death flowers ain't it. If Frances is home, I might go over and let her do the mother hen thing, fix me a cup of hot, too-sweet tea and let me gorge on Milano cookies. But first I have to collect my child. And while I'm at it, this probably would be a good time to reassure my tenants—I shudder—that they're not being kicked out on the street.

As I said, my father, sister and I moved in with my grandparents after my mother's death, at which time our old house was converted into the two apartments. For the most part, the smaller duplexes like ours only converted well into one-bedroom apartments, or small twos at the most. But with a little clever maneuvering and an eager young contractor, Leo managed to make the bottom apartment into a three-bedroom, by turning the finished basement into a living/dining/kitchen combo and then making over everything on the first floor into bedrooms and bath. The top apartment they made into a very nice one-bedroom, where Mr. and Mrs. Nguyen live.

When I tell Mrs. Nguyen that nothing's changed, except she'll be making her rent check out to me instead of my grandfather, the soft-spoken sixtyish woman looks torn between sympathy and extreme relief. She expresses her condolences, sings my grandfather's praises for several seconds, then asks me in careful English if we need any food. I decline; then, after several obviously tormented seconds, she apologizes for the bad timing, but she can't get her kitchen faucet to shut off all the way and the dripping is starting to get on both her and her husband's nerves.

I tell her I'll take care of it. Of course, I have no earthly idea what I mean by that, but I'm sincere. Somehow, I will take care of it.

Then I go downstairs to get Starr. Mrs. Gomez—a former beautician, I think my grandfather had said, a few years older than me, very pregnant, very pretty, with curly brown hair caught up in a ponytail—takes one look at me and lets out a soft gasp. Our relationship is maybe a Level 3—with Tina being a 1 and the guy at the newsstand I say "hi" to every morning being a 5—so we exchange the odd pleasantry now and again, but we're not close by any means. Maybe not quite a 3, now that I think of it, more like a 3 ½. Anyway, she reaches around her enormous belly and pulls me inside.

"You've been crying? Of course, you've been crying, what am I saying? Can I get you anything? A cup of tea or coffee…?"

"No, no, thanks. I just came to get Starr. And to tell you you don't need to worry about the apartment. Nothing's changing as far as that goes. Well, except that I'm your landlord now, I guess."

Like Mrs. Nguyen, she looks torn between regret and relief. "Thanks. This wouldn't've been a real good time for us to have to look for a new place."

My gaze strays to her belly, barely contained underneath her sweatshirt. A little twinge of nostalgia sneaks past all the other flotsam floating around inside my head, memories of the fear and excitement and anticipation, wondering who this was inside me, would we like each other, would I be able to answer her questions, be what she needed me to be…?

"Mickey and I thought maybe you'd sell up and leave the neighborhood, actually. Your grandfather mentioned something about you working in fashion, maybe moving to Manhattan at some point…." Then her cheeks pink. "Listen to me, going on about the house when your grandfather just died!"

"No, no, really…it's okay. And I'm not going anywhere right away, so please, don't think another thing about it."

After a moment, she nods, then says, "You sure you won't have that cup of tea? It would only take a sec—"

"No. Thanks. I really need to get back—"

"Sure, sure, I understand. Well," Liv says, turning and starting slowly up the stairs, "your daughter's been trying to teach my seven-year-old how to play checkers for the past hour."

"Is it working?" I say when she stops to get her breath—oh, how well I remember that.

"I have no idea." She resumes the climb. "All I know is, they've been quiet. Locito conked out about a half hour ago on my bed, and it's been Heaven. I'd almost forgotten what it was like to start a thought and actually finish it, too!"

The Gomezes have the two boys, seven-year-old Andy and a three-year-old named Erik who they mostly call Locito—little crazy one.

We reach the doorway to the boys' room, which is your standard bunk-beds-and-wall-to-wall-toys space. On the dresser sits an aquarium with something furry molded to one corner, sacked out. In the middle of the chaos, Starr and Andy are sprawled on their bellies, feet in the air, chins in hands, as Starr explains—for what I have a feeling is not the first time— the rules of the game.

"She's very patient," Mrs. Gomez whispers. Unlike her husband, she has no trace of an accent. "Maybe she'll end up being a teacher someday."

"Since she's already convinced she knows everything, I wouldn't be surprised."

Starr looks up, scowling. As if I'm an interruption. "C'n I stay a little longer? He's just about got it, I think."

"I'm sure Mrs. Gomez has other things to do—"

"Of course you can stay, sweetie," my tenant assures her. "I'll just show your mommy the nursery while you finish up, okay?"

"Honestly, I don't want to impose—"

"Don't be ridiculous," she says, steering me into the next room, which is as pretty and pink as the boys room is messy and blue. "And please, call me Liv. Short for Olivia," she explains with a grimace. "Anyway, Andy and your daughter get along better than he does with his own cousins. Or any other kid on the block." She hesitates a moment, then says, "He's a little slow. His kindergarten teacher noticed it first, but just brushed it off to him being one of the younger ones in the class. But they did some tests on him last year, and found some problems. Nothing major, they don't think, but he needs some extra attention." Guilt swamps her pretty features when she looks at me. "With the new baby coming, I don't know how much time I'm going to be able to give him. And it's not like we can afford special tutors. So trust me, your little girl is a blessing. She can come over anytime she wants. Anyway…"

Her bright smile back in place, Liv turns back to the room. "We found out it's a girl and I guess, after two boys, I sorta went berserk with the pink."

There's an understatement. Still, I've never seen a happier room, with the white crib and all those bunnies dancing along the top of the walls. My grandfather has always given his tenants permission to repaint the rooms any way they liked, as long as it wasn't a dark color. If I were a baby, I'd be tickled, well, *pink* to be brought home to this room.

"It's great. Have you named her yet?"

"My mother's name is Danielle, so we're thinking the Spanish version—Daniella. But then, she might not be a Daniella, so we'll have to wait and see."

I glance over at Liv, wearing that serene look mothers sometimes get when the house is quiet and/or the baby inside them is close to coming out. And man, I could really use some serenity in my life right now.

"You know," I say, "maybe I'll take you up on that tea after all."

She beams. "You got it."

Eventually, I'm going to have to deal with both my grief for a man I absolutely adored, and the consequences of his not being here anymore. But not right now. After all, putting off the inevitable is what I do best, isn't it?

chapter 11

Later that evening, I'd come to the conclusion that not doing anything, funeral-wise, for my grandfather feels very…unfinished. As though I've been cheated, somehow. Or as if I'm destined to go through the next several weeks sure I've forgotten something.

However, despite there being no funeral or wake or shiva-sitting, my house is full of flowers. And food. Oh, God, the food. I have Frances to thank for that. Or blame, I think as I stand here, staring into the open refrigerator. There are no less than four deli chickens in here. Not that I don't love deli chicken, but Starr won't touch it and, um, I'm the only other person in the house? Must see about palming some of this off on other people. I'm sure the Gomezes could use one. Or two. Don't know about the Nguyens, though. They don't strike me as deli chicken types.

Starr's in bed, asleep. I've encouraged her to talk about how she feels, but she just keeps saying she's not ready. Oh, well. She knows I'm here, ready to listen whenever she's ready to talk. I can't do any more than that.

And earlier, I'd gone through Leo's desk and phone book, searching for a clue as to who this Sonja Koepke is. But I couldn't even find a cryptic "S" or "K" with a phone number. Very weird.

Taking into account Leo's regular Sunday afternoon outings, I assume this is some sort of secret romantic thing. But why? Why did he keep it a secret, I mean. After all, my grandmother's been dead for more than a dozen years. Yeah, they'd been married since their early twenties, but did he think this would bother me? Or, given the possibility that the relationship went back to when my father was still alive, that Norm would have had a problem with it? Then again, maybe because my father never went out with another woman after my mother died, Leo couldn't bring himself to flaunt his happiness in front of his son.

Of course, I could simply be romanticizing the whole thing and this Sonja person could be…his insurance agent or somebody.

Right.

I'll say one thing, I muse as I begin the slow, deliberate annihilation of the seasoned, now rewarmed, bird in front of me (I may be depressed, but my appetite isn't), this whole Who is Sonja Koepke? business is keeping me from obsessing about Leo's death. Tina's strangeness. Losing this job opportunity.

I strip the meat off an entire drumstick in one bite.

The phone rings. Why does the phone always ring when you're on the toilet, your mouth is full or you're on the verge of orgasm? Not that I've had to deal with the last one in a while, but it has happened.

Wiping my hands and chewing double time so I can swallow, I check the Caller ID, but it's a number I don't recognize.

Something upstate. The machine clicks on, and I hear Luke say, "Hey, honey, it's just me—"

I grab the phone off the hook, startling both of us. Him, because I shrieked "I'm here, I'm here!" in his ear. Me, because I sound like some fourteen-year-old who hasn't yet learned the finer art of answering a boy's phone call.

"I just heard," he says. "God, I'm so sorry, El."

"Thanks," I say, my throat thick with emotion and half-chewed chicken.

"I'd be there in person, but Pop sent me to do this bid upstate and I didn't know until Mom called me this morning. Then my damn cell service went out and I had to drive halfway to Poughkeepsie before I found a phone that worked. Are you okay? What am I saying, that's a stupid question. Do you want me to come home? 'Cause I will if you want."

Yes! is the first thought that flits through my brain. I let it keep on flitting while I finally swallow the chicken puree in my mouth and say, much more calmly, "Thanks, but I'm fine, really."

"Don't bullshit me, El. You were crazy about that old man. And with good reason. There is no *way* you're fine."

"There are degrees of 'fine,'" I bravely say. "Which you of all people should know. There's 'fine' when you really *are* fine, and 'fine' meaning, yeah, I feel like crap right now but I'll get over it and then I'll be the *real* 'fine.'"

I can hear crackling on the line. So much for high-tech fiber optics. Or whatever they're touting these days. Then he says, "How's Starr?"

"I don't know, to be honest. I'm not sure I know what her definitions of 'fine' are yet. My assessment is...sad but coping."

"Poor thing," Luke says. And I somehow don't think he's talking about Starr.

You know, I'm not sure my brain can take any more weirdness right now. In fact, I know it can't. Even as we speak, I can feel it pressing against my skull, looking for a weak spot to break through and explode all over the ceiling. Tina was talking smack, I know she was, yet…

Yet here I am, hearing nuances in Luke's voice from two hundred miles away. At least, thinking I'm hearing nuances in Luke's voice.

Wanting to hear nuances in Luke's voice?

"You sure you don't want me to come home early?"

You have no idea.

"Positive. It's not like there's anything you can do here, for heaven's sake. Except maybe fix the Nguyen's leaking faucet."

"Tell Pop, he'll take care of it. Then when I get home, I'll show you how to do some of that stuff." A pause. "Unless you're gonna sell the houses anyway."

"No, I'm not—"

The canned operator cuts in, demanding more money.

"Shit, I'm outta change. I'll see you Sunday, and you take care, okay?"

And he's gone.

I sit back at the table, facing my mutilated chicken. There's not much left. Although in my defense, it was a small chicken.

One puny little tear sneaks out of my eye and wriggles down my cheek. And, because being sad about one thing always seems to lead directly into the Bad Memories storehouse in your brain, I start thinking about Daniel.

He was my first grown-up—or so I thought at the time—love affair. Or maybe it was just that I wanted to believe I was in love, that I finally had a boyfriend. A *lover.* I hadn't been a virgin for some time, but I'd never even gone steady with a boy. Two, three dates, and *pfft.* Usually by mutual consent.

But Daniel…Daniel was different. At first, anyway. He made me laugh, he paid attention to me, he made me feel desired and important and like a woman on a very basic level. Which might sound trite, but when you're twenty-two, you don't know from trite. That first night, after we left the bar, we walked all over the Village until two in the morning, talking. Just talking. I suppose at first I was simply besotted with his English accent. Or his being six years older than I was. Or that, as a photojournalist, he had a real career, not just a job, doing something he loved. Why he was attracted to me, I have no idea. And I've given up trying to figure it out. Just one of those things, I guess.

Anyway, he didn't try to get me into bed right away. In fact, we'd been out four or five times before he asked—almost shyly, I thought—if he could make love to me.

What can I say, I'd already gone on the Pill. And was I ever delighted to discover he knew how to push a lot more buttons than those on his trusty Nikon.

I was not in a real place, I know that now. But I was having too much fun—and far too many five-star orgasms—to care. Even about his having to be away so much, or that he maintained apartments in both Manhattan and London. When he had to go back to England for a month, I was a mess. And I was too young or naive or whatever to realize that feeling as if my own life was in a holding pattern until his return wasn't such a good thing.

So when he returned, and asked me to move in with him— as long as I understood that he couldn't make any promises— I said yes in a heartbeat. At that point, I wasn't after promises; I was after full-time sex.

Not to mention being able to finally move out of Queens.

I told Leo and Dad I'd found a male roommate, which wasn't exactly a lie. Even though they didn't try to stand in my way, I know they worried about me. Now that I'm a mother, I realize just how much. I'm also sure I wasn't fooling anybody but myself.

About a lot of things.

Like Daniel's insisting we each have our own cell phone,

rather than getting a land line. And that I was expressly forbidden to answer his, even if he was just in the shower. He said it was because he'd be charged for the minutes and that many of his calls were from overseas.

But then, when he was away? I had to let him call *me*. Again, he made some excuse about his schedule being so wacky, it was just easier that way. Which was true. You could set clocks by my comings and goings in those days—I was always back in the apartment within thirty minutes of getting off work. Waiting for his call. Pathetic, I know.

Then I started talking about babies, and the shit started edging a lot closer to the fan.

I wasn't even aware I was doing it—at that point, I certainly wasn't thinking about having any of my own—until Daniel irritably brought it to my attention one day. We were out for a walk in Central Park; I saw a toddler in a stroller and made googoo eyes at it. He went nuts.

"Don't get any ideas, Ellie," he said, yanking me away.

"About what?"

"Kids. As in, you and me having them. Because it's not going to happen."

I believe I laughed. "Oh, for heaven's sake, Daniel—I was just *looking* at the kid! I don't plan on having children for a very long time—"

"You're not listening, Ellie." In hindsight, I now realize he could get very paternalistic at times. And his jaw would start working, making his beard bob up and down. "I don't want them *ever.*"

I got the message. But since having children was one of those vague, maybe-some-day-down-the-road kind of things, anyway, I thought no more about it. And said no more about it, and all was well.

On the surface.

As the weeks went by, though, he started getting weirder.

Nothing I could really put a finger on, but he'd get short with me over nothing, usually right before he'd take off on one of his trips. Then he'd come back and things would be all lovely and multiorgasmic again, and I'd convince myself I'd been imagining things. Then, one day, I got a wedding invitation from one of my girlfriends, which set Daniel off. About how marriage was such a crock and only idiots let themselves get suckered into it and I was never, ever to even think about us getting married, was that clear?

Of course I *said* I totally understood, but deep down— God, this is embarrassing—I somehow assumed I'd be able to change his mind. Given time and a long enough lever. In my blissfully ignorant state, I assumed all men felt this way about marriage initially, but that, when the right woman came along, their objections melted away like ice in the Sahara. And I had no doubt I was Daniel's right woman. He just didn't realize it yet.

Except I should have realized how serious his aversion to marriage was when he refused to go to the wedding with me. Actually, he'd somehow always manage to wriggle out of going anywhere with me that included friends or family. Said he didn't want to share me with anybody, which I actually thought was very sweet.

At first.

Shouldn't his refusal to even hold hands with me in public have rung some sort of alarm? Or his wincing the first time I called him my boyfriend?

"A bit juvenile, love, don't you think?" he said.

The last thing I'd want anyone to think me, God knows.

So I played by his rules, a small price—I rationalized—for having this man want me in his life. And his bed. In fact, when we accidentally ran into his brother, Alan, one afternoon at a post-modernist exhibit at the Met, Daniel frantically whispered to me—as his smiling, older, what-the-hell-was-he-doing-in-New-York-for-Christ's-sake? brother rapidly closed the space between us—not to let on to Alan that there was anything serious between us, otherwise his brother would torment him mercilessly. I was tempted to point out how juvenile I thought *he* was being, but I played along. Even told Alan, when we were introduced, that I was one of Daniel's photography students (how handy that he was teaching a seminar at the New School at the time). I didn't even catch on when, seconds later, Daniel excused himself to take Alan off to the side for a "quick word" about some family crisis or other.

I thought it was odd, but I let it slide. I let it all slide, because I wasn't about to do anything to screw this up.

Or so I thought.

We'd been together for about six months when, one morning, Daniel's phone rang. I could hear him finishing up in the bathroom, so I figured, this is nuts, the guy's right here, I'll just answer it. A very prim, English-accented child's voice asked to speak to "Daniel Stein, please." But before I could reply, an equally prim, English-accented, grown-up woman's voice cut in.

"Sorry about that, my little boy's just learned how to use the phone!"

"Oh, that's quite all right," I said. "How old is he?"

"Four," she said on a laugh. "I'm so sorry—he must have pressed one of the autodial buttons—whom did he call?"

"Daniel Stein. At least, this is his phone. I'm not Daniel, I'm Ellie. Your son asked to speak with Daniel, though."

There was a pause, which I assumed had something to do with the satellite transmission.

"What time is it there?" she asked, the lovely voice suddenly rather frosty around the edges.

"Around seven-thirty in the morning, why?"

"I see." A pause. "Is Daniel available?"

"Sure, just a sec."

I called him; he came out of the bathroom, saw his phone in my hand, blanched, then reddened. Fury darting from his eyes, he grabbed the phone and stormed back into the bathroom, slamming shut the door. Five minutes later, he emerged, screaming at me, *how* many times had he told me *not* to answer his bloody phone!

And at long last, the penny dropped.

"Ohmigod. You're married."

He didn't answer.

"And…you've got a son?"

"Bloody hell! You talked to him, too?"

"He made the call, actually."

"Great. Just bloody great. Thanks a lot, Ellie, for completely bollixing things up!"

"Because I answered the phone?" I said, then burst out laughing. He looked at me like I was nuts. But it was all so absurd. Not only that he would be living two lives, but that I would be too stupid to not figure it out.

I moved back to Richmond Hill that morning, but I'd forgotten my hairdryer, which Daniel left with Carlos, the day doorman, according to the terse message left on my cell. When I went to get it a few days later, Carlos told me Daniel'd moved out right after I left. Whether he went back to England, or patched things up with his wife, or got eaten by a lion on the African plains, I have no idea, since we never saw or talked to each other again.

I did not, as you may have guessed, find the situation amusing for long. For weeks, I wallowed in a sea of humiliation and self-pity unparalleled in the history of mankind. I had no idea one's first breakup could be so brutal. Or the extent of the incredibly stupid things one might do under the influence of abject misery and self-loathing.

Then, three weeks to the day I discovered the man I thought I loved was already married, I realized my period was late.

* * *

I've sat here so long, the chicken's gone stone-cold. I stuff the last bite into my mouth, clean up and wander out into the living room, unable to fathom that only yesterday my grandfather sat in that chair, alive. That his scent will eventually fade, as will his image from my memory. I no longer remember exactly what my mother and grandmother look like, unless I look at their photographs.

I lift Leo's sweater from the back of the sofa and slip into it, even though I'm already wearing two layers of clothes and it's not all that cold in the house. Cocooning myself inside it, I lower myself into his chair, my legs crossed, my eyes closed. For a moment, I remember how it felt when he'd hold me in his lap when I was little, reading to me or watching a Jimmy Stewart movie with me. *Harvey* was his favorite. There were lots of hugs, when I was growing up. From my parents, from Leo. My grandmother was the reserved one in the family. Her embraces were fleeting, brittle things—

The phone rings again. Since I'm not peeing and my mouth isn't full, I pick up.

"There is no way you and Starr get *everything* and I end up with half of a fucking life insurance policy!"

Ladies and gentlemen…meet my sister.

She was never real generous with her hugs, either.

chapter 12

You may remember my mentioning Jennifer, my older sister, a while back. Or maybe not. I didn't make a big deal of it. But then, she hasn't made a big deal of the rest of us, either, especially since she married some hot-shot investment banker and moved to Lawn Gisland, where she's apparently settled quite nicely into her role as an Oyster Bay matron. Not that I know of this personally, but from Shirley Webster, Jennifer's one-time best friend who I see maybe once a year when we happen to be in Grand Union at the same time. Shirley herself only hears from Jen sporadically, usually by means of an invitation to some event to benefit this or that Jewish charity on which board my sister serves.

Which might be commendable, except when you consider—from what I remember, at least, since it's been ten years since Jen and I lived under the same roof—that my sister's regard for religion in general and Judaism in particular ranked several notches below last year's shoes. According to her, God was something for the weak and deluded to pin the rap on. Granted, maybe nobody in my family (except for my grand-mother) was exactly big on the synagogue thing, but if the rest of us schlepped our Jewishness around like a squeaky, slightly bent grocery cart—a little rusty, but still useful when the need arose—Jen had given hers away to Goodwill.

Until, apparently, she realized sometimes you need a gro-cery cart, after all, so she went right out and bought a shiny new one. That doesn't squeak.

As, apparently, she realizes there are times when you need your family.

I.e., me.

I always got the feeling that Jen was convinced she'd been plopped into our little circle by mistake (no argument there) and realized early on that she would shrivel and die, like an orchid planted in the desert, if she didn't transplant herself somewhere more conducive to her delicate, hothouse tem-perament. Or maybe she was just pissed about the burial plan graduation gift. Something tells me she was thinking more in terms of all-leather interior and a sunroof. In any case, I have literally talked to the woman once since her wedding, and that was at our father's funeral. At which she arrived ten minutes late because of a conflict in her schedule.

Anyway, here she is again, fuming nicely on the other end of the line. Funny how a relative's death can reestablish those family bonds.

"You're not exactly getting *nothing*," I say, figuring since she dispensed with the usual amenities, I might as well follow suit. "Twenty-five grand, tax-free, is nothing to sneeze at."

I hear the snap of a cigarette lighter closing, the whoosh of an angry inhalation. Like Tina, Jen has smoked since she was fourteen, prompting an impulse—which I somehow resist—to point out that if she's really that afraid of dying young, let alone ending up with skin like a Slim Jim casing, perhaps she should rethink a few of her lifestyle choices. "Big fucking whoop. Like that's gonna do me any good."

Uh-huh. I think back to Jen's wedding, which Stuart—Jen's much older husband—bankrolled. At the Pierre. Ice sculptures, open bar, a cake that deserved its own wing at the Met. And let's not even get into the ring, which practically needed its own zip code. Somehow, I'm not feeling many sympathy pangs, here.

But then, Jen isn't after sympathy. She's after blood. Mine, apparently, since Leo's dead.

"We were his only grandchildren," she says, huffily. "By rights, his estate should have been divided equally between us."

"Yeah, well, and I'm your only sister," I retort, figuring, what the hell, if you can't resurrect a grudge at times like these, when can you? "Although it seems to me that didn't exactly count for much ten years ago."

There is actually silence on the other end. Then I hear the whoosh of smoke being exhaled and realize the pause wasn't due, as I had sanguinely hoped, to a pang of conscience. "Oh, for God's sake, Ellie! I cannot believe you're still hanging on to this after all this time. I was trying to protect you, you know that! It would have broken my heart, seeing you embarrassed…"

"What was embarrassing was having your own sister tell you that you were too fat to be in the bridal party!"

"I never said that!"

"No, you just said you didn't think I'd be 'comfortable' in the dress you'd chosen for your attendants."

"Well, would you have?"

"I could have altered it, Jen! Or gotten the fabric and made up something else!"

"And wouldn't that have been even worse," my sister said in her version of "soothing," "standing up there in a different dress because it was obvious you couldn't wear the same one everyone else was?"

I wouldn't've cared, I want to say, but why bother?

"Never mind," I say wearily. "Let's just drop it, okay?"

Her relief positively shimmies through the phone to give me a hug. "I'm so glad to hear you say that, honey—"

Honey?

"—I mean, it's not healthy to keep dwelling on the past. Unresolved resentments do *terrible* things to our immune systems." I hear her take another drag on her cigarette. "But as I was saying…there must be some mistake. With Grandpa's will, I mean."

Who the hell is this "Grandpa" dude? *Leo,* I want to scream. *We called him Leo.* "There's no mistake. The will is completely legal, signed and witnessed and everything. Although I had no idea what was in it before I saw my copy, either—"

"Oh, don't give me that, of course you knew! It says you're the executor, how could you not know?"

"That doesn't mean I had anything to do with what's *in* the will! I just have to make sure everyone gets what's coming to them!"

"Yeah, well, who was sucking up to the old man for years? You can't tell me that didn't count for something!"

"Living with the man's not the same as sucking up to him! And yes, it counted for something! Starr and I were his family, Jen! You know, when people share lives and living space and actually give a damn about each other?"

"How do you know how I felt about Grandpa? I'm absolutely devastated, Ellie. *Devastated.*"

"Right. And when was the last time you actually talked to him?"

"I've been…busy. You have no idea what my life is like."

"And you have no idea what mine is like," I say softly, suddenly too drained to fight. Like she knows from devastated. "Or Starr's. Or Leo's, before he died."

After a beat or two passes, she says, "So when's the funeral?"

"You're in luck," I say. "There isn't going to be one. So you don't have to worry about fitting it in."

"What do you mean, there isn't going to be one?"

"Just what I said. Leo doesn't want a service, it's right in the will." *Which you'd know if you'd read the whole thing instead of just the part that had your name in it.*

Because if she had, you better believe Sonja Koepke would be a serious part of this conversation.

"That's just not right," Jennifer says, "not even honoring the man after his death—"

"Jen? Go one step farther down that track and I swear I will kill you."

"It's so sad," she says, "the way you've changed."

"No, what's sad is that you haven't."

After a couple of brittle moments, during which I can feel her thinking evil thoughts, she says, "I have to clear up some things on my schedule, but then I'm coming in, so we can talk."

"If you're coming to see me and your niece, fine. If you're coming to give me a hard time about the will, save yourself a trip. The houses are mine and Starr's, the bonds are mine, the bank account is mine. You don't need it. We do."

She hangs up on me.

Nice to know some things haven't changed.

Like a St. Bernard sitting on my chest, lethargy pins me to the overstuffed armchair in my bedroom.

It's taken a couple of days, but grief has finally found its way home. I still haven't really cried yet, but I think that's because it would take more energy than I have to really let go.

I hear Starr getting herself breakfast: a chair scraping over the linoleum, the sound of the fridge slamming shut, her favorite plastic Peter Rabbit bowl clattering onto the kitchen table. I should be down there with her, being strong and comforting and motherly. That my five-year-old daughter is clearly functioning better than I am is unnerving, to say the least.

I know I need to shower, to make my bed. Talk to my daughter. Except all of that implies a commitment to getting on with things. I don't want to get on with anything, except maybe crawling back into bed and sleeping for about five days straight.

Depression does that to me. Especially this time, combined with the soul-sucking revelation that there's absolutely nobody else to share the decision-making process with anymore, nobody for me to lean on and shoulder the sorrow with me, that I'm completely alone.

It may be a while before I get out of this chair.

"You gotta eat."

Starr's voice, whisper-soft and irritatingly commanding at the same time, startles me out of my stupor. Before I can say anything, she plops a bedtray on my lap with a bowl of Cookie Crisp in way too much milk and a half-filled glass of orange juice. She thrusts a spoon in my face, the Baby Gestapo in a faded powder blue hoodie and sparkly gunmetal leggings. And those red boots, the only shoes she will now wear. Her glasses sit crookedly on her nose. "That's all the juice," she says as I take the spoon in self-defense. "We gotta buy more."

I nod and force my hand to scoop up a spoonful of the dreadful cereal and carry it to my mouth. "Thanks, sweetie pie," I say, trying not to gag.

My child perches primly on the edge of my unmade bed for several seconds, her gaze unwavering, until—apparently satisfied that I have at least eaten enough to stave off imminent starvation—she gets up and pads silently over, wraps her arms around my neck and kisses me, then leaves, shutting the door behind her.

My throat closes, refusing to let the soggy bite of cereal

pass. Alone? Why on earth would I think that? I'm not alone at all.

I set the breakfast tray on the floor and go take my shower.

Leo's been gone a week now. Recently enough that I'm still thinking, "A week ago, we…" or "Just the other day he said…" But the thoughts aren't making my stomach twist inside out quite so much anymore. I am, however, sick to death of everybody trying to boost my spirits. My spirits don't want to be boosted, they want to grieve. They want to milk my sorrow for all it's worth. I want to be left alone to let the memories wash over me, like lying on the beach in the warm sun and feeling the water gently lap at my legs until I feel healed.

Wearing my grandfather's gray, shawl-collared cardigan— I have rubber bands around the cuffs to hold them up, otherwise they hang more than six inches below my fingertips—I check on Starr for the third time since I put her to bed an hour ago. It's all I can do not to get her up to play or watch a video or make brownies. We can do that tomorrow, when she's supposed to be awake. When she's not as likely to guess her mother's hanging by the thinnest of threads to what's left of her sanity. Except I'm not really that bad off, I don't think. I mean, wouldn't I know I was losing it if I really were?

Maybe I don't want to know the answer to that question.

I find myself wandering from room to room, like a restless cat. The worst thing is the silence. No, that's not quite it, because I've been in the house plenty of times when no one else was here, or when Leo and Starr have both been asleep. But there's the silence of peace, and the silence of a void. That where something—or in this case, someone—used to be, now there's nothing.

And it's making me batty.

I end up in my grandfather's room, thinking maybe I'll start going through his things. Except the instant I set foot on the worn carpeting, the ache of loss is so sharp I nearly cry out with it. This isn't the first time I've been through this, looking at or touching personal items I know will never be touched or looked at by their owner again. Why the pain should be so searing this time, I don't know. Maybe because it's taken me three times to really, truly understand just how ephemeral this all is. Our individual lives, I mean. After eighty years, what's left? Memories. And a bunch of stuff that will either rot away or end up being owned by someone else who'll have no idea of its significance.

Creeped out by my own moroseness, I leave the room and its shadows. Tomorrow, or maybe the next day, or next week, when I can lift the shades to let the clear, cleansing early spring sunshine chase away the heebie-jeebies, I'll come back and do what I have to do. After all, there's no hurry.

I finally realize I'm *afraid* to cry. Afraid if I let out the sorrow, I won't be able to stanch it.

I go back downstairs and put a mug of water in the microwave for tea. Soothed by the appliance's benign hum, I become so thoroughly engrossed in reading the Celestial Seasonings box I flinch at the ding. I make my tea and put away the few dishes in the drainer, dismayed to discover, when I glance up at the clock, that all of five minutes have passed.

Okay, I need to do something. Anything. Hugging my tea to my chest, I wander out into the living room and poke through my video collection, bypassing the Jimmy Stewarts for *Sex and the City*. I shove in a tape at random, then plop onto the sofa. Only, before I can press Play, there's a soft rap on the front door. It's Luke, weighed down with grocery bags. And commiseration.

I'm grateful and apprehensive, both, for the comfort of his familiarity, the gentleness in his dark eyes. As with no one else, I can be with him and still be alone, which is exactly what I need at the moment.

I want to throw myself into his arms. Desperately.

"You're back," I say.

"I'm back." He somehow frowns and smiles at the same time. "How you doing?"

I hitch my shoulders.

"Yeah. Same here." He jiggles the bags. "I come bearing carbs. We got your ice cream and Sara Lee crap in this bag—" he holds one aloft "—and Entenmann's and chips—" he lifts the other one "—in here."

"Oh, God. You got any idea how much food I still have in my refrigerator?"

"I can guess." He heads back to the kitchen; I follow, telling myself I don't really want to bury my nose in that beat-up leather jacket of his. "I figure we can trade," he's saying, "since right now you're probably wondering how on earth you're going to eat it all before it goes bad."

Unfortunately, this is not turning out to be as much of a problem as I'd previously thought. My mouth waters as he unloads a copious supply of goodies onto my counter.

"You've been well trained."

His movements hitch. "I remember you and Tina used to be able to really pack this stuff away."

Only Luke could think of somebody else's pain while his own is still so raw and new. Especially as—I suddenly realize—this breakup is the first really bad thing to happen to him. For good or ill, loss is nothing new to me. I at least know what to expect, how to weather the stages. But all-in-all, Luke's led a pretty charmed life—no major setbacks, no deaths, except for one grandparent a few years ago. So this is totally new territory for him.

"Your mother put you up to this, didn't she?"

"You kidding? My mother would have a cow if she knew I was here."

Frowning, I look up.

"Because she read me the riot act," he says, "about how both of us are vulnerable right now."

A moment of profound silence follows. I know what he's thinking, because so am I: *She has no idea.*

"Are we ready to talk about this?" I say.

A glance, fleeting as a dream. "Are you?"

I think about it, then shake my head. "No. Not until…things are a little more settled."

"Yeah, that's what I thought, too."

"I don't suppose we can avoid it for much longer, though."

"Soon," he says. "I promise."

I shift, folding my arms over my stomach. "So why *are* you here?"

"Because if you feel half as crappy as I do, you probably don't need to be alone right now. We're both lousy company, so we might as well be lousy company together. So—" He indicates the loot. "Any preference?"

I feel a smile tug at my lips at his perception, as our unfinished business once again disintegrates like a soap bubble between us.

"Anything with chocolate."

Luke rips open a box of Entenmann's chocolate donuts, plunking one on each of two plates, then scoops chocolate chocolate chip ice cream into the middle. This is good—I recently read that it takes the body longer to convert carbs to sugar if you consume protein at the same time. Which confirms my long-held suspicion that ice cream is the perfect food.

"Wanna watch a video while we eat?"

"Yeah, sure."

We grab our plates and forks and head for the living room, although he grimaces at the *Sex and the City* video case on the coffee table. "What's up with women and this shit?"

"What's up with men and pro wrestling?"

"Better than listening to nonstop whining for two hours."

"Oh, as opposed to the grunts of rutting hippopotamuses?"

"Yeah, that's what I'm talkin' about." He thumps his chest with his free hand. "*Man* noises."

I roll my eyes. "Whatever. But anyway, that's not whining. That's exploring their feelings."

Hanging on to his plate with one hand, he takes a half-hearted swipe at my head with the other. And for some reason, I feel better. Like maybe I'll get through this. Like we're kids again and life is simple and death and mistakes and regrets are things we won't have to deal with for many years to come.

"Tell you what," I say, settling into the sofa. "Next time I'm at your place, we can watch whatever's in season, okay? But no way, nohow is this TV getting anywhere near ESPN tonight."

We both let my "next time I'm at your place" comment sail off into the sunset before Luke says, "Whatever happened to the gracious hostess letting her guests choose the entertainment?"

"Remember the lousy company thing?"

With a sigh, Luke drops onto the opposite end of the sofa, toeing off his sneakers and plopping his feet up on the coffee table. I hit Play and Sarah Jessica Parker prances across the screen. "So which episode is this?" he says.

"*Which* episode?" I rear back and look at him. "You've actually watched *Sex and the City?*"

He shovels in a bite of donut and ice cream. "Tina made me," he says around a full mouth. "Said I might learn something."

"And did you?"

"Yeah. That there's a damn good reason men have performance anxiety. Christ—do women really want all that stuff?"

"All what stuff?"

"You know. The sex stuff."

"Beats me. I just watch it for the clothes."

That gets a chuckle. "Yeah, right."

Of course, fate picks that moment to treat us to a no-holds-barred sex scene. Samantha enjoying the hell out of herself.

Maybe this wasn't such a great idea, after all. I mean, yes, it's just Luke, but then…it's just Luke.

My cheeks get so hot I seriously consider slathering ice cream all over them. Or I would have if there'd been any left. Still, I come up with, "Okay, maybe most women don't want all of it. But I think a lot want more than they're getting." I scoop up the ice cream residue with my finger and stick it in my mouth. "And I'm talking quality, not quantity."

He doesn't reply. Just as well. For several minutes, we sit there in the flickering darkness, separated by the width of a sofa cushion and our thoughts, stuffing our faces with enough calories to fuel the space shuttle. Then suddenly Luke says, "It's funny. You'd think most women would care less about a guy's equipment and more about how he feels about her."

I can't stand it. I reach over and squeeze his arm. "Most women do."

His eyes veer to mine, his mouth lifting at one corner. He's got a small blob of ice cream on his upper lip, making him look about eight. Eight is good. Eight I can handle. It's *twenty*-eight that's giving me trouble.

There. I've said it. I could dance around this issue from now to Doomsday, and God knows, I've learned enough from past mistakes not to do something stupid—like launch myself at the man—but okay, fine, Tina's right, I'm attracted to the guy. And I'm tired of pretending to myself that I'm not. I also know—and here's where Tina's wrong—nothing's going to come of it. And that's not pretending, that's facing reality.

And from now on, reality is my new best friend.

We both turn our attention back to the screen. Another long silence follows, during which I realize that we've been watching the show for a good ten minutes and haven't so much as chuckled, even though I remember howling with laughter the first time I saw it. Not because I ever personally related (I mean, please—those chicks go through more men in two episodes than I even know) but because of the whole single woman solidarity thing, I guess. But tonight, I suddenly do relate. At least to the quiet—and sometimes not so quiet—despair trembling at the edges of their lives.

As if I'm not depressed enough already.

I point the remote at the TV and click it off.

"Why'd you do that?"

"Lost interest."

Luke skootches around, pushing himself back farther into the corner of the sofa, one arm stretched out over the back. "This doesn't change anything between us," he says, and my eyes jerk to his.

"What?"

"Tina and me breaking up. I know you and she are buddies and all, but I'm not disappearing just because…" He swallows. "Just because things didn't work out between her and me."

"Oh." He obviously doesn't know that Tina and I haven't spoken since that last conversation. She sent flowers for Leo, but she didn't call. So I guess it's safe to say we're not exactly tight anymore. "I guess I hadn't thought about it."

"It's just…" His eyes meet mine for a fraction of a second, then skitter away. "It would kill me to lose both of you at the same time, you know?"

Nothing like being thought of as a spare tire.

But I smile gamely anyway, silently repeating my reality-is-my-new-best-friend mantra. Besides, it would have killed me to lose both of them at the same time, too. "It's okay. I'm not going anywhere, either. Anyway, having you around's a no-brainer. And I don't have too many of those these days."

"Yeah. I know what you mean." The air thickens between us, but for different reasons. Luke gets up, taking my dish from me and carting both his and mine back to the kitchen. I rise and follow; he's already at the sink, rinsing them off. Frances has trained her boys well. We decide which food he should take (I swear, it's multiplying in the fridge); I wrap things up in foil, plastic, old margarine dishes and stuff the grocery bags he brought.

But when he glances at me, it's clear we both know it's not true, about nothing changing between us. It's already changed, just by Tina no longer being a factor in the equation. As long as she was, Luke was part of my life by default. But let's get real: Luke will last about as long on the open market as a six-room Riverside Drive apartment for two grand a month. And what are the chances of him hooking up with somebody willing to tolerate another woman in his life, childhood buddy or not?

Yeah, that's what I think, too.

As for that hooey from Tina, about Luke really wanting me instead of her? Right. Man can hardly say her name without choking on it, he's still so torn up about what happened.

"Guess I should get going," Luke says, heading down the hall. "You decided when you're going back to work yet?"

Work. Blech. Yeah, yeah, I got this twenty-five grand coming, but at the rate Starr's going, I might need that for her college tuition like, next week. "Soon. Gotta figure out the day-care thing first."

"Hey—" His jacket back on, Luke bends slightly at the knees to meet my gaze, his expression earnest. "You know, if you need anything, anything at all, I'm here, right? I mean, to help take care of the Twink—"

"We're fine," I say, too quickly and for reasons I'm not sure I fully understand.

"What you are," he says, straightening up, "is a pain in the ass."

"Sweet-talker."

That gets a smile, even if it's a little blurred around the edges. Then: "I'd better get going. Oh—by the way, Mom expects the two of you for Sunday dinner, no excuses."

My throat tightens with emotion, for everything I've lost.

For everything, I think sappily, I still have. Frances is still my surrogate mother. She just wouldn't want to be my mother-*in-law*. Never known a Scardinare yet who didn't marry a good Italian Catholic girl and make good Italian Catholic babies.

"Sure, fine, we'll be there."

With a wave, he's gone. And when I can't hear the sound of his car anymore, I go upstairs and check on my little girl one more time. Her somewhat smelly Oscar the Grouch strangled in her arms, she's softly snoring.

It's the sweetest sound in the whole world.

I wake with a start sometime later, my heart pounding. It's just beginning to get light: everything looks like a TV picture when the brightness dealie's turned too far down.

"You 'wake?" I hear beside me.

I turn and gather my wide-eyed child, as well as Oscar, into my arms. Starr's collected all the characters from *Sesame Street,* but decided—at three, mind you—that Oscar was grouchy all the time because maybe he didn't get enough love. And that it was her mission to remedy that situation. Well, she might not have used those words, but the toy definitely has that well-worn, slightly gross patina that demonstrates her devotion.

"Snuggle?" she says, skootching closer.

"Sure." I yawn. "Did you go potty?"

She nods against my chest, then backs up to frown into my eyes, her little myopic brown ones slightly unfocused. At least, I think that's what she's doing, since my big myopic ones aren't doing much better.

"So," she says, "now what?"

"Now what?" I repeat, stalling until something sparks to life inside my skull.

That gets a little huffy sigh. "I *mean*…what happens now? Are we gonna stay here? Are you going back to work? And who's gonna take care of me when you do? And does this mean we definitely can't get a puppy now?"

I shut my eyes in an attempt to keep my shrieking brain from bolting from my head. When I open them again, Starr's still frowning at me, patiently awaiting any words of wisdom I might be inclined to share. Unfortunately, I'm fresh out.

"Don't know, Twinkle-girl."

"About *any* of it?" You'd have to be here to get the full impact of her incredulity.

"Well, I pretty much have to go back to work," I say, "since otherwise, we'd eventually starve."

"But why do we have to buy food when people keep bringing it to us?"

I chuckle. "They won't do that forever, honey. That's just something people do when…when a family's going through a tough time."

"You mean because Leo died."

"Yeah."

She rolls out of my arms and onto her back, her hands folded over her tummy. The heat hasn't kicked on yet; I pull the down comforter up over her, then wrap my arm around her, just for a second wishing there was somebody to wrap an arm around me, to make me feel warm and safe and secure. It suddenly hits me that I'd never expected, at twenty-eight, to be either a parent or an orphan. And I'm not real sure what to do with the fact that I'm both.

"Why do people have to die?" she asks and I close my eyes again, thinking it's way too early for these kinds of questions. Not before coffee. Or another couple of decades of trying to figure it out myself. But somehow, when I open my mouth, out comes, "Because everything does, eventually. Everything that has a beginning, has an ending. That's just a law of nature."

Dark eyes meet mine. "Can God die?"

God? How the hell did He get into this conversation?

"Of course God can't die. God's...God, for goodness sake."

This gets one of those astute, assessing looks that scares the crap out of me. The you-don't-really-know-so-you're-faking-it-aren't-you? look. To distract myself from the panic threatening to cut off my air supply, I remember all the goodies downstairs that Luke brought over last night. Surely there's something I can feed the child that won't invoke the wrath of the Good Mother police.

So I swing my legs out of bed as if I'm actually awake and perky. "You hungry? Uncle Luke brought a whole bunch of donuts and stuff last night—"

"Is God even real?"

Would someone tell me how I got a kid who puts her spiritual awakening ahead of sugar and fat calories?

I twist around. "I'd like to think so," I say, since unless and until I get incontrovertible proof that He isn't, I don't think it's in my best interests to deliberately piss the old guy—or gal—off by denying Him. Or Her.

"Then why does He let bad stuff happen? I mean, if he's God, isn't he supposed to be like all-powerful and stuff?"

I make a mental note to find out who the kid's been hanging out with.

"Unfortunately, since I'm not, I don't have all the answers. In fact, I don't have most of them." I pause, then add, because it seems like a good idea at the moment, "But maybe if you keep asking, God will answer them for you Himself."

"How?"

"Honestly, Starr—how do I know? Now do you want donuts or not?"

Her eyes get very...deep, is the best way I can describe it. Starr almost never cries, never did very much even as an infant. But she does the wounded look better than anyone I've ever known. And she's got it on full display now, boy. I let out a loud sigh, then scoop her up into my lap, trying to pat her tangled hair out of my face before it makes me sneeze.

"I'm sorry, sweetie. But I'm a little frazzled right now and you're asking me questions I can't answer. And I get frustrated because I do want to be able to answer them. I just can't. Does that make sense?"

She nods, then says, "I have an idea."

"About?"

"Leo's things. In his room? Maybe I could help you go through them, and then we could say something about each thing, to help us remember him?"

"I think that's a great idea. How'd you think of it?"

"Dunno. It just came to me."

I glance up. *Um...if You're up there, or wherever, and talking to my daughter? Would You mind not leaving me out of the loop?*

We get on our robes and slippers and go down to the kitchen, where it hits me that I think I've just said my first honest-to-God prayer. Is that weird or what?

Although not nearly as weird as what's pitching a fit at my front door.

chapter 13

"Yes?" I say politely to the unfamiliar blonde glowering at me through the glass.

"Oh, for Christ's sake, Ellie, let me in. It's freezing out here."

"Jennifer?"

The glower deepens.

Okay, in all fairness, I didn't recognize my sister at first because a) she was brunette the last time I saw her and b) she had a nose. I stand back and let her inside, biting back the urge to say, "Ooooh, we've been hitting up WASPS-R-US, haven't we?"

What can I tell you, grief brings out my surly side. Which, if I were in a more charitable frame of mind, I might say was the reason behind my sister's foul mood. Since a) I'm not and b) she's always been like this, what's the point?

Jennifer stops and stares at Starr for a moment, as if she's startled to find her here. Then, without so much as a "hello" for her niece, she turns back to give me the once-over.

"Well, don't you look like hell."

Aaaand, we're off.

"Who're you?" Starr says.

At this, Jen turns and bends at the knees, a pained smile stretched across her face. "I'm your Aunt Jennifer, honey. Your mommy's sister."

Starr shoots me a is-she-serious? look. When I nod, her eyes veer back to her aunt. "How come I've never seen you before?"

"Starr, sweetie? Would you do me a huge favor and go watch TV for a bit while Aunt Jennifer and I…chat for a few minutes?"

"C'n I have juice first?"

"Sure, baby." I pour her some Tropicana and send her on her way, then turn on—I mean *to*—my sister.

"It's not even seven-thirty," I say, hoping the morning halitosis is strong enough to reach her, "I just got up, I wasn't expecting you, and what was the other thing? Oh, right—I've been mourning our grandfather for the past week." I shuffle to the fridge to get out the coffee, then let my eyes slide up and down Jennifer's DKNY'd body. "And your excuse is…?"

"Don't be catty."

"It's a big kitchen. There's plenty of room for both of us."

She ignores me because apparently there's a much bigger crisis looming on the horizon. "You use *Folger's?*"

Under other circumstances I might even be enjoying this. Especially when she gets a load of the tower of goodies left from last night. Filled with equal parts pity and disgust, her eyes once again rake over my body.

"People have been bringing food," I say, clicking on the coffeemaker. "Feel free to take some home with you if you like." I turn, my arms crossed. "Why are you here, Jen?"

"My name," she says, "is *Jennifer.*"

Beelzebub to your friends, I think but do not say.

"So why are you here, *Jennifer?*"

"Two things, actually. First, I want to know what your plans are. About the house."

I frown. "You came into town at seven-thirty to ask me about the house?"

An airy little wave precedes, "I have a meeting at nine in the city. I thought I might as well kill two birds with one stone."

My God, she's so blond she practically glows. Next time there's a blackout, I'm sticking with her, boy.

I haul myself back to the present. "And what plans, exactly, did you have in mind? Some home improvements, maybe? I was thinking maybe we could use a new coat of paint—"

"I'm not talking about home improvements!" She actually stamps her foot. But gently. So as not to break off the pretty little stacked heel on her I-don't-wanna-know-how-much-it-cost pointy-toed boot. "I'm talking about selling!"

"Jennifer, hellooo? I can't sell this house, remember? It's in trust for Starr."

Her eyes—a peculiar, colorless color, like platinum—turn cold. "I know that. I'm talking about that *ridiculous* condition about not being able to sell the other house as long as the tenants want to stay. As if that's a problem."

I shut my eyes. I don't even want to know what she's thinking.

"Jen…ifer, you're talking about peoples' homes. And the Gomezes are expecting another baby within a matter of minutes."

"I bet you don't even know what the property's worth."

"Since it hasn't exactly been a top priority to find out…nope. Haven't a clue."

"Take a wild guess."

You know, there really ougghta be a law about letting people like her loose this early. I'm thinking the next millennium would be good. But if I have any hope of her going away and letting me enjoy my despondency in peace, I might as well play along.

"Couple hundred thou?"

Her laugh—shrill and slightly maniacal—startles me. "Are you kidding? A duplex in this neighborhood, and with the improvements Grandfather made on it…you're looking at four hundred grand, easy. Maybe even five."

I refuse to let my jaw drop.

"Did you say…four hundred thousand dollars?"

"Maybe five."

Even in my early morning stupor, I can translate that into *half a million freakin' dollars.* Kinda takes the sting out of being pissed that the she-devil actually got one up on me.

"And any halfway decent Realtor," Jen is saying, "would probably be able to unload that puppy in a snap. So what do you think?"

"About what?"

"Selling. Think of all the things you and Stella could do with that much money."

"Who the hell is Stella?"

Jennifer laughs, a breathy, irritating tinkle. "Your *daughter?*"

My eyes narrow. "Her name is Starr." Then they narrow farther. "And why are *you* getting so excited about what would be *my* money?"

You'd have to know Jennifer to catch the subtle signs, but since I do, I did. Her smile starts to droop, just slightly. And the merest hint of a crease appears between her brows. And she's always had this habit, when she gets nervous, of rubbing the thumb and forefinger of her left hand together.

"Stuart lost his job," she says in a low voice, her eyes averted, as if the shame is too much to bear. For a second, I feel a small swell of sympathy. It passes. Especially when this news is followed by, "And, I just thought, you know, if you did sell, that maybe we could get a small loan?"

Ah. "How about instead Stuart gets another job? Or better yet, how about *you* get a job?"

Jennifer lets the second part of my suggestion sail over her two-hundred-dollar highlights. "Believe me, he's trying. With the economy the way it is, though…" Her lips thin. "And you wouldn't *believe* some of the lowball figures he's being offered. With no bonus. It's absolutely outrageous. So we're kind of strapped," she says, crinkling her Michael Jackson nose. "But honestly, all we'd need is, say, a hundred grand to tide us over. And we'd pay it back with interest, you know we would—"

"A hundred grand! Are you out of your *mind?*"

"It's just for few months, until Stuart finds a decent job."

"Who the hell needs a hundred grand to *tide them over?* For a *couple of months!*"

"Your voice is getting all shrieky."

"You bet your ass my voice is getting shrieky! If you and Stuart are having so much trouble, here's an idea—why don't you sell *your* freakin' house?"

"We can't do that! It's our *home!*"

"And my tenants? Those aren't their homes?"

"That's different! They're just renting, for God's sake!"

"I somehow doubt they'd agree with you."

Her mouth goes all thin. "So you won't even consider it?"

"I didn't make the will, Jennifer. Our grandfather did. If you've got a problem with it, you'll have to take it up with him."

"That would be a little difficult, considering he's dead."

"Keep this up, and it won't be a problem."

That gets a cartoon affronted gasp, immediately followed by slit eyes. And a very strange, I-know-something-you-don't smile.

I should know better. But I say it anyway. "What?"

"You have no idea, do you?"

"About what?"

"Not what. *Who.* Sonja."

Crap. I'd forgotten all about her. "You know who she is?"

"Oh, yeah. I know who she is, all right." Jennifer puffs herself up. "She was Grandfather's mistress."

I let out a sigh. "That's not exactly a shock, you know. I mean, Nana's been gone for more than a dozen years—"

"Oh, nonononononono," my sister says, waving her finger in front of me. "Sonja wasn't *after* Nana. Sonja was *during* Nana."

Wow. She's just full of surprises this morning. "Are you sure?"

"I guess Nana never told you, did she?"

No, Jen and my grandmother were the best buds in the family, I always assumed because Jen was much more Judith Levine's…type. So I guess it was only natural they shared the odd confidence now and again.

"So you're telling me Nana came right out and said, 'Oh, by the way, your grandfather's screwing somebody named Sonja Koepke.'"

Jennifer looks pensive for a moment, then says, "Yeah, pretty much. Only she was much too much of a lady to say 'screwing.'"

"Unlike her favorite granddaughter."

"Fu—" She catches herself, practically turning purple from the effort of swallowing what she'd been about to say. Since it's early and all, I would appreciate knowing where my sister's going with this. But from years of experience, I know she'll get there eventually. And it's mildly amusing to watch how she works. But eventually, she tosses her hair—she's such a cliché, I can't stand it—and says, "Still think our grandfather's the wonderful man you always thought he was?"

"You mean because Nana told you something that might not even be true?"

Her eyes go to ice again. "Sonja's in the will, isn't she?"

"Yes, she is. Which reminds me—you wouldn't have any idea how to get in touch with her, would you?"

"No!" She actually recoils. "And even if I did, why on earth would I want to hand over what should have been part of our inheritance to some woman who couldn't even keep her hands off another woman's husband?"

Whether I like it or not, my gut cramps. In the dictionary,

next to the word "shrew," is my grandmother's picture. Or Jennifer's, depending on what edition you have. If Leo really was cheating on her—and if Jennifer heard her name from our grandmother's lips, there's probably at least some truth to her accusation—I can't really find it in my heart to condemn him. Yet still, it stings, that he didn't trust me to even mention her, not once in the twelve years since my grandmother's death.

But I can't take my frustration and anger out on Leo, because he's not here.

My sister, however—my vindictive, hateful, always-looking-for-ways-to-get-a-dig-in sister—is.

"Get out," I say quietly.

"What did you say?"

"You heard me."

She grabs her purse—Kate Spade, what else?—and impales me with her gaze. "I cannot believe you're being this rude when I'm only trying to be helpful, for God's sake—"

I grab her arm, which provokes a satisfying yelp. "Honey, you wouldn't know *helpful* if it bit you in your Pilated butt. You think *helpful* is coming around and stirring up trouble—"

"That's not true!"

"—and then you look at my daughter like she's a puddle of something disgusting on the subway platform, you don't even bother to speak to her until she forces the issue, and you're calling *me* rude?"

Jen jerks her arm from my grip and flounces out of the kitchen and down the hall in a flurry of natural fibers, yanks open the front door and stomps down the stairs, beeping her Beemer unlocked from twenty feet away. I follow, because I'm obviously still not awake, so I'm right in the line of fire when she turns and says, "You know, Nana was right. You're just like our mother, nothing but a two-bit, dumb-as-dirt Southern hick!"

The car is too polite to actually roar when she guns the engine and shoots down the street, but I get the idea.

Starr comes up behind me, watching Jen's vapor trail.

"Geez. What's her problem?"

"Beats me, honey," I say, trying to control the shaking. Then we go inside and gorge on donuts until we almost make ourselves sick.

I finally get around to sorting through Leo's things that afternoon. Frances and Jason have come over to help, turning what could have easily been a morbid activity into, well, something less morbid. I'd like to say I'm over my set-to with my sister, but her words cut deeper than I'd thought they could. Especially after all this time.

I never quite understood the enmity my grandmother felt toward my mother, who might have been Southern but was no hick, believe me. And God knows, she wasn't dumb. Maybe it was because my mother was about as *goyish* as you could get. Or maybe it was because Judith was simply jealous of my mother, that she couldn't stand seeing her son's loyalties diverted. Because there was no doubt Dad adored Mom. As she did him. But whatever my grandmother thought of Connie Griffith Levine, she knew to keep her trap shut about her in front of my father. I even heard him say, one time when I was supposed to be asleep but had crept out to the landing because I heard them arguing, that he hadn't married my mother to please Nana, but to please *himself.* And if she couldn't deal with that, that was just too damn bad.

In her place, I would've been thrilled to know my son had found someone to make him so happy. Not to mention I can only hope Starr has half the guts her grandfather had, to go after what she wants, as well as the courage to defend her choices, no matter what. But that's just me.

And here's hoping I remember that the first time Starr brings home somebody that makes my heart drop into my shoes.

"God," Frances says, dumping a load of boxes on the floor.

She's in jeans and a ratty old brown sweater, she's not wearing a drop of makeup, her hair's a mess, and she's gorgeous. "Could this room be any gloomier?"

I've lifted both sets of blinds and tied back the sheers, but it's still murky in here. Forget what I said about letting in the spring sunshine, since it started raining—a miserably cold deluge—right after Jen left and hasn't let up since. Frances turns on every light in the room, including the overhead, so now everything's a pale urine color. I could do without the interrogation room ambiance, but I'm not about to argue with someone who's volunteered to go through an old man's underwear, for Pete's sake. Some of which I'm convinced predates the New Deal.

Two hours later, although our conversation's been pretty much limited to the occasional "What do you want to do with this?" or "You think this is worth hanging on to?" we've made good progress. Everything's been sorted into three groups: the few things I want to keep; the stuff that should've been tossed ten years ago; and the rest into boxes and bags for Frances to take to her church's thrift store, a task she's undertaken for my family four times in fifteen years.

But we don't mention that.

However, it hasn't all been morose. As Starr and I agreed, many of the items sparked an impromptu memorial, which more often than not got the two of us laughing, much to Frances's obvious relief. The idea of giving most of Leo's possessions away to strangers doesn't seem to bother my daughter at all. In fact, she's only keeping a trinket or two that sat on his dresser, as well as his watch and a pair of silver and onyx cufflinks I'd given him when I was ten. I tell her we can have them made into earrings one day, if she likes.

I, on the other hand, have held back a tweed sportjacket, all the sweaters the moths haven't half devoured and two pairs of nearly new corduroy pants we'd just gotten for him at Christmas.

After Jason hauls off the first box of clothes for the thrift store, Starr climbs up onto Leo's bed, slowly inspecting my choices.

"How come you wear men's clothes so much?"

Frances looks over, clearly interested in what my answer's going to be. Especially as I'm still wearing the same cardigan I've been in all week. Yes, because it still smells of my grandfather and it's helping me to ease into the idea of his not being here. I'm well aware of what I'm doing. And why I'm doing it.

"Because they're comfortable. And wearing Leo's or Grandpa's clothes helps me remember them. But I don't just wear men's clothes, I wear my grandmother's, too, you know."

Which might seem odd, considering my relationship with her. But hey—I can't fault the woman's taste. And we were close to the same size. It seemed a shame to just toss them simply because of a few negative association issues. Besides, I have a real strong feeling she'd pop her girdle if she knew I was wearing her duds. A good reason if ever there was one to strut around in them from time to time.

"You should wear that pretty red dress," Starr now says. "The one with the big skirt." She means one of my grandmother's fifties outfits from when she was still in her twenties, a cranberry duppione silk I will cherish until the day I die. "You look like a girl in it."

Again with the girl stuff. Although I notice her obsession seems to be focused on me, not on herself. "Question—how come I have to look like a girl and you don't?"

"Because you're the mommy," Starr says, with a is-she-slow-or-what? glance at Frances.

"Frances is a mommy. Why doesn't she have to wear dresses?"

"Because she looks just as pretty in pants."

Ouch.

"Hey," Frances says, her chin lowered as she points at my

daughter. "You watch your mouth, little girl. Your mommy looks just fine the way she is."

But Starr lets out one of those sighs that lifts her shoulders several inches. Clearly, we don't get it. Although someday, I suppose I'd better make an effort *to* get it.

My cell rings. I find it under one of the piles, frowning when I see my work number. Have you ever noticed how you're allowed exactly one week to recoup from a family death—especially when it's a "routine" death, like that of an aged relative—after which you're expected to buck up and get on with your life? Or rather, on with whoever's life your personal problems have disrupted?

Nikky gave me seven days exactly. And showered me with sympathy—not to mention flowers and a fruit basket—during that official grieving period. But now we're on Day Nine, in which case my sorrow is now on her time.

"Hello, darling," she says, her voice laced with I-don't-mean-to-prod-but-where-the-hell-*are*-you? kindness. "Just calling to see how you're doing."

"Oh...I'm getting there."

"Any idea when you might be coming back?"

"Soon," is my oblique answer. Funny how I was okay with this job until Mari dangled the other one under my nose. However, since that's now moot, and this is the job I still have, and need, it's not as if I can afford to blow it off. And I do miss the city. But the fact is, I'm not ready to go back to that madhouse and I don't know when I will be. So there. "I still have to arrange for child care." Starr's eyes dart to mine, accusing.

"Child care?"

"For my daughter?" Okay, fine, maybe I don't litter every conversation with the kid, but it's not as if I've never mentioned her, for God's sake. I walk over to the window, out of earshot. "She's only five," I say in a low voice, "and since her grandfather was her main caregiver when I wasn't around, this might not be the easiest transition."

"Oh, kids are more resilient than we sometimes give them credit for," Nikky says brightly. "Look at my two—they've had nannies and caregivers from the time they were babies, and they turned out just fine."

What's sad is that she really believes that. "That may be, but I'm not going to rush things. Of course, if it's really a problem and you need to find someone to replace me—"

"No, no!" A nervous twitter tickles my ear. "Take all the time you need, dear. We'll just…muddle through as best we can until you return. But keep me posted, will you? And by the way…I have a surprise for you."

"Oh? What?" Another Return To Vendor shipment, no doubt, that she wants me to convince a department manager or buyer to take back.

"You'll see. Just as soon as you come back."

Then she hangs up. I stand there, staring at the phone, vaguely aware that Starr's gone off with the returned Jason, leaving me with Frances. Who takes the phone from me and sets it aside, then gently pulls me down to sit on the edge of the bed with her, looping an arm around my shoulder. "Do you really need to go back there?"

"I need the money. Not to mention Manhattan."

She ignores the second part of my sentence. "The rent money from next door isn't enough?"

"Barely. And some of that goes back into maintenance, of course. But I don't know…" I look at her. "My sister was here the other day, did you know?"

Her eyes widen. "Jennifer? You're kidding?"

"Nope."

"God. It's been, what? Eight or nine years?"

"Ten. She was trying to figure out a way to somehow circumvent the will so I could sell the rental house."

"Why? It was left to you, not her."

"Ah, but she thinks if I sell, she can get a loan." I explain the whole business about Stuart losing his job, etc., watching as Frances's mouth gets increasingly thinner. Then she blows out a harsh breath.

"That girl always was a piece of work. If I hadn't had six kids of my own, so I know how different siblings' personalities can be, I'd swear one of you was switched in the hospital. And my money'd be on Jennifer." Frances stands, hauling one of the boxes up onto the bed to tape it closed. "Anyway, there's no way the will can be broken, right?"

"Not according to the lawyer. Is it true, though, that the houses are worth around four hundred thou a piece?"

She nods, ripping off a piece of packing tape with her teeth. "That's a pretty fair ballpark figure, yeah."

So if Starr decides to sell when she reaches twenty-one, she'll have a nice little investment. A pretty stable one, too. And one that nobody—like, say, greedy, self-serving aunties—can touch.

Good old Leo.

Which reminds me…

"You ever hear Leo mention somebody named Sonja?"

Slowly, Frances looks up, then brushes her bangs out of her eyes with the back of her wrist. "Was that her name?" she says softly.

"Are you saying…you knew about her?"

Strong, capable hands stretch the tape across the closed box. "I wouldn't exactly say I *knew* about her. Suspected, maybe. Jimmy and I were closer to your parents than we were your grandparents. Mainly because I don't think your grandmother liked me all that much." She shrugs. "Not that I cared. But we had them all to dinner from time to time, you remember, when you and Jennifer were little? Anyway, I'd pick up on these…clues that something was going on. You know, when somebody says something and glances shoot across the table? That kind of thing. Suggestions, nothing more. But I'd catch your grandmother giving your grandfather these looks." Another shrug. "For a long time, I decided it was just my overactive imagination. Until Jimmy said he thought there was something funny going on, too." She sets the box on the floor, closes up the next one. "Why are you bringing this up now?"

"I didn't tell you everything about the will. Like that my grandfather apparently left this Sonja person a money market account worth a nice chunk of change."

"Really?" Then she grimaces. "Bet Jennifer loved that."

"You have no idea."

Frances smiles, then says, "You think Leo was still seeing this woman?"

"Who knows? He rarely volunteered where he was going when he went out, and I never asked. I always assumed he was just going to Pinky's or someplace. Or the senior center." With a small smile, I add, "He never came back smelling like perfume or anything like that."

"Maybe she didn't wear perfume."

Good point. I get up; the boxes are all ready to go. Which means the bed is cleared.

The bed still made up with the linens my grandfather slept in.

Frances looks over, waiting for me to make the first move. I reach for the top of the hobnailed bedspread; in seconds, we've stripped the bed, the sheets dumped into a laundry basket.

"You want me to wash those for you?" Frances says.

"No, I'm fine."

"If you're sure." I nod, my throat closing. Then she says, "Where do you keep the vacuum? This floor is a mess."

"That's okay, I'll do it later—"

"Ellie. Where is it?"

"Hall closet by the kitchen."

A minute later she returns with the vacuum. I see the cord twisted in the figure-eight pattern and burst into tears.

Frances holds me until the storm passes; eventually, I wipe my eyes and blow my nose, then say, "Guess I'm not as over it as I thought."

"Who says you have to be?"

I smile and blow my nose again. A second later, the vacuum cleaner roars to life. I watch Frances pushing it around, wondering again who this Sonja is, how she'd take Leo's death, if she knew.

Does she know?

Another dangling thread, leading nowhere. Which seems to be the theme of my life these days.

chapter 14

The next several days are spent in a marathon session of investigating all the day-care options within a reasonable radius of the house, ninety percent of which I reject out of hand. Especially the "loving care in my home" ones I find tacked up on assorted local bulletin boards. But eventually I narrow it down to a couple of places that seem clean, well-run, with smiling caregivers and children who aren't huddled in the corners, rocking and sucking their thumbs while staring blankly into space.

Of course, there is the issue of Starr getting along with other children. Liv's testimonial of how well my daughter deals with Andy notwithstanding, having been raised with adults, she's just always preferred adult company. She can tolerate children for an hour or two, then becomes bored with them, like a cat with a dead mouse. Forced to endure their company for nine hours a day could be a challenge for all concerned.

Be that as it may, I realize I can't put this off any longer. Especially as Nikky's taken to calling twice a day. At this rate, she'd be less of a pain in person. So, in a nasty drizzle I'm convinced will never stop, off Starr and I go to check out what I can only say is the least offensive place, someplace called Precious Seedlings (gag), close to the subway stop. One little hand shoved into the pocket of her puffy pink parka (only a shade lighter than Mrs. Patel's flamingo, today attired in a shiny emerald green top hat and matching vest), the other clamped tightly around a matching umbrella, she stalwartly crosses the street, slightly ahead of me. And not a single word does she utter on the way there. Once we arrive and are ushered into the director's office, she sits primly across from the smiling, dark-skinned woman, her mouth set, answering Mrs. Harrison's questions with as little enthusiasm as possible.

The humidity has done a real number on Starr's hair, poor baby.

"Well, Starr," the director says, "would you like to spend a few hours with us and see what you think?"

Shoulders hitch. "Fine, whatever."

We walk down a short, brightly lit hallway to a glass-paneled, double door leading to the main classroom. A cheerfully lit room filled with bright colors and several dozen active, boisterous, chattering children. Normal children. Probably very nice children. Just nothing like Starr.

"It's free play time, which they normally have outside," Mrs. Harrison says apologetically. "But the weather's so awful, we decided to keep them in." She smiles. "In twenty minutes, you'll be able to hear a pin drop in here."

Starr, the child who will play quietly by herself for hours, who has no problem with being alone, looks up at me, betrayal in her eyes.

I lean down and whisper, "Do this for me, and there's a puppy in it for you."

"Deal," she says, striding into the melee like a soldier into battle.

When I pick her up at the end of the free trial session three hours later, she seems resolute. Although, frankly, none the worse for wear. It occurs to me that it won't kill her to learn to interact with members of the human species her own age. She's going to have to do it anyway come fall, when she starts kindergarten.

Kindergarten. Aiyiyi.

"So how was it?" I ask as we walk home. The drizzle has turned into a fine mist. I tell myself it's great for the complexion.

"The art stuff was okay, but they made us sing these stupid songs. And most of the kids are such babies."

"Oh, Starr…"

"Well, they are. Some of them still like *Teletubbies,* for crying out loud."

Not much I can say to that. Then she slips her hand in mine, a tiny show of vulnerability. "C'n we go get a puppy this afternoon?" When I don't answer, her eyes lift to mine. "You said."

"I said you could get one. I didn't necessarily mean this afternoon."

She faces forward, her mouth set.

*Dam*mit.

"I guess there's no real reason we can't do this today." And yes, I am the world's wussiest parent. "Especially as I'll have to go back to work on Monday."

Either she doesn't hear that last part, or she's choosing to ignore it, because her head jerks up, a wide, baby-toothed grin splitting her skinny little face in two. Just like a real little kid, even. Itty-bitty water droplets frost her lenses.

"Ican'tdecidebetweenasmallfuzzydog, orsomethingreally-reallybig—"

"Small is good," I interject, but she's on a roll.

"—andIlikethosedogswiththebigfloppyears, what'rethey-called? Orthosedogsthatgetdressedupon.*SesameStreet*—"

"Honey," I say as we near the house, "I think we'll just have to wait and see what's there, okay?" I see Jason sitting on the stoop, looking miserable and cold. Of course, he always looks miserable, but the cold part is new.

"Why on earth are you sitting out here?"

"F-forgot my k-key. G-got locked out. Thought I was g-g-gonna freeze to d-death. You got any ssssoup or some-thing?"

I unlock my front door, push it open. "Yeah, I got soup. But aren't you supposed to be in school?"

"T-teacher's meeting or somethin'—"

"We're gonna go get a dog after lunch!" Starr interrupts as we all stumble inside and head for the kitchen. Even though the heat's on, Jason twists on the gas burner and holds his hands over it. "Wanna come with us?"

While it might be a stretch to say he actually perks up at this news, there's a definite flicker of interest in those dull brown eyes.

"Whatever," he says, yanking his hands away from the flame. Two seconds later, he finds a can of tomato soup in my cupboard and hands it to me.

The promise of a fun-filled afternoon stretches in front of me like a highway in the desert.

There are roughly four million dogs in this place, all yapping their heads off and calling attention to themselves like desper-ate actors at a cattle call. The sound is deafening; the smell, unbelievable (I know they do the best they can, but with four million dogs, poop happens. Frequently.). But what really gets me is my reaction. I realize I haven't been avoiding the dog issue because I don't want the extra responsibility; it's because another five minutes in here and I'll want to take them *all* home with me.

I'm telling you, there are far too many big, brown, pleading eyes in here.

So I hang back with Jason (the better not to get sucked in by all those big, brown, pleading eyes) watching Starr slowly make her way from cage to cage. The dogs are going nuts, trying to get her attention. But she remains expressionless as she walks, her hands stuffed into her coat pockets. Almost as if she doesn't even see them, although obviously she does.

"Whoa," Jason says in a monotone beside me. "Scary kid."

I roll my eyes, just as Starr suddenly stops in front of one cage near where we're standing.

"This one."

Jason and I exchange glances before we both move closer.

"Dude," he says. "Serious candidate for Extreme Makeover."

Truer words were never spoken. Although I'm just trying to wrap my head around the most startling aspect of her choice. No big, brown, sad eyes here. Instead, more like the color of old pee.

"But honey…I thought you said you wanted a *dog?*"

Starr shrugs. Mind you, I've yet to see one iota of excitement over her choice. A feeling, or lack thereof, which seems to be reciprocated by the choice itself, which I can only describe as the feline answer to the Phantom of the Opera. Without the mask. And, I strongly suspect from the malevolent glare currently aimed in my direction, without the soul.

"I changed my mind," she says, then adds, "Besides, cats are easier to take care of than dogs, right?"

The cat glares at me again, as if in challenge. The protruding fang is an especially nice touch.

"In theory, yeah," I begin, only to have my breath catch in

my throat when my child leans her forehead against the cage. I have visions of the thing's head spinning around, or something. Instead, it bumps Starr's head, then lets out a long, mournful noise more like keening than a meow.

"Why?" I ask her.

Her eyes meet mine, full of that not-so-patient indulgence one uses with the slow. "Because if we don't take him, who will?"

And for this I'm about to shell out a hundred bucks. Unbelievable.

I have to admit, after two weeks stuck in Queens, I'm almost giddy when I come up out the of the subway station at 34th Street on Monday morning. And believe me, only a diehard New Yorker would find anything on 34th Street and Seventh Avenue worth getting giddy over. Glamorous, this part of the city ain't. Still, as I dodge guys shoving racks of plastic-shrouded garments down the filthy, cracked sidewalks, I'm nearly overcome with the urge to do a little jig.

Not that my troubles have gone far away, by any means. I still worry about Starr (Will day care scar her for life? Will she scar the other kids for life? Should I worry that she's fallen in love with the ugliest cat in the history of the species?), about Luke (Is he okay? How much do I dare care whether he is or not? Where do we go from here?), about Tina (Should I call? Should I let things ride? Should I stand by her or let her drift out of my life?), about how little I know about being a landlord and what my sister's next move might be—because, believe me, there will be a next move—and what the whole story is behind my grandfather's relationship with the mythical Sonja Koepke.

But right this minute as I'm whizzing along with the quadrillion other people whizzing along (a young woman passes me, yelling, "You're a fucking *asshole,* Marty!" into her cellphone) the city's energy goes to my head like champagne. Still clinging desperately to my high minutes later, I get off the elevator and wish a stunned Valerie/Vanessa (she's still there, imagine that) good morning, then sweep into the—oh, yes— devastated showroom.

Uh-uh. I refuse to let a few crumpled garments crumple my mood.

I go on back, where we go through the brief, uncomfortable, obligatory sympathy thing (Jock sees this as a convenient op- portunity to hug me a little too closely for longer than socially acceptable: either it doesn't take much to arouse this guy or he's mainlining Viagra); then everyone returns to what they were doing, leaving me with a positively beaming Nikky. Who takes me by the arm and swoops me off to the farthest recesses of the floor, where, carved out of a corner next to the door lead- ing to the service elevator, stands—

"Your office!"

So it is. A desk, some file cabinets, a computer, a chair. No window, and the walls are only five feet tall, but hey. It is, in- deed, an office.

Nikky looks like a little kid waiting to see what Mommy's reaction is to the lopsided vase she made in summer camp.

"Wow," I say. "Thanks. This is great."

"I realize it's a little bare bones, but it was the best we could do on short notice."

Only Nikky would consider more than a year short notice. But far be it from me to look an office-horse in the mouth.

"It's great. Really."

"And," she says, "since you've been here for a while, I think you deserve a raise. How's an extra twenty-five dollars a week sound?"

"Fifty," I hear myself say.

Whoa. Had no idea that was coming.

Neither, apparently, did Nikky.

"F-fifty?"

"I have to pay for day care now. If I don't get it, I'll have to look for another job." She has no idea I don't have housing expenses, or what my budget is. Nor is it any of her business. This isn't about what I need, it's about what I deserve. And around here, I think as Harold starts screaming about God knows what, what I deserve is freaking combat pay.

Underneath enough foundation to support a fifty-story building, she blanches, as if I've threatened to hold her Paxil hostage. Of course, I'm totally bluffing. Yeah, this may be about what I deserve, but it's not as if I can walk away if she says no. Or that there aren't a hundred other people eager for my job.

"Thirty-five," she says.

Do I dare do this?

"Nope." Apparently, I do. "It's gotta be fifty."

She narrows her eyes at me. "You've got another offer, don't you?" Then one expertly manicured hand shoots up before I have to lie. "Fifty it is. Just don't tell Harold."

Not a problem.

"And I won't be able to work Saturdays."

Nikky looks at me, agape. Agog? One of those. Then her mouth snaps shut, she says, "Fine," and walks away.

I sit on my new chair in my new office until the dizziness passes.

The first week back passes without major incident. I go to work, I save Nikky's butt, I run interference between Harold and the rest of the world (literally—we've got suppliers in every continent except Antarctica). Now that I have an office, everybody seems to take me more seriously. I take myself more seriously. Hey, I'm a survivor. Sixteen months and counting, and I'm still here. I even suggested a way to rework that dress to flatter more figures, and Nikky thought it sounded like a good idea.

By the second week, however, things aren't so hot. Nikky seems crazier, Harold louder and I'm spending twice my net salary gain on taxis to make sure I pick up Starr before six-thirty every night so I don't get slammed with a hefty surcharge. And since I don't have five minutes to learn how to do even the simplest maintenance tasks, it seems like everytime I turn around, I'm calling a repair guy. More big bucks down the tubes.

And then there's the time issue. As in, I need a clone to get everything done and still be there for my child. The child who, while not exactly saying she hates day care, is being uncharacteristically clingy. Which isn't a good thing since I'm now behind on Heather's dress. And I still haven't even thought about the bridesmaid's dresses. So Heather's freaking, my tenants are getting nervous and my child's expression when I drop her off every morning is tearing me up inside.

Then there are the phone calls. From the tenants (although honestly, it's not their fault the old house has picked now to fall apart, piece by piece); from Heather or her mother or her sister, wanting to know when she can have her fitting, when we can go fabric shopping, when they can see the bridesmaids' sketches; from the day-care center (*"Please talk with Starr about getting along with other children." "Please talk with Starr about the need to participate more." "Please talk to Starr about what it means to be in a group."*)

And naturally, Harold manages to be around every single time I get a personal call.

Like now.

"Ms. Levine? It's Mrs. Harrison. From Precious Seedlings?"

As if I don't know where she's from by now.

Harold is standing by my officette, glowering. I turn my back on him. "Yes, Mrs. Harrison—?"

"If that's a personal call, young lady, tell them you'll call back later."

"Excuse me," I say to the director, then cup my hand over the phone and swivel back to Frog Man. "It's my daughter's day care. Trust me, they're not calling to shoot the breeze."

"Make it snappy, then. I'm not paying you to talk on the phone all day."

Never mind that *he* doesn't pay me at all. But at least he goes away. Would that he would *stay* away, but that much luck, I don't have.

I sigh and return my attention to the phone. "I'm sorry. You were saying?"

There's a little pause. Which is worrisome because if it's one thing Mrs. Harrison is not, it's a prevaricator.

"There's been…an incident."

My hands go ice-cold. "What kind of an incident? Is Starr—"

"Oh, no, no, your daughter's all right." A pause. "That is, she's not injured. Exactly."

"What do you mean, *exactly?*"

Another hesitation. "I don't think this is something we should discuss over the phone. Would you mind coming right away? I'll keep Starr in the office with me until you get here."

Ohmigod. Ohmigod, ohmigod, ohmigod. My heart now lodged in my throat, I grab my bag from the bottom drawer of my desk and tear out of my office and through the workroom.

"Hey!" Harold yells, following me out to the elevators. "You can't just leave! What about all those orders on your desk?"

"I'm sorry." *Not.* "It's a family emergency."

"That's the trouble with you working mothers," he says as the elevator arrives. "Can't get a decent day's work out of you, because it's always something with the kids."

I get on and turn around, flipping him the bird as the doors close. Judging from Valerie's expression, I just made her day.

Mrs. Harrison is trying to maintain her composure, but her eyes tell another story. The please-God-don't-sue-us story.

As well they should.

Starr's out in the playground with one of the workers while

I sit here, trying to make sense of the director's nervously spoken words. Apparently, my baby girl's been sexually molested, by some boy who exposed himself to her in one of the bathrooms. Granted, the kid was only five as well, but a good six inches taller and thirty pounds heavier than Starr.

But what I'm finding nearly impossible to digest is that today wasn't the first time. It was, however, the first time that anybody believed her.

"We all knew she wasn't happy, that she was having a difficult time adjusting," Mrs. Harrison is saying, obviously not wanting to meet my gaze. "And children as bright as Starr have a pattern…of coming up with stories they believe will be their ticket out of here."

"You thought she was *lying?*"

The woman looks like she's having a hard time keeping her lunch down. "She was so calm about it, when she told us…I didn't think—"

"You didn't think it was worth finding out if she was telling the truth. You just assumed she was making it up."

"I'm so sorry, Ms. Levine, I can assure you nothing like this has ever happened before."

"That you know of."

Color floods the woman's cheeks, turning them almost maroon. "If you feel Starr needs to talk to somebody about this— a professional, I mean—I'll be happy to pay for it. Out of my own pocket," she adds, clearly keen on not involving the center's name if she can help it.

I let out a sigh. While I'm pissed beyond belief that nobody listened to Starr—and wondering why on earth she didn't tell me, either—neither do I want to blow this out of proportion. Show-and-not-tell is a fairly standard game around here in this age group. I should know. Seems to me I was around that age when I accidentally saw my father's penis as he was getting out of the shower. I thought it was strange and ugly and immediately asked Luke if he had one. He obliged my curiosity by yanking down his pants and showing me. I believe I said, "Oh," he pulled his pants back up and we continued watching *He-Man* without giving it another thought.

Of course, Luke and I were friends and touching wasn't part of the equation.

"We've already notified the boy's parents, of course," the director says. At my raised eyebrows, she adds, "He won't be returning."

I can tell there's more. "And…?"

She pauses, then says, very gently, "Ms. Levine, to be perfectly honest, I'm not sure this is the best environment for Starr, either. Her…unique personality seems at odds with the typical day-care setting."

"She wasn't fitting in, you mean."

That gets an apologetic smile. "Not very well, no." Then she says, "She's extraordinarily bright, which I'm sure you know. Have you had her tested?"

Inside, I cringe. I am so not ready for testing and all that implies. "No. Not yet."

"I can recommend somebody, if you like." She stands. "And I meant what I said. About footing the bill for her to talk to a professional, if that seems necessary. And it goes without saying, we'll refund you for the week."

Damn straight.

After I liberate my daughter, we decide ice cream is in order.

"C'n I get a sundae?" she says when we slip into the coffee shop booth.

"You can get whatever you want."

Starr orders a hot-fudge sundae with extra whipped cream. I order a vanilla egg cream. Leo used to buy these for me all the time when I was little. And not so little. My insides knot with missing him, with wanting to talk to him about this, ask his advice. Except if he'd been around to talk to, none of this would've happened, anyway.

"Were you scared?" I ask while we're waiting for our order.

My baby's delicate little brows crinkle behind her glasses for a moment, then she shakes her head. "I didn't like it, but I wasn't scared." She makes a face. "It looked like a fat, icky worm, though. Gross."

And God willing, she will keep thinking that for a very long time.

"Did he try to touch you?"

Another head shake. "He wanted to kiss me, but I wouldn't let him." Her expression tells me she found this prospect even more disgusting than the fat, icky worm business.

"So how come you didn't tell me?" I say carefully.

She shrugs. "'Cause I didn't want you to worry, I guess."

My insides cramp. "Starr, sweetie, I'm your mother. I'm supposed to worry. And you're supposed to tell me anytime somebody does something bad or mean to you, you got that?"

After a long, steady look, she nods. "Okay."

Our treats arrive. She hands me the maraschino cherry—she hates them—then starts her methodical annihilation of the whipped cream. "Are you going back to work?"

"Not today, no."

After a second, she says, "Do I have to go back there?"

"Never."

"Never ever?"

"Never ever."

"Then who's going to take care of me when you're at work?"

I open my mouth to say…what? That I'll find someplace else to send her? Even though I'm reeling right now, I know what happened today isn't the norm, that most accredited day cares provide safe, loving environments for the children entrusted to them. At least, I want to believe that, for all those parents who don't have a choice, who have to trust someone else to take care of their babies for part of the day. But the fact is, I already know this was the only place I could afford. And as it was, I wasn't coming out ahead, even with my raise.

I am not by nature an impulsive person, as we all know, save perhaps for the series of events that brought about Starr's existence. And even now, despite what I'm about to say, I question whether I'm being protective or *over*protective. If giving in to my fear might do Starr a disservice in the long run. But right now, I don't give a damn about the long run. I only care that she's safe and happy *now,* when she's five and has just lost her great-grandfather and needs to know her mommy cares more about her than anything else in the world.

And what I might want, or need, will just have to take a back seat. I also don't know how I'm going to make ends meet, but I'll figure it out.

So I reach across the table and wrap my hand around hers. "I'm not going back to work, at least not until you start school. I'm going to stay home with you."

"Cool," she says with a little smile, as worry sloughs off her tiny shoulders like a mudslide.

chapter 15

My kitchen faucet is lying in about a hundred unidentifiable pieces all over my sink and counter. Luke hands me a wrench.

"Now you put it back together."

Right.

With all the events of the day, I'd totally spaced that he was supposed to come over tonight for my first Ms. Fixit lesson. My initial reaction was to plead a headache or something and send him away. Partly because the last thing I feel like doing right now is reconstructing something that looks only marginally less complex than the innards of the Space Shuttle. And partly because I'd really like a few minutes to sort out my thoughts, not to mention my life, before everybody else jumps in with their two cents.

Except no sooner had he walked in the door than Starr piped up with, "Mama quit her job and I don't have to go to that 'scusting place anymore." Followed by, before I could stop her, "They called Mama to come get me—"

"Starr…"

"—cuzsomeboyshowedmehiswienie."

I now know how much noise a fully loaded toolbox makes when dropped onto a wooden floor.

I thought the man was going to explode. Then he dropped to his knees and hugged Starr so tightly I was afraid he'd crack a tiny rib. Then, just as abruptly, he held her out at arm's length and asked her if she was okay.

"Uh-huh," she assured him, her head cocked. Frito (Starr named the cat, don't ask) came up and writhed around her skinny legs as she patted Luke's shoulder. "It's okay, really. 'Specially since Mama's staying home now." Then she twisted around and asked if she could go over to the Gomezes' for a little while.

Which is where she still is, an hour later. And here I am, having an intimate personal relationship with assorted metal and rubber bits, while Luke continues to emit sporadic bursts of steam like a faulty iron.

"What the hell kind of place lets somethin' like that happen?"

I remind him of our little show-me-the-goods experience. Not a subject I would have brought up, God knows, if I hadn't had to make a point.

He doesn't look convinced.

"Oh, come on," I say, stacking one piece on top of another— I glance at Luke, he nods his approval. "She may have been a little grossed out, but I don't think she's traumatized for life or anything."

"You hope."

"They were *kids,* Luke."

"Wait—" He hands me one of the other pieces. "This one comes next."

"Oh. I knew that."

"Liar."

I smile.

"So. Were *you* grossed out?"

"About what happened to Starr? Sure—"

"No. Not today." I look over. He's trying his damnedest to look cool. "Back then. Us."

"Oh. That." I shrug. Hey, he's not the only one in the room who can do cool. "Please. We weren't even in grade school. Besides, I asked to see it, remember?"

"I do. *And* I seem to remember you were impressed."

"Male selective memory strikes again. Hey!"

He's lightly thunked me on the head with a roll of paper towels. I grab for the towels, we tussle for a minute, my heart rate goes up and my nipples tighten, then we both seem to realize what we're doing and back away from each other.

I return to my silver puzzle. Luke's made a diagram of the exploded faucet for me, but since his drawing skills suck, most of the real pieces bear little resemblance to the ones on the diagram.

"No, the gasket comes next. The *gasket,*" he says, handing me some little round thing that looks exactly like all the other little round things. Somehow, I don't think plumbing is my calling. "So what'd your boss say about your quitting?"

"I, um, haven't exactly told her yet."

"Ellie. Jesus."

"Hey. This is going to take a little finessing, okay? She's not going to be happy that I'm leaving, especially without giving notice."

"But you were gonna leave anyway if you'd gotten that other job."

"At least I could've eased her into that. Not dropped a bomb like this is going to be."

"El, honey...oh, for godsake, lemme have that, this is making me nuts...." Like I'm gonna argue with the man. "It's not like it's that big a deal. I mean, it was just an assistant's job, right? Not like you're interrupting some big career or anything."

Why should this take my breath? It's not as if he's saying something I didn't know. Nor does he mean to be hurtful. All he's doing is rationalizing things in order to make this easier for me. Still, knowing something and hearing somebody else say it are two different things.

"Yes," I say quietly, my arms folded over my middle. "Not like I'm interrupting any big career."

"So maybe this'll give you some time to think about what you wanna do next."

While I stand there, pondering what he means by that, he lowers himself to my floor, which isn't exactly pristine, then disappears underneath the sink. From underneath comes, "You gonna be okay, though? Financially?"

"I don't know," I say to faded denim knees and chamois-colored workboots. "Figuring that out was on my agenda for this evening." I bend over, tossing words in the general direction of his head. "Until you showed up."

He finishes whatever mystery thing he was doing under there and emerges. His hair's grown out a bit in the last few weeks; now it's sitting up in little startled spikes all over his head. Concern tightens his mouth as looks up at me.

"Hey. Like I said before, you need anything, I'm here."

"I know. And thanks. But I'm sure I'll be fine." As long as nobody gets sick because—it hits me—I no longer have medical coverage.

Luke gets to his feet with an agility I can only envy, frowning as he wipes his hands on about six paper towels. Then he stuffs the trash can and cleaning paraphernalia back underneath the sink, banging shut the cabinet door. I've known him too long not to read his body language.

"What?" I say before he can start with me. "You don't think I can pull this off?"

"Not if you can't learn to do some of this maintenance work yourself. These houses are old, they take a lot of upkeep. You can't be callin' a plumber or electrician every five minutes."

"Tell me something I don't know. But maybe tonight wasn't the best time for me to try learning something new." When he grunts, I add, "I'll figure it out, okay?"

"Right."

"I will! For God's sake, Luke, at least give me a *chance* to work through some of this!" At his continued expression of disbelief, my face warms. "Hey," I say, poking his chest. "How about a little support here, huh? Like trusting me to stand on my own two feet."

His brows inch even closer together. "I worry about you, okay? So sue me."

I let out a sigh. "I'm not going to let you make it easy for me to lean on you, Luke. Not like—"

I stop myself, but it's too late.

"Not like I did Tina," he finishes. "No, it's okay, I already knew where you were going with this. Even if you didn't." The tools make a dreadful racket as he tosses them all back into his metal box, then turns the water on to wash his hands. "But that's why you're the smarter one here."

"What are you talking about?"

He flicks the excess water off his hands, then uses another six towels to dry them. Honestly.

"You've always been able to see things I couldn't, even if they were starin' me in the face. Like with Tina and me." He stops, the towels crumpled in his hand, and squints at me. "I've had a lot of time to think about things the past several weeks. Things I couldn't see for squat as long as Tina and me were still together." He pauses. "You knew all along I was makin' her dependent on me, didn't you?"

Oh, boy.

"I thought that's what you wanted," I say quietly.

Luke watches me for a moment, then balls up the towels, yanks open the door under the sink and tosses them into the trash can. "Yeah," he says on a heavy sigh. "That's what I thought I wanted, too. Now that I've got a little distance, though, I'm thinkin' maybe that was stupid."

"You loved her," I said. "That wasn't stupid."

"Because I figured she needed me to love her. That if I didn't, nobody else would." He turns to me, his eyes fathomless. "How lame is that?"

"Some people might call it noble."

He smirks. "I should've known you'd say something like that. Pitying somebody isn't the same as loving them. And sure as hell makin' 'em dependent on you isn't. But it wasn't until I realized she was lying to me that it dawned on me what I'd been doing to her."

My eyes pop open. "L-lying?"

"Oh, come on, El—you didn't honestly believe all that crap about her havin' somebody else, did you?"

I swear, the blood's pounding through my veins so hard they're going to burst. "*You* did!"

"For about five minutes. Okay, maybe for a little longer than that. But once she moved to Jersey…you didn't know she'd moved to Trenton?" I shake my head. "Yeah," he says, "a few weeks back. So I'm back at my old place. Anyway, once I got to thinking about things, I realized there were several pieces of her story that weren't fitting together right. I told you, the marriage was falling apart way before she lost the baby. If you ask me, that whole it-wasn't-yours business was just her way of putting the final nail in the coffin."

So he still doesn't know about the abortion. For about two seconds, I think of telling him. Until I realize it's not my place to come clean for Tina.

"It worked, didn't it?" I say. "You let her go."

"Yeah, it worked. But not because I believed her story. Because, when I realized I didn't believe it, I also realized just how badly she wanted out." He bangs his hand on the edge of the sink, then lets out another one of those heavy sighs. "Of course, the irony of the whole thing is that all I wanted to do was protect her, you know? Make things a little easier for her, because she'd had such a bad time of it."

"And I repeat—that's not a bad thing."

His eyes are hooked in mine; I know what's coming. Knew from the moment he hugged Starr so hard, a little while ago. "Yeah, it is. When it makes you screw over other people you care about, makes you ask somebody else to keep a secret that shouldn't be kept, it sure as shit is a bad thing."

And there it is, peeking out from its burial place after more than five years.

"What would you have said?" I say, reclothing an old argument. "It was crazy, what happened between us. We agreed at the time, it was crazy. That there was nothing to tell Tina…"

Luke's arm swings toward the house next door, where Starr is playing. "You call a child *nothing?*"

"And I told you then, I couldn't be sure—"

"Except you said the jerk always used a condom, even though you were on the Pill. But even so, even if Starr hadn't happened, what we did was a fact. A fact I decided that the woman I'd convinced myself I loved, because she *needed* me, couldn't handle. And in doing so, I screwed over my best friend. What kind of a man does that make me?"

I take my own deep breath. And don't think the "my best friend" part of all that went over my head. One problem with dragging something out into the open is that a whole lotta other junk gets dragged right out there with it. Junk you thought for sure you'd chucked out ages ago.

"One who thought he was doing the right thing, at the time," I say softly. "Don't beat yourself up, Luke. In the grand scheme of things, it's not worth it."

"But we have to tell her."

I don't know whether he means Starr or Tina. But my answer's the same, whoever it is. "Eventually, yes. Not now. Not until…"

"Not until when?"

I feel what I realize is a not-so-little prickle of irritation. "I don't know!" I snap, then look at him, seeing my own uncertainty mirrored in his eyes. And regret, that despite our best intentions, we still screwed up.

I press my fingers against the spot between my eyebrows, then let my hand fall. "I don't know," I repeat, wearily this time. "My life's in shreds right now, okay? How about giving me a minute to figure out what to do next?"

Remorse instantly contorts his face. "Christ, El, I'm sorry, I don't mean to pressure you, babe, you know that—"

"Go home, Luke," I say, turning him around and prodding him toward the hall. "The longer you stay, the more confused I get."

When we get to my door, he frowns into my eyes. "Yeah. Me, too," he says, then disappears into the chilly spring night.

Being a grown-up sucks.

Especially when you do something that proves you really weren't as much of a grown-up as you'd thought.

I call the Gomezes. Liv, who still hasn't had this baby, answers, begs me to let Starr stay for another hour or so, the kids are having a great time. I say fine—I need to encourage her getting along with other kids as much as possible, right?—but I'm secretly disappointed, that she's not coming back right away. Then again, maybe it's not so much that I want to see her, as I want the distraction from my thoughts.

You think?

In any case, I wander out into my quiet, child-free living room and plunk myself in the middle of the sofa, riding out the ache at not seeing Leo sitting here, playing Nintendo or watching TV or reading the *Post*. And arguing with it, I think with a half smile, pulling a drawing pad off the end table and flipping through a half-dozen sketches I'd made—and re-jected—for Heather's bridesmaid dresses. Although I'd sug-gested different styles for the different figures, she really wants them all to be alike. So—I sift through the detritus on the end table until I find a pencil with an actual point—all alike, they shall be.

I turn to a clean page and begin sketching, lightly delineating a pair of figures—one thin, one…not so thin. Then I stare at them, trying to visualize the perfect dress, hoping against hope I can distract myself enough to ward off the memories of some-thing not worth remembering.

It doesn't work.

I may not have learned much about life, but I do know this: The more you'd like to forget about certain events in your past, the more you can guarantee they'll come back and haunt you.

I draw the first line, only to immediately erase it.

To be perfectly honest, if I could expunge my twenty-second year from my history, I'd be a happy camper. However, since The Months Ellie Forgot She Had a Brain aren't going to go away, and since those months produced a child who isn't going to go away, either, I knew I'd have to face the issue of who her father is at some point. I was hoping on my deathbed, when I'd be too riddled with pain to see the agonized look on her face.

My second attempt at a neckline goes a little better. No, ac-tually—I erase it again—it needs to be lower. All those boobs, might as well show 'em off a little, right?

I don't suppose our little revelation back there came as any big surprise. But hard as anyone might find this to believe, we honestly thought we were making not only the most logical, but the kindest, decision we could have, given the circumstances.

Which were? you might ask.

Pause for a big sigh here. As well as a tiny plea in my own defense, which is that I had never before, and have never since, slept with two men within a forty-eight hour period. Nor have I ever engaged in pity sex. Pity gorging, yes, but not pity sex. However, after Daniel's bombshell, I was lower than a smashed roach on a subway track. I barely remember getting home, although I do remember refusing to sob on the train. Then, both because I still possessed a shred of pride and because I couldn't bear the thought of listening to my father's and grandfather's threats against Daniel's life for the rest of mine, I sort of gave them the impression that I was the one who broke it off. Unfortunately, in my zeal to avoid recriminations, I also left myself with no visible means of sympathy. For a woman with freshly pureed emotions, this was not good.

Hmm. The sleeves. Gotta have sleeves of some kind, too many wobbly upper arms in this bunch...

My stoicism, aided by copious infusions of cheesecake and Cherry Coke, worked well enough for the first twenty-four hours. (Sugar highs—the poor woman's Percoset.) However, unbeknownst to me, while my heart was being ripped asunder by Daniel The Schmuck in Manhattan, Luke and Tina had split up in Queens, a fact I discovered on Day Two.

Wrist length? No, elbow length for June. And something...yeah, like that.

It was early April. Opening day at Shea Stadium. Dad and Leo had gone out to the game (an annual ritual they were far more likely to observe than donning yarmulkes and prayer shawls at Yom Kippur) leaving me alone in the house with a new cheesecake. I had my fork poised for that first, exquisite bite when our doorbell blatted out the opening notes of the *Star Wars* theme.

Luke.

Word gets out fast around here. However, I certainly didn't expect him to show up in the middle of the afternoon. Or that, when I opened the door, I'd actually flinch at how awful he looked. On some men, scruffy looks sexy. On Luke, the impression is more that of a stray dog needing a bath and a flea dip.

"Tina and I split up," he said, which was about the only thing right then guaranteed to jolt me out of feeling sorry for myself.

"Oh, my God!" I grabbed his hand and dragged him into the house, only to immediately drop it and subtly put some distance between us. He didn't smell all that great. "Why?"

The picture of abject misery, he sank bonelessly onto the sofa. Fillet of James Dean. Three days past his sell-by date.

Big, soulful, sad brown eyes (hmm…maybe now I understand the wanting-to-take-all-the-dogs-home phenomenon) looked up at me. "Dunno."

Actually, I did know, but I wasn't sure whether this was the time to mention it. He and Tina had been going together for nearly seven years by then. So she was getting pretty anxious for a ring. Yes, they were still really young, but as she so succinctly put it, how long can you keep screwing somebody without getting married? Which, translated from Tinaese, meant Please God, don't let me end up like my mother.

Trouble was, as ready as Tina was to get married, I knew Luke wasn't. Not that there was anybody else for him, I don't mean that. Despite all that stuff he said in my kitchen a little while ago, the fact was, and forever shall be, that at that point he only had eyes—among other body parts—for her. So it wasn't Tina he wasn't ready for, it was donning the cloak of Husbandhood that was giving him palpitations. See, despite his mother's tenacious grip on modern life, Luke was solid nineteen-fifties. You know, when a *real* man supported the wife and family and he damn well didn't get married until he could. And Luke couldn't, not then.

But apparently, Tina didn't want to wait—

Fuhgetabout a waist, half these girls don't even have waists…

—so she'd broken it off, taking what I suppose she thought was a calculated risk that he'd come to his senses. Which actually, for Tina, was a pretty gutsy move.

Anyway. The guy was, literally and figuratively, a mess. We think women take breakups hard? I've seen more upbeat bloodhounds. At least women rant and sob and generally give voice to their feelings (which Tina did, later that night. But I digress.) Luke just…sat there. Boneless and morose and smelly. So, in desperation, I spewed out the one thing I figured might take his mind off his misery: my cheery news about Daniel.

Just like that, Just Shoot Me Luke disappeared. Color flooded sallow, unshaven cheeks; fury set dull eyes ablaze.

"The sonuvabitch was *married?*" He jumped up from the sofa, nostrils flared, fists clenched. "Is he still there, back at the apartment? 'Cause I'll go right over there and whip his ass if you want—"

Just like that, the sobs I'd been holding back for two days gushed forth like lava from a volcano. And once they started, I couldn't stop.

Here's where things get blurry. I remember sitting on the floor, bawling like a three-year-old, and Luke making like he was going to hold me only I must have recoiled or something because he didn't, and then we were breaking into my father's bourbon stash, which, judging from the layer of dust on the bottle, hadn't been touched for some time. I might have fleetingly wondered if bourbon gets stronger as it ages. Or maybe not. Anyway, from then on, we're talking fragmented images involving Luke realizing how bad he smelled and wanting to take a shower, only then I was somehow in the shower with him because he was too drunk to do it himself and I was afraid he'd fall over and crack his head open or something. And then my clothes were all wet so I took them off, too, totally forgetting— or not caring?—that I was undressing in front of Luke. Who was rapidly sobering and hardening, right there in front of me.

And then we were kissing, and the water was pouring over us, warm and soothing, and I think we were both crying a little, I couldn't tell with the water running down our faces, but I was very aware that Luke is an excellent kisser, and suddenly, there we were, having hard, frantic sex. In my shower. Standing up. Not the first time I'd had an orgasm there, but definitely the first time I'd had company for the occasion.

Then it was over. Oh, boy, was it over. Luke unwrapped me from his waist and set me down, looking at me as though he'd never seen me before, then nearly ripped the shower curtain off its rings in his split to get out of the tub.

He was dressed and gone before I even had a chance to get dried off.

I look down at the sketch, only to rip the page out of the book and crumple it up. A warm, unpleasant flush creeps over my skin; I can't quite catch my breath, as if my lungs have shrunk or something.

I can't do this, I can't....

How on earth did I get through that evening, when Tina came over to cry on my shoulder? And did I really squeal with excitement a week later when she showed me the adorable little engagement ring Luke had given her?

I suppose I did. After all, that's the way things were supposed to work out. Luke didn't ask me not to tell Tina what had happened, but he didn't have to. Our soggy tryst was nothing more than a moment of drunken insanity. In theory, he hadn't been unfaithful to her, since they weren't together at the time. But I know he felt he'd betrayed her trust as much as if they'd been married. And had I not gotten pregnant, I doubt either of us would have ever mentioned it again.

Tina'd had enough crap dumped on her in one lifetime. The last thing either of us wanted to do was hurt her. I mean, if you could have seen how radiant she was in those weeks leading up to her wedding, her obvious relief at finally, finally having something good come her way…how could Luke or I even think of bursting her bubble? Especially since—we told ourselves—we didn't actually *know* it was Luke's baby. Whoever's baby it was, the whole thing was a fluke (or so I thought, not knowing then what I do now, that, uh, yeah, you *can* get pregnant while on the Pill. Odds may be slim, but slim is a helluva lot different than nonexistent.).

Except that Daniel had indeed insisted on also using a condom every time we had sex. And that Luke and I didn't, since I don't normally keep a stash next to the shampoo.

My father and grandfather accepted my news—when I finally got up the nerve to tell them—with equal parts shock and resoluteness. But once I started showing, they both really got into it, one or the other bringing home something for the baby almost every day, it seemed like. Starr may not have been planned, but she's always been loved.

But by nobody more than the man who's always assumed she's his daughter.

I'll be the first to admit this is a bizarre situation. And one a lot of people aren't going to understand, whenever the truth comes to light. Especially our never finding out for sure whether or not Luke *is* Starr's father. I guess neither of us saw much point, since Daniel—even if I had known how to contact him—had made it crystal clear he wasn't interested in the daddy bit. At least, not again. And not with me. But now, more than five years later, we've got this huge, tangled mess I'm not sure we can ever fully untangle. Try to loosen one knot, and you only tighten all the others.

"Mama!" The front door slams shut. "I'm back! Where are you?"

"In here, honey."

Starr clomps into the living room in her boots, her smile drooping when she sees me. "What's wrong?"

I plaster on a smile of my own and shake my head. "Nothing. Just…frustrated with my drawing, that's all."

"Oh." She comes over and plops her skinny little butt beside me on the sofa. Before I can stop her, she's found the wadded up sketch and unwadded it, smoothing it flat against her thighs. "What's wrong with this?"

"It didn't come out the way I wanted it to, that's all."

"I think it's pretty. I wish I could draw as good as you."

"As *well* as me. And I'm not really that good."

"Well," she says.

"Well, what?"

She huffs one of her little sighs. "You said good instead of well. Like I did."

"Oh. No, when I said good, it was right."

"That doesn't make a bit of sense."

Does anything?

"You need to go get ready for bed, sweetie."

"Yeah, in a minute," she says, scrutinizing the sketch like an art expert a Rembrandt. "C'n I have this if you don't want it?"

"Sure. Live."

She beams at me as if I've just given her the moon—if not a real Rembrandt—then scampers out of the room. Seconds later, I hear little boot thuds against the stairtreads as she goes up to her room.

I turn to another clean page and start over.

Maybe this time, I'll get it right.

chapter 16

A laid-back, slightly exhaust-scented spring breeze teases the new blue-and-white checked café kitchen curtains as I scrape out the canned spaghetti sauce into a pot on the stove. Rap music blasts from an apartment across the way, competing with a loud, rapid-fire argument in some unrecognizable language. An ambulance screams up Atlantic Avenue; every dog in Richmond Hill starts howling.

Ah, spring in the city. Gotta love it.

"Whatcha making?" Starr asks at my elbow. Worry lurks at the edges of her words.

"Spaghetti."

I don't have to look at her to see the frown. Or that the cat, whom she's got in a death grip, is mirroring her expression. The late-afternoon sun has turned the freshly painted white walls—I finally got rid of the pumpkin-orange—a pretty peachy color. A color that makes me happy, I decide, adding it to my mental "things to be grateful for" list. All in all, despite the million and one unresolved issues littering my brain, it's been a good day. Since seven o'clock this morning, I've unclogged a toilet, unstuck a stubborn window, finished the mock-up of Heather's dress before she has a cow, gone grocery shopping and planted pansies in the two new window boxes I bought. And now I'm making dinner for my child. I am hot stuff.

"Leo didn't make it like that."

Okay, *warm* stuff.

However, I refuse to let a five-year-old with a serious lack of diplomatic skills destroy my good mood. I peer into the Dutch oven on the back burner to see if the water's boiling yet. It isn't.

"I know. But it'll be fine," I say, as I've said at least three dozen times since Leo's death.

Frito squirms to get down; after a second or two of clashing wills and some kitty cussing, Starr finally concedes. "So how come you don't know how to cook?" she says as the cat stalks off, his fur all spiked like a punk rocker.

"Hey. I cook." As if to prove my point, I stir the sauce. "I put stuff in pots, you get hot meals. Besides," I say before she can poke holes in my theory, "you don't cook either."

"Hello? I'm five? I'm not allowed to touch the stove?"

I have no comeback for this.

"When's Luke coming back?"

"I don't know, baby." My stomach's jumped at her question, but I don't let on. He's been gone most of the past couple of weeks, overseeing the plumbing installation for some corporation's new headquarters in New Paltz. I dump half a package of dry pasta in the boiling water. "This week sometime, maybe."

She nods, then wanders out of the kitchen. Frito jumps up onto the microwave stand to stare at me. This is his thing. Staring. For hours. At me.

Now with Starr, he's cuddly and purry. Me, he stares at. With barely tempered disgust. Why, I have no idea. I feed the damn thing. Change his litter pan. I even went out and bought him this cushy little faux sheepskin-lined bed. Which he never sleeps in. Forked over nearly three hundred bucks to the vet when the stupid animal scarfed down a length of thread with a needle attached to it. And still, after a month, he stares. Oh, and if I try to pet him? He flinches. I'm good for food and a clean pan, but God forbid I should *touch* him.

So maybe I'm not exactly a cat person. Especially cats who could give Freddy Krueger a run for his money. But I'm doing my best here. Why doesn't he get that?

And while I'm thinking this, the damn thing jumps off the stand straight at my chest, shaving five years off my life and knocking over a half-full can of Diet Coke I'd left there earlier. I watch in helpless rage as soda spatters all over the floor I'd just washed. Okay, so maybe I hadn't *just* washed it, but it was a helluva lot cleaner than it is now.

"Stupid cat!" I yell, but all I get is this smug, yellow-eyed glare that clearly says, *"Hey. It wasn't me who left the can there, was it?"*

By the time I finish cleaning up the mess, the sun has shifted, the glow from only minutes before all but gone.

Just like the glow from my earlier contentment.

As the last of the peachy color fades from the walls, I toss the Coke-soaked paper towels into the garbage and sigh. Aside from still missing Leo like crazy, it's not as if this past month has been horrible or anything. On the whole, I have nothing to complain about. I might miss going into the city, but I sure don't miss Nicole Katz. And while I'm still no threat to Emeril in the cooking department, I'm proud to say that—thanks to Luke—I can now change out the inner workings of a toilet, stop a leaky faucet and do minor electrical repairs without batting an eye. Or frying myself. But here I am, once again feeling…unsettled. As though I'm marking time.

Do all stay-at-home moms go through this, feeling as though they're treading water in the middle of the ocean, having no idea where the nearest land is? Or is this just me, being weird?

Maybe I don't want to know the answer to that.

But seriously, how did Frances do it, with six boys? And Liv, who's still in the middle of it? She finally had her baby last week, by emergency C-section. Since her husband couldn't take that much time off, and since no other family members were available for various reasons, I volunteered to take up the slack. So suddenly I had a houseful of boys during the day. Yes, I know, there were only two, but two boys in a house is a house *full* of boys. How can two measly little kids manage to be in fifty places at once? I don't get this.

Just as I don't get why I'm stewing over something that's not even the real problem, and I damn well know it. It's not being home full-time, or being a mother full-time, that I feel so unsettled about. It's this whole Luke and Tina business that's got me ready to scream.

The spaghetti's done; I carefully upend the full pot over the colander in the sink, wishing I could somehow steam my brain open. Up until a few weeks ago, our roles were more or less clearly defined. But now I have no idea how I'm supposed to act, what I'm supposed to feel—or let myself feel—what I'm supposed to *think*. It was easy—well, maybe not easy, but predetermined at least—when Tina (who I keep thinking I should call, but what would I say?) was in the picture. I simply ignored my attraction to Luke. Stuck my fingers in my ears whenever it tried to jump up and down and get my attention. And for the most part, it worked. Not all that hard when despite Tina's assertion otherwise, it's one-sided. Maybe I can't help what, or how, I feel about somebody, but I sure as hell can choose what to do about it. Up to this point, my control over my emotions has relied heavily on a combination of denial, never being alone with the man and keeping busy.

Since the first two of those are obviously shot to hell, I'm left with number three.

At least there's Heather's wedding. Otherwise known as The Circus. Even with Tina officially out of the wedding party (her decision), we're up to fifteen attendants now. *Fifteen.* I swear she's dragging 'em off the street. But besides needing the work (since picking through the trash for aluminum cans doesn't appeal) if this doesn't take my mind off the Great Luke Dilemma, nothing will.

Except I wonder...*and then what?*

Yes, things are peaceful (relatively) and on an even keel (for which I should be grateful), but why do I feel as though I'm in the eye of the storm? That for all the changes and upheavals I've been through in the past few months, I ain't seen nothin' yet?

"Is dinner ready?"

"Yeah, sweetie," I say to my kid. She comes to the table and slips into her chair—she's finally tall enough not to have to step up on the rung first—her expression resolute. I've really got to learn how to cook. As in, chopping and measuring and all that fun stuff. However, I no sooner set her milk and bowl of spaghetti in front of her than the doorbell rings. Her eyes light up.

"Maybe it's Luke!" she says, bolting from her chair and streaking down the hall to the door.

But I can tell, through the sheer-curtained glass pane, it's not Luke. Starr undoes the three locks with a dexterity a concert pianist would envy and yanks open the heavy door, only to let out a moan of disappointment.

"Hi...honey," Jennifer says to my kid with an expression not unlike Starr's when she had to eat those stewed tomatoes. Her linen jumper is wrinkled just enough to prove no polyester was used in the making of this garment; her white T-shirt is the finest gauge cotton Stuart's money could buy; her clunky Mary Janes are hideously trendy. "Guess you were expecting someone else, huh?" Then she turns her stiff smile on me. And opens her arms.

Just as I notice the mountain of classy taupe luggage stacked behind her.

Uh, God? You and I need to have a *serious* talk.

I desperately want to believe I'm dreaming, but I've pinched myself three times already and all I have to show for it are a trio of red welts on my arm.

And my sister, sitting at my kitchen table.

Where she obviously plans on staying for a while.

My sister, who wanted nothing more to do with this house, this borough, this family, has moved back in. And I have six pieces of Gucci luggage in my foyer to prove it.

"Only temporarily," she says, sipping from a bottle of Dasani. I offered her dinner, but I guess canned Hunts spaghetti sauce isn't high on her list, either. *Quelle surprise.* "Until Stuart finds another job."

Starr is sitting at my side, shoveling in her spaghetti, silently taking this all in. Probably better than I am.

"And where is Stuart again?" I ask.

"Chicago. Uh...excuse me," Jen says, then sneezes loud enough to stun Hackensack. "But he's off to Indianapolis tomorrow—" her smile fades "—then Lansing."

Lansing? Oh, how the mighty have fallen.

Seems they had to sell the house after all, before they lost it. The good news was, a buyer snatched up the property within forty-eight hours of their putting it on the market, proving that *somebody* still has money out there. The bad news was, the new owner wanted to take immediate possession. Not being in any position to argue, my sister and brother-in-law agreed. So, while Stuart is doing the grand tour of the Midwest in search of a new job, my sister is—dare I say it?—homeless.

Or she was until she remembered she could suck it up and come back here.

Not that sucking up's one of Jen's strong points, but I imagine she'll improve with practice. We all do.

"Where's your furniture?" We're talking a five-thousand-square-foot house. Or so I hear. I've never actually seen it (and now I guess I won't). Gee, you could wander around for hours and never see the person you were living with. Which might account for the longevity of my sister's marriage.

Long, heavily coated lashes drift down onto pale, perfectly made-up cheeks, followed by a despondent sigh. "We were able to store some of it in Stuart's parents' garage, since they're down to three cars now—"

Don't say it, Ellie.

"—but we had to sell the rest." Another sneeze. "At a loss, as you can imagine."

The resultant silence, in which I try desperately—well, maybe not desperately—to drum up a smidgen of sympathy for the obviously distraught blonde in front of me, is shattered by my daughter's slurping up the last of her spaghetti. Delicately blowing her nose into a tissue, Jennifer looks at Starr, whose gaze is nailed to her aunt.

"Don't you know it's rude to stare, little girl?"

"Sorry," she says, not moving.

"And don't you ever smile?"

"When there's something to smile about, sure."

God, I love this kid.

Jen and Starr glare at each other for several seconds, then Jen swings her attention back to me. Her eyes are beginning to get kinda puffy.

"I suppose you're wondering why I didn't simply find an apartment or go to a hotel while we're waiting—"

You might say.

"—but Stuart thought it made more sense to set aside the proceeds from the sale of the house and furniture so we can start over once he finds a new position." She sneezes again, then says stuffily around her tissue, "What's the sense of wasting it on rent when I can live here for free?"

Of course, what Stuart didn't take into account when he came up with this amusing little plan was that living under the same roof with my sister for more than, oh, twenty minutes might well drive me to hire a hit man.

Then again, maybe he did.

Frito picks that moment to meander back into the kitchen, all pigeon-toed macho swagger. Cat and sister catch sight of each other at the same time; they both freeze, their expressions equally horrified.

"Ohmigod! Ohmi*god!*" Jennifer shrieks, grabbing a napkin and holding it over her nose. "No wonder I'm sneezing! I can't have a cat in the house! You know I'm allergic!"

Ah, yes. Now I remember. We couldn't have any pets because both my grandmother and Jennifer were dander-intolerant. For the first time since this cat's taken up residence, a surge of genuine affection sweeps through me.

"Well, since you didn't exactly clear your stay with management," I say as the cat yawns, stretches, then begins to slowly, torturously head in Jennifer's direction, "there wasn't a whole lot I could do, was there?"

About two feet from my sister, Frito decides to sit down and do the bath routine. But not before I catch what I swear is a wink.

Jen, however, hasn't so much as twitched a muscle. The slightest nudge, she'd topple over and shatter.

"Jen? He's not a dinosaur. Not moving won't trick him into thinking you're not there."

This apparently prompts the woman to leap from her chair and scream, *"Get him out of here! Get him out of here! Get him out of here!"* whilst flailing her arms enthusiastically about and hopping up and down as though stomping grapes.

Frito glances up from his bath, apparently finding this all

highly entertaining. As do I. And Starr, who's not even trying to suppress the giggles.

Lest you think me cruel and unfeeling, however, let me relate a particular incident from several years back, when I was eight and Jen twelve.

Our parents had left her to baby-sit while they ran a few errands. Jen locked herself into the bathroom—our only bathroom, remember—to take a bath. Where she stayed for two hours. And I had to do Number Two. A fact of which I apprised her, to no avail. And I'd been expressly forbidden to set foot outside the house by myself, so I couldn't go next door to Leo's and Nana's or the Scardinares. *And* when our parents returned to find me sobbing hysterically because I'd messed my pants, Jen insisted she never heard me ask to get in.

Granted, my parents didn't believe her for a second, so it wasn't as if she got away with it. But her punishment at my parents' hands—an apology (insincere) and having to clean the toilet every day for a solid month—didn't go nearly far enough, in my opinion, to negate the pain and humiliation to which I'd been subjected.

Nor did it stop her continued torture of me, via methods increasingly nefarious, for the rest of the years we spent under the same roof. Ergo, I am totally enjoying her misery. I have been waiting many, *many* years for this.

The cat yawns again, then somehow curls his lip, a shard of light glancing off his snaggletooth. He takes a leisurely survey of the room, then refocuses on the yelping, possessed person in our kitchen. Finally, after due deliberation, he once again hauls himself off his fat haunches and continues his journey. By now, Jen is backed up against the counter and shrieking her head off. Unperturbed, Frito swerves to swipe up against her shins. Jen looks at me, terror shining in her now reddened eyes, and says, in a very small voice, "Please?"

I sigh. It was a sweet moment, but we all know how fleeting those are.

I scoop up the cat; Jen heaves a huge sigh of relief. Of course, she has no idea there's half a can of tuna in it for this rumbling furbag in my arms.

Oh, yeah, he and I are compadres now, boy.

Sagging against the sink, Jennifer sneezes, three times in rapid succession. My conscience twinges.

"Starr, honey—maybe you should take Frito to your room for a bit." When child and cat are gone, Jennifer says, "I don't subbose you could fide someplace else for himb to stay while I'm here?"

I said *twinges.* Not *goes over to the other side.*

"Jen, moving back in was your idea. And I suppose, when it comes down to it, this is still your home. If you want to stay here, fine. But I'm not turning my life, or my daughter's, upside down for you. The cat stays."

Her chin lifts, making her nearly swollen shut eyes look even slittier. "I can't believe," she says, blowing her nose, "that you'd choose that hideous creature over your own sister."

"I'm not. I'm choosing my *kid* over my sister." I cross my arms, feeling close to victory for the first time since Starr opened the door to Jennifer earlier this evening. "If that's a problem, you can dip into that nice little capital gain you and Stuart have just realized and go to a hotel."

She sniffs. Twice. "Where's the nearest all-night drugstore?"

Not exactly the words I'd hoped to hear.

"Over on Atlantic Avenue," I say.

Like I said, God. *Serious* talk. So pencil me in.

chapter 17

The cat got tuna, anyway. Hey, he gave it his best shot, right? And I have to say, it's nice to know somebody around here is looking out for my best interests.

Damn thing still won't let me pet him, though. Miserable beast.

The next morning, Starr and I left Jennifer making strange thumping noises in Leo's old room (I don't want to know) and went over to the Gomezes', since it occurred to me this new baby's nearly ten days old and I haven't given her a present yet. All I had to do was wrap it, though, since—after the third girlfriend gave birth within as many months a couple years ago—I finally realized how much time and energy could be saved by simply buying baby gifts in bulk every year or so. The first time I plunked a half dozen white sleepers with little androgynous creatures scampering about and as many teething rattles at the Macy's checkout, the saleswoman looked at my stash, then at me, and asked if it was hard getting enough sleep with sextuplets.

Liv is fully dressed but reclining on the sofa in the living room, the baby observing the world from her little bouncy chair on the floor. Starr plops down cross-legged on the floor to watch her, elbows on knees and chin in hands, whereupon Erik, the three-year-old, begins regaling us with a minute-by-minute account of everything the baby's done since they all got up that morning. Definitely an argument for stopping after one kid.

Blissfully ignorant that half the babies born in Queens in recent years have cut their teeth on this very model of teething ring, Liv oohs and ahhs over the gift, then thanks me for at least the tenth time for taking the two older boys off her hands after little Dani's birth.

"Oh, please," I say, "fuhgetabout it, it was no big deal."

Really, the tic in my left eye is hardly even noticeable anymore.

Still, here I am on her floor, tickling the baby's chubby tummy and making all those idiotic sounds people make at babies. Barely visible over chubby cheeks, slate-blue eyes stare back at me, unimpressed. Between the cat and this kid, I'm batting zero.

"Did I have that much hair?" Starr asks.

"Much" is an understatement. This poor kid looks like she's wearing a cheapo Dracula wig—black, stiff and dangerously flammable.

"Remember the pictures in your baby book? You were so bald I had to tape a bow to your head so people would know you were a girl."

That gets a priceless look, as Liv says, "So, I see you have company."

This is like saying Attila the Hun's evil sister dropped by for a visit. But since Starr is sitting here, I simply say, "My sister. Jennifer."

"Oh. And?"

I let the baby grab hold of my finger. Her eyes get bigger, but that's about it. Frankly, unless they're your own, babies are kind of boring at this stage. Like goldfish but without the charisma.

"We're—" I glance at Starr, who's totally mesmerized by the multilimbed blob in front of us "—very different."

"Gotcha," Liv says. And I have the feeling she does.

The kids troop upstairs to play; a minute later, Liv's grandmother, who's apparently returned from wherever she'd been when Daniella was born and who tells me to call her Dolly, everyone else does, scoops the baby out of her seat and whisks her off for a bath, leaving nothing behind but a blurred impression of an impossibly red beehive and a hot pink track suit. After she's gone, though, I catch Liv's frown.

"Is something wrong?"

Her eyes shift to mine. "Your grandfather took care of Starr, didn't he?"

My chest gets tight. "Yeah. Why?"

"Did you ask him to, or did he volunteer?"

I laugh. "More like he refused to even consider anybody else doing it."

"See, that's the way Dolly is. She lives for these guys, especially since she quit working several years ago, but I'm beginning to worry that taking care of them is getting to be too much for her. At the same time, I know she'll be hurt if I even suggest getting someone else in to help. She was really upset about not being here when Daniella was born, but my uncle had gotten her this nonrefundable, nonchangeable plane ticket so she was stuck. Oh! Damn, I think my brain's leaked out through my tits…." Liv carefully propels herself off the sofa, then gingerly makes her way across the room to a small roll-top desk. "It finally hit me that today's the fifth of the month and I'd totally spaced the rent check. Why didn't you say something?"

"I figured you had other things on your mind." I look at the check she hands me, my gaze zinging to hers as she lowers herself back onto the sofa. "What's this?"

"Something extra for watching the boys that week. And no arguments." One side of her mouth lifts up. "I know you said it was no big deal, but these are my kids we're talking about. They can be just a bit rough on the nerves."

"I was just doing you a favor, for God's sake—"

"I know you were. But I don't like taking advantage of people if I can help it." She grins. "Even landlords. And by the way, once I get the wind back in my sails, if you ever want me to, um, trim your hair or something…"

I blow my bangs out of my eyes. "Trying to tell me something?"

"Don't take it personally. I'm so desperate to do something besides wipe poopy butts and play cow I offered to cut the *paperboy's* hair today!"

Which I guess answers my earlier question. About stay-at-home moms feeling just a bit…stifled. Occasionally.

A little bit later, after I've gathered Starr and we head back over to our place, I think, Why couldn't I have gotten a sister like that? A thought immediately derailed the minute we step inside and Starr says, "C'n we get a baby someday?"

"Honey," I say, hanging up our jackets, "you were pushing it with the *cat.*"

She lets out one of her sighs, but she knows better than to press the issue.

Jen's been here for about a week now and we haven't killed each other yet. A positive sign, I'm thinking. Of course, this might be due partly to my having sequestered myself in the basement to figure out this damn bridesmaid dress (Heather's wedding is eight weeks from today; she's coming for her first mock-up fitting later this afternoon and if I don't have sketches to show her, she's going to freak), and Jennifer not being here much. All in all, a highly agreeable arrangement. Would that we'd thought of it as kids. Might've made childhood a tad less hairy.

Speaking of hairy, both literally and figuratively: since it's Saturday, Jason doesn't have school, which means he's been over here since just before lunchtime. Which means my kindness-to-moony-teenage-boys allotment for the day is just about used up. He keeps looking at me like he wants to tell me something; I keep acting like I'm too busy to talk. Because I have a real strong feeling I know what he wants to tell me, and an even stronger feeling I don't want to hear it. I've been down this path before (believe it or not), with Ricky Carver, in the ninth grade. Fleshy, myopic and pimply, Ricky trailed after me like a homeless mutt, always managing to somehow cross my path even though we didn't have the same schedule. Finally one day he cornered me after gym class and confessed his love. I'm not sure which of us was more humiliated. I do know that I never want to go through that again.

I don't get it—it's not as if I'm wearing hot pants and a low-cut halter top. Or ever have. In fact, it's kind of chilly today, so I'm in a sweatshirt and baggy drawstring flannel pj bottoms, my hair's in a ponytail (and anyone who's ever tried to put layered hair in a ponytail knows how attractive *that* is), my face devoid of makeup. I'm even wearing my glasses. Last time I caught my reflection in the mirror, I looked like one of those tabloid photos of some star under a Her Sad, Final Days headline.

And yet here Jason is, like a seagull hovering over a garbage barge.

Why can't the kid be like any other boy his age, jerking off over some X-rated Internet site or something? How fascinating can it be, watching me swear at a sketchpad?

Actually, now that I mention it, he's not watching me at all. Actually, he's slumped down into one corner of the couch, eyes shut, gently nodding to whatever he's plugged into. Frito's on his lap—of course—kneading the baggy denim lying in folds around his knee, fang glittering in the soft light from the lamp by my desk.

Maybe the kid gets off on just...smelling me?

I spread out the sketches I've done. Or at least, the ones that don't make me gag. There are twelve, six of which I'll show Heather. The others I intend to burn. Now I remember why I didn't major in design. I mean, really—does the world really need another sucky designer?

So why am I looking at these sketches and thinking...I want more? To do more? To *be* more?

"Hey, dude—what's wrong?"

Startled, I realize Jason's come up beside me, giving me the oh-God-don't-be-unhappy look. I'm even more startled to discover my cheeks are wet.

"Nothing," I say, wiping my eyes on the hem of my sweatshirt. "Just that time of month."

Usually a guaranteed male repellent.

Except for this time.

Before I can say, *"Holy crap!"* Jason's yanked me against him so hard I nearly lose my balance. Since his hoodie smells like week-old Mickey D's, this is not a pleasant experience. Especially as my breasts are squished into his ribs. If this is giving the kid a woody, however, I have no idea, because believe you me I've got my butt jutting out so far you could fly a squadron of fighter jets between our pelvises.

Which doesn't stop him from kissing me.

I allow myself precisely one hundredth of a second to debate the don't-want-to-hurt-his-feelings vs. must-stop-this-NOW issue. Hands clamped on his shoulders, I push back, trying not to yelp when inertia keeps his mouth moving after me like a heat-seeking missile.

"Jason?" I try to sound gentle, since I doubt screaming *"What the hell do you think you're doing?"* would do a whole lot for his obviously fragile self-esteem. "What was that all abou—?"

"*Jason!*"

That's not good.

We both look over; Luke's standing at the foot of the stairs, holding my grinning, blessedly clueless, daughter in his arms. Luke, however, is not grinning. He whispers something in Starr's ear, then sets her down. She goes skipping up the stairs, leaving Luke free to glare and fume.

"Go home, Jase," he says softly.

"I was just—"

"Home. Now."

"Luke," I try to get in as Jason says, "She was crying—"

"I was not!"

"—so I was just trying to make her feel better, was all." Jase hangs his head like a Beagle who's just piddled on the carpet. An apt description, considering how he smells. "Geez, I didn't mean anything by it."

I'm not sure how to take that.

"Go home," Luke repeats. "We'll deal with this later."

"Hey!" I stomp around the table to get up in Luke's face— okay, chest—hands on hips, breasts up and out. Woman on warpath stance. "Whatever this is, or isn't, it's between Jase and me, okay?"

Luke lifts one eyebrow, only to immediately frown. "Jesus, Ellie, you *were* crying. What's wrong?"

Isn't this where we came in?

"Nothing, for God's sake, I was just feeling a little blue— I'm entitled—but I'm fine now. So can we just forget the whole thing?"

"So," Jason says behind me, "can I stay?"

"No," Luke and I say at the same time. Understandably enough, the kid looks crushed. And confused.

"If you were on Luke's side to begin with," he says, shoving his stringy hair out of his eyes, "why'd you pretend you weren't?"

Why do kids always think people have to be on *sides?*

I let out a little sigh, then walk over and lay my hand on his arm. "Jason, honey? Please don't take this the wrong way, but you need a life. Of your own. And hanging out over here all the time ain't it."

His whole body sags. "Thought you liked it when I came over."

"I do," I say, squeezing his arm. "Every once in a while. But as long as you're here, you're not out there. Making friends and all that stuff." I refrain from adding "your own age." I'm not that stupid. Or mean. I angle my head to look up under the shaggy hair. "I can't be your girlfriend, Jason. And I know we need to talk about this—"

"Forget it! Just…forget it!" Hair flying, he cuts through the room and storms up the basement stairs. When the reverberations stop, I turn to Luke. The caveman scowl is still firmly in place; his gaze remains fixed on the stairs for several seconds before it shifts to me.

"You okay?"

I go back behind my table, laying out the sketches to glower at them some more. "I think maybe you should be asking Jason that, not me."

"He ever try somethin' like that before?"

"No. And I doubt he'll try it again, so unknot your boxers. No boy in his right mind would deliberately embarrass himself like that twice. Oh, for crying out loud, Luke," I say when the scowl deepens. "It was just a kiss. From a kid who's seventeen and confused and horny."

"It's the horny part that worries me."

"Why? Because you're afraid I might succumb to temptation and end up having a hot and heavy affair with your baby brother?"

"Don't even *say* that."

"I don't believe this! How could you even think I'd—" For some reason—Luke's crazed expression, my precarious emotional state, the fact that Mme. Attila has moved back in—I burst out laughing. When the hysteria subsides, I say, "Luke, sweetie? For one thing, I can take care of myself. So you can unplug the Damsel Defense System, okay? For another, you're wasting brain cells on something that ain't gonna happen, in this or any other lifetime. Although…" I lean across the table. "You might want to take him under your wing and give him a few pointers. His seduction technique is from hunger."

Luke gets this funny look on his face. "Oh, and like mine's so great?"

I am such an idiot.

But not so much of an idiot as to pursue this line of conversation.

Apparently, neither is Luke, who walks over to the sofa and flops into it with a loud, worn-out sigh. "I'm just worried about Jase, is all. Mom told me he's been acting weird lately."

"Lately?"

"Okay, weirder than usual. I mean, come on, El—none of the rest of us moped around like some sad-eyed mutt all the time."

I bite my tongue. There were periods during Luke and Tina's tumultuous relationship when Luke made Jason look downright jolly by comparison.

"He's got a crush on me, Luke. That's all. And he's… sensitive."

"You saying the rest of us aren't?"

"You really want to go there?"

Luke makes a face, then says, "Yeah, well, he better damn sight snap out of his *sensitivity* before he finishes school and comes to work for Pop."

A piece slides into place. "You're assuming an awful lot, aren't you?"

"Whaddya mean?"

"Maybe Jason's been acting so strange lately because he knows everyone expects him to go into the family business, only he doesn't. And he can't figure out how to tell you guys."

Luke angles his head. "He say something to you?"

"No. Just speculating."

"Well, that's nuts," Luke says with an incredulity usually reserved for Elvis sightings and adding three inches to one's penis. "We've all gone in with Pop, why wouldn't he? Besides, what else would he do?"

"Maybe that's for him to decide? I mean, really, does he look like somebody who'd be happy unclogging toilets?"

"Got news for you, babe—*nobody* likes unclogging toilets. Except maybe J.J."

Jimmy, Jr., Luke's oldest brother. We both smile. Then I glance at the clock, realizing that Heather, et al., will be here in less than an hour. Terror pulls up a chair and plants its big old butt right next to me. I glance over the sketches, my heart racing, then hold one up so Luke can see it.

"Whaddya think?"

I'm too far away for him to see clearly, so he has to squint. No self-respecting Scardinare male would ever let a little thing like nearsightedness come between him and his machismo. "It's a dress. So?"

"But do you think Heather will like it?"

His dark gaze shifts from the sketch to my face. "And I repeat—it's a dress. What do I know from dresses?" He shrugs. "Other than it's easier to mess around when a woman's wearing one than when she's wearing pants."

I throw a plastic S-curve template at his head. Well, in the general direction of his head. Blood's such a bitch to get out. Luke yells "Hey!" and ducks, just as Jennifer ventures downstairs.

Which is odd, because Jennifer never ventures downstairs. And never did, even when she lived here for real. Dad and I must've played a million games of Ping-Pong, but Jen never joined us, not even once. But here she is now.

My sister and Luke do the cold, hard look thing for a few seconds. As you may have guessed, they weren't exactly chums when we were kids. She's not quite all the way down the stairs, one spiked heel still poised on the step above, as if she's contemplating flight.

If only.

She crosses her arms over something tiny and silky and expensive. "Hello, Luke."

Maybe it's just me, but I don't know another living soul who actually says, "Hello." Not around here. Hi, hey, yo…but never "hello."

"Jennifer," Luke says with a big, laconic grin, stretching his legs out and crossing them at the ankles. "Our rose among the thorns. How's it goin'?"

I can tell she's holding back a bristle. "Fine. I hear Petey's getting married?"

"Yep. In a cuppla months."

She nods, hesitates, then comes all the way down the stairs. "And, um…I'm really sorry about, you know. You and Tina."

Wait a minute. This is my sister. Sounding as if she actually cares. About somebody else.

Did somebody suck out her brain and replace it with a human one?

Luke looks equally wary. With good reason. All our lives, Jennifer was only nice to any of us when she wanted something. Then the minute we'd hold out an olive branch, she'd rip a chunk out of our butts.

"Thanks," Luke says. "But maybe it was for the best."

"You two were so close, though. It must've been hard."

"Uh, yeah." His eyes bounce from her to me then back to her. "It was."

She sits beside him on the sofa, one foot tucked up under

her tush, her cheek resting on her knuckles, her expression positively dripping with sympathy and genuine interest.

"What happened?" she says softly, and the hair lifts on the back of my neck.

"Lu-uke!" Starr shrieks from the top of the stairs. "You said you were going to play Nintendo with me!"

Luke shoots up off the sofa like he's been goosed, mumbles something about "Gotta go," and does. Taking the stairs two at a time, in fact.

"He's really devoted to her, isn't he?" Jen says.

It takes a second. "Oh. Starr. Yeah. He is."

"Almost like a daddy."

Maybe that was simply an idle comment, maybe not. Maybe she was coming on to Luke, maybe I'm reading things into what was nothing more than a simple, concerned inquiry. But I have neither the time nor energy to get into any of it with her now, not with Heather due any minute.

"Starr's lucky to have Luke in her life," I say.

Jen gives me a funny look, then gets up and walks over to the mock-up of Heather's gown, which I've arranged on the mannequin. I can't approximate a tulle skirt from muslin, but even so, it looks pretty damn good. If I do say do myself.

"Heather's dress mock-up," I say. "She's coming for a fitting in a few minutes."

Wordlessly, Jen skims a finger over the décolletage, then pivots, catching sight of the sketches on the table. She picks one up and studies it, her expression stony, glances at the others, then at me, then leaves without saying another word.

Not that this is any surprise. Her criticisms of my designs when we were younger were ruthless. And she had no qualms about entertaining the few friends she had at my expense: to this day, I can see Stacey McMillan and Eve Graciano, sitting with Jen on her bed and hooting with laughter over the sketches I'd thought I'd safely hidden under my mattress. What does surprise me this time is her lack of comment, since I've never known my sister to sidestep any opportunity to put me down.

What the hell is she up to?

chapter 18

"Now remember," I say to Heather's reflection in the three-way mirror I bought for cheap from some going-out-of-business dress shop over on Lefferts Boulevard, "this is only muslin, so it's stiffer than the satin and tulle will be. And if you don't like something, go ahead and tell me, it's okay, I can fix it."

Once again, bosoms abound in my house, since Heather has brought half the female population of Richmond Hill to the fitting. I'm getting used to it.

"Ohmigod, Heather, turn around so we can see—"

"Christ, if it looks this good now, can you imagine what it's gonna look like in the real stuff?"

"Holy shit, you look absolutely freakin' *gorgeous!*"

Then Heather's grandmother—four-foot-ten, droopy stockings and droopier boobs, six strands of boot-polish-black hair yanked back into a bun, pokes me in the arm like the witch testing Gretel to see if she's fat enough and says, in a Harvey Weinstein voice, "Is good."

I breathe a major sigh of relief.

"Turn around, for God's sake," Sheila says, impatiently wagging her hands, only to let out a gasp when Heather does.

"Christ," Joanne intones, and the room falls silent.

Heather bursts into tears.

Wait. What?

Then I get the wind knocked out of me when Sheila hauls me into a Giorgio-laced hug. For a second, I wonder if I'll live to see tomorrow, until she holds me back, tears shining in her eyes. "It's perfect," she says. "I don't know what you did, but it looks ten times better than the one in the magazine. Am I right?" she asks the rest of the room, and everybody agrees.

I turn to the bride, who's once again ogling herself in the mirror. It's true, I took a few liberties with the design, like angling the waist and widening the neckline and adding a wide collar to emphasize the girl's lush, creamy shoulders and cleavage. See, the minute I looked at her, I thought of those Dutch masters paintings, with all those rosy, round ladies about to burst out of their corsets, their necks and shoulders and tops of their breasts alluring and innocent at the same time. "Heather?" I venture. "What do *you* think?"

"What do I think? Ohmigod—I look *totally* hot in this." She grins at me in the mirror. "Hey—d'you think you could maybe make up something like this top for me to wear with jeans or something?"

I hadn't thought of it, but…"Sure. Why not?"

"So," Sheila asks. "You got the fabric yet?"

"Just swatches." I cross the room to get them. "I wanted to make sure it worked before I invested in thirty yards of tulle."

"Really? That much?"

"That much. I got a piece of lace, too, but I'm not sure we

still want it. What about beading on the collar instead, with paillettes sprinkled across the skirt here and there?"

Five faces go blank.

"Trust me," I say.

"And what about the bridesmaid dresses?" Heather asks.

Ah, yes. The moment of truth. I pick up the sketches and hand them to Heather. "Bride first," I say when the horde tries to crowd around. "Because if she hates them, there's no point in continuing the discussion."

"Hate them?" Heather says, leafing through them. "Why would I hate them? They're fabulous. Especially this one. I can so see everyone in this, can't you, Ma?"

She hands it to Sheila, who's immediately swarmed by everybody else. Including me, since I have no idea which one she's picked.

"Yeah," Sheila says, nodding. "This could work."

"Lemme see," Joanne says, snatching the sketch out of my view. Waxed eyebrows lift. "I'm not sure about this rose…"

"I like the rose," Heather says.

"And all that chiffon…I dunno. It's so…bridesmaidy."

"Well, duh."

The girl is learning. Her sister, though, is doing the narrow-eyed, you-lied-to-me look. "But I thought you said we'd have something we could wear again?"

"Like my attendants are gonna look like they picked their dresses off the markdown rack at Macy's."

"But you *said*—"

"Hey." One square-nailed hand, daintily speckled with little rhinestones, lands on a hip complete with early-onset cellulite. "My wedding, my choices. Deal with it."

Oops. I think maybe I know who got my sister's brain.

Anyway, I finally see which gown they picked, a no-waisted dress that should—in theory at least—work for the fat girls, the skinny girls and the pregnant girls, ankle-length, uneven hemline, three layers of chiffon, draping at the left shoulder, fluttery little sleeves to mask wobbly upper arms, but still airy enough for June.

Joanne is sulking, but Heather is thrilled. "Can we do this in pinks and mauves?"

"You have got to be kidding?" Joanne says, as the maid-of-honor (Tiffany) squeals "Yes!" and Sheila presses her hand to her bosom and says, "Christ, this is gonna be so beautiful!"

"What about your redheaded cousin?" I ask.

"Cissy?" Heather shrugs. "Two words: *Loving Care.* Well?"

Guess it's settled. God knows *I'm* not gonna cross Bridezilla.

I show her the sample card I begged off the wholesaler on 47th Street before I quit my job at Nicole Katz. Sixty-five colors of polyester chiffon with coordinating taffeta for the lining, more shades of pink than a sunrise in the Bahamas. I suggest we use three different colors for the layering; we pick them out, I calculate how much the fabric will cost, add on for my labor, and give Heather a price for the dresses. Since I can get the fabric for cheap, and I'm not going to charge her full price for my labor since this is such a big order, each dress will probably cost about the same as they'd pay pretty much anyplace else.

"But I'll have to pay cash for the fabric upfront, so…"

"Not a problem," Sheila says, getting out her checkbook.

Gotta admit, I really like this part.

I take Tiffany's and Joanne's measurements, then tell Heather to make sure the other girls call me within the next week so I can get theirs. It's not until they've gone that it hits me:

I now have to make sixteen (yes, they added one more) dresses in eight weeks.

By myself.

Am I out of my MIND?!

Stupid question.

* * *

"Did you know you have sixty-seven bottles of nail polish?"

I look up from the dress form, where I've been trying to figure out this pattern that looked like a piece of cake on paper, and over at Starr, who's come downstairs after I could have sworn I'd put her to bed. I attempt to process the myriad thoughts her comment provokes, but they all collide in my head and are now lying prone like the Three Stooges after a pratfall.

"No I didn't, why are you up, and how long have you been able to count that high?"

Settling cross-legged on the sofa and yanking her Snoopy nightshirt over her knees, she huffs a sigh. "Since I was three. Honestly, Mama, where have you *been? Actually, I can count to a thousand. Wanna hear?"

God, no.

"Not right now, honey, okay?"

"Okay. Anyway, I'm up because it was boring in bed."

"That's kind of the whole point of going to bed, isn't it? I mean, who wants to be stimulated when you're supposed to be going to sleep?"

"What's stimulated mean?"

"Excited."

"Oh." Obviously, she chooses to ignore her mother's lame attempt at logic, instead getting up and padding over to the cutting table, clutching the forlorn Oscar to her chest. "Whatcha doing?"

"Making a pattern."

"Oh. Is it fun?"

"It is, actually. Like putting together a puzzle. Except when the pieces don't fit. Then it's not so much fun."

"Oh." Silence. Then: "How come Aunt Jennifer cries so much?"

I stab myself with a pin as my eyes shoot to hers. "What're you talking about?"

"She cries in her room, sometimes for a really long time. Don't you hear it?"

I shake my head, as if doing so will settle this new revelation into place among the five million other ones. "No. Is that why you can't sleep?"

"Sometimes, yeah." Starr reaches down to scratch her butt through the thin flannel. "But mostly it's because my head's too full. So I have to keep thinking until it's empty, and then I can go to sleep."

She thinks *her* head is full? Right now, mine's like a Dumpster that should've been emptied a week ago. But somewhere in there, it occurs to me we haven't had to deal with any monsters recently. Yay.

"What's your head so full of you can't sleep?"

One shoulder bumps. "I don't know. Stuff." After a moment, she says, very softly, "Leo." Her eyes lift to mine and my throat gets all tight. "I really miss him," she says.

"Yeah. Me, too." I hold out my arms. "C'mere, stinker." She crawls up into my lap, no mean feat since I'm already precariously balanced on this stool. Then we just sit and cuddle for a few minutes, not talking. Or crying. There's a sniffle or two, but that's about it. Should I be worrying, that she still hadn't really cried?

I try to smush down her hair, but it just sproings right back. "Do you think Aunt Jennifer knows you know she's been crying?"

"Nuh-uh. 'Cuz she keeps her door closed. Except one time she didn't, and I saw her. I was gonna ask her what was wrong, but she got up real fast and shut the door." Her mouth screws up. "I don't think she likes me very much."

"I'm not sure Aunt Jennifer likes anybody very much, sweetie. Don't take it personally."

"Do *you* like her?"

"She's my sister. I'm supposed to like her."

"That's not what I asked."

"No," I say. "Not very much."

"How come?"

"Because she wasn't very nice to me when we were kids."

"Andy says Jesus says we're supposed to love everybody, even the people who are mean to us."

Oh, brother.

"That's a nice philosophy—"

"What's that mean?"

"Um…a way of looking at things. But it's not always easy."

"Oh," she says on a huge yawn. Hallelujah. I am much too tired to go any farther down this road tonight.

"You ready to get back in bed?"

"C'n I sleep down here on the sofa until you're ready to go up?"

"Sure." She crawls back up onto the sofa and basically passes out. I cover her with an old afghan; Frito climbs up on it and does this kneading routine, purring like a jackhammer for several minutes until he curls up against Starr's legs and also passes out.

You got any idea how hard it is to stay awake with two sleeping bodies six feet away? After another twenty minutes, I realize this is pointless—I can't drape if I can't see. So I shut everything down and off, then heft my daughter upstairs—although not before Frito and I exchange several heated words—to tuck her back into bed. Then I pause, listening to Starr's deep, even breathing, Frito's purring…and the faint but unmistakable sound of weeping next door.

Once in the hall, I stand outside Jen's door for a good minute, trying to decide what to do. I may not be all that big on religion per se, but I got the basics down. I know all about turning the other cheek and the Golden Rule, but…

But I'm tired. And I'm no saint. If wanting to save my own hide, for once, is a horrible thing, so be it. If Jen wants to tell me what's going on, fine. I'll listen. After all, I'm probably the best damn sounding board in Queens.

There's something to carve on my headstone, huh?

So I tiptoe to my own room, where I peel off my clothes and fall into bed, wondering how the hell I managed to accumulate sixty-seven bottles of nail polish when I haven't even worn the stuff since I had this kid?

Mrs. Patel's flamingo is decked out for May in a lovely wreath of plastic daisies and a fetching little straw hat, perched at a jaunty angle. The bird looks rather pleased with himself, actually, as Starr and I pass with our creaking grocery cart, filled from our Saturday morning shopping expedition. I find this somehow reassuring, Mrs. Patel's removing the burden of my having to remember what season it is. Of course, this didn't used to be a problem when I actually ventured out into the world every day, but these past few weeks there's been so little difference in my days, I need these little reminders to keep me grounded.

And I swear to God, I'm not whining again. No, seriously. I've got a lot to be grateful for—getting to hang out more with my kid, watching Heather's gown blossom from idea to reality, not having to bust my butt to make the train every morning. And there's a lot to be said for going to work in old sweats. Or my jammies. It's just that, well, the days do tend to blur into each other a bit. And sometimes it gets to me, that's all.

For instance. It suddenly hit me yesterday that it's been three weeks since Jennifer moved back, and I still don't know what her plans are. If any. She spends most of her time in her room, occasionally venturing out to go potty and eat. Sometimes she leaves the house for several hours, but she doesn't volunteer where she is going. Or say anything when she comes back. I suppose this is a good thing, right? I mean, it's not as if I *want* to talk to her. But her avoidance is beginning to bug me. If anybody's supposed to be avoiding anybody else, it should be *me* avoiding *her.* She's taking all the fun out of it, dammit.

And there's something else that's setting my teeth on edge. While I've had plenty of occasion to see Jen pissed, or affronted, or irritated, or just plain wacko, never once that I can remember have I actually seen her identifiably *unhappy.* Which she obviously is now, and which obviously makes her—I don't believe I'm saying this—human.

I have no idea how to deal with that.

As we near our house, I see Dolly, Liv's grandmother, hustling out the door to Liv's apartment, looking a little flustered. I haven't seen her in a couple weeks, since Liv has been functioning on her own with the kids for a while now. The old woman's beehive is as red as ever, her lipstick as fluorescent, but she seems to be having difficulty negotiating the steps.

"Dolly!" I call out when we get closer. "What's the matter? Are you hurt?"

Her silvery green gaze jerks to mine. Then she smiles. "Oh, no, sweetheart! My knees act up a bit when it's going to rain, but nothing serious." As we approach the stoop, she says, "I came over because Liv's got some sort of tummy bug, I'm just on my way to the corner to get some Coke for her, she never keeps it in the house, you know—"

"Oh, don't do that. Come on inside, I'll get you some."

"I don't want to put you out—"

"You're not putting me out, I've got plenty." Starr and I haul the full grocery cart up the stairs like a dead body, then Dolly and I troop back to the kitchen. Starr clomps upstairs, calling for the poor cat. If he's smart, he's halfway to Guatemala by now.

"This is so nice of you, but I'll pay you for it—"

"Don't be ridiculous, it's just a couple cans of Coke, for heaven's sake."

I toss the just-purchased ice cream in the freezer, realizing the soda's all in the basement. I explain to Dolly that I keep a small fridge down there filled with goodies so I don't have to keep coming back upstairs while I work. Although considering the way my butt is spreading since I've been home all day, maybe hauling said butt up and down the stairs a few more times a day wouldn't hurt.

I think about this for a moment.

Naah.

"Work?" Dolly says. "What do you do?"

"It's just temporary, I'm making a friend's wedding gown and her bridesmaid dresses. So I'll just zip down—"

"Could I see?"

Terror strikes deep in my heart. My work area is not a place one allows sweet old ladies to see. As I've (unfortunately) always suspected, I'm definitely one of those creative types who thrives in chaos. And believe me, I don't mean a few threads and fabric scraps lying around. I'm talking the-trailer-park-after-the-twister devastation.

"Um, gee…"

"If you don't mind, that is. I just love wedding dresses."

"Uh…you sure you're up to more stairs?"

"Actually, the more I exercise, the less problems I have."

Figures.

"Okay," I say as we descend into Hell. "I have to apologize, it's a little messy…."

I flip on the light.

"Oh my God, sweetheart! Call 9-1-1! You must have had a break-in!"

For a second, I'm tempted to let her believe this. But I shake my head. "No, it's okay. I'm not a very neat worker, I'm afraid."

"*You* did this?"

But I realize Dolly's no longer talking about the rampant disarray, but Heather's nearly completed gown, on display on the dress form in one (clean) corner of the room. When she gets closer—think forging through the rain forest—she says, "But this is *beautiful*. Did you use a pattern?"

"See the photograph on the bulletin board behind it? I took it from that."

"I'm sorry, but I'm only seeing one photo…"

"Yes, that's it."

She turns to me. "You honestly think this dress is the same as that one?"

I frown. "Well, I did make a few changes—"

"No, you designed a whole new dress, sweetheart. Yes, yes, they both have tulle skirts, but other than that… And your workmanship…my God! Not a single pucker along the piping, even at the curves. Absolutely exquisite."

Curiosity overrides my blush. "Do you sew?"

"I used to," she says softly, her gaze fixed on the dress. "But not since Liv's wedding dress. And you said you are doing bridesmaid dresses, too?"

"I've only got the pattern and one mock-up I did from some old drapery sheers to make sure it would work." Then I laugh. Slightly hysterically. "Although how I'm going to get sixteen of these done—in ten different sizes—in six weeks, I do not know."

"Did you say…*sixteen?*"

"Yes. And each one has three layers of rolled chiffon hems. What *was* I thinking?"

Dolly looks at me, her mouth twitching in amusement. "God alone knows. So. You need help, yes?"

For a second, I think she means help as in the kind where you go lie on a couch and barf up your past to some stranger. Then I realize she's talking about another pair of hands. Specifically, hers.

"Oh, no…I couldn't ask you—"

"You didn't ask, sweetheart. I'm volunteering. Because you'll never make it otherwise and I didn't realize…" Again, she looks around. "I didn't realize how much I missed it until just this minute. So. I'll bring my machine and you'll give an old lady something to do, yes?"

I think I need to sit down. "Ohmigod, I don't know…I mean, I'm not sure how much I could pay you, but—"

"Did I ask for money?"

"Well, no. But I don't want to take advantage of you."

Something in her eyes goes strangely…brittle. But it passes so quickly I think perhaps I imagined it. Except then she says, "That will not happen. Believe me. Once upon a time, I might have let myself get into situations that put me at a disadvantage, but I learned from my mistakes. Now I call the shots," and I realize I didn't imagine it at all.

God, I love these tough little broads. I can only hope this will be me, one day.

"You've…worked with chiffon before?"

Her smile is enigmatic. "Chiffon, organza, velvet—you name it, I've handled it. So. Do we have an agreement?"

"I…guess so."

"Good. Then if you will give me those Cokes, I will go. And if Liv doesn't need me tomorrow, I'll be here at nine?"

Oy. My blood doesn't even start pumping until ten these days. But I smile and say, "Nine is perfect."

After I've seen her to the door, I go back downstairs and sit on my stool, staring at the mess and thinking, Dude—I've got an assistant.

Hot damn.

Next Sunday, five o'clock, the Scardinares. Starr (on my right) and I are totally scarfing down the manicotti while Jen (on my left) is picking at it like a member of the bomb squad disabling a particularly sensitive device.

Yes, that's right. Jen is here. At least, her body is. What's left of it, anyway, since she's lost, I'm guessing, a good fifteen pounds since she moved in. No telling where her head is, though. All I can say is, her defenses must have really been down when Frances ambushed her yesterday. But she's not exactly fitting in, if you know what I mean. Oh, once we got past the shocked expressions—it's been years since Jen's been here, after all—everyone tried to draw her into the conversation. Except conversation with the Scardinares is a little like getting too close to the wrong side of a jet engine. So perhaps Jen's reticence is the more prudent choice, after all.

Especially since I'm picking up on all sorts of weird vibes today, lurking like a poison gas underneath the deafening, incessant chatter about Heather and Pete's wedding. Primarily from Luke and Jason. Understandable, since this is the first time I've seen or talked to either of them since the Jason Kissy Face incident. I have no idea what Luke's problem is, but something tells me Jason's ill humor has something to do with his brothers razzing him about having a girlfriend. Or rather, his not having one. Especially since Scardinare testosterone tends to kick in around kindergarten.

At the latest.

Poor kid. He keeps shooting me these looks, but what am I supposed to do? Explain that their baby brother's juices are flowing just fine, they're just leaking for the wrong person? Oh, yeah, telling Frances her son's got the hots for his half-Jewish, eleven-years-his-senior neighbor oughtta go over *real* big.

But if he doesn't stop staring at me, I may scream. Doesn't he care that somebody might notice?

Finally he leaves the table, along with several of the older nieces and nephews who, with Starr, barrel out into the backyard to play. An eyeblink after they leave, Jennifer whispers, "The way Jason was staring at you was really creeping me out."

As I was saying.

I am also amazed that my sister has initiated a conversation in which she is not the focal point. So, as an experiment, I decide to see how long she can keep it up before she cracks under the strain of thinking about somebody else.

"He's got a crush on me," I whisper back, then explain about the kiss.

"Oh," she says, getting up to help clear the table. "That explains it, then."

"That explains what?"

But she hustles her butt out to the kitchen without clarification.

Well. It was only five words, granted. But I can officially say that Jen got through *an entire conversation* without mentioning herself once.

Family and guests disperse throughout the house as they always do—women to the kitchen, men to the living room to watch sports. This is the way it is in this house; rabid feminists need not apply. Especially since the trade-off is the men watch the babies and younger kids while the women do the dishes. Sounds fair to me. Besides, who can talk dirty with a bunch of men in the room?

Once in the kitchen, the women take up their appointed tasks like a precision military machine, getting dessert plates and forks, making coffee, scraping dishes and filling the dishwasher. I've been a dish-scraper ever since I was deemed old enough to join the women, around when I turned eighteen. Of course, there weren't as many of us back then, since only Jimmy Jr. was married at that point. Just me and Frances and Julie, J.J.'s wife.

And Tina. Whom I miss today with a sharpness that takes my breath away.

I glance over at Jennifer, standing apart from the swarming mass of estrogen. She asks Frances if she can do anything, but it's a futile question, since it's obvious there's no place for her. Maybe I'm transferring my sadness over losing Tina's friendship onto my sister, or maybe the manicotti has put me in a very good mood, but I say, "Come here and help me scrape."

She looks as pleased as a kid picked for the best team. Jesus.

"So what's for dessert?" Kristy, Johnny's wife, asks. At twenty-four, she's the youngest daughter-in-law, still thin after delivering twin boys a year ago. We would all hate her, except it would be like hating Mother Teresa. If Mother Teresa were gorgeous, had seventies hair and was, you know, alive.

"Jimmy made his chocolate cake," Frances says, and we all pause for a moment of awed and respectful silence.

"With the chocolate buttercream frosting?" This from Monica, Vinnie's wife, her brown eyes like saucers underneath maroon-highlighted bangs.

"Of course, what else?" Frances says, and my guess is that more than one of us comes perilously close to orgasm.

Still, despite the camaraderie, for all that my position as après-dinner dish-scraper is mine for as long as I want it, it occurs to me that I'm still on the outside looking in with this family. Never mind that I know the intimate details of their sex lives, their finances and their menstrual cycles, that Julie had a benign cyst removed last year and Monica feels guilty about wanting another baby when she and Vinnie already have three kids. I *know* these people, but I'm not *part* of them. I used to think it was because I'm not actually related, either by blood or marriage, but more and more I'm beginning to think it goes deeper than that. And right now, as I scrape and salivate in anticipation of this cake, it hits me—I've got ethnicity envy. Not because they're Italian, specifically, but because they *are* part of something. Except for Jen and me, everyone in this room knows who they are, where they come from, what's expected of them. An Italian meeting another Italian—or a Jew another Jew, a Greek another Greek, whatever—shares an immediate bond. They get the inside jokes. They know the secret handshake. It's like they're sirloin tip roast and I'm…meatloaf.

Not that there's anything wrong with meatloaf. It's just you don't always know what you're getting.

And whilst I'm wandering down these philosophical paths, and the cake is sliced and passed around while we wait for the coffee to brew, they all stop their good-natured significant-other bashing long enough to wax rhapsodic about Heather's dress.

"All I have to say is," says Julie, "if I ever get married again?" Her fork jabs in my direction. "You are so doing my dress. Come to think of it, it might be worth dumping J.J. just so I *could* get married again!"

We all hoot with laughter as Frances yells, "Hey! That's my kid you're talking about!", especially as we all know Julie wouldn't dream of doing any such thing. Especially not with four kids including a four-month-old.

"But are you really sure the bridesmaids' dresses will be ready in time?" Heather asks, longingly eyeing the cake the rest of us are "sampling." Everybody else except Jennifer, that is, who's again retreated to her spot by the kitchen sink, her arms crossed over her stomach, watching but not participating. If I'm on the sidelines, Jennifer is in a whole 'nother stadium.

"No problem," I say around a full mouth, thinking if they don't have this cake in Heaven, I'm not going. Then I tell them about Dolly and her offer to help. Which she's been doing for the past week, making herself immediately indispensable. "It turns out she worked in the costume department of the Metropolitan Opera for years. Isn't that wild?"

"And she's working for you for free?" Frances asks.

"Everytime I try to talk money, she threatens to quit. Says I'm doing her a favor by giving her back something she used to love."

Jason comes into the kitchen for a glass of water; Monica pretends to come on to him just to get a rise out of him. He blushes furiously and once again glances at me.

And this time, *everyone* notices.

Including Frances.

I shrug as if to say, "Sorry, haven't a clue."

He leaves; conversation resumes. But I keep feeling these speculative glances pinging off the side of my face. I'm not sure if nobody's saying anything because they don't believe it, don't want to believe it, or are afraid of being the one to look like an idiot, accusing Jason and/or me of something so totally outside the realm of logic. Finally everybody moves en masse back out to the dining room with cake and coffee; Julie bellows, "Dessert!" as the older kids come trooping in from outside. In the ensuing chaos, I slip down the hall to the john. Only when I come out, Jason ambushes me and drags me into Frances's office.

And shuts the door.

"Jason, what the hell—?"

"Dude, I've been trying to get your attention all night! Didn't you see me looking at you?"

"Honey, *everybody* saw you looking at me! Jase, you've got to get over this. I told you, nothing's going to happen between us."

"What?" He actually looks confused. Then the light dawns. "Oh. Dude, that's not what I wanted to talk to you about. It's just I've got something I need to tell my folks, and I've got to get it out, like, *now,* before I chicken out. And I thought maybe you could help me figure out what to say an' stuff, because I'm afraid Pops is going to be real disappointed when I tell him. And I mean, hey, you must have some experience in that, huh?"

I frown, trying to digest all these scraps of information. "Experience in what?"

"Giving bad news to grown-ups, dude."

Why do I not feel flattered?

However. If this isn't about him and me (big sigh of relief, here), then I'm going with my other hunch, that he doesn't want to go into business with his dad. Especially when he says, "See, I finally realized it wasn't fair to anybody, my keeping this to myself, you know? Trying to act like I don't feel certain things, just because I'm afraid I might hurt somebody? Pops, especially, he really needs to know this so he doesn't start expecting something that's not going to happen."

He pauses. I take that as my cue to encourage him. "Then you just have to come right out and tell him. Because you're right, it's not fair otherwise."

Relief washes over his features. "You really think so?"

"Yeah. I do."

"Dude." His hand goes to his chest as I idly contemplate how many teenagers would become mute if "dude" were stricken from the English language. "I'm so glad to hear you say that. Because I thought, y'know, I didn't want to do what you've been doing, y'know, like lying to yourself about how you really feel about stuff? I mean, the last thing I want to do is get to be as old as you and think, whoa—I just spent my whole life living a lie—"

His next words—and my *What the hell are you* talking *about?*—are lost in the deafening shrieks from down the short hall. We both race out of the room to find out that, after five years of trying, Vinnie and Monica are expecting Bambino Number Four. Much hugging, much crying and kissing.

Jen sidles up to me and says, "Why couldn't our family be like this?" as Luke gives me a weird look from across the room and Jason gets up on the coffee table and says, *"I have an announcement to make, too!"*

Um, methinks the kid's sense of timing could use a little work?

His father looks up at him, his round face creased in a frown as Luke wends his way over to me and mutters, "You got any idea what this is about?"

"I was right," I whisper. "About his not wanting to be a plumber."

"You sure?"

"He said he had to say this, even though your father would be disappointed—"

"Jason," Jimmy says, "for godssake, whatever it is, it couldn't wait for a few minutes?"

"No. No, it can't." The kid's shifting from foot to foot on the coffee table like he's gotta pee. "I gotta say this now, in front of everybody so there's no confusion—"

"Jason," Frances says, her mouth steely. "Get off my coffee table. And you're being rude to your brother. Someday, it's gonna be you making an announcement like this and I'm sure you wouldn't want anyone else stealing your thunder—"

Jason's high, hysterical laugh cuts Frances off in midbreath. "No, no grandbabies here," he says, and Luke mutters "shit" and grabs my hand.

My eyes zing to the side of his face. But his attention is riveted to the little drama unfolding in front of us. Which means I guess he has no idea he's rearranging the cellular structure of my hand. Let alone my brain.

"What's that supposed to mean?" Jimmy says, as all eyes play Ping-Pong between the two of them.

"It means," Jason says, looking for sure like he's about to crap his pants, "that I'm gay."

chapter 19

Understandably enough, a long moment of stunned silence follows. A silence broken by yours truly when I blurt out, "So what the hell was that kiss all about?"

"That's what made me realize I was gay," Jason says.

Well, there's a first.

Luke is now cussing up a storm under his breath, although he's mercifully let go of my hand. Presumably to use it to keep his head from falling off. The rest of his family is still doing the stunned silence thing—astonishing when you consider the number of Italians per square foot in here—which apparently awakens some deep urge inside my sister to raise her hand and ask, "Anybody want coffee and cake?"

"I think I need to sit down," Frances says.

Taking advantage of what we all know is the calm before the inevitable storm, Jason climbs down from the coffee table and makes his way over to me as Luke wanders away. "Dude,

I'm like really, really sorry I used you. But I thought, y'know, if I, like, kissed you, I'd stop feeling so confused. Except—" he shrugs "—I didn't feel anything."

Somehow, I swallow the laugh. "Uh, honey? I hate to break this to you, but I didn't feel anything, either. And trust me, I'm not gay."

Grinning like I have *never* seen this guy grin before, Jason leans over and whispers in my ear, "That's because we weren't kissing the right people." Then he giggles and holds up his right hand, showing off a thin gold ring. "His name's Connor."

And my first thought? That this may be the first time in history the straight girl advises the queen on *his* wardrobe. Because God knows the poor kid'll be eaten alive if he comes out of the closet dressed like that.

I glance around, realizing that all the Scardinare wives have ushered the children elsewhere—to where the cake is, judging from the sound of forks pinging off plates in the next room— leaving a mass of glowering, über-macho Italian jocks behind. And me, the only nonfamily member in here. But nobody seems to notice as Jason's brothers all light into him at once.

"Whaddayou, nuts?"

"No brother of mine is gonna be queer, goddammit—"

"Is this some kind of sick joke?"

"How the hell can you do this to Pops, huh—?"

"Leave the kid alone," Luke says quietly from where he now leans against the wall beside the fireplace, his arms crossed. When his brothers wheel on him, accusing him of everything from being a wuss to being gay himself, Luke calmly holds up one hand. Amazingly, they all shut up.

"It took balls, him telling us like this," Luke says, giving his baby brother a considering look. "He could've taken the easy way out and kept it a secret. But he didn't." He walks over to Jason and extends his hand. "I'm proud of you, bro."

"Oh, don't be ridiculous," Frances says from a few feet

away. "This is just one of those adolescent phases, the kid's no more gay than I am." She goes up to Jason and smacks him in his arm. "So you had a crush on Ellie and she didn't return your feelings. So what? That doesn't make you *gay,* for God's sake, it just makes you young and stupid. Besides, nobody on either side of this family has ever been gay, and they say it's hereditary—"

"Your uncle Carmine," Jimmy says softly from the sofa. Where he'd sunk like a stone earlier.

Frances whirls around. "What did you say?"

Jimmy lifts bag-cradled eyes to her. "I never told you this, but Carmine once made a pass at me. Before we were married. In your mother's kitchen."

"*What?* Don't talk crazy, Jimmy, Carmine wouldn't've done any such thing."

"You weren't there, babe," Jimmy says with a half smile. "Trust me, his hand didn't land where it did on accident."

"Ohmigod—"

"Oh, for crying out loud, Franny, he was just foolin' around. Flirting, y'know? He didn't mean nothin' by it. Actually—" he grins "—I was kinda flattered, if you wanna know the truth. Those guys tend to be real picky."

"Jimmy, for God's sake! What a horrible thing to accuse somebody of!"

Jimmy shoots to his feet, his stomach jumping as he bellows, "It's the *truth,* for chrissake! So what's so terrible about your uncle being a homosexual?"

"He baby-sat for our boys when they were little! If what you're saying is true…" Her hand flies to her mouth, her eyes huge behind it. "Ohmigod!"

Okay, this is really freaking me out. Frances is one of the most open-minded people I know. Well, except when it comes to her daughters-in-law. But still, I've never heard her once utter a homophobic remark. I glance over at Luke, still standing beside Jason, and I can tell by the looks on their faces that they're feeling the same way.

"So ask 'em," Jimmy says, turning to his sons. "Tell us the truth, now—did Carmine ever pull any funny stuff with you?"

"No, Pops—"

"Uh-uh, never."

"Don't you think I'd've said something if he had? Jesus."

"He was the best baby-sitter we ever had," Luke says with a smile. "Unlike Nonna 'ducci."

"Oh, Christ!" Vinnie says with a laugh. "I'd totally forgotten about her!"

"Probably one of those, whaddyacallits?" says Peter. "Suppressed memories or something. Swear to God, my left earlobe is longer than my right because of her."

Frances is looking from one to the other, flummoxed. "You saying my mother *hurt* you guys? For God's sake, the woman barely weighed ninety pounds!"

"Ma," J.J. says, chuckling, "the nuns at school were girlygirls in comparison."

"Yeah," says Vinnie. "And the thing was, she always knew how to inflict the kind of pain that didn't leave any scars."

"Except emotional ones!" adds Pete, and they all crack up.

The laughter dies down, though, as one by one, Jason's big brothers force their gazes to his. Then, even though they're obviously still uncomfortable with this news, they approach him one by one, again, giving him a hug, shaking his hand, acknowledging his courage. Finally, Jimmy Sr. embraces his youngest son in a bear hug that makes Jason grunt, then says, "I just gotta say one thing—" he points in Jason's face "—anybody gives you any trouble, you come to us and we'll beat the crap out of 'em for you, you got that?"

Jason pushes his hair out of his eyes, then laces his fingers and cracks his knuckles, posturing like some gangster in a two-bit Mafia movie. "Hey. I can beat the crap out of 'em my-self, you know."

On this note, I finally realize I've been hanging around long enough in this private family scene. So I slip out to the dining room, signaling to Starr that it's time to leave. I catch Jen's eye, gesturing for her to stay, if she wants, but she opts to come with me.

"Time to get ready for bed," I say to Starr when we get back home.

"It's still light out!"

"It won't be by the time you get your jammies on and teeth brushed and I read to you. So go on." She tromps up the stairs, muttering under her breath. Beside me, Jen actually laughs.

"She's going to be something when she hits puberty."

"Tell me about it," I say, going to the kitchen for something to drink, more than a little surprised when Jen follows. So does the cat. But since Jen's been getting her allergy shots, cat and sister can now share breathing space with impunity.

Whether Jen and I can, however, for any length of time, remains to be seen.

"You've really got it good, you know that?" she says softly behind me, and I nearly crack the glass on the spigot when I turn around.

"Me? Why?"

She shrugs. "I don't know. Lots of reasons. Because you've got a kid." Huh. I'd always assumed Jen had remained child-less by choice. But maybe not. "Because you appreciate what you have. Why are you looking at me like that?"

"No special reason. Other than wondering what the hell Jimmy put in that cake tonight." I take a gulp of my water, then lift the glass in her direction. "After what you just witnessed, you still wish our family was more like the Scardinares?"

"I could think of worse things."

"Why?"

"Because…because no matter what, they're still there for each other, aren't they?"

"Yeah, I suppose so." I pause, then say, "Are we actually having a normal conversation?"

Her mouth tilted in a half smile, she pushes her hair back over her shoulder, then crosses her arms. "Does it feel as strange to you as it does to me?"

"Stranger." I take another sip of water. "Pardon me for being skeptical, but why are you being nice to me?"

"I think the question is, why are you being nice to *me?* You could've thrown me out, when I showed up a few weeks ago."

"Don't think the thought didn't cross my mind."

"So why didn't you?"

"Beats the hell out of me."

Frito jumps up on the counter. Next to Jennifer. Who scratches him behind the ears.

And he lets her.

"Did Jason really kiss you?" Jen asks.

"Yep." Damn cat—who's purring like crazy, by the way—is smirking at me, do you believe it?

"Was it awful?"

I break my I'll-deal-with-you-later eyelock with the cat, returning my gaze to my sister. "When was the last time you kissed a seventeen-year-old boy?"

"That bad, huh?"

"In spades."

Her smile is sad. So I say, thinking to perk her up, "So. What do you hear from Stuart?"

"Oh." Is it my imagination, or are her cheeks red? "Not much, actually. That is to say, not much on the job front. It takes time to find a good position these days, you know? Anyway— I'm pretty pooped, so I think I'll head up to bed, if that's okay?"

And she's gone before her words finish echoing inside my skull.

If that's okay? Since when does my sister care whether or not what she does is okay?

A minute later, Starr calls from the top of the stairs that she's ready. Cat and I troop upstairs, where I check her teeth (I'm not wholly convinced she doesn't just smear toothpaste on her teeth rather than brushing, since that was one of my tricks at her age), and settle in to read the next chapter of whichever the heck Harry Potter book we're on. When we're finished, she finally asks the question I know has been simmering in her overactive little brain ever since Jason's announcement.

"What was Jason talking about? When he said he was gay?"

And for once, I'm ready. More or less.

"It means he likes boys instead of girls."

Starr frowns. "Does that mean he won't like *me* anymore?"

"No, sweetie. It just means instead of having girlfriends or wives, like his brothers do, he'll have boyfriends."

"Oh." Her whole face puckers. "Is that bad?"

"No. It's just the way he is."

She crosses her arms. "Brandon said it was disgusting."

Brandon's J.J.'s oldest. Brandon is a pain in the butt. "Brandon," I say, "will get over it." I hope. Then I add, "Sometimes people feel threatened by things, or people, they don't understand."

"You mean somebody might be *scared* of Jason?" She giggles. "That's nuts."

"Yes, it is. And now you need to go to sleep."

We do lots of hugs and kisses, I check for that damn monster (who's decided to come back, the turd), turn out the lamp by her bed, then start out of the room. It's almost dark, the charcoal light eking through the sheers cottony and soft.

"Mama?" Starr says in a stage whisper when I get to the door.

"What, baby?"

"When I get bigger, will I like girls or boys?"

Why does my heart clench at this question? "I don't know,

sweetie. Probably boys." Or maybe both, but no way am I going there. For both of our sakes. "You'll just have to wait and see."

"Okay," she says, flopping over and yawning. "Night. Love you."

"Love you, too, Twinkle."

When I get downstairs, I nearly jump out of my skin at the sight of a shadow in my living room window, followed by Luke's soft, "It's me," through the screen. I've got bars on the downstairs windows, but still. Skulking shadows do bad things to the heart.

"What do you want?" I say through the screen.

"Is the kid down?"

"Yeah, I just turned off her light."

"Then come outside, sit with me a minute."

His words echo through my memory, words spoken hundreds of times during our lives. I grab a sweater off the coat tree and join Luke outside on the stoop, thinking how many spring and summer evenings—even a few winter ones—we spent out here, shooting the breeze about nothing. Everything.

"How's Frances?" I say.

He blows out a breath. "Hard to tell. Still in shock, I think."

"Here Jason was so worried about your father's reaction. I guess he never even considered how much it might upset Frances."

"Yeah, her reaction kinda surprised me, too. But…I don't know, El. Mom's not a homophobe." He pauses. "But other people are. My guess is, she's scared."

I can hear the undertones of anxiety in his voice, too. And for good reason. This may be New York, and the twenty-first century, but still. What I told Starr is, unfortunately, still very true.

I prop my elbows on the step behind me, listening to the constant buzz of traffic and other people's radios and babies crying, inhaling the scents of a dozen different suppers, exhaust, Mrs. Waxman's little lilac bush across the street.

"That took a lot of guts," I say, "you standing up for him against your brothers. I'm sure he appreciates that."

He grins down at his hands, folded between his knees. "My brothers don't scare me. Besides, the one with the guts is Jase. And he needed to know at least somebody in that room understood that."

I sit there, staring across the street and thinking about Jason's comment, about how he couldn't stand the thought of spending his whole life "living a lie" like I had. I'm not entirely sure what he meant by that, since there's an awful lot he doesn't know, but that doesn't negate his comment's accuracy.

"Why do we waste so much energy on being afraid to admit the truth?"

I can feel Luke's gaze veer to my face, the intensity of his expression sending itty-bitty shock waves coursing over my skin. Then he looks away.

"Because sometimes," he says softly, "we know the truth is gonna hurt. So we think it's better to keep things to ourselves."

"Or from ourselves?"

"That, too."

I sigh, knowing what he wants me to say.

"This is about wanting to tell Tina about Starr, isn't it?"

He nods. "I know you said you needed some time, but…I'm sorry, El. This is gonna eat away at me until I come clean."

I think about what *I* know that I can't talk about, and feel sick.

"There's no sense telling her anything without finding out for sure," I say, annoyance rising like bile in my throat.

"Then we'll find out for sure." His voice seems very far away. "But don't you think she deserves to know?"

That, I can't answer. But Luke certainly deserves to know. As does Starr. And I suppose, on some level, I do, too. Yet here

I sit, getting more pissed by the minute. And hating myself for it because I don't understand *why* I'm so pissed.

I get up, brushing off my butt. "Fine. Whatever you want."

"El? What's wrong?"

"Nothing," I say, heading for the door. "I just don't want to stay out here too long, in case Starr wakes up and comes looking for me—"

I gasp when Luke's hand tightens around my arm. "Why the hell are you so upset? I thought this was what you wanted, to finally get this out in the open?"

"I never said that!"

"You didn't have to."

Even in the weird orangey glow from the streetlamp, I can see remorse camping out in his eyes. For some reason, this makes me even crazier.

"Oh, so now *you've* decided everybody should know, it doesn't matter what I think?"

"What are you talking about? Of course it matters what you think! It always did—"

"Did it? Did it, Luke? When I told you I was pregnant, whose idea was it not to tell Tina?"

His brows dips. "It was both of ours—"

"No, it wasn't. Not at first. You asked me if we could keep it a secret, and I agreed, because I loved—" my voice catches "—both of you. And now—"

I stop myself, before I say too much. Before I feel too much.

"Ellie…" His breath leaves his lungs in a rush. "All I'm tryin' to do is fix things."

"Why?" I say, my eyes burning. "Because now that Tina and you won't be making babies, it's safe to acknowledge Starr as yours?"

Like tiny, poisonous darts, the words are out of my blow-gun of a mouth and embedded in their target before I even knew I was taking aim.

Just what I needed tonight, to connect with my inner bitch.

"Shit, Luke, I'm sorry, I didn't mean—"

But the devastation in his eyes stops dead in its tracks whatever I thought I was going to say.

A second later, he's gone.

See, this is why we keep the truth to ourselves, if we even acknowledge it at all: because it simply hurts too damn much. It hurts to hear it, it hurts to say it...

It just hurts. Period.

chapter 20

Okay, I've got a question: When the hell did my daughter and my sister bond? How did I miss this?

I've clearly been spending way too much time in this basement. But when I asked Starr about it, all she said was, "Because she looked like she could use a friend."

Oh, to be five again.

Anyway, I made this rather startling discovery this morning when Jen asked me if she could take Starr to the mall with her, and Starr said, "Please, Mama?" and before I could mutter, "Uh, sure, I guess…" they were gone. I was half concerned Jen would forget she had a child in her care and leave her someplace, but since they both returned an hour ago—whispering and giggling—I guess my worries were groundless.

Some things, you don't try to understand, you just accept. Like gravity. Or that strange redheaded dude who does the 1-800-CALL-ATT commercials.

Now, as I sit hunched over the cutting table (Dolly went home an hour ago), pinning the size Large pattern to many layers of chiffon and trying to ignore the cramp in my gut brought on by my conversation with Luke last night, my daughter is imploring me to "come see what Aunt Jennifer's doing in the kitchen."

I remember the kitchen. Sort of. That's where the coffeepot and microwave are, right?

"Come *on*," Starr says, grabbing my hand to drag me off the stool. I trudge behind her, yawning, fabric fluff and thread bits clinging to my T-shirt and hair.

My house smells like Heaven. And my sister, when I reach the kitchen, looks…happy. If a little possessed, flitting from counter to table to oven, mixing and checking and peering at cookbooks. So somebody really does use those things. I always wondered about that.

"Don't worry," she says, grinning. "You'll never even taste the arsenic."

"I didn't know you cooked," I say, standing in the doorway since I'm afraid I'll get trampled if I step any farther inside.

She glances up, her smile…shy? Something. "One of the few things I *can* do. But I hadn't felt much like it before now. Besides, I didn't want to intrude."

I frown.

"It's your kitchen, after all."

Starr and I look at each other and burst out laughing. Jen smiles. I think she gets it. Then she says, "Everything should be ready in about twenty minutes. I thought maybe we'd eat in the dining room?"

"With candles and the pretty dishes?" Starr pipes up.

"If it's okay with your mom."

Honey, right now I don't care if I eat in the street.

Twenty minutes later, all I can say is…my sister sure knows her way around a chicken breast. The chicken's been pounded thin and is rolled around a stuffing with…stuff in it. Cheese and crunchy bits and things. Whatever, it's terrific. Even Starr's eating it (I guess if you deprive a child of real food long enough, she'll eat anything). When Jen brings out a bottle of wine, though, I shake my head.

"None for me, I have to work tonight."

"No, it's okay, it's nonalcoholic," she says, expertly uncorking it and pouring it into a pair of Waterford wineglasses that were my grandmother's pride and joy. "I seem to recall you and alcohol don't do very well together."

"How would you know that?"

Jen glances at Starr, who's busy picking the mushrooms out of her green beans, then says in a low voice, "Like I didn't know what was going on that night when you were fourteen? You know, when Tina brought you back home?"

"Ah. And I suppose you took great delight in ratting on me."

"Oh, absolutely. Only Mom said your misery was punishment enough."

"That would have been my take on it." I hold up my still-clean bread plate, a simple ivory Lennox pattern with gold trim. "These were the meat dishes, remember?"

"Ohmigod, you're right, I'd forgotten. From the Kosher phase. How long was that, anyway?"

"Two years? Three?"

"No, it must've been four, because I remember it was two years before Mama died that Nana went into Jewish overdrive."

I don't say anything, not wanting to spoil the mood. I mean, not only am I enjoying the food, but I'm actually enjoying my sister's company. Since I have no idea when the potion's going to wear off, I intend to make the most of it.

"I'm done," Starr announces. "C'n I be excused?"

I glance at her plate. "You ate three bites."

"Four. And I'm full."

Swear to God, the kid is an airfern. How I've managed to keep her alive this long is beyond me.

"Yeah, okay," I say, waving her off. As she scrambles down out of the chair, Jennifer calls out, telling her there's chocolate mousse for dessert.

"You do realize," I say when Starr's gone, "you're making it very hard to remember why I don't like you."

She looks genuinely hurt. "Still?"

"Jen, get real. It's gonna take more than one meal and a couple of noncombative conversations for me to trust you." I take a sip of the wine. It's good, but even I can tell it's missing something. Like fat-free ice cream, it's just not the same thing. "I mean, can you blame me?"

"No," she says on a sigh. "I suppose not." She takes a small bite of her Chicken Whatever—I've noticed she doesn't eat much more than Starr, which is why I suppose she's not much bigger than Starr, either—and says, "I'm not here because Stuart lost his job."

I tense. "You're...not?"

Sad eyes meet mine, a second sigh drifting across the table like goose down. "No. Oh, he lost his job. And he's somewhere in the Midwest. Well, I suppose he is. Actually, he could be on the moon, for all I know. Since the divorce papers came from an attorney in Syosset."

"Oh, Jen...I'm so sorry." And I am. No, really. As much as I can be for someone I don't totally trust, anyway.

Judging from the look on her face, there's more.

"And there's more," she says, getting up from the table and disappearing into the kitchen, returning seconds later with a glass and my grandfather's bourbon. Yes, the same bottle from nearly six years ago. Should be *real* potent stuff by now. She pours herself a ladylike inch in the glass, only to knock it back like a trucker. "When I first came here, though, I had no idea what was on his mind. Which was, apparently, to dump me. And clean me out. Everything was in both our names, and he took it all. And canceled the credit cards. Except for my jewelry, my clothes and the car, it's all gone. I wouldn't have any cash at all if it weren't for the money from Leo."

"So...the money from the sale of the house...?"

"Gone." She pours herself another shot, downs it in one. "Honest to God, I didn't plan on staying here for more than a week or two." Her eyes get all teary, although whether to the booze or her situation, I'm not sure. "But now I've got no place else to go. I'm *homeless,* Ellie. I'm fucking *homeless.*"

No, you're not, your home is right here with Starr and me, is what I should be saying, right this very minute, my hand over hers, soothing and reassuring. Except right this very minute, a little me is running around inside my brain screaming *Aiiiiiiiieeeeeeeeeeeeeee.*

Oh, poop. Now she's crying. Big, honking sobs into one of the linen napkins I never use because they're a bitch to wash and iron.

Damn. I'd really wanted to finish my dinner.

Oh a sigh, I get up and go around the table, kneeling beside her and taking her hands. I can't believe I'm about to say this, but here goes:

"You've always got a home here, you know that. You can stay as long as you need, until you figure out what your next step is."

I figured I might as well plant the idea that there needs to *be* a next step, although my comment is met with a wailed, *"What the hell kind of 'next step' is there for an unemployed t-t-trophy wiiife?"*

Hey, she said it, not me. But I'm guessing a liberal arts degree from Queens College, followed by ten years of hosting charity dos and business dinners have not exactly rendered my sister a hot commodity, employment-wise.

My knees are killing me, so I get up while I still can. "We'll figure something out."

"You sure?"

Oh, God. She looks so hopeful. So naive. So miserable.

"Sure I'm sure," I lie, returning to my seat. If I hurry, I can finish up my meal before the chicken gets that icky, gooey stuff all over it. Does this make me a cold, unfeeling bitch? Or just starved—and grateful—for decent food?

Over the next several seconds, her sobs turn to sniffles, then hiccups. She belts back another shot of booze and says, "Maybe I c-could write a bo-ook."

I tell myself not to go there. If she thinks I didn't hear her, maybe she'll move on to something more practical. Like becoming a paratrooper. But nooo, apparently *this* is the idea that catches fire in her underutilized brain.

"I could get an agent, and he—or she—could get me an advance, and then I could get my own place, nothing too fancy, maybe a cute little one-bedroom on the Upper West Side, where I could look out at Central Park while I write."

I'm not making this up, I swear.

"What would you write about?"

Her brow crinkles. For about two seconds. Then she brightens like the sun coming out after a storm. The classic symptoms of alcohol-induced manic depression. "My life as a trophy wife, what else?"

And with that, she pops up from her seat and begins snatching dishes off the table (when she goes for my plate, I grab it and growl at her), prattling away about titles and chapter headings and God knows what else, ending with, "Can I borrow your computer? I might as well get started right away, while the idea is still fresh."

Wow. I didn't even know she typed. Except then she says, "It does have ViaVoice, doesn't it?"

"What the hell's that?"

She sighs, but it's the sigh of someone confronting an unexpected, but otherwise minor, obstacle to her goal. "I suppose I'll just have to make do," she says, then sweeps into the kitchen, her hands full of plates, only to turn back and say, "But don't think for a minute I'm going to mooch off you and not keep up my end of the workload. From now on, think of me as…as your housekeeper!"

I just manage not to choke.

Heather's wedding is two weeks away.

Jen is now the fastest hunt-and-peck typist on the Eastern seaboard (and cooking fabulous meals every night—this, I could get used to), I'm up to my eyeballs in chiffon and taffeta, and I keep shoving the Luke/Starr issue to the back of my brain like that sparkly sweater on the top shelf of my closet that Leo gave me five Christmases ago. The one I either need to give away or wear, already.

I called Luke and apologized for being an unreasonable, hysterical, pain in the can. He said it was okay, he understood, but considering he immediately said he was busy and rang off, my guess is he hates me. Since I'm none too thrilled with myself these days, I can't exactly blame him.

And it's hot. The first week of June and the temperature's already hovering around ninety. With humidity somewhere in the thousand percent range. Rain forest without all the pretty birds. I put in a small window air conditioner down here out of deference to Dolly, but the cool air stops precisely ten feet from the appliance. My work area is precisely a foot and a half beyond that. Even with a six-foot tall industrial fan blowing right on me, it's like sitting in a vat of stew. Why would anyone in their right mind love summer? Call me crazy, but I prefer seasons where I don't worry about mold growing under my breasts.

Except for Jennifer, who, even without the booze, is in a state of euphoria with this book of hers, my black mood has apparently infected everyone around me. The cat won't even stare at me anymore. Starr spends more and more time at the Gomezes', or with Jennifer, which is making me feel more and more guilty—about dumping on Liv, about being too busy to play with my child, which was the whole reason for my staying home to begin with—which in turn is making me even crankier.

Even Dolly is making me cranky, which only goes to show how close to the edge I am. Being cranky with Dolly is like being cranky with Mrs. Santa, for God's sake. Besides being a crackerjack seamstress, she's one of those people who just never seems to get upset about anything. Which is probably what's annoying me about her. Bitching is meant to be a group sport, dammit.

I glance across the room, where we've rigged a pipe over a pair of ladders to hang the dresses that are nearly finished so their hems will "grow" before we finish them, and some of the crabbiness dissipates. I have to say, seeing the gowns all in a row like that, they're really pretty. And I'm proud of them, that I made them from scratch. Of course, it's a fluke, this design—remember all the ones I tossed?—but all the girls look good in it, and Heather's happy, and that's all that matters.

What's strange, though, is that, as much as I'm looking forward to getting this project out of my hair, I think—I can't believe I'm saying this—I'm going to miss it, too. In other words, I wouldn't mind taking on another wedding, or making a prom dress now and then. At least until I figure out what I really want to be when I grow up.

You can stop laughing now.

My cell rings; at the sight of Liv's number, my heart jumps into my throat. I was never like this before I had a kid, always expecting the worst. And what's crazy is—knock on wood—Starr's never had anything worse than a skinned knee or a cold. Liv has boys, Liv sees gushing blood on a regular basis, yet she doesn't get as flustered with her three as I do with my one—

"Aren't you going to answer your phone, sweetheart?" Dolly asks.

"Hey, Liv," I say calmly into the phone. "What's up?"

"I really hate to bother you, but my kitchen sink's stopped up and I can't get it unclogged, no matter how much Liquid-Plumbr I put in it. I think maybe one of the boys dropped something in the drain. And Mickey won't be home for hours."

Since nowhere in there are the words "your child is unconscious," all is well. Clogged drains, I can handle.

"No problem, I'll be right over. Just run lots of cold water in the sink to dilute all that Liquid-Plumbr, okay?"

Telling Dolly I'll be back soon, I gather up my (Leo's) handy-dandy toolbox and head next door. The apartments really don't take much of my time, as it turns out, although I noticed the other day all the windows need new screens. Some of them have holes big enough to let Bigfoot through. Theoretically, I could make them myself. I mean, really—how is this different than making a dress? You cut the screening, you fit it to the frame, right? Piece of cake.

Once there, feeling oddly proud of myself, I shoo everyone out of the kitchen, don my heavy rubber gloves, goggles and face mask in case of splashing Liquid-Plumbr (ah, if they could see me at Nikky Katz's now) and take my trusty wrench to the pipe trap under the sink. A few minutes later, ta-da!

"What was it?" Liv says from the doorway.

I hold up a half-decomposed chunk of plastic. "I'm guessing a Lego guy."

Liv sighs, then says, "Is Dolly working today?"

"Yeah. Why?"

Liv gets her purse down from a hook by the back door and digs something out of it. "Would you mind giving this to her? She bought some groceries for me the other day, I need to reimburse her."

"Sure, no problem."

Liv hands what turns out to be a check to me, faceup. On pure reflex, I glance down at it.

And nearly faint.

chapter 21

"Is everything okay?" Dolly says from her machine when I return. She's feeding a layer of chiffon through the hem-rolling attachment; when I don't answer, she looks up, giving me a puzzled look through her glasses. "With the sink, I mean?"

"The sink's fine."

"Then what—?"

"Liv gave me something to give to you." I walk over and hand her the check, my heart pounding. "I take it Dolly's not your real name?"

She starts, then slowly, carefully folds the check and slips it into her apron pocket. "It's my nickname. Nobody's called me Sonja for years."

"Except my grandfather?"

"What…what makes you think—?"

"You're in his will."

On a soft gasp, she turns away, her hands trembling like frail, indecisive insects. When she speaks, it's barely above a whisper. "He wasn't supposed to do that...tell anybody..."

"Is that why you never said anything to me?"

Her hands, still shaking, smooth the chiffon, over and over. "Why would I have said anything if I thought you didn't know?"

She has a point.

"But people suspected," I say gently. "You have to know that."

She stills. "And what, exactly, did they suspect?"

"That my grandfather was having an affair."

"I see." Her voice sounds far away; the oddest little smile tilts her lips, as though this news actually pleases her a little. She finally looks at me, worrying her lip in her teeth for a moment before asking, "You said I was in his will?"

"Yes. You're the beneficiary of a mutual fund. A fairly nice one, according to the lawyer—"

"I don't want it. You keep it, save it for Starr."

"I can't. It's yours by rights. I mean, you can do whatever you want with it, give it away, whatever—"

"Yes, yes, I see."

Her mouth pulls tight, a clear indication this whole conversation is making her nervous. But she says, staring hard at the rumpled chiffon under her hands, "It was a long time ago."

"Was it?"

Several seconds pass. "I loved your grandfather. But I'm not proud of what we did. Of how...we handled things."

I don't mean, or want, to sound judgmental. I only want to find out what happened. But I know, no matter how carefully I ask the questions burning inside my head, or how I phrase them, she's going to think I'm condemning her.

"Were...either your husband or my grandmother still alive when you—"

"No!" Her head whips around, her eyes on fire. "Not in the way—" Leaving the chiffon panel pinned to the sewing machine like a butterfly specimen, she bounds out of her chair, sending a box of straight pins delicately clattering onto the linoleum. "I can't...I'm sorry," she says, fumbling for her purse from beside the sewing machine. "I'm...not feeling well, I need to go home...."

"But the will—"

Her sharp, achy gaze cuts me off. "Not today, sweetheart. Please."

After she leaves, I grab the magnet I keep for just this purpose, squatting down to gather the pins. If Dolly—Sonja—didn't want me to know her identity, why'd she insinuate herself into Starr's and my life? To maybe, somehow, reconnect with Leo? I sigh. Who knows?

Crazy. All those years Liv's lived next door, all the times I'd seen her grandmother come and go, and I'd never suspected—

Oh, for heaven's sake. Am I slow or what? Liv and Mickey getting that apartment wasn't some random occurrence. And all that about my not being able to sell the house as long as the original tenants wanted to stay...

I go over to Dolly's machine and finish off the rolled hem, then remove the chiffon panel from the machine. My head is spinning. Now that Dolly knows I know, will she eventually tell me more?

Or will I even ever see her again?

I suddenly can't quite catch my breath. What if she never comes back, and I'm left with all these bridesmaids' dresses to finish on my own?

Sorry. That just sort of slipped out.

As do a couple of tears. Okay, maybe I don't know all the particulars—or any of the particulars, when you get right down to it—but I knew Leo. And Dolly might be a bit eccentric (who isn't?), but she's sweet and generous and kind. I can see why my grandfather fell in love with her. Especially as sweet and generous and kind were never qualities I associated with my grandmother. God, how awful it must have been for Dolly to have heard about my grandfather's death without even being able to talk to anybody about it. Or even react. It's all so romantic and tragic, I can't stand it—

"Ellie?"

I grab a tissue to wipe my cheeks, then look up to see a glowing Jennifer standing at the foot of the stairs, waving a sheaf of papers in her hand. "I finished Chapter One!"

Ohmigod. Jennifer.

She'll be thrilled to bits to hear this news, doncha think?

"I see," my sister says when I finally tell her that night, after I put Starr to bed. We're in her room, me cross-legged on the bed eating an apple (yes, I do occasionally eat G-rated food), her twisted around in the chair in front of the old desk where she's set up the laptop she bought after she sold off a tennis bracelet.

"That's it?" I say when nothing else seems to be forthcoming. I'd expected ranting, raving. Foaming at the mouth, at the very least. Instead, I'm facing a picture of total calm.

Creepy.

Jen frowns. "What am I supposed to say? Am I happy about her working for you? No. Is this important relative to the mess my own life is in right now? Again, no."

Ah. Once again, it's All About Jen. Have to hand it to her, though—she sure knows how to prioritize.

I take a bite of my apple. "We don't know for sure that either of them were actually unfaithful."

"Tell me you're not that naive."

"There's a difference between naiveté and accusing someone without proof."

Jen gets up, grabbing her ever-present bottle of Evian and joining me on the bed, where she piles pillows behind her back and settles against the old maple headboard, legs stretched out, feet crossed at the ankles. Her toenails, peeking out from beneath the hems of a pair of raw silk drawstring pants, are a brilliant rose color, reminding me of how long it's been since I painted mine. She takes a swig of her water, screwing the top back on before saying, "Do you think I'm self-involved?"

Uh-huh. This from a woman who, in less than five seconds, for no discernible reason, switched the subject from Dolly and my grandfather to herself.

"What is this, a trick question?"

The old Jennifer would have probably scratched my eyes out. The new Jennifer, however, simply smiles wryly. "Let me rephrase that. If I told you I've been thinking about why I am the way I am, would you listen?"

"As long as you didn't expect immediate absolution, sure, why not? Could be amusing."

She takes another sip of water, her eyes fixed on my face. "You're not perfect, either, you know."

"No arguments there. But at least I never acted like I was."

After a moment, my sister rises and crosses to the open window, removing the screen. For a second I think, ohmigod, she's going to jump, only to realize, since she'd just land in the grassy side yard two stories below, she'd be doing well to get a broken ankle. Which would hurt. And I can't see Jennifer willingly inflicting pain on her own person. Then she fishes a package of cigarettes out of her purse, putting up one hand when I let out a squawk.

"Don't worry, I'm not going to sully your airspace." She lights up, settling her rear end on the window ledge, dangling the cigarette outside. Somewhere a pigeon is coughing. "I know, I know. I've gotta quit."

"Did I say anything?"

"You don't have to. Nonsmokers have it stamped on their foreheads. And I actually had, for a few months. Then my life went to hell in a handbasket." One shoulder hitches as she takes a drag. "What can I tell you? Backsliding happens." Her eyes scan the room. "You have any idea how much I used to hate this house?"

"You didn't exactly keep it a secret," I say, munching and feeling very virtuous. About the apple, I mean.

"No, I suppose not."

"Although…I always thought it was *me* you hated. Not the house."

She looks at me for a moment, then shakes her head. "I didn't hate you, Ellie. I was jealous as hell of you."

I nearly choke on the bite in my mouth. "*Jealous?* Of *me?* Why?"

"Because…I don't know. Because you never seemed to be afraid of anything."

"You're not serious."

"No, really. Think back, how you were always the first one to make friends with anyone new in the neighborhood, how you'd stand up to all the Scardinare boys. Even your clothes." She waves at my outfit, a gauzy man's Indian shirt over a black tube top (that I swear shrunk since last summer) and turquoise paperbag pants. "It takes guts to dress the way you do."

Or poverty. But she doesn't need to know that.

"Is that supposed to be a compliment?"

"Yeah, it is. Because ever since you were little, you've never given a damn what anybody else thought." She shakes her head. "Unlike me, who's *always* worried about what other people would think. Not that it ever did any good, since you were the favorite, anyway."

Another piece of apple gets lodged in my windpipe. After I cough it up (and let this be a lesson to me: Nobody ever choked on ice cream.), I finally get out, "You are totally nuts, you know that?"

"Oh, Ellie," Jennifer says on a sigh, "Mom and Dad always looked at me like there'd been a mix-up at the hospital. No matter what I did, I never felt like a real part of the family. Why do you think I cozied up to Nana so much?"

I resist the impulse to point out that Jen might've fit in more if she'd stopped with all the weird shit. And, sorry, the same goes for my grandmother. Although, if I really think about it, it's not all that clear which of us were the "normal" ones, and which were the misfits.

"Okay, so you and Nana were different from the rest of us. But that doesn't mean Mom and Dad didn't love you, for God's sake."

"Loved me, sure. Because I was theirs. Understood me, no."

"Is that why you acted like a brat?"

She shrugs, unoffended. "Isn't that why most kids act like brats? To get attention? To compensate for everything they think they don't have?"

"Compensate for what? Because…I got along with the Scardinares? Because I dressed strangely? What?"

"Because you were so damn talented, why else? Jesus, Ellie— I used to look at your sketches and want to scream, wondering why *you* were the brilliant one while I was so totally useless."

For several seconds, I can't speak. "You *are* nuts. Why do you think I dressed the way I did, acted the way I did? Not because I didn't give a shit, but because I *did*. I've got news for you—it hurt, that our grandmother fawned over you and couldn't've cared less about me. And that I could never figure out why. So the clothes, the attitude…don't you get it? It was all a front! Because I couldn't compete with my beautiful, smart, older sister on her level."

"Oh, right!" Jen blows her smoke out the window, then lets out a dry laugh. "I was so smart that after four years of college, I'm not qualified to do a goddamn thing. So what did I do? I got married. *That* really worked out, huh?"

Notice how she didn't dispute the *beautiful* part of my observation. But I scramble onto my knees on the bed and say,

"And like my life has? I didn't exactly plan on being a single mother, you know. Especially at twenty-two. And excuse me? *What* talent? No offense, but you don't have a clue what you're talking about."

She points to *her* outfit, a chic, perfectly coordinated raw silk confection. Dior is my guess. Last year's, but still.

"Okay, so you've got a good eye," I grudgingly admit. "But that doesn't mean—"

"Oh, and like somebody else designed those dresses in the basement?"

"Those were a fluke."

"Were not."

"Were too!"

"Were *not!* Oh, for Christ's sake, what is this—the Who-Fucked-Up-More competition?"

I actually laugh. Then I crawl to the other side of the bed and sit on the edge. "Jen, look—I think it's very nice, if a little bizarre, that you're trying to bolster my ego like this, but nobody exactly encouraged me to pursue a design career. Nobody at FIT…not even Mama."

After a moment, she turns back to the window. "No surprise there."

"What's that supposed to mean?" I say, even though the words are barely out of my mouth before I know exactly what she means. I hold up one hand. Yet even as I say, "Because she never got her own career off the ground?" something nags at the back of my brain, like a half-remembered dream.

"And did you ever wonder why? She was really talented, El. Don't you remember hearing her sing?"

"Sure," I say, although I don't really. Not clearly. "So maybe she was trying to protect me, Jen. It's hard, trying to make it in the arts." But that niggling half thought is still there, just out of reach. "Besides, she never tried to talk me out of a career in fashion, just in design—"

"For God's sake, you were only thirteen when Mom died! Don't you think that's a little early to be making judgment calls about someone's prospects? Besides, you know as well as I do there are a helluva lot less talented designers with very successful careers, because they've got the drive and determination *to* make it!"

"But it takes more than that—"

"Dammit, Ellie—look at me! I've got nothing! *Nothing.* All I know how to do is cook and give parties and blow jobs." She smirks. "And apparently, I don't even do that very well, according to Stuart. Now I have no husband, no marriage, no money and no skills."

Seconds pass before I say, "You have your book."

"Oh, right. *My book.* Talk about a piece of crap. Okay, so maybe it's got some therapeutic value, but please. The chances of anyone actually wanting to buy it are slim to none. Whereas you have a great kid and so much talent it's unbelievable, not to mention a man who's crazy about you, and you're sitting here with your thumb up your ass, not doing a damn thing about any of it. So who's the pathetic one here, huh?"

"Whoa, whoa, whoa—" I'll deal with the "pathetic" remark later. *"A man who's crazy about me?"*

"Hello? Luke?"

"That's crazy."

"No, *you're* crazy. You're in love with the guy, you've always been in love with the guy, and why the hell you let Tina move in on him, I do not know. Dammit, Ellie, I put the moves on him right in front of you, and you did *nothing.*"

"I did *nothing* because…wait—you were *testing* me?"

"I was bored. I thought it would be amusing. Except then I just got mad. That you can't see what's right smack in your face."

I get up from the bed, my stomach roiling. "I don't want to talk about this—"

"Which is the whole problem with this family, isn't it?"

Almost to the door, I turn back around. "What?"

"I said, that's the whole problem with this cockamamie family. Nobody ever wants to talk about anything. Or admit anything. Or make waves. I mean, Jesus, whatever was going on between our grandfather and this Sonja, it was pretty obvious nobody was happy about it. But it was easier to pretend that everything was fine, rather than actually doing something about the situation."

Well, at least we're finally back on topic. Not that it's helping. God, I'm so confused. Life was much easier when my sister didn't have a train of thought to keep up *with.*

"And what were they supposed to do? Divorce their spouses and marry each other?"

"How the hell should I know? But it would've been a damn sight better than living a lie!"

I angle my head at her. "You better be careful. If you get any deeper, you're gonna drown."

On a breathy half laugh, Jen threads one hand through her hair and sinks back onto the edge of the mattress. Then she lifts her eyes to mine. "See, it wasn't until I could admit that Stuart's leaving was at least partly my fault that other things began to make sense, too. Sure, maybe he only wanted a trophy wife and after ten years he got bored. And maybe I had a hard time accepting that he'd been an asshole for some time, because there were a lot of perks to being a trophy wife, even to an asshole. But maybe if I'd put more effort into my marriage, maybe if I hadn't *acted* like a trophy wife, if I'd forced myself out of my comfort zone, maybe I'd still be married today. Or maybe I wouldn't have married Stuart to begin with, or would have found the balls to leave *him,* and would actually have a life by now. But it's scary on the other side, isn't it? Who knows what sorts of monsters and icky things lurk past those boundaries?"

"That's your problem, not mine—"

"Bullshit, Ellie. Our excuses may be different, but in the end, it all comes down to the same thing—we're petrified of facing who we really are, because we're both petrified of failing. Just like our mother was. And damned if she didn't infect both of us with her fears."

Outside, somebody walks by with a boom box so loud my teeth rattle. How it doesn't wake Starr is beyond me, but she's always been able to sleep through anything, even as a tiny baby. Eventually, the reverberations from hip-hop music die down, leaving in their place Jen's words, pounding viciously inside my skull, their meaning every bit as distorted and indecipherable as the words to the rap song had been.

"But the way I figure it," Jen's saying, apparently oblivious to the fact that I'm falling apart over here, "I can't get much lower than I am now. I mean, come on—coming back to live in this house again? If that's not failure, I don't know what is. But even though I feel like last week's garbage, you know what? My heart's still beating. I'm still in the game, even if I have no idea what the rules are. And I'm going to finish this book and start sending it out, because what have I got to lose? My pride? *God!*" She bounces up from the bed. "I feel as if I've been anesthetized for the past ten years, like I was living in a world that was only half-real, you know?"

She doesn't elaborate. Thank God, since I'm way too wrung out to deal with any more of Jen's liberated consciousness tonight. Especially since she seems hell-bent on dragging mine to the meetings right along with hers.

Now her hands are on my shoulders, her gaze locked with mine. "I realize this is about a decade too late—"

I shut my eyes. *Please, God, make her go* away…

"—but I'm really sorry about my wedding. Not letting you be part of it, I mean."

What is this, double-coupon day at the Salvation Store?

"Oh," I say.

"That's it?"

"What do you want me to say? You treated me like crap the whole time we were growing up. In fact, you treated me like crap up until a month ago—"

"Please don't hate me, El," she says in a small voice. Her eyes well up. "You're all I've got left."

Do you believe this?

"I don't want to hate you," I say. "I never did. But I'm not all that wild about being thought of as a last resort."

"I didn't mean it like that!"

"Then learn to choose your words more carefully. Or reconcile yourself to the fact that this is going to take some time."

"God. You're really going to make me grovel, aren't you?"

"That was the plan, yep."

"I see." A sigh. "I suppose that's better than telling me to fuck off."

Only marginally, but I don't tell her that.

In any case, our little exchange has left my sister après-mud-pack radiant (sloughing off dead skin cells, sloughing off a couple decades worth of bad blood—all the same thing). While I, on the other hand, feel as though I tripped in the middle of the street while crossing Times Square at rush hour. And nobody noticed.

I leave her to her radiance and her book and return to my room. I should go back to work, but it ain't gonna happen tonight. Instead, I rip off my clothes and toss on an old sleep T (sleeping nude is no longer an option when a small child pays regular visits to your bed at night), yank back the covers and collapse on my stomach across the bed, staring at Frito, who's perched on the two-foot-high pile of discarded clothes on the only chair in my room, giving me the evil eye for having turned on the lamp and disturbed his sleep.

"So sue me. You're supposed to be with Starr. Besides, you sleep twenty hours a day."

He narrows his eyes. *So whatcher point?*

I flop onto my back to stare at the overhead light fixture, delicately frosted in cobwebs. The overhead light fixture I was supposed to change out for a ceiling fan two years ago. Where the hell is that thing, anyway? I distinctly remember buying one. And bringing it into the house. After that, it's a blank. I suppose I should clean off the cobwebs, except the only way I can reach the fixture is to move the bed, and if I'm going to move the bed, I might as well put up the ceiling fan. Wherever it is. Except the fan blades would collect even more cobwebs than the fixture does, which means I'd have to just keep moving the bed, and that's a pain in the butt, so maybe I should just forget about it.

I think I just solved a problem. I'm just not entirely sure what.

I let out a yelp when a large, furry, rumbling thing lands on my stomach. I lift my head—the rest of my body being pinned beneath the large, furry, rumbling thing—to see Frito massaging my belly with a goony look on his face. Apparently cotton jersey turns him on. Terrific. Now he's in my face, letting out these strange *errnking* sounds and bumping my chin. Would someone please explain to me how a cat that only gets dry cat food can have fish breath?

Gingerly, I reach up to scratch his head. He actually lifts up to bump my hand, his eyes becoming slits of ecstasy as I scratch.

"What is this, reconciliation week?" Frito opens one eye, smiling that smug you-should-only-know cat grin just as my cell phone rings on my nightstand. I nearly dislocate my shoulder trying to reach it without disturbing the twenty-pound furbag settling in for the duration on my stomach.

"Hey, El. It's me. Tina."

I should have guessed.

chapter 22

"I can't believe Jason's gay," Tina says the next night, seated across from me at one of a half dozen bistro tables crammed into three square feet of sidewalk space in front of Pinky's, out of deference to their smoking customers. We've been here for about a half hour; the heat rising from the pavement is slowing searing my butt through the tiny metal chair. I'm wearing the minimum amount of clothing I can without risking arrest, but mugginess clings to my skin like a film of exhaust-flavored Pam.

"I know. The last thing I expected him to come out with. As it were," I add, and we both laugh.

On the surface, we're just a couple of friends catching up, falling back into old patterns of conversation as though nothing's changed. But it has. For me, anyway. And judging from Tina's shredded cocktail napkin, the way her eyes never quite meet mine, my guess it has for her, too. We sound the same, we look the same, but we'll never feel the same.

I've filled her in, about Leo and the childcare incident and how I'm home now, at least for the time being. I tell her about Jennifer's moving back, but not about our most recent conversation, since I haven't processed that one myself. I tell her about Sonja.

In her turn, Tina tells me she's got a good job, a better job, doing payroll for some machine parts manufacturer in Jersey. And a really nice apartment. With a pool. And a washer-dryer right in the kitchen. She's thinking about getting a dog. Something little, like one of those itty-bitty poodles or something.

Nobody's mentioned Luke. Yet. But he's here as surely as if he were sitting at the table with us.

A couple goes into the bar, releasing a puff of booze-scented air-conditioning. I inch my chair closer to the door, wincing as the metal seat rips the top layer of skin off the backs of my bare thighs.

"So how's Starr?" Tina asks.

"She's good. My sister's staying with her tonight."

Tina nods, then lifts one hand to toy with a strand of newly copper-highlighted hair. "And...Luke? Do you see him much?"

Ah. Bouncing my straw up and down in my Coke, I say, "Not that much, no. We've both been busy."

"So...you haven't...?"

"Haven't what?"

"You know. Gotten together?"

I see the hopefulness in those clear blue eyes and get sick to my stomach. Which is stupid because I have no claim on the man and never have. No matter how I feel about him, the fact is he's never given me any indication that my feelings are reciprocated. And why should he? Whatever his motives for marrying Tina, the fact remains that he did. No matter how you slice it, our getting together now would be weird.

I look hard at my drink. "Of course not, don't talk crazy. Even if..." I stir the Coke frantically, releasing all the little bubbles. Then I look up at her. "I don't do rebound relationships, Tina."

No, just ten minute trysts in the shower that might have resulted in my daughter.

I cannot tell you how relieved she looks, even as she says, "It's not like I could've said anything, you know, if you two had started up something. I mean, it was me who practically shoved you into his arms, right? But then I got the final divorce papers to sign, and I don't know…" Her voice trails off. She takes a swallow of her gin-and-tonic and meets my gaze.

My stomach pitches. "So all that you said before…?"

"I was hysterical, you know? All the hormone swings after…" She reaches over, grabs my hand. "You never told him, did you? About the abortion?"

Since I don't dare open my mouth right now, I settle for shaking my head. Tina lets out a huge sigh, pressing her palm to her rampant cleavage. A pair of guys I've never seen turn the corner. I see the one poke the other, then point at us. Subtle. Sure enough, they make a beeline for us.

You know, it was bad enough when we used to have to fend off the freaks *inside* the bars. Now with this no-smoking thing, we gotta deal with the ones outside, too.

Thank you, Mayor Bloomberg.

"Hey, ladies," the shorter one says, not even pretending to look at my face. Funny how on some guys a soul patch is just not attractive. "What are you two beautiful women up to tonight?"

Okay, zero points for creativity, but I'll give him two for directness. Except then his buddy gets a negative ten with, "Yeah, wanna go back to my place and, you know, get it on?"

Am I wearing a Hard Up sign around my neck or what?

Except then Tina reaches over and takes my hand. "Sorry, guys," she says, winking at me, "but we've got our own private party planned for later."

"Hot damn!" Soul Patch says. "Chick on chick action!"

"Yeah," his buddy puts in. "Can we watch?"

"I dunno…" Tina's eyes slide to mine. "Should we?"

"Oh, I think we definitely should," I say. And as the turkeys high-five each other, Tina and I simultaneously grab their waistbands and pour our ice water down their crotches.

As the string of obscenities fade into the night—as does the laughter and applause from the other tables—Tina turns back to me, grinning. And I know that no matter how much things might have changed between us, or how much we might grow apart, that nothing will ever be able to completely sever the threads of lunacy and love that have always held our wacky friendship together.

Not even our being in love with the same man.

And I can see in her eyes that she knows this, too. Not just the nothing-will-ever-rip-us-apart part, but the we're-both-in-love-with-Luke part.

"I want another chance," she says, her eyes never leaving mine. "With Luke."

Funny how knowing something's going to hurt doesn't do diddly to alleviate the pain when it strikes. "What happened? Did you get cold?"

Her brows pucker. "Cold?"

"Yeah. Now you want your coat back."

The blossoms of bright red clash with the burgundy contouring under her cheekbones. "I'm sorry," she says to her drink. "I just had no idea how much I'd miss him."

A bead of sweat trickles down my back, making me twitch. "And what if Luke and I *had* started something?"

After a moment, she again lifts her gaze to mine. "Then I would've backed off."

"Really?"

Her brows nearly meet. "Yeah, really. But since you didn't, why are we even talking about this?"

"I don't know. Especially since whether the two of you get back together isn't up to you or me alone, is it?"

"But you could help. Like you always have."

I drain the last of the Coke from the glass, then fold my arms across my stomach, rattling the half-melted ice cubes at the bottom of the sweaty glass as I nurse the white-hot kernel of anger sizzling in my gut.

"Okay, cookie, it's like this," I say, watching her eyes go wide. "Maybe the coast is clear—although to be honest, I have no idea what Luke's thinking—but no way am I going to help you with this. All I can promise is that I'll stay out of your way. But if you want him, *you* figure out how to make that happen."

After a moment, she pushes out a heavy breath. "Okay, okay…you're right, this is something I've gotta do on my own."

"Only…" I can't believe I've got the nerve to say this. Because God knows, I don't have the right. "Don't you think you should tell him about the abortion?"

All the color drains from her face. "You know I can't do that!"

"Tina, honey…how can you even consider trying to pick up where you left off without fixing the problems that broke you up to begin with? Luke deserves to know exactly how strongly you feel about not having kids." I reach over and take her hand. "Just like you deserve someone who'll love you whether you want children or not."

Her mouth thins; she yanks her hand from mine, then gets up and tosses a few bills on the table. Déjà vu. Only this time, I follow suit, so that we hit the sidewalk at the same time. "And you know damn well," she says as a sudden, lung-suckingly hot breeze whips our hair, "there's no chance in hell we'll get back together if I tell him. And just where do you get off, anyway, judging me because I don't want kids?"

"I'm not judging you! Whether you have kids or not is totally your choice! But what's the point of trying to resurrect something with someone who *does?*"

When she tries to walk away, I grab her hand and pull her back around, locking our gazes. "Secrets are like cancers, Tina. Believe me, I know."

"You don't know shit—"

"Tina—" Oh, God. After everything I said, about waiting until I knew, about not being ready…Luke's going to hate me for this. But then, since he already does, what have I got to lose? "There's a chance Starr is Luke's."

For a long moment, her face registers nothing. Then her mouth quirks into a humorless smile.

"Tell me something I don't know," she says, then wrenches herself from my grasp, spins on her rope-soled wedgie and storms down the sidewalk, her tiny pleated skirt flouncing angrily with each step.

In spite of the loudest orchestra this side of Secaucus blaring from the stage, it's everything I can do not to lay my head down on the banquet table and take a little snooze. I doubt anyone would notice, since the dress I spent so long (two minutes) picking out to wear to Heather's wedding happens to be a perfect match for the seafoam green tablecloths.

My daughter is in here somewhere, having the time of her life. Even if she, too, is wearing a dress. When she found me curled up on the sofa in the basement at six this morning (I'd finished up the last bridesmaid hem at five) she'd patted my hand, told me I looked like holy hell and to go fix myself up before I scared somebody.

Nice kid I'm raising here.

Anyway, so here I am, somewhere in Great Neck, surrounded by five million wedding guests and dressed like a banquet table, sans the centerpiece. Whenever I'm tempted to doze off, somebody else comes up and tells me how gorgeous the dresses are and then asks me for my card. Which, if I had a grain of sense (or foresight) I would have had made up. I've taken all their numbers and said I'd get back to them.

I just didn't say when.

The minute this shebang is over, I'm down for three days straight. And when I wake up, I am on the A train, boy, headed straight for Manhattan. Pure torture, that's what it's been, knowing the city was less than an hour away and not being able to get to it. And you know what's really great about going into Manhattan? Getting to leave Dolly and Tina and Jen and Luke and all the rest of them *here*. Well, *there,* since I'm not *here* at the moment.

Okay, I'm gonna just prop my chin in my hands here, like this, and shut my eyes for a second…

"There you are! Smile!"

I jerk awake just in time to be blinded by the flash from one of the disposable cameras Heather's so thoughtfully left on the tables. By the time the dots stop dancing in front of my eyes, the picture-taker has disappeared. A good thing, I'm thinking, since I'm feeling a touch murderous right now.

Suddenly a golden image materializes in front of me. Frances, looking foxy as all get-out in this clingy gold jersey number that ninety percent of women *my* age can't wear. It's so unfair.

"Hey, baby," she says, leaning over to give me a hug, then sitting beside me. "You don't look like you're having much fun."

"Sure I am," I say covering a yawn with my hand, then blinking. "Can'tcha tell?"

She chuckles, then says, "You did fantastic. It's all anybody can talk about, how good you made everyone look."

I frown. "I thought that was the point."

"No, I'm serious. Look at Elissa over there. I've never seen her look so pretty. Or happy."

The size 24. It is true. She does look good. In fact, she looks fabulous.

Thanks to me.

I grin. It's a little wobbly, and I feel another yawn coming on, but I definitely grin. "I did that, huh?"

"Yes, you did. You know, baby, anybody can make a skinny girl look good." She lowers her voice, talking out the side of her mouth. "But it takes talent to make most of *these* women look good."

"Remember to tell me that again when I'm awake, 'kay?"

"You got it. Oh, look…Luke's dancing with Starr. Isn't that the cutest thing you ever saw?"

I look over. And because being next door to comatose leaves me with no emotional defenses whatsoever, longing swamps me, so swiftly and suddenly I can hardly breathe. Whatever's going on—or not—between Luke and me, he's refused to let Starr suffer for our sins. Or my sins, whatever. And the sight of him in a classic Christian Dior tux, holding Starr—in her frilly powder blue dress and black patent Mary Janes—up in his arms so she won't get stepped on, nearly takes me under. I imagine I can hear her laughter all the way over here. I can definitely see it, though.

Oh, yeah, I can definitely see it.

I've been too busy to think about anything but getting these damn dresses finished—Jennifer pretty much took over the house and the kid, much to my shock and profound relief—so I have no idea if Tina's spoken to Luke or not. If she has, Luke hasn't said word one to me.

I feel Frances's arm go around my shoulder; she presses her temple to mine and whispers, "All I want is to see all of you happy." She lifts her glass of champagne to her lips, then chuckles. "Even that one," she says, gesturing with the glass to Jason and…what's his name. Connor, that's it. He looks like a nice kid. If very Irish.

"Now if he were just Italian," Frances says, pulling away, "I'd be much happier about the whole thing."

As I said.

I look over at her. "Are you really okay? About Jason being gay?"

Frances is quiet for a moment, then says, "You know, I always thought, what's the big deal? People are who they are, right? Until suddenly it's one of your own you're talking about."

She takes my hand in hers, her wedding rings glinting in the overhead light. Her fingers are long and strong; she's recently started wearing false fingernails. Tonight they're polished a glimmering champagne color, putting mine (I was doing well to scrape a nail file across them before we left) to shame.

"You know what upset me most that night," she says, "when Jason came out? Well, besides finding out about Uncle Carmine," she says with a half grimace. "It wasn't so much that Jason was gay, but my reaction to it. I felt suckerpunched at how much I didn't want to believe it. Scared the hell out of me, like I didn't know who I was anymore."

"And now?"

One shoulder shrugs gracefully under the gold fabric. "I keep telling myself, he's the same kid he was before." A smile tilts her lips. "Better, actually, since he's not carrying around this huge, dark secret anymore." Then the smile droops a little. "But I worry. Because he's still so young. And young males aren't known for always making the smartest decisions, you know?"

I notice her gaze has shifted back to Luke, still dancing with Starr, and a slight chill crawls up my spine. Is she talking about Luke's marrying Tina? Or his letting the marriage die? Or—grinning, Luke spins Starr around, making her giggle— does Frances suspect more than she's ever let on?

"Why is it," I wonder aloud, "that nobody warns you *be-*

fore you have kids how much you're gonna worry about them?"

Frances chuckles, a dark sound I've always loved. "Oh, they do. We just don't hear them. Otherwise, nobody'd ever have kids." Then she squeezes my hand. "Things always have a way of working out, baby. Maybe not always the way we hoped, but they do."

"Oh, no."

"What?"

"You've turned into an old wise Italian woman, dispensing sage advice at the drop of a hat."

"Bite your tongue, little girl," she says as she gets up. "I've got a long way to go before I'm even close to old!"

With a wave, she's once again swallowed up by the crowd. I'm thinking of rousing myself enough to go find something else to eat—we already had dinner, but I can see there's munchies over by the cake—when Luke suddenly appears in front of me. Without my daughter.

I get to my feet, trying to see behind him. "Where's Starr?"

"Monica took her to the bathroom, she's fine." He holds out his hand, his eyes huge and sexy and unreadable. "Wanna dance?"

"Luke, I—"

"Dammit, just come dance with me. Before somebody's fourteen-year-old cousin gets any bright ideas."

I smile. "Maybe…that's not such a good idea."

"Why?" One eyebrow cocks. "Afraid I'll try to feel you up on the dance floor?"

I laugh, as something goes "*Hel*-lo" inside me. "No. Afraid I'll keel over on the dance floor."

"C'mon." He comes around the table and takes my hand, placing his other one on the small of my back to steer me out to the dance floor. "I won't let you keel over. I promise."

Underneath his palm, about a million skin cells have just

been startled awake and are now running around in confused circles and crashing into each other. "And about the other?"

"That," he says on a grin, his breath teasing my moussed-to-death hair, "I won't promise."

I tell myself—and my libido—to get a grip. This is Luke. Flirting is what he does. It doesn't mean anything, and never has. Please, we've been trading sexual banter since forever. Granted, there was a period there right after the shower episode during which we could barely look at each other, let alone banter. But once he settled into marriage, oddly enough, things eased up again. Even when Tina was around, he'd do this playful teasing thing with me. But he always kept it light and friendly, with absolutely no room for misinterpretation. He'd never do—and never did—a single thing to give Tina the idea that I was in any way a threat.

Which begs two questions: One, was she really not surprised when I told her about Starr, or did she just say that to save face?

And two, is she back in the picture?

Up until this moment, I hadn't realized just how weak my legs were. Logic tells me it's only exhaustion; my libido, however, is howling with laughter. The good news is, it's a slow dance, which requires a minimum expenditure of energy on my part. The bad news is, it's a slow dance, which requires bodily contact.

This is obviously not a problem for Luke, who pulls me close, tucking our linked hands against his chest, his other one still at the small of my back. Which, by the way, happens to be a major erogenous zone for me. A fact I'd totally forgotten until this very moment.

Keep it light, keep it light.

I look up and grin. "A word of warning—my hair could inflict serious injury, so you might not want to get too close."

"Yeah, I kinda noticed that. What the hell did you use on it? Superglue?"

"As good as."

"Women," he mutters, pulling me closer. Uh-oh. I'm about a millimeter away from the there's-nobody-here-but-us zone. Not good. Then he says, "Don't take this the wrong way, but the bags under your eyes don't go with the dress."

"Smart-ass."

He grins, but his brows are saying something else. "You look like you're ready to drop."

"Good call."

"Starr told me she found you asleep in the basement this morning."

I shrug. "No big deal."

Luke doesn't say anything for several seconds. Then: "You know I don't know anything about sewing or dresses or any of it, but I know everybody's really happy with what you did for them. Heather, especially. You're good at this, El. Damn good."

I try to smile, but it's getting wobblier by the second. Especially since my eyes are stinging. "You wouldn't kid around with a sleep-deprived person, would you?"

Suddenly, his expression goes serious. "I don't bullshit, Ellie. You know that. At least..." He takes a breath. "At least, not anymore."

"Oh."

Then his expression softens. "You can go ahead and lay your head on my chest, if you want. Unless you think your hair might make holes in the tux."

"No, I think we're safe."

Safe? Who the hell am I kidding? I'm slow dancing with a man I've had a thing for since I was six, a man with his hand planted firmly on an area of my body with, apparently, a direct link to my woefully neglected clitoris (Yeah, I know all about taking care of myself, but the thing about masturbation is, there's no one to cuddle with afterwards, is there?) and I'm so tired I can barely stand up. But not so tired that I don't think to say, "Doncha think people will get ideas if we look, you know, too cozy out here?"

He glances around. "Yeah, maybe you've got a point," he says, then leads me across the floor and outside a pair of French doors, onto this flagstone patio that overlooks the pool. It's nearly dark, the sky a luscious, diamond-studded violet edged in persimmon at the horizon. One of those summer breezes you can sense more than actually feel wicks the moisture off my skin; I shiver as Luke dances me over to a pocket of shadow, out of the line of sight.

"Now you can lean on me all you want, and nobody will know."

So the question is, is he being protective of me (for whatever reason) or himself? And why can't I push that question from my brain to my lips?

I look up at him. "But *I'll* know."

A funny little smile plays over his mouth, then he—cautiously—presses my head to his chest. My hair crunches like cellophane as I settle in. I should be thinking about all of this, trying to make sense of it, but my brain has gone night-night. So we just move slowly to the music, some ballad from before my time, my hair crunching, Luke humming (off-key), and this very pleasant warmth washes over me, a feeling of possibilities I'd never allowed myself to feel before, I realize.

I decide, because this is what I want to believe, that Tina's not back in the picture, because this is cozier than Luke would let us get if she were. Right? Of course, we *are* in the dark and he *hasn't* made a pass. A significant observation, I'm thinking. But then, why would he?

How's he gonna know it's okay to take a giant step if I don't say *Yes, you may?*

I think of all that stuff Jen said about our family always

playing it safe, not taking risks. And to somebody on the outside looking in, maybe it seems obvious that I should just tell him how I feel, already. But aside from the fact that he's just come out of a *very* long-term relationship, there's the little matter of my not being hot on the idea of sounding like some pathetic loser who's been pining away for him for a million years. Not that I *have* been pining, although I'm not going to pretend the seed hasn't been lying there, dormant and waiting. But timing is everything, you know? And speaking of seeds…

"Did you know," I say into his chest, "that we can order a paternity test kit online and get results in like a week?"

He squeezes the hand close to his chest. "You sure?"

"I checked several sites—"

"No. About doing this."

"Yeah," I say on a gust of breath. "And I really am sorry I freaked on you the other night. There's no excuse for how I behaved. Or what I said."

"Other than my behavior over the last five years? Ellie, you had every right to say what you did. Especially as I'm thinking maybe you weren't all that far off the mark. Maybe, subconsciously, I dunno…maybe Tina and me splitting up did have something to do with the timing."

There's that word again. I swallow.

"I have a confession to make—"

"You told Tina. That Starr might be mine."

My eyes bounce up to his. "How'd you—?"

A dry chuckle sifts through the humid air. "I told her, too. Which is when she told me you already had."

Shit.

"Oh, God, Luke—I'm sorry, I shouldn't've said anything without your knowledge—"

"Yeah, well, same here. So we're both blabbermouths."

Like I can dance with all these questions zipping around my

sleep-deprived brain. So I stop, staring at the white glow of Luke's pleated shirtfront.

"When did you talk to her?"

"About a week ago. I would've told you, but Mom told me how busy you were—"

"She didn't sign the papers, did she?"

Luke lets out a harsh sigh. "She wants to get back together, El. And there's too much history between us for me to just blow her off. I figure it's time I start figuring out how to fix problems instead of running away from them—"

"There you are! God, I've been looking all over the place for you!"

Luke practically pushes me away as his pregnant sister-in-law, my daughter in tow, make their way across the patio toward us. "Poor kid," Monica says as we emerge from the shadows. "She must've eaten too much and got sick."

"Sweetie, ohmigod!" I drop to my knees in front of her, my heart twisting at the miserable look on her face. "Did you make it to the bathroom?"

At that, her face crumples. "N-no. An' now everybody thinks I'm disgusting."

"Hey," Luke says, bending down, close enough for me to feel his body heat. My brain does an instant replay of his last words, and I kinda feel like tossing a few cookies myself. "Everybody gets sick sometimes," he says to Starr, "especially at things like this. Nobody thinks you're disgusting, okay?"

Holding my quietly weeping daughter, I look up at Monica. "Do I need to get it cleaned up?"

"Are you kidding? Like ten people swooped out of nowhere, had it taken care of so fast nobody even noticed, hardly." She touches Starr's hair. "So don't you worry about this another minute, sweetie, okay?"

Starr nods in my arms, but I can tell she's not convinced. She looks up at me. "C'n we go home now?"

"Sure, baby, right away. Let me just go find my purse—"

"I'll call you later," Luke says behind me.

I turn, just as the first clear thought I've had all night occurs to me. Which is that there are no absolute guidelines for how, or when, or even if, to tell the truth. That there's no point in saying *Yes, you may take a giant step* before, and unless, someone asks if he may. All I'd be doing is confusing the issue even more. If Luke's on the fence about this, then…then he's just going to have to decide which side to climb down on all by himself. Besides—and here's where being a basically honorable person is a real bitch—I did promise Tina I'd stay out of her way. So that's what I've gotta do.

"Luke, please—" Feeling my throat go tight, I haul my smelly daughter up into my arms. "Just…just leave me out of it, okay?"

Then I walk quickly away before I fall completely apart.

chapter 23

My mother absolutely adored Manhattan.

When Jen and I were kids, Mom used to take us into the city at least once a month, sometimes to shop, but mostly to go to the museums or to sightsee—she couldn't wait to take us up to the top of the World Trade Center the year it was finished; she insisted she could see our house from the observation deck. And of course, there was always the Radio City Music Hall Christmas show, with hot chocolate at the Rockefeller Ice Rink afterwards. Admittedly, all schmaltzy, touristy stuff, but I ate it up. To Mama, Manhattan was another word for "magic," and my sister and I caught her enthusiasm like it was a benign, and incurable, virus.

And like all good little carriers, I fully intend to infect my child as well.

The tail end of a tropical storm swept through the mid-Atlantic states a couple days ago, leaving behind clear blue skies and temperatures that feel more like mid-September than late June. "A perfect day to go to the Central Park Zoo!" I announced to Starr when I got her up this morning. "And while we're so close, you wanna go to FAO Schwartz?"

Most kids would have been hopping around like a flea at the prospect of going anywhere, especially anywhere that potentially involves animals, toys and/or junk food, but Starr simply said "Whatever" as she shrugged into a long-sleeved purple T-shirt with glittery butterflies on it and a pair of yellow capris. And the boots. Never mind that they must be hot as hell.

"But we're going into *the city!*" I said, wondering what I was missing here.

She patted my arm, solemnly said, "You'll make yourself sick if you get too excited," then calmly went downstairs for breakfast.

How is this my daughter? How?

Anyway, we're on the train at last, me fidgeting in my seat, Starr still as a mouse next to me, impassively studying the other passengers. We'd invited Jen, but she said it would kill her to go into the city and not be able to go shopping (apparently it's harder to resist the flagship stores in Manhattan than their miniclones in the mall?), so she decided to stay home and go through several boxes of Leo's papers she'd found in the closet in his room. She actually asked if I minded. Like I'm dying to sort through forty years' worth of paid Con Ed bills.

"So what do you want to do first? The zoo or the toy store?"

Starr shrugs. "Whatever."

This is her new word. Which unfortunately is much easier to work into the conversation than *esoteric,* which was last week's fave. Then my middle-aged baby snuggles up next to me, her arm threaded through mine. And I wonder, will she remember this moment twenty years from now? Or even five?

Memory's such a bizarre thing. When you're in the moment, you think it'll be emblazoned on your brain forever. But although I remember the fact of snuggling up to my own mother like this, I don't actually remember doing it. The *feel* of it. And other memories, especially from when I was littler, are fragmented and out-of-focus, like looking down through twenty feet of water at shards of pottery scattered along the ocean floor. Occasionally snippets of a conversation float through, or the vague impression of the look on her face or the sound of her voice, but very little that I can actually define. Which leads me to wonder just how much is actually memory, and how much is imagination.

The human brain is one bizarre organ, that's for sure.

For instance…when I finally recuperated enough from the weeks leading up to Heather's wedding to address cleaning the hellhole that used to be my basement, I realized that, despite the exhaustion and the craziness, I really had gotten a real kick out of making all those women look good.

And that, maybe, just maybe, I wouldn't mind doing it on a regular basis.

Do I perceive a collective rolling of the eyes? A chorus of "Oh, brothers"? Okay, fine. But here's the thing: I still haven't got what it takes to make a splash in high fashion. That's not fear, that's fact. My brain simply doesn't work that way. However (it occurs to me) there's a lot of real women out there, with real breasts and real hips and rounded bellies from having kids (or not) and not a whole lot of designers catering to their needs. And I think—maybe—my brain does work *that* way.

In theory, I could do this. In fact, the other night after I put Starr to bed I was suddenly attacked—that's the only word that fits—with a whole bunch of ideas. I was up until nearly three in the morning, sketching my fingers off. A lot of the designs were crap, but some of them weren't too bad, I don't think. A few more, and I'd actually have enough for a modest start-up line.

Even so, coming up with the ideas—even for me—is the easy part. It's making the damn clothes that's a killer. Hey, I felt bad enough about basically ignoring Starr for the last few weeks while Dolly and I pushed to get those dresses finished. I sure as hell couldn't do that to her—or me—week after week. But as I sketched, and the more possibilities came into focus, so did that nebulous almost-memory that had hovered over my conversation with Jennifer several weeks ago.

I was still pretty little, maybe Starr's age, and we were all over at my grandparents'. I can't recall if Jen was there or not, which might account for why she didn't mention this when we were talking the other day. Either that, or her memory's crappier than mine. In any case, Nana was riding my mother about her failure as a performer—and taking great delight in it, as I recall—when Mom noticed me standing in the doorway, taking it all in. With a smile, she held out her arms to me, scooping me up into her lap when I ran over to her.

"I didn't *fail,* Judith," she said calmly, her breath sifting through my hair as I cuddled against her chest. "I simply chose my children over something that would have taken me away from them more than I could bear. Maybe when they're older, I'll start up again...."

If my grandmother had a rebuttal, it's been mercifully expunged from my memory. And of course, Mama never got her second chance at a career. Did she regret her choice? I have no idea. I doubt she would have admitted it even if she had. But even though this may sound selfish, I certainly didn't. I interpreted her sacrifice as her not wanting to do anything that she saw as hurting Jen or me. Unlike Tina's mother, for instance, whose kids didn't even rank a distant second in her life, let alone first.

Of course, I now know there's a balance. That having a job or career has nothing to do with how involved someone is with her kids. Take Tina's mom, for instance—she was always around, but she sure as hell was never *there,* if you know what I mean. But there's a huge difference between starting up a clothing business, and a job that has regular hours and weekends off and paid vacations and benefits. Nobody succeeds in the rag trade without working their butt off and putting in long hours. If I don't, I'll be lucky to last ten minutes. Aside from the tremendous financial risk (Start-up capital? *What* start-up capital?) there's an even bigger risk that I'd never see my daughter again. Her finding me asleep on the couch downstairs once might have been amusing, but any more than that…no damn way. Look at Nikky and her relationship with her kids, for God's sake. Do I really want to end up like that? Or worse, for Starr to end up like zombie-girl Marilyn?

Maybe I didn't choose to get pregnant, but I definitely chose to become a mother. A choice which, for better or worse, impacts all my other choices, for the rest of my life. I know this. More to the point, I've accepted it.

Then why won't this crazy, impractical, totally unfeasible idea simply lie down and die, already? The idea is to make my life *less* complicated, not more. The idea is…

I suck in a breath, willing the knot at the back of my throat to go away.

The idea is to not let myself ache for things I can't have.

By the time we reach Manhattan, I've talked myself back down off the ledge. Even if I hadn't, though, just walking into FAO Schwartz would've done it. There's just something about three floors full of nothing but toys that makes me feel all Christmasy and giddy and goofy inside. Even if most normal— and sane—people wouldn't dream of paying several hundred dollars for a life-size stuffed tiger, or as much for a toy car as a real one might cost. There's just something about the place that turns everyone who comes in here into a kid again.

Even, amazingly enough, *my* kid.

She's dragged me up and down the escalators three times, looking for the perfect (as in, I won't have to sell *her* in order to afford it) reward for her being so good while I was swamped with work these past weeks. Of course, she doesn't know it's a reward, but far be it from me to pass up a guilt-assuaging opportunity. At last, she picks out a chubby, grinning stuffed hippopotamus (not life-size, unless there are foot-long pygmy hippos roaming around somewhere); the cashier's ringing up the sale just as I hear:

"Ellie?"

I turn, frowning, unable at first to link the voice—low, male, English-accented—to any of the roughly ten thousand bodies in the store. A second later, however, a smiling, familiar-looking dark-haired man appears in front of us.

"I'm sorry, maybe I have the wrong person?" he says. My brain dimly registers the open-collared black linen shirt, the casually rumpled Dockers, the expensive-looking tan bag slung over one strong-but-slim shoulder. That I'm looking *up* at him. Even in shoes that add half a story to my height. "It is Ellie Levine, isn't it?"

"Yes…"

"You don't remember me, do you?" Damn. His eyes—a stunning silvery gray, long lashes—actually sparkle. "We only met once, and for all of ten minutes at that. It's Alan. Stein? Daniel's brother? We ran into each other at the Met several years ago?"

Oh, boy. I now know you don't have to be staring *death* in the face for your life to flash before you. In a pinch, your former lover's brother will work just fine.

Okay, God? Not to be a pain in the butt or anything, but how is this less complicated?

"Alan!" I say, smile frozen in place like a ventriloquist. "What a surprise! What on earth are you doing here?"

"I'm in New York on business—"

(If I ever knew what he did, shock has totally eradicated it from my memory.)

"—and I thought I'd pop in here to get my nephew a gift."

I'm guessing that's the little darling who made that life-altering trans-Atlantic call six years ago.

Grinning (the dimples now register. Oh, boy), Alan says, "You look fantastic! Your hair's…shorter, isn't it?"

I nod, simultaneously wishing the floor would swallow us up and thanking my grandmother for drumming into my head that you never know who you might see when you're out, so you should always look your best. Of course, her definition of "best" and mine probably wouldn't jibe (I can't exactly see Nana in baggy, bright red monkey print overalls), but that's neither here nor there. Then I realize Alan's smile has drifted down to my daughter, who has been quietly sizing him up. My hot dog (with everything) from lunch threatens to make an encore appearance. "And who's this?" he asks.

Since I've been holding her hand the entire time, I don't suppose he'd buy that I'd never seen her before.

"This is…Starr."

"Is she yours?"

I can't exactly deny it. At least not while she's within earshot. So I nod, praying he won't ask her how old she is.

Alan tells her she's got a lovely name and promptly asks her how old she is.

"Five," she says with all the ennui she can muster as the clerk hands me back my charge card and our purchase and I pray like hell the guy's math challenged. Starr cocks her head. "How old are you?"

Alan laughs while I make one of those embarrassed I-have-*no*-idea-where-she-gets-this-from faces. "Thirty-eight."

It takes a second. Then, right on cue, platinum eyes bop back up to mine. Brows lift. Questions hover. Expletives burst like fireworks in my brain.

"Well, hey, it was terrific running into you," I say, dragging my poor child through the throng and away from all the hovering questions, "but I'm afraid we've got to run—"

"Ellie! Wait!"

Alan stumbles through the revolving door and outside right along with us. I could make a run for it, I suppose, but Starr and I barely have one decent set of legs between us. So I blow out a resigned breath and squint up into a face creased with concern. A face obviously wrestling with how to ask those questions, since the object of the questions is standing right beside me with, I imagine, a few of her own.

"Daniel doesn't know, does he?"

"Who's Daniel?" Starr says.

I sigh. Remember what I said about wanting to forget my twenty-second year? Well, lemme tell ya—my twenty-eighth ain't exactly shaping up to be any great shakes, either.

"We were on our way to the zoo," I say. "Care to join us?"

On a Monday afternoon in early summer, the zoo is crowded enough to muffle our conversation, but not so crowded that I have to worry about letting Starr skip ahead a few feet in front of us so Alan and I can talk. Would, however, that that was the only thing I was worried about. Aside from the still very real threat of the reappearing hot dog, I'm having the strangest reaction to Alan's cologne. As in, it's turning me inside out. That isn't supposed to happen.

Is it?

Well, I'll have to get back to myself on that one, since I've got just a few more pressing issues to deal with right now. We hit the sea lion exhibit right at feeding time; Starr's right up at the glass, but Alan and I hang back to continue our conversation. I've told him a truncated version of the truth, glossing over the bits that make me sound like a slut. Alan's listened thoughtfully, only occasionally interrupting for clarification. Now he says, kindness oozing from his pores, "And you've been beating yourself up over this ever since, haven't you?"

"Wasn't exactly my finest hour. Or, in this case, forty-eight hours."

He shifts his bag on his shoulder and shrugs. "Everybody fucks up, Ellie." From his lips, the word sounds elegant. "But you're hardly the first person to—" he lowers his voice "—use sex as a therapeutic after being hurt by someone."

By all rights, this conversation should be embarrassing the hell out of me. But when I force myself to look up at Alan, I see such openness there—a quality I now realize I never saw in his brother's eyes—that embarrassment doesn't even get a toehold. Now he frowns at Starr, his arms crossed. "But are you sure she's not Daniel's? She looks uncannily like he did at that age. The hair—"

"My father's mother had hair just like that. So it could easily have come from my side."

"And her eyes—"

"We all have—had—brown eyes." I feel a blush coming on. "I know what you're getting at. But it just doesn't seem very likely that Daniel's her father."

After a moment, Alan says, "If you'd known for sure that Starr *was* Daniel's, would you have told him?"

"Even if I'd had a clue how to contact him? What would have been the point? Especially as he wasn't exactly loyal to the kid he did have, was he? Sorry, not really somebody I'd want my child to call Daddy."

Alan seems to consider my words before saying, "When we all met up that day in the museum, I hadn't seen Daniel for several months. He told me he was separated from Caroline, and since I knew they'd been having problems, I saw no reason not to believe him. Only then I ran into *her* when I got back and quickly realized he'd been lying."

"And you didn't say anything? About me, I mean?"

"Good God, no. Car's a wonderful girl. I wouldn't hurt her for the world. I did, however, read my good-for-nothing brother the riot act when I next spoke with him."

"And he said?"

"To bugger off." I can sense there's more; I give him room to finish. "Especially as he'd already…indicated that it would end soon enough, not to make a big deal out of nothing." He glances over. "Sorry. I've never been much good at soft-pedaling."

I actually laugh. "It's been more than five years, I think I can handle it. Besides, it's nothing I hadn't already figured out. Even then." One of the sea lions comes right up to the glass where Starr's standing; she laughs and turns around.

"Look, Mama! Did you see that?"

"Sure did, Twink!"

Beside me, Alan says, "She's a great kid."

"If she's a kid at all." At his puzzled look, I add, "Let's just say she's not…typical."

"Who is?"

I chuckle, then ask, "Are they still together?"

"My brother and Caroline?" Alan shakes his head. "As it happens, you weren't the only one."

"Why am I not surprised?"

The dimples—deep, sexy creases, actually, in slightly beard-hazed cheeks—pop out. "Car's not the long-suffering type, I'm afraid."

"No, I wouldn't think so from the one time we talked." The shopping bag strings are cutting into my palm; I switch hands, then say, "This may sound nuts, but I feel a lot worse for her than I did for me."

"Then you'll be glad to know she's happily remarried with another baby on the way."

"She is? Well, go, Caroline!" I shield my eyes from the sun with my hand. "And…your brother?"

"Off being a photojournalist somewhere. I suppose. Actually, no one's heard from him in more than three years."

"He doesn't even contact his son?"

"No."

"Well, that certainly gives me one less thing to feel guilty about. That's really crappy for his kid, though."

"It was, until Car met Timothy. Her new husband is crazy about the boy."

"That's good." Then I blow a stream of air through my lips. "I was twenty-two, Alan. Right out of school. Your brother was…my first serious relationship. At least, I thought so at the time. Looking back, though…it's not that I wasn't hurt when I found out he was married, but I think it was more that I was angry with myself for being so stupid."

"You can't blame yourself for his dishonesty, Ellie."

A moment passes before I say, "But I haven't exactly been honest, either."

"With this other bloke, you mean?"

"No, he's always known there's a strong possibility Starr's his. But…" I wait out the pang I've been trying, with little success, to dodge ever since Heather's wedding, that I haven't heard from Luke. I explain about Tina and the timing and how neither of us wanted to hurt her. Alan says, "I see," in that way people do when they don't see at all. Not that I blame him. It barely makes sense to me, and I've been living in the middle of this mess for six years.

"But now you're planning on finding out for sure?"

"Yes. Very soon, in fact. And we've both confessed to Tina."

"A little air-clearing?"

I nod.

We back up to let a herd of strollers pass. Then Alan says, "When you find out…I'd like to be kept in the loop."

I look up, my stomach bebopping again at the expression in his eyes, the set to his mouth. Alan's not handsome in any classic sense, but everything just…works, somehow.

"You didn't even know Starr existed a half hour ago."

"True. But…" He glances over at her once again, then back at me. "If she's my niece, I'd like to know. That's all."

I break eye contact, calling Starr to come on.

"But what I don't understand," Alan says softly as we continue, "is why you've put this off for so long. Surely you must realize how much harder it's going to be on Starr, the longer you wait."

"Of course I realize how hard this is going to be, I'm not a total idiot!" I've stopped, making him turn back to face me. "But you weren't there, and none of this was your decision to make. So I'd appreciate not being judged for something about which you basically know squat."

"You tell 'im, girlfriend," some woman says as she passes.

Alan and I face off for a few seconds, during which the signals inside my brain go totally kerflooey. No doubt about it, the man gets my juices going. Only thing is, I can't tell if it's because he turns me on or pisses me off. Neither of which I need in my life right now.

At last Alan pushes out a breath. "I apologize. You're absolutely right, I've got no business badgering you about this." Then he gives me this little sideways look, accompanied by a half grin. "At least not until I get to know you better—"

What?

"—but I've hit on a sore point, haven't I?"

I let out a sigh of my own. The man is hopeless.

"No. Maybe. Oh, hell, I don't know anymore. I just kept thinking…if by some chance it *is* your brother, what if Starr decides to look him up one day, and he rejects her?"

"You don't know that." At my snort, he adds, "Stranger things have happened, Ellie."

"Right. And somewhere, somebody still thinks he can turn iron into gold."

Another grin slides in my direction, followed by, "And if it is this other man?"

"Jesus, Alan…I don't know!" I rummage in my purse and find a 3 Musketeers miniature, which I frantically unwrap and cram into my mouth. "I'm kind of a one-step-at-a-time chick, okay? First we get the results. Then we figure out what to do with them. And pray I haven't scarred my kid for life. You think I don't worry about this? Criminy—what if she never trusts me again? What if this in some way warps her relationships with men?"

Alan gives me a strange look.

"So maybe that last part's a little far-fetched."

"Just a little. My God—how do you sleep at night?"

"I don't. Next question?"

We've left the main zoo and are standing out by the glockenspiel, waiting for the hour to strike. I've tried to impart to Starr how great this is gonna be, but I can tell she's not real impressed.

"Are you still in touch with…what the bloody hell is his name, anyway?"

"Luke?" My stomach feels like it used to after eating my grandmother's matzoh balls. "Yeah, we've known each other our whole lives."

"And…Tina?"

"We were all best friends," I say quietly.

"Were?"

"Things aren't the same as they used to be. And I'd appreciate it if you'd let it go at that."

"I understand."

Again, I doubt it. But as long as he doesn't try to root around in my brain for a more substantive answer, I'm good.

The clock chimes two; the animals begin their measured, dignified dance around the base. I look over; Starr's standing with her arms crossed and her head tilted to one side. Taking it in but not reacting. Figures. Afterwards, she wends her way back through the crowd and slips her hand into mine.

"I'm *exhausted.* I tell you, my legs feel like they're gonna give right out from under me."

Alan chuckles, then offers her a piggyback ride.

"Oh, God," she says, "I would *kill* for a piggyback ride."

That gets a roar of laughter from Alan. And a great sigh from me.

We pass an ice-cream cart; Starr tosses me a hopeful look. She's not a whiny child, doesn't beg for everything she sees. But she's always had this uncanny sixth sense for knowing when I'm in pushover mode. I say okay, she picks this god-awful blue…thing. When I go to pay, however—I do not want to even think about what this is going to do to her intestines— Alan shoves a five-dollar bill at the vendor before I can even get my wallet out of my bag.

One arm wrapped around the man's neck, Starr looks over at me and gives me a thumbs-up.

"So," Alan says when we get going again. "I take it you're on your own then? With…" He angles his head back slightly to indicate Starr, who's about to garnish his hair with sticky, bright blue highlights.

"More or less. Although my sister's living with us at the moment. And we were living with my grandfather until a few months ago."

"Were?"

"He passed away in March," I say carefully, trying not to disturb the ache in my chest. Wrong.

"I'm sorry," Alan says, and I nod.

"But there's Frances and them," Starr puts in. "And Luke. An' Dolly. So we've got people coming out of our *ears.*" She takes a big lick of her treat, then sticks out her tongue, cross-ing her eyes trying to see it. "Is it blue?"

"Like the Mediterranean," I say. "You rule, little girl."

That gets a huge, blue-tinged grin.

"So, Starr," Alan asks, tilting his head back. "You and Luke are friends?"

I'd give him a dirty look, but he can't see me.

"Totally," Starr says around her last bite. "C'n I get down now? I'm done."

"How about a somersault dismount?" Alan asks.

"Cool!"

My heart stops while Alan grabs her around the waist, then flips her over his head and onto her feet. Starr wobbles for a second, then hikes over to the nearest trash can to dump her denuded ice-cream stick.

Alan gives me a considering look. "So…are you okay? Moneywise, I mean. Just because my brother's a jerk doesn't mean I couldn't help out if you need—"

"We're fine," I say, too quickly, stunned by his willingness to take responsibility for something that has nothing to do with him, as Starr plays imaginary hopscotch on her way back to us. We've come out of the park at 59th Street, across from the Plaza. Alan reaches inside his shirt pocket and pulls out a slim wallet, from which he extracts a business card. "I'm here for at least six weeks. My cell number's on the card. And why don't you give me yours?"

I stare at it dumbly, like some time traveler who has no idea what the heck is going on.

"Um…so you can reach me when you find out?"

"Oh! Right."

As I give him my number in return, it dimly registers that we've stopped at the Plaza because *this is where he's staying*. A horse-and-carriage drops off a couple in front of the hotel; Starr is now transfixed by the horse, a dapple gray with plastic daisies threaded through its bridle.

"Ellie?"

My gaze snaps back to Alan's. Who's got this funny, do-I-dare-ask-this? look on his face. He laughs, a little nervously, then says, "You're undoubtedly going to think I'm totally daft, but…will you have dinner with me sometime?"

"What?"

Oh, yeah, Miss Cool, that's me.

This time, his laugh is full and rich and my toes are tingling and I'm thinking there is no *way* this man is Daniel's brother. "I thought I'd asked you out?" One dimple plays peek-a-boo with me. "I mean, it's been a while, but I didn't think the modus operandi had changed that much—"

"No, no, it's not that, it's…"

"It's what?" he prompts when speech fails me.

"I'm not sure."

"I'm sorry…did I misunderstand? I didn't get the feeling there was anything between you and this Luke person, really…."

"There isn't," I say so quickly I startle myself. Well, there isn't, is there? And I doubt there ever will be, Tina or no Tina. If I'm going to turn over this new leaf about facing reality, then it's high time I do just that and get on with my life.

Luke Scardinare will never be more to me than he's ever been.

And this torch I'm not carrying is about to break my back.

"We're just friends," I say. With conviction, even. "But why…I mean, I don't get…" I huff out a sigh. "Look, if this is because you might be Starr's uncle—"

"No, Ellie, it's not that. I swear." As I stand there, trying to process all of this, he says, "I know this is rather bizarre, our meeting by chance and your having been…involved with Daniel and all that, but I could spend the next six months thinking about the propriety of it all before asking you out, by which time you will have moved on—"

Yeah, like that's gonna happen.

"—and I would have lost out. And then I'd be miserable because I'd prevaricated about something I'm not going to feel any differently about then than I do right now. And I don't much like being miserable, actually. I mean, unless you don't want to go out with me, in which case I can find out now and get the misery over with, instead of worrying about it for another six months."

I laugh. "You're crazy."

Alan's grin warms me all the way to my…never mind. "So

I've been told." Then he lifts his hand to brush a strand of hair off my cheek, and I can hardly breathe. Speaking of crazy. "The older I get, the faster time seems to go. And the more I'm inclined to act on my impulses. My half brother was a fool—"

Half brother! I knew it!

"—but he's always had excellent taste in women." His shoulders rise, then fall. "I like you. In fact, I was intrigued by you that first time we met. I thought then I'd like to get to know you better. But I never dreamed I'd get that chance." He frowns for a moment, then nods and says, "Yes, I think that pretty much covers it, don't you?"

Covers it? My poor bedraggled ego is stretching her achy limbs and positively *bathing* in it.

"So…is tomorrow evening too short a notice to get a baby-sitter?"

"Uh—"

"Never mind," he says, and I think, well, hell—so much for that. Only then he says, "I'll give you a call later. If a baby-sitter's a problem, we'll just plan something to include Starr, that's all." Then he offers me a chagrined smile. "Sorry. You haven't exactly said yes yet, have you?"

"I'd love to go out with you," I say, and his whole face lights up. Then he checks his watch and lets out, "Damn, I had no idea it was so late. Look," he says, "I'm terribly sorry to leave you like this, but I've got a three o'clock meeting at the Winter Garden with my director, and I've still got one sketch to finish up—"

Lightbulb time! I remember, I remember—he's a stage designer!

"—but here, let me give you taxi fare…"

"Oh, no, forget it, we'll take the subway back—"

He crams a pair of twenties in my hand. "You will do no such thing," he says, and I decide that much of a fool, I'm not.

Then, with a wink, he backs away, swiping his hair off his face as he calls out goodbye to Starr.

Is this an Audrey Hepburn movie moment or what? Man, oh man—when was the last time I *intrigued* a man? Confused them, yes, but intrigued? This is good stuff.

On the taxi ride home (a real sacrifice), I tell Starr that Alan's asked me out, which apparently prompts nothing more worrisome in her mind than my needing to do *something* about my hair. In any case, I'm feeling pretty damn mellow when we get out of the taxi and climb up the steps to our house.

Until Jen grabs me the instant we set foot inside and shoves a tattered manila envelope into my hands.

"You're not gonna believe this," she says.

The way my life's been going lately? Try me.

chapter 24

However, Jen's right. I don't.

But there it is, in black-and-white. Or, since the documents
are so old, charcoal gray and beige:

Dad's adoption papers.

Along with what must be an amended birth certificate with
my grandparents' names on them.

Suddenly, thoughts of Alan and dimpled smiles and an actual date (where the guy pays and everything) get knocked
right out of the ballpark. Not to mention the hundred and one
other worries that have been traipsing after me all summer like
a bunch of stray dogs.

"Do you think he even knew?" Jen whispers, handing me a
glass of iced tea. Starr's gone up to her room; Jen and I are in
the kitchen, the shades drawn against the late-afternoon sun.
This is, without a doubt, the closest I have ever felt to my sister. Would that it were under more auspicious circumstances.

"I have no idea. Although I doubt it, since nobody ever said anything. Lemme see the rest of the papers," I say, shuffling again through the brittle documents until I find Leo and Judith's wedding certificate. Jen busies herself by bolstering her tea with a good-sized dollop of Canadian Club. Since it doesn't appear she's been boozing it up all afternoon, I let it go. Especially since I'm half-tempted to indulge in some bolstering of my own. Jesus. And Mary and Joseph and Abraham and anybody else you want to get in there. "According to this, Dad was born only four months after the wedding."

"And adopted when he was three days old."

We blink up at each other. "Which begs the question," I say, "why would a newly married couple adopt a baby?"

As if we both haven't leaped through hoops to the same conclusion. Jen raises her glass in a surprisingly cheerful salute and says, "Is this family fucked up or what?"

You might say. I glance down at the documents, shaking my head. "I suppose we could ask her…"

"I've already invited her for dinner," Jen says, taking a swig of her tea. She glances up at the clock, then back at me. "You've got three hours to prep."

Terrific.

Since we have no proof that Dolly was Dad's birth mother, she could have easily dismissed us as two crazy women with overactive imaginations. But although Jen's and my craziness is a given, the woman we now know is our biological grandmother hasn't denied a thing. If anything, she seems relieved that it's finally all out in the open.

We didn't bring it up until after dinner, although how either Jen or I got a crumb of food down our throats, I'll never know. Once Starr was safely ensconced in the living room watching the latest teeny-bopper movie (Jen really did think of everything—I'm beginning to think there's hope for the girl yet), I brought out the papers and presented them to Dolly.

Who cracked like an overripe walnut.

She's been telling her story for several minutes now, caressing the adoption certificate over and over, as though it's an old, beloved pet. At first, her words emerged haltingly, cautiously, like disbelieving prisoners newly released after decades of wrongful incarceration in a dark prison cell. But the longer she talks, the more secure she sounds, someone who's turned her burden into a strength.

She's told us how she and Leo became lovers when he was only twenty-one, she seventeen. But their families were adamantly opposed to the relationship because she was Catholic and he Jewish. Never mind that Leo wasn't practicing even then: his parents were convinced a good Jewish girl would straighten him out. Naturally they were horrified when he started seeing Dolly. But as appalled as my great-grandparents were, that was nothing compared with Dolly's family, who wouldn't hear of her being involved with a Jew.

"If he had been willing to convert," she now says, "there might have been some hope. But your grandfather's disaffection for organized religion wasn't limited to his own faith. He thought all of it was bunk. However, he'd already said I could raise our children any way I liked." A sad smile crosses her lips. "From the beginning, he wanted to have babies with me. Although…not the way it happened.

"When I discovered I was pregnant, I foolishly thought my parents would *have* to let us marry. I was very wrong. Your grandfather wanted to elope, but I was too young, and too scared, and we didn't have a cent between us. So my parents sent me away to cousins in Buffalo to have the baby. Then…give it up for adoption."

Her head moves slowly from side to side, her brows sinking behind her glass frames as she rests the side of her face in one palm, once again skimming her index finger over the papers. "I hear the words come out of my mouth, but they don't sound quite real. As if it's not my story, but something that's familiar because I've heard it over and over again so many times." Her gaze lifts to mine. "But it did happen to me. All of it. Including your grandfather's pestering everybody we knew until he found somebody finally willing to tell him where I was. And what my parents planned."

Her shoulders, suddenly delicate and insignificant-looking underneath a brightly patterned blouse lift, then drop. "If he couldn't have me, he was determined to at least have our child. As I'm sure you understand, my parents very much wanted to keep my *embarrassment* a secret. It was bad enough that I dated a Jewish boy, but to then get pregnant on the wrong side of the blanket..." She shakes her head. "Things were so different then. My family enjoyed some social standing in the community. People trusted my father and admired my mother. So my parents saw me as their failure. Your grandfather knew this, knew how little they wanted their shame to become public knowledge. So he...made a bargain with them—that they would let him adopt our baby, in exchange for his keeping his mouth shut."

My eyebrows shoot up a full inch. "He *blackmailed* them?"

Dolly smiles. "I think *damage control* is a better term, don't you?"

"Still, you had to give up your baby—"

"Better that than have him go to strangers and never have any idea where he was or how he was doing. Remember, there was no such thing as open adoption then. This way, I would at least know he was with his father. Maybe even see him, from a distance at least, from time to time."

"But..." I frown. "To stand by and watch Leo marry someone else..."

"Nearly killed me," she says. "But there was no other way

he would have been allowed to adopt. Not then. And I knew he wasn't in love with Judith."

Jen and I exchange glances, then Jen says, "How do you know that?"

"Leo had told me about Judith when we were still seeing each other, that their families wanted them to marry, that he suspected she had feelings for him. Feelings he couldn't return. When he found out about the baby, however, he knew he had to marry quickly. So he proposed to Judith, but with two conditions— that she understand it was solely to help him raise his baby, and that she could never tell a soul who Norman's real mother was."

From the living room, I hear Starr's laughter, a bizarre counterpoint to the sadness that has suddenly swamped me like a dense fog. My ginger-encrusted salmon from dinner is boogeying in my stomach.

"But…" My sister's voice sounds furry and distant. "People knew you and Leo had been seeing each other. Wouldn't somebody have put two and two together when Leo adopted your baby?"

"The story was that the child was an orphan, born to a young widow—a distant friend of the family—who'd died in childbirth, and that Judith and Leo had taken on the child so soon after their marriage as an act of charity. A *mitzvah,* he later explained to me."

"And people actually *bought* that?"

"Apparently, disgrace brings out a family's creative side."

"Jesus."

The disgust in Jen's voice leads me to believe her salmon's having a high old time, too. But at this point, I'm perfectly willing to let her ask the questions. A burden she seems perfectly willing to accept.

"Why on earth would anyone agree to such a horrible arrangement? Nana, especially. It wasn't like she was ugly or anything, that she couldn't have eventually found someone else."

"She didn't want someone else. She wanted Leo," Dolly says matter-of-factly. "And apparently, she was willing to do whatever she had to to get him. She saw the marriage as an opportunity, that being a mother to his child would eventually win him over. And that someday they'd have babies of their own, and his feelings for me would fade."

Jen collapses against her chair back, her arms folded. "How would you know—?"

"She told me."

"Wait—our grandmother *talked* to you?"

"Only once. Shortly before her death, right after my husband died. We ran into each other in the supermarket. I tried to avoid her, but she made a beeline for me, offering her condolences, asking if she could take me to lunch. Stupid me, I thought she was extending an olive branch, that she'd finally reconciled herself to something none of us had any power over. Instead, she…" Dolly inhales deeply. "It was like having all the old wounds torn open all over again. On both sides. You tell yourself, you've made your bed, but…" Her eyes lift to ours. "Who could blame her for being bitter?"

Not me.

Hey. I adored my grandfather, so I'm probably not the most objective person to be sorting through all this. And I personally never witnessed him being anything less than considerate with my grandmother. Judith, I mean. But if there was never anything *more* between them than consideration…well, hell. No wonder my grandmother had a bad attitude. Yeah, I understand that in order to not lose his son, Leo's choices were limited. But the fact remains that someone else suffered greatly because of the choice he did make.

And it's making me sick.

From what seems like a great distance, I hear Jen ask Dolly about her own marriage, then Dolly's response—about her desperate need to have more babies after giving up Dad, that in spite of everything, she hoped she'd made George a good wife.

"He was a kind man," she says. "Very generous, crazy about his kids. I missed him terribly when he died, the way you'd miss a wonderful friend."

"Did he know about Leo?" Jen asks.

"Only that I'd been deeply in love before, and that it ended badly. George seemed to…honor my feelings, is the best way I can put it. And in a way, that made me more fond of him, you know?"

"But you cheated on him?"

She recoils at Jen's accusation. "I saw Leo from time to time, yes. I wasn't strong enough to give him up entirely. But I swear to you, we weren't…intimate while our spouses were alive. I made sure, the few times we met, that it was someplace where nothing could happen. At a restaurant in Brooklyn, or Coney Island in the middle of the day. It was torture, but I'd made as full a life as I could with my husband. I wasn't about to jeopardize that. Not after what I'd already lost."

Do I believe her, that they were never lovers while they were both still married? But then, what does it matter? Especially now. It's all over and done with.

Or is it?

I finally pull together enough brain cells to ask, "So how did Liv come to be Leo's tenant? And after he died, and you volunteered to help with me with the dresses…" I pause, not even sure what I'm trying to ask.

Dolly smiles. "The first was a coincidence, believe it or not. And your grandfather wasn't happy about it when he found out. Except once she was in…" She shrugs. "Well. You know your grandfather."

Do I? *Did* I?

"As for the other…" She looks down at her hands, then

back up at me. "I never got to know my son. I wasn't going to turn down the chance to get to know my granddaughter."

"But you weren't going to tell me—us—who you were, were you?"

"Probably not."

"Why?"

"Because of exactly what I'm seeing in your eyes right now. All that anger and hurt…" Her head moves from side to side. "Oh, years ago, after both George and your grandmother were gone, I wanted to get this out in the open. But Leo wouldn't hear of it. Too afraid of somebody digging around and discovering the *whole* truth, I suppose. And eventually, I began to think maybe he was right, maybe it wasn't such a good idea, maybe it was better in the long run to leave the truth buried. If you hadn't found those papers, I probably would never have said anything. But when we met, and I realized you needed help with the sewing, and then Jennifer came home, too… Well, I thought maybe this was some small reward for keeping my mouth shut for more than fifty years."

I swear, I think my heart is going to break.

Not long after, the little party breaks up, leaving the hows and whens—and ifs—of breaking this news to our families for another discussion. Jen offers to give Dolly a ride home, while I do the good roommate thing and clean up after dinner. But once in the kitchen, putting things away in assorted plastic dooflatchies, I realize just how tenuous is my hold on my already stretched thin emotions.

My grandfather was a fraud.

No matter how I, or anyone else, might try to justify it, the fact remains that his actions made not one, but two women miserable. Judith was stuck in a loveless marriage, saddled with a child that reminded my grandfather every day of what he'd had to give up. But at least he got to see my father every day— Dolly never saw him at all.

The leftover salmon I've just scooped out of the baking dish blurs as my eyes fill with tears: How was that a good thing for any of them? What was the freaking *point?*

"So. What was that all about?"

I spin around at the sound of Starr's voice, sending the salmon flying off the spatula and onto the floor. Frito pounces on it, only to rear back and hiss at me when I yell at him to get away. Wiping my eyes, I squat to clean up the splattered fish.

"What was what all about?"

"Dolly and Leo."

I look up to see her give me The Hands. Palms up, fingers spread. She has clearly been hanging around the Scardinares too much lately. "You were supposed to be in the living room," I say.

"You guys talk too loud."

Shit. I finish picking up the fish, tossing a piece of it into Frito's food dish. "I don't want to talk about it right now."

"But—"

I whirl around a second time, advancing on my daughter so fast she stumbles backwards. "I *said* I don't want to talk about it right now! For God's sake, Starr—give me a freaking *break!*"

I have never yelled at her. Ever. And when I see the stunned, hurt look in her eyes for that instant before she takes off, I die inside. I run after her, catching her before she hits the stairs.

"Let go of me!" she screams, sobbing.

"Oh, God, Starr, I'm so sorry, baby, I'm so sorry…" I sink onto the stairs and pull her awkwardly into my lap, wrapping my arms around this kid I didn't have to give up, that I chose to have, and keep.

"You yelled at me!"

"I know, Twink." She's all jutting limbs and frizzy hair, her skin so soft I can barely feel it. "It's not your fault, I was upset—"

But she's way too upset herself to hear me, I realize. "I want

L-Leo!" she says on a wail, throwing her arms around my neck and plastering herself against me. "I w-want him to come b-back! I hate that he's d-dead and I'll never see h-him again and I hate G-god for taking him away from m-me!"

"Oh, sweetie…" I hug her even more tightly, my shirt getting soaked in the tears she's held in so valiantly until now. Who knows, maybe my yelling at her finally gave her permission not to feel she had to be tough for her basketcase mother. But as I sit there, my own tears running down my cheeks, I realize I feel the same way, angry at God or who/whatever for taking away my grandfather. Not his body, but my idealized notion of who he was.

For the next several minutes, we just sit there, weeping, me saying whatever mothers are supposed to say at times like this. Gibberish, mostly. Lots of apologies. Except when she tries to elicit a promise that I'll never yell at her again, I tell her I can't do that.

What I can do, however, is tell her as much of the truth about her grandfather and Dolly as I think she can handle. Which basically boils down to letting her know that Dolly is actually her great-grandmother, that Liv and the boys are her cousins. And I tell her (because this just occurs to me) that maybe someday Dolly can tell her stories about her grandfather from when he was a young man that might help her not miss him so much.

Because it occurs to me that I *don't* know what was going on in my grandfather's head, that it's quite possible his choices made him miserable, too. And who the hell am I to judge him? You know, all that stuff about casting the first stone. After all, as Alan so succinctly put it, everybody fucks up.

Something I sincerely hope this little girl remembers when she eventually finds out a few things about her mother.

* * *

As she's done since she was tiny, Starr has opted to be by herself for a while, until, she says, "I feel like me again." So I'm alone in the living room, feeling appropriately morose and moody, when Alan calls.

Morose and moody go sailing out the window as the dating alarm goes off in my head. You know, the total panic generally accompanied by ripping everything you own from the closet, followed immediately by the realization that you cannot, short of hacking off a limb, lose twenty pounds in less than twenty-four hours.

Yes, I know, how very high school of me. Well, honey, since it's been nearly that long since I've been on a date, deal with it.

Anyway. So here the man is, on the other end of the phone, making plans. And here I am, on this side, feeling conflicted.

So what else is new?

I'll tell you what else is new. That I feel flattered as well as conflicted, that's what. I mean, holy crud—when was the last time a man showed enough interest to actually go after me? 'Tis a strange and wonderful feeling. And yes, I know there was Daniel, but since I'm doing my best to ignore that part of my life, work with me here.

He's insisting on picking me up tomorrow, then whisking me off for a romantic evening in town. Or, if Starr has to come, a Mets game. The man is a keeper, I tell you. Not sure if he's my keeper, but he sure as hell is somebody's. Although at some point I should probably find out why, since he's thirty-eight, nobody's kept him yet.

See? I'm learning.

We talk for a few minutes more, I find out he was the set designer for a hit London musical now coming to Broadway, that he's here supervising the adapted sets for the Winter Garden; he goads me into telling him about my designing and making the dresses for Heather's wedding, my decision to stay home for Starr, my being a landlord of sorts. Then he gets another call and we say a hurried good-night, leaving me with that delightful what-the-hell-am-I-*doing?* feeling.

Jen comes in the door and drops her keys on the hall table, which is the first time it occurs to me how long she's been gone.

"Everything okay?" I say.

"Yeah. Dolly invited me in for coffee." She comes over and sinks onto the sofa, crossing her legs and slapping one mule against her bare sole. "She's got pictures of us, do you believe it?"

"You're kidding?"

"Nope. A whole album full. She said Leo gave them to her after Nana died." Then she leans her elbow on the arm of the sofa, her fingers plowed through her hair, staring at a spot over my left shoulder.

"What are you thinking?"

"I'm not sure." Her eyes focus on mine, but slowly, as if she didn't expect me to be there. "All that lost opportunity crap, I suppose. I mean, here are two people who couldn't be together, and other people who probably should never have been together..." Her brow puckers. Very delicately, though. "You gotta wonder... If Leo was so dead set against anyone ever discovering the truth, why did he leave those adoption papers where they could be found?"

A question I'd already asked myself. "Guess we'll never know the answer to that one."

"Guess not." Then her expression changes, as though she's tired of that subject. "So...I never got a chance to ask, how was your trip into Manhattan?"

This new Jen is like upgrading your computer system. Gonna take some getting used to, I can tell. Granted, it's much more interactive, but do I dare download new data to it without freezing the whole shebang?

"Actually...I kinda met someone there."

She perks up. "As in, a man?"

"Yep. And he asked me out. For tomorrow night."

That gets a frown. "And you're *going?* Out? With a total stranger?"

"Actually…he's not a total stranger. We met before. Briefly. A friend's brother. Actually."

Now, Jen and I have never *actually* had a heart-to-heart about old Danny boy, but she knows nobody left Starr in a basket on my doorstep. And even though I don't think Daniel's actually her father (yet), and since we can't talk about who I think *is* her father, The Man Who Sucked Out Ellie's Brain wins by default. And somehow, I don't think Jen's gonna be exactly wild about my going on with The Man Who Sucked Out Ellie's Brain's brother. I'm not even sure I'm all that wild about it, frankly. So I decide not to *actually* tell her the truth.

Yet.

She narrows her eyes. "I know who this is, don't I?"

Little sigh of relief, here. "No, you don't. His name's Alan."

"Alan what?"

Damn. "Stein."

"Jewish?"

"That would be a safe guess, yes."

"Stein, Stein…" After a moment of careful puckering, she shakes her head. "Nope. You're right. Don't know him."

"Which reminds me…could you baby-sit?"

"Of course I can baby-sit, don't be silly. I mean, my God, how often does this happen, you going on a date?"

"Okay, that was just you injecting a little levity into the subject of my pathetic love life, right? As opposed to being snide and cruel, like I'm used to?"

She just grins. "So what does this mean?"

"Nothing. Other than I've met a nice man who wants to take me out and I'd be an idiot to turn him down."

"O-kaaay… As long as you're happy, right?" While I mull

this over—*Happy? Who the hell knows?*—she gets up, stretching out her lower back. "I'm pooped. Think I'll call it a night." Halfway out of the room, however, she turns back, her hands in the pockets of her pale pink linen shorts. "By the way, I've started job hunting."

Not sure how many more of these shocks I can take in one evening. "Job hunting? But I thought—?"

"The book?" Her smile slants to one side. "Isn't going to feed me. At least, not for a very long time. If ever. Something about finding those papers, hearing Dolly tonight..." She shakes her head. "I'm long, long overdue for a few lessons in facing facts. And the first lesson is, nobody's gonna support me but me. Whether I ever get married again or not. So I think I'm going to go see what I can dig up in the city with some events planners. Maybe someone could use a very classy assistant, whaddya think?"

Smiling, I tuck my legs up under me. "You're just doing this because you can't stand living here any longer."

"Boy, can't get a thing past you," she says, and we laugh. Then her smile fades a little. "Although it's not nearly as bad now as it used to be."

"Meaning?"

"I'm not sure. But it's as if..." Her gaze takes in the room. "There's more light in here now or something."

"That's what generally happens when you turn on a lamp."

That gets an eye roll. "No, I mean, it's not dark and heavy anymore with all these secrets, you know? I actually don't mind being here now, not like when we were kids. But it's just...I need my own home. Someplace I choose to live, not where I have to live. Does that make any sense?"

"Yeah. I think so," I say, even as I'm wondering if maybe that was partly why I wanted to get away from here, too, even if I wasn't actually conscious of it. All these secrets, threatening to bury me alive...

Jen nods and leaves, high-fiving Starr as they cross paths. High-fiving, for cripes' sake. Wouldn't've believed it if I hadn't seen it with my own eyes.

"Are you feeling like 'you' again?" I ask my little girl.

Tiny shoulders hitch. "Close enough."

I pull her into my arms. "Still mad at me?"

"No. But you're *much* scarier when you're mad than that stupid old monster."

Unless I'm mistaken, there's a smidgen of pride behind her words. One of those "my mama can beat the crap out of you" kind of things. Hey. Whatever works.

Suddenly, I want to talk to Frances. I *need* to talk to Frances. "Go find your flip-flops and let's go next door, see what Frances and Jimmy are doing."

"All *right*."

Five minutes later, Starr's down in the Scardinares' basement watching Jimmy tinker with something that Frances swears is gonna blow up in his face one day, and I'm in the kitchen with Frances, baring my soul. Or at least as much of it as I'm gonna. I tell her about meeting Alan and him asking me out, about Dolly, about Jen's turning over a new leaf and looking for jobs and stuff. The whole time I'm blathering on, she sits there with her chin in her hand, watching me, listening but not talking much. Her eyebrows go up a few times, but other than that nothing I say seems to surprise her. Not even the stuff about Dolly. But when I'm done, she gets up to get a couple of cans of root beer out of the fridge.

"I've got some vanilla ice cream—wanna float?"

Frances has a serious thing for root beer floats. As do I. But since nobody at my house likes root beer much, I only ever have them here. "You have to ask?"

She gets down a pair of heavy stemmed glasses from the top shelf, the move exposing a sliver of her bare back underneath the hem of her sleeveless cotton top. Her arms are sinewy and strong and reassuring, the muscles flexing as she scoops ice cream into first one, then the other. An unruly hunk of hair flops into her eyes; she pushes it back with her wrist, then glances over at me.

"So. What's this guy like?"

A reasonable enough question. And one I invited by telling her about Alan to begin with. Yet, even as I answer—English, witty, gainfully employed, attentive (I leave out the Daniel connection)—I get this icky feeling inside.

"And he knows about Starr?"

"Uh-huh. They've even met."

More eyebrow lifting. "And he's okay with this?"

She should only know. Then again, maybe not. "Oh, yeah."

Frances pours the root beer over the ice cream—carefully, so the heads get nice and high but don't do the overflowing lava number, the way I usually make them—then carries them to the table, takes her seat and says, very gently, "Now quit the b.s. and tell me why you're really here."

"I have no idea—"

She jabs her spoon at me. I blow out a breath.

"Okay, fine." Into my mouth goes a huge glob of float fluff. "It's been two weeks since I've heard anything about Luke and Tina and the suspense is killing me and I thought you might know something."

Frances sucks on her spoon for a second, then says, "Guess that shoots any hope I had of finding out what *you* knew."

"You haven't heard either?"

"Not word one. And when I call, all I get is his answering machine."

"You think he's screening his calls?"

"Who knows? Maybe." She licks a chunk of ice cream off her spoon, then shrugs. "Maybe this is Luke's way of saying he's gotta work this out on his own."

Which is exactly what I've been saying all along. So why,

now that he's apparently doing just that, is his silence driving me nuts? After all, who told him to leave me out of it?

Then Frances says, "Tina didn't really have a miscarriage, did she?" and I miss my mouth and smear ice cream across my chin. Frances hands me a napkin.

"W-what makes you say—?"

One eyebrow lifts; I dissolve like a wet cracker.

"Oh, God, Frances…if she finds out you know she had an abortion—"

Frances's stunned expression stops me cold. "An abortion? I assumed she'd faked the pregnancy, that's all."

The room starts spinning; I drop my head on my arms, muttering, "Shit, shit, shit," under my breath. Frances's hand lands between my shoulder blades, gently rubbing my back.

"Don't worry, I won't say a word, I promise. But that explains a lot."

After several seconds, I lift my head. Tenuously. "Even so, how did you figure it out? That she hadn't had a miscarriage, I mean?"

"Intuition, I suppose. The way she didn't seem all that excited when they told us they were expecting." Frances chugs the last of the ice-cream laced root beer from her glass, then locks her gaze with mine. "Then she *loses* a baby, and suddenly she wants out of the marriage?" Leaning closer, she says, "I love Tina, and I know she's good at heart. But nothing's ever motivated that girl except fear and neediness. And who can blame her? What else did she know, growing up? Only problem is, whichever one is stronger at the moment, that's the one she listens to. And that's not good."

I stare at what's left of my float. Hell, fear's probably what motivates most people's decisions, when you come right down to it.

"When…when Tina told me she wanted to get Luke back…" I look up into Frances's eyes again, hating myself for having such a big mouth, relieved I finally have someone to share the burden with. "I told her she really needed to think about telling him."

"Really?" I hate that I can't read Frances's expression. "It'll kill him, you know that."

"Not any more than the false hope that maybe they'll have kids someday! I mean, hey, if Tina's who he really wants, if they can work this out..." My spoon clanks against the glass as I dig for the last bit of ice cream. "Fine and dandy. But I can't stand the thought of him going back into that relationship, knowing what I know. And knowing that he *doesn't* know."

Dammit. My hands are shaking.

And Frances misses nothing. She leans back in her chair, letting out a long breath. "You know, it's a real bitch, knowing your kid's miserable and not being able to do a damn thing about it." Then she gets up, removing my empty dish. "So you've been carrying around this secret for all these months. That's horrible."

All I can do is nod. She goes away, returning seconds later with a tissue, which I silently accept. I'm not crying as much as leaking, as if it's all too much to hold in anymore.

"So what are you going to wear tomorrow for this big date?" she says, again sitting across from me.

Frances doesn't mean to hurt me, I know that. But with her single, seemingly innocuous question, it's as if she's taking me by the shoulders and whispering in my ear, "See over there? Why don't you focus on that, honey?"

And I can hardly breathe through the pain.

Starr comes racing in, however, before I can answer, babbling on about what Jimmy's doing in the basement, I gotta come see, right now. I get up to follow my child, telling myself that no matter what, the instant she's in bed, I'm going online and ordering that paternity test kit.

chapter 25

I know this sounds silly, but I wasn't all that comfortable with Alan seeing this place. This is someone used to staying at the freaking *Plaza,* after all. And while I'm not ashamed of my home—and I did manage to put a reasonable dent in the dust bunny/fur ball population—I figured it's a little more plebeian than Alan's used to.

Once again, I was wrong.

He's standing in the middle of our living room, graciously ignoring my sister, child and the cat sitting in a row on the couch. By the way, he's already given me flowers—a mixed bouquet, not roses, good choice, roses would have been pretentious—and complimented me on my outfit, an aqua sixties sheath with silver embroidery around the neck (my mother's), with silver fishnet stockings and nosebleed-inducing ankle strap sandals that are an exact knockoff of a pair of Manolos I saw in the March *Vogue. Exact,* I'm telling you. Twenty-four ninety-nine at some hole-in-the-wall shoe store on Eighth Avenue. And my hair…ohmigod. I'd rushed over to Liv's and promised her my child if she could make me look good, and after falling on my neck and hugging me and calling me "cousin" like a character from a Jane Austen novel (although for some reason she didn't seem interested in my offer of another child), she sat me down and performed an absolute miracle. I am blown and fluffed and moussed within an inch of my life and dammit, I look *good.*

And you know what they say: if you act like you're having a good time on the outside, you'll start to feel that way on the inside.

"It reminds me a lot of where I grew up," Alan's saying, "before Mum died and Dad remarried. We lived in a semidetached much like this, all the rooms feeding into each other. Even down to the dark wood molding and cornices and the flowerboxes."

He turns to me and smiles, all casual Hugh Grant-ness in an unconstructed charcoal silk blazer. We are going to look so hot together, I can't stand it. "I've nothing but good memories of those times, and that house. Now if there's a local where we can get a pint, we're in business."

"There's always Pinky's," Jen puts in from the couch.

"What's Pinky's?" Alan says as my eyes cut to my sister.

"Just some neighborhood bar," I say, "believe me, you wouldn't be interested—"

"Not at all! After all, how often do I get a chance to experience the real New York?" At what must be my horrified expression, he laughs. And misinterprets. "Don't worry, we've still got dinner reservations for eight-thirty at this terrific little place I stumbled across on East Seventieth. But I've always found the best way to get to know a person is to see them in their real element."

This is me, being thrilled.

Then Starr jumps up from the couch and grabs Alan's hand, exhorting him to come down to the basement to "see Mama's stuff." Since protesting might lead the man to believe I've got bodies stored down there, I cringe and follow, muttering something about it's being a pee-poor workroom, but it was just makeshift and all—

—and then I remember I'd left out my last batch of sketches.

And of course Alan gravitates toward them like Frito to carbs.

"Ellie…" He lifts one up, brows drawn speculatively, then glances over at me. "These are quite remarkable."

"You're very kind."

A puzzled frown crosses his features. "*Kind* is what I am to old ladies who need help getting a can down off the top shelf. But I don't flatter. And I thought about taking a stab at a fashion career, before the theater bug bit me and I discovered I preferred working on a larger scale. I do have some idea of what I'm talking about. So believe me when I tell you these are good. *Very* good."

"This one's my favorite," Starr says, handing him one of a pants set, a mandarin collared duster over slender, too-long pants.

"These are all designed for larger women?"

"Um, yeah. I didn't figure the size twos needed another designer."

He smiles. "I daresay you're right." Then he crosses his arms, the sketch dangling from his hand. "Why on earth haven't you pursued this as a career?"

It's as if a sudden storm flares up inside my skull, opposing ions repelling and colliding or whatever the hell it is they do. I open my mouth, fully expecting all the excuses to come flying out—that I don't have the talent/money/means to do this, that I have a kid, that I can't take the risk. Instead, all I hear is, "I guess the timing just hasn't been right." I don't even know what that means, but at least it puts the kibosh on the interrogation.

Ten minutes later, we're threading our way through the clot of bodies seated outside of Pinky's. The heavy summer night air is redolent with the scent of ten-buck cologne, cigarette smoke and hope; inside is no different, except for the cigarette smoke, and the fact that the air-conditioning's up so high my lip gloss instantly congeals.

"Classy joint, huh?" I yell over the blare of the jukebox, the roar of conversation.

As we slide onto a pair of just-vacated bar stools, Alan dips his mouth close to my ear. So I can hear him. "It's terrific," I think he says. Brother. And I think *I* don't get out much.

I introduce Alan to Jose, who plunks our order—a Diet Coke for me, a German beer for Alan—in front of us before answering a signal from the other end of the bar. Within the next two minutes, no less than a half dozen people I went to school with make it a point to say "Hi" and exchange a few words. A few are in here by themselves, or with dates, but I'm surprised by how many are here with their spouses. And how relaxed and happy and content they seem. These aren't losers trying desperately to validate their existence by making a transitory connection with another human being, but perfectly normal people simply out having a good time.

Perfectly normal people who've lived their entire lives in this neighborhood.

And are perfectly okay with that.

"Looks as though I'm out with the popular girl," Alan says, tipping back his brew. This guy makes chugging beer from a bottle look elegant. I am seriously out of my league here.

"Hardly," I say, stirring my swizzle stick in my Coke in order to get rid of some of the carbonation so I don't belch after drinking it. "Just hit the right night, that's all."

I can feel his eyes on the side of my face, but before he can say anything, I hear, "Ellie! Hey, girl!"

I turn around to see a grinning Lisa Lamar, in a miniskirt and one of those skimpy tops where the whole point is to show off your purple lace Victoria's Secret bra, hanging on to some new guy's arm. This one has hair, at least. So much hair, in fact, the medal around his neck is nearly swallowed up in it.

"This is Sal," she says coyly, forking her fingers through her long, tiger striped hair.

I make introductions; Alan and Sal shake hands, Lisa sizes Alan up without being predatory about it. She always was good that way. Then she makes appreciative noises about my outfit, before—and I can tell it's been killing her to hold back—shyly extending her left hand, on which sparkles a fairly impressive solitaire. Round cut, simple platinum setting. I doubt we're talking Tiffany's here, but not bad. Not bad at all.

"I don't mean to brag," she says as I make appropriate excited-for-you noises, "but Sal just gave it to me for my birthday last night and I'm still in shock! We're gettin' married in November!"

The guys shake hands, Lisa and I hug. Then she asks me about doing her wedding dress, since she knew someone who'd gone to Heather's wedding and it was all she could talk about, how gorgeous the dress was.

"An' I want to look classy, you know? You can do that, right?"

Well, yeah. But before I can figure out how to tell her I can't exactly do something for a couple hundred bucks, she says she's been saving up for this since she was sixteen, price is no object.

"Define 'no object,'" I shout.

"Sal," she says, lightly smacking him in the arm to interrupt his conversation with Alan, "you got somethin' to write with?" He hands her a matchbook and a pen; she scribbles on it and hands it to me, saying in my ear, "I didn't think I should exactly be shouting this figure at the top of my lungs, you know what I mean?"

I'm staring dumbfounded at the number on this tiny piece of cardboard. Uh, yeah, I know exactly what she means.

"So. This would work?" she says.

I take the pen from her and write down my cell number on the matchbook and hand it back. "Call me," I say, and she squeals. Although we really need to talk about the tiger-striped hair, I think as the happy couple squeeze their way back to their table. Maybe I'll bring Liv in on this one.

"Drumming up business?" Alan says, grinning.

"Apparently so."

"You want to be careful, though."

"About what?"

Somebody's put on some ancient Rolling Stones number (it's been a while since the music selection's been updated, but nobody seems to mind), so he has to lean over again in order for me to hear him. Damn, he smells good.

"If you get too busy making wedding dresses for your friends, you won't have any time or energy to develop your own line."

Now, would somebody tell me why that totally supportive comment is sending prickles of irritation along my skin? Why I'm prompted to shoot back, "But I *like* making wedding dresses for my friends"?

And mean it?

I see Frances and Jimmy come in and wave them over. In her tank top and slinky, ankle length skirt, Frances looks like a teenager, which I tell her.

"Which only goes to show," she says, climbing up on the stool perpendicular to mine, "if the room's dark enough, anybody can look good."

"Ain't that the truth," Jimmy says, hauling himself up onto the stool next to his wife and signaling to Jose to bring them a couple of beers. "Soon as I come in, some chick sidles up to me and says—" he lifts his voice into a breathy falsetto "—can I have your autograph, Mr. Clooney?"

We all laugh, not because Jimmy's corny joke is funny, but because he's so damn sincere about it. And as I make introductions, a wave of tenderness washes over me for these people, immediately followed by a twinge of conscience for how much for granted I've taken their presence in my life. If I were drunk, this would be where I'd drape myself around their necks and blubber, "I love you guys!" Since I'm not, I settle for talking and laughing and munching munchies for the next few minutes, until I suddenly catch Frances focusing on something, or someone, beyond me. Without thinking, I twist around, at the precise moment all the bodies part, giving me a clear shot of the booths. And there, in the same back booth where Tina and I had our little chat way back in January, I see her again. Only this time, she's sitting across from Luke.

Her gaze flies to mine as though answering my call, but her expression gives nothing away. A second later, Luke—whose back is to us—rises and goes to the restroom; when he's gone, Tina lifts one brow, smiles triumphantly and gives me a big thumbs-up.

I twist back around, briefly catching Frances's eyes. But I refuse to hold her gaze, refuse to let myself see the relief I know will be there.

"Ellie?" Alan asks. "Is everything okay?"

I look into his kind, concerned face and think, *For God's sake, Ellie—snap out of it.* Here I sit, out on a date with a wonderful, funny, together guy who—for whatever reason—is fascinated with me and who treats me like gold. And who, as far as I know, isn't still attached to some other woman (although I should probably ascertain that for sure before much longer). Maybe the circumstances surrounding our being together are a little off-the-wall, and maybe we'll end up hating each other by the end of the evening. But if this isn't a sign that I need to start enjoying what's put in front of me instead of pining away for the one thing that's not on the menu, I don't know what is.

"Yes, everything's fine," I say, giving him a bright smile. "But we should probably get going, don't you think?"

Alan's eyes narrow, just a fraction, but he gets out his wallet and leaves a bill on the bar as we make our excuses to Frances and Jimmy. Frances grabs my hand and says, "Have a great time, you two." Then, in a lowered voice to me, "You deserve it, baby."

That much, I can definitely agree with.

Three hours later, I think it's safe to say Alan and I don't hate each other.

In fact, I think it's even safer to say he's one of the nicest guys I've ever met. And since he hasn't stuffed me in a taxi and thrown money at the driver, I guess he doesn't think I'm too strange, either.

And that's not me putting myself down. That's just the way these things work, sometimes. You can put two perfectly nice people together and still end up with zip chemistry. Like trying to put cream cheese on a kielbasa. Nothing wrong with either one, they just don't work together. Although, come to think of it, I remember going over to visit Luke in his apartment a couple months before he and Tina got engaged, and discovering he'd put all his leftovers in one pot and then heat them up whenever he got hungry. Spaghetti, peas, chicken, whatever. Totally disgusting—

Do you *hear* this? I swear, I should be taken out and shot.

In any case…to get back on topic (which is, in case I'm interested, the man with whom I'm currently strolling down Park Avenue), if one can judge a date by the conversation, then this one has been great. At least, nobody's eyes have glazed over yet. Always a good sign. Of course, we're talking typical first-date stuff, but still. Having been on first dates where stepping out in front of a moving bus held no small appeal, this one's a dream.

It's a lovely summer night, the sidewalk's empty enough to hear our own footsteps, the humidity low enough that you can't really smell the dog pee from the gutters. On either side of us, graceful old apartment buildings and sleek office complexes soar, majestic and silent. I look up; you can't really see many stars from the middle of Manhattan, but there's a full moon, reflected a thousand times in as many windows. Alan follows my gaze.

"It's quite magnificent, isn't it?"

"From this perspective, yes," I say. "Even if it's only an illusion."

"But does that really matter?" I shift my gaze to his, soft and enigmatic in this light. "If something's beautiful, if it makes you feel good, what difference does it make whether it's an illusion or not? After all, isn't it all perspective? Whether something's real or not?"

I laugh. "Whoa. Too deep for me."

"Sorry. A good meal tends to make me wax philosophical. So on a more *pedestrian* note…" He looks down at my feet. "How on earth can you walk in those things?"

"Practice. I've been wearing heels since I was fourteen, when I realized this was as long as my legs were going to get."

"I thought today's women were all about accepting that they come in different shapes and sizes?"

"Oh, I accept my body fine. But short legs are a real pain when you're standing in a crowd. And I find wearing high heels is a helluva lot more practical than hauling around a step stool. Not to mention if I had on flats, we'd have to yell at each other to be heard."

He laughs, then reaches over and takes my hand. His is warm and dry and smooth. It's…nice. "Have you always been this open and honest?"

Guilt spikes through me. "Am I?"

"Compared with most of the women I know, yes. You are. Which is why I know, when I ask you what upset you back at Pinky's, you're going to tell me."

And here I'd thought we'd avoided that little land mine.

"I saw Luke and Tina."

"And that rattled you?"

I'm so screwed. There's nothing I can say that won't either

incriminate me or make me look like an idiot. Or a liar. So I don't say anything.

"I thought you said there was nothing between you?" Alan says softly.

"There isn't."

"Then…?"

I slip my hand out of his. "Look, it's complicated, okay? And I can't explain it, because it doesn't make any sense, and it's my problem to deal with and nobody else's—"

"Sh, sh, sh, it's okay," he says, taking my hand again. "Now I know where things stand, that's all."

I try to remove my hand from his again, but he holds on tight. "And what's that supposed to mean?"

"It means," he says, smiling, "whatever your conflicts, you're still here with me, aren't you? It means, I'm not going to turn back simply because the road looks like it might get a bit bumpy."

My brows knot. "You're awfully confident, aren't you?"

"Not really. But I do like challenges."

"So how come you're not married?"

Have *no* idea where that came from. None. Alan, however, seems to take my erratic behavior in stride. "I was, briefly. A long time ago."

"What happened?"

There's a fountain in front of an office building nearby; he steers me over so we can sit on the pool's ledge. "My career, in a word. I love what I do, but I'm rarely in one spot for longer than a few months. Next year alone, I've got commitments here, in London, Milan, Houston, San Francisco and Prague."

"A lot of people would find that exciting."

"To tell the truth, it's often boring. And incredibly lonely. Especially after so many years." He pauses, then says, "Marlys and I fell madly in love while we were still at university. And got married. But I went straight from school to working as an assistant to a top stage designer, which meant I was rarely around. After a while, Marlys began to wonder what was the point of being married if we were almost never together?"

"I'm so sorry."

"Don't be. She basically asked me to choose between her and my work. And I chose my work. See, she was all for making a cozy little nest in a semidetached in Reading, just as our parents had done. While everything I'd done to that point had been with an eye to escaping cozy little suburban nests. Only now…" He releases a sigh. "I'd kill to have a cozy little nest in Reading. Or a Pinky's to slip off to whenever I felt like it."

"You must be kidding. With all the traveling you do?"

"And do you know what that makes me, Ellie? The outsider. Everywhere I go. Hell, I can't even really call London home anymore. When I am there, I'm either jet-lagged or sleep-deprived, or so busy getting sketches and models done for the next project I rarely have time to go out. Most of my friends have given up on me. And with good reason."

The air between us reeks of his loneliness. "And Marlys?"

"Happily remarried with a pair of brats and a chocolate Lab," he says with a wry smile. Then he cocks his head at me. "I don't know why I'm dumping on you like this. Not exactly stellar first date etiquette."

"S'okay," I say, linking my hands around his arm. Then I add, as if trying to make him feel better, "I don't actually go there very often. Pinky's, I mean. Especially since Starr was born."

"Really? That's a shame. They seem like good people. Good friends."

"They are." To my surprise, tears gather at the corners of my eyes. I blink them back. "Question—if you hate your life so much, why do you do it?"

"Habit?" he says with a slight shrug. "Ego? And the money's not bad, not at my level. But frankly, I'm damn close to chucking it all for a teaching job at some college with a great little theater program. How's that for ambitious?"

"I think it sounds a damn sight better than continuing to do something that's making you miserable."

He twists around to smile into my eyes. Then one hand brackets my jaw and his mouth drops to mine. He's a good kisser, gentle but thorough, and for a moment I feel swept up in something sweet and magical, as close to a fairy tale as I'm going to get. But when he breaks the kiss, even though he then touches his lips to my forehead and strokes my cheek with his thumb, even though he's doing everything exactly right, I can't say that anything's really fizzing here. Yes, he's a nice man who can kiss well, but I'm not really meeting him halfway.

He gets up and pulls me to my feet, keeping my hand in his as we walk back to the garage where he parked the Lexus. I glance up at the thousand moons, and realize it's only magic if I believe it is. That, if I'm being honest, Manhattan is just a place like any other. Its power to mesmerize, to seduce, to excite, is in direct proportion to my willingness to be mesmerized, seduced, excited.

That it really is all about perspective.

On the drive back to Richmond Hill, Alan talks a lot about his work, I bore him to tears (I imagine) with Starr stories. I get the feeling the kiss didn't exactly fire his jets, either. Not that I'm surprised. Or disappointed. Like I said, either the chemistry's there, or it isn't. No harm, no foul.

"You don't have to see me in," I say when we pull up in front of my house, and Alan chuckles.

"Was it that bad?"

I flush up to my roots. "No, it wasn't bad. At all. It's just…I don't want to waste your time."

He angles his body to lean his forearm on the steering wheel. I can only half see his expression in the light from the halogen streetlamp, but I can tell he's smiling. "I didn't think they made them like you anymore."

"Like what?"

"You'll slug me."

"No, I won't."

"Old-fashioned."

I slug him. Well, try to. He's got great reflexes. And a selective memory.

"I'm not sure I'd call a woman who doesn't know who the father of her child is exactly old-fashioned."

He shrugs. "An aberration." Then he reaches over and fingers one of the earrings. "So. Was that kiss as boring for you as it was for me?"

"You would have to ask that."

"Then I guess you'd probably think me completely daft for wanting to ask you out again."

"Uh, yeah. Why?"

"Because I enjoy your company. And I could use a friend in New York."

Yep, that's me. Miss Port in a Storm.

"I can't believe you don't have other friends here."

"I have professional colleagues. And acquaintances. But trust me, nobody I can talk to the way I did to you tonight."

I feel my mouth stretch tight. "I'd be using you, Alan. How fair is that?"

"I'd be using you, too. So we're even."

I think about this a minute, then say, "Define 'friend.'"

He grins. "Define 'using.'"

"Maybe I should get back to you on that."

"Fair enough."

He kisses me again—okay, so maybe something stirs this time, but nothing to write home about—and I get out, watching as he drives away. Then I look over at Mrs. Patel's flamingo, spotlighted from opposite angles. Even though Independence Day was a week ago, the little fellow's still dressed in his Uncle Sam attire, complete with a striped top hat. He's also still standing like a happy drunk, which somehow seems at odds with his patriotic attire. And I'm sorry, but this is really bugging me. So, being the good neighbor that I am, I troop across the street, hike my skirt up to my crotch and carefully climb over the spiked wrought iron fence to straighten him up.

Which is when an alarm worthy of Leavenworth goes off.

Lights go on, windows fly open, a string of Hindi assaults me.

"It's just me, Mrs. Patel," I shout over the alarm as I shield my eyes from the glare of a extra-high-powered flashlight beam. As if the spotlights weren't enough?

"Who is me, please?"

"Ellie. Levine. Um…you might want to turn off the alarm before you piss off the neighbors?"

She disappears from the window; five seconds later, the alarm mercifully dies. Although my ears will be ringing for a week. Then she pops back at the window. "Ellie? What are you doing out there, please?"

"The flamingo was crooked." A giggle bubbles up in my throat. "I was just trying to fix him, that's all."

"Oh. Oh, I see. Well, thank you. But next time, perhaps it would be better if you just told me and let me do it?"

"I'll do that, Mrs. P." I say, hefting my form back over the fence. "'Night."

"Good night, dear," she says, and the window slams shut.

Brother, I think, as the giggles take over. I can't even straighten out a meshuggah plastic flamingo without screwing things up. How the hell am I supposed to straighten out my life?

chapter 26

The kit arrives the next day. During the very five minutes I'd zipped next door to check out a "funny noise" in Mrs. Nguyen's kitchen, which turned out to be a rattling wok on top of her refrigerator.

As promised, the box is discreetly labeled. However, since Ellie Never Gets Packages, and since clearly nobody, including the cat, has a life, a trio of eager, curious faces greet me upon my return.

"What is it?" Starr asks.

I really thought I was ready for this.

Ha. Ha.

"It's a test."

"For what?"

Oh, boy.

"To help us find out who your father is."

My sister's head spins around so fast I'm surprised it doesn't launch into orbit. Starr, however, just frowns.

"How does it work?" she says. Hmm…maybe she doesn't understand how babies happen as clearly as I thought she did. My heart rate ratchets down a notch or two as I calmly explain the cheek swabbing process. Although I suppose I kinda give the impression that I only need her sample in order to find out.

Starr speculatively eyes the box in my hands. "Will it hurt?"

"Not at all."

Not physically, anyway.

"And then we'll know?"

"After the results come back from the lab, yes."

"Does this mean he'll come live with us?"

Oh, God. I squat down and take her hands. "I don't really know what's going to happen. But I doubt anything's really going to change."

"Just checking," she says and leaves the room.

I turn to my sister, sitting on the sofa, clutching the cushion welting on either side of her thighs as though afraid of being launched into orbit after all. Figuring I might as well get this part of things over with, I sit down beside her and wait. Sure enough, she glances around to make sure the kid's not within earshot, then whispers, "I don't know what's more unbelievable—that you don't know who Starr's father is, or that you waited this long to find out! Jesus, Ellie—what were you *thinking?*"

"Jen? If you think you can possibly make me feel worse than I already do, fuggedaboutit."

"But *why?* Why would you do something like that?"

Bile rises in my throat as I see in her horrified face a sample of what I'm going to face dozens of times over the next little while. I get up, walking over to the window with my arms tightly crossed over my roiling stomach.

"All I can say is, I had my reasons. Reasons which I thought made sense at the time. And believe me, it's no picnic knowing that no matter what I do now, or what I did then, *somebody* is going to hate me for it, or think I'm stupid or selfish or a total twit." I turn to her, tears fogging my vision. "That Starr will think that, one day."

"Oh, shit," Jen says, getting up to wrap me in her arms. She has never, to my knowledge, hugged or held me before, and it feels very strange now.

"Honey," she says into my hair, "if you're stupid or selfish or a total twit, where does that leave me?" She loosens her hold to grimace at me. "It's just…a shock, you know?"

"Yeah. I know." Then I think, oh, what the hell, and tell her the rest of it.

"Luke?" she squeaks, her eyes huge. *"While he was married?"*

"Give me *some* credit, for God's sake! Of course not! It happened before. And it was one of those drunken insanity things."

"But you're not sure?"

Now it's my turn to grimace. "I'd slept with Daniel two days before."

"Jesus." She pauses. To recoup, I'm guessing. Then: "Does Luke know? That she might be his?"

"He can count, Jen." At her flummoxed expression, I add, "For what it's worth, the decision to keep this secret wasn't just mine."

She lets go of me, crossing her arms. "Let me guess. To protect Tina."

"Yeah." At her snort, I add, "But you weren't around then, you didn't know—"

"Trust me, once a manipulative little bitch, always a manipulative little bitch. And before you jump to her defense, remember who you're talking to." Her mouth pulls to one side. "We're like alcoholics, you know. We're never really cured."

I open my mouth to defend Tina anyway, only to remember all too clearly our last conversation. And back before that, how she always knew exactly how to get our sympathy, how adept she was at playing Luke, knowing where his soft spots were. Are.

Mine, too.

"God. You must think I'm a weenie of the first order."

"Sometimes. But that's only because you want to see the good in people. And be helpful. And be liked." When I wince, she says, "Which is one of the reasons I hated your guts when we were kids. Because you *were* liked. By pretty much everybody."

I let out a sigh. "Guess those days are over."

Jen slings an arm around my shoulder. "Welcome to my world, babycakes."

Over the past twenty-four hours, I've left four cryptic messages on Luke's various answering machines, fielded a call from some woman named Renee Tomaszewski who'd been at Heather's wedding who has a dress shop in Forest Hills and would I maybe be interested in whipping up—her words—a few gowns for her more zaftig patrons (I told her I'd get back to her), allowed Alan to talk me into going out with him again (I need the diversion) and thought a lot about what Jen said about Tina.

A lot.

See, the thing is, I'm finally beginning to realize most of the mess I'm in stems from my being an approval seeker of the first order. In school I was a major brown-noser; in every job I ever had, I'd knock myself out just to eke out a word of praise from my superiors. What can I tell you, working for Nikky Katz fed my ego. So basically, I'd do anything—and overlook anything—in order to ensure I stayed in someone's good graces.

Now I think I can finally, maybe, accept that not everybody is going to like me, no matter how much I want them to. That I might have to occasionally tick off somebody in order to save my own neck. And that, amazingly enough, I'll still probably be able to have a relatively okay life. However, what I hadn't fully understood (before Jen so eagerly shoved my face in it) was that in my zeal to keep Tina as my friend, I guess I did sorta overlook her tendency to be a mite on the manipulative side now and then.

Like every chance she gets.

That's not to take away the times she was there for me. Or that her childhood really was crummy. Nor do I think she's "bad" because she had an abortion, or because she doesn't want kids. But she knew damn well that Luke and I felt sorry for her, and she milked it for every drop.

And she still is.

What I'm going to do about this, if anything, I have no idea. But I think I just snipped another thread tethering me to someplace I no longer need to be.

Whee.

I try Luke's number again. Still no answer. Finally I take the bull by the horns and call Frances, figuring if anybody would know where Luke was, she would.

"He's gone away with Tina for a few days, baby—didn't you know?"

Okay, that does it. I'm tired of trying to fix this all by myself, tired of worrying about hurting this or that person's feelings, tired of the whole stinking deal. So, after I hang up with Frances, I pack up the kit, with Starr's sample safely tucked inside, schlep the damn thing to the post office and mail it to him. Whenever he gets around to taking care of it is fine with me.

Meanwhile, I've got a life to live.

Somewhere in here.

Two days later, he calls.

"What the hell's the big idea, *sending* this to me?"

"I got tired of leaving messages. So sue me. Why? Is she there?"

"Who?"

"Tina, who else?"

"Tina?" He actually sounds confused. "No. Why?"

"Just wondering."

He sighs into the phone. "Let me guess. Mom told you we'd gone away."

"Well, yeah, when I couldn't get hold of you, I asked her. I guess she didn't figure it was like this big secret or anything." Criminy—what's with the reversion to teenybopperdom here? "So anyway, I figured sending it to you was the easiest thing, that's all. The instructions are in it, just send it on whenever you're ready—"

"She told me."

My heart skips a beat. "She told you what?"

"That she had an abortion."

"Oh, Luke—"

"And that you knew."

He doesn't sound angry as much as...worn-out.

And hurt.

My insides get so twisted up I can barely breathe. "It wasn't like I *asked* to know. But once I did, what was I supposed to do? Do you guys have any idea how often you've stuck me in the middle with all these secrets—?"

"Yes," he says. "I do. And now..." He lets out another sigh, then says, "Funny thing. All these years, the three of us thought we had this unshakable relationship, when actually...I dunno, El. Were any of us ever totally honest with each other?"

But before I can figure out what to say, he says, "I'll send this out tomorrow, okay?" and hangs up.

I nearly crumple from the sudden emptiness I feel inside, a void so great and vast and cold I can't imagine how I'll live through it. Because maybe Luke didn't say that was the end, but I could hear it in his voice. That our friendship had been like a sweater with the first rows off-kilter, so the more we kept adding to it, the more off it got. And now we have this huge, ugly, unwieldy *thing,* but no one in their right mind could call it a real sweater.

And who has the energy to rip it all out and start over?

Frito jumps into my lap; I hug his mangy, furry body to my chest and hang on. He doesn't seem to mind. In a way, this is almost harder than having someone die. Because at least that's final. Yeah, it hurts like hell, but there's nothing you can do about it except grieve and move on. But this…

This just sucks.

A week later, when Jen's gone into the city for a couple of job interviews, Dolly calls and invites Starr and me to lunch. I eagerly accept, since I've determined that I am *not* going to sit around and mope about Luke like some dorky adolescent. Or eat myself into oblivion. So, since moping and eating were taken off the schedule, that left me with cleaning and fixing.

The house actually *sparkles.* I even cleaned behind the refrigerator (found an earring I haven't worn since tenth grade, among other things). And the rental house not only has all new screens, but I've got most of the wood trim around the porch scraped and ready for new paint.

I am hot stuff when I'm depressed, let me tell you.

Anyway, so Dolly asked us to lunch, and we accepted. She and I have talked a few times since the Big Revelation (according to Liv, after the initial shock, the family's really rallied around their mother/grandmother. Oh, and by the way? Dolly's mother, grandmother and maternal aunts all lived well into their nineties. So maybe I've got a little more time to figure things out than I'd thought.) and Dolly's taken Starr for an outing or two, but this is the first time I'll have spent any real time with her since then.

We make quite a picture, we three. If there's a color in the rainbow not represented somewhere on our bodies, I don't know what it would be. And we're all wearing hats—me, a cute little straw with a turned up brim; Starr, a bright yellow ball cap crammed onto her frizz; and Dolly, a purple, floppy-brimmed number, secured under her chins by means of a gauzy, floral scarf. But you know, she looks twenty years younger. And, she says on the bus going up to Jamaica (she says there's this great little Italian place she's been wanting to try, but she doesn't like eating out alone) she's lost ten pounds.

"Without even trying," she says, beaming, her face slightly lavender underneath the purple brim. "There's a lot to be said for shedding a burden you've been lugging around for fifty years."

So that's the secret? Ditch your problems, lose your butt? Who'd've thought?

Anyway, we have our lunch in this joint, it's nothing special, I'm not sure I see what the big deal is. I'd also like to know why my daughter keeps giving me this furtive little grin, like something's going on. Sure enough, after Dolly pays the check, she says, "There's something I want to show you, a couple blocks up."

Starr's smile widens.

"Oh? What?"

"You'll see," my daughter says, slipping her hand into her great-grandmother's. We start out down Jamaica Avenue at a dignified, full-of-pizza pace, (so much for not eating myself into oblivion), but my grandmother and daughter suddenly pull out in front, urging me to get the lead out, already. Now I can see someone, a woman, standing out on the sidewalk, obviously watching and waiting for us.

Frances?

Then a second woman appears.

Jennifer?

"What's going on—?"

"Promise you'll keep an open mind," Jen says as Frances unlocks the door to the tiny, nondescript three-story building, flanked by a shoe repair shop on one side and a florist's on the other. It's your basic little store, retail space in front, complete with a few leftover racks and display cases (as if the previous tenants stole away in the middle of the night), storage room/office in back, tiny bathroom, kitchenette. A pair of minuscule dressing rooms. Two large floor-through apartments upstairs, Frances says.

It's not even officially on the market yet, she says.

And an unbelievable bargain.

So we'd need to move fast.

I look at her. "What the heck are you talking about?"

"Oh, for heaven's sake, Mama!" Starr huffs. "Get with the program, already!"

"It *would* be perfect," Frances says as I gawk at my daughter. "You could have a shop down here, but convert the second floor into a workroom."

"And I could rent the top floor," Jen says.

I'd sit down if there was someplace to sit. They've all gone mad. Mad, I tell you.

Dolly slips her arm around my waist. "It *would* be perfect, wouldn't it?"

"Perfectly insane! I mean, yes, it's great…" I look around, thoroughly annoyed with myself that I can already visualize what the place would look like fixed up. And I haven't even seen the upstairs yet. "But I can't possibly *buy* a building and go into business, just like that! And certainly not on this scale!"

"Well," Jen says, "you certainly can't keep working out of our basement."

"Especially since the city'll get on your case about having customers come to the house in a residential zone," Frances says. "Besides, you can take out a second mortgage on the rental house to swing the down payment. If Dolly's investment won't cover it."

My eyes swing to my grandmother. "Your what?"

"I've been thinking about this for a while," she says, her mouth set in a fierce, don't-even-think-about-bucking-me line. "And I decided I want you and Jen to have the money your grandfather left to me. I didn't expect it, and I don't really need it. And I'd love to invest that money in your new business. With the stipulation that you make me the head of your workroom."

"And," Jen says, positively fizzing with excitement, "I'll throw a totally awesome launch party for you!"

This is surreal.

I sit down anyway, right on the tatty root beer slush-colored carpeting, trying not to think about what might be crawling around in there.

"And Jimmy and I talked it over," Frances says, "and we wanna help, too. So our accountant and lawyer are yours until you start showing a profit."

Tears crest in my eyes as Starr plops into my lap. "Why?" I say. "Why do you want to do this for me?"

Frances crouches in front of me, taking my hand. Her dark eyes bore into mine. "Because we love you, you nitwit. And we believe in you. Even if you don't."

I burst into tears. Because I don't know what I've done to deserve having all these people love me this much, because I'm petrified to take such a huge risk and let everybody down.

Frances gets on her knees and takes me in her arms as Starr wraps hers around my neck, practically choking me. "What's the worst that can happen, huh?" Frances says, smoothing my hair out of my face.

"I screw u-up and l-lose everybody's money?"

She laughs. "We all know it's a risk, baby. We also have every confidence that if anybody can make this work, you can. And so what if it doesn't?" I pull a face. "No, really. What's the worst that can happen? You sell the building at a great profit, right? Far as I can tell, this is a total win-win situation."

I blow my nose and look around through watery eyes. "Oh, God, Frances…I don't know…"

"Tell you what. If you want some time to think it over, put a bid on the place with a couple thou earnest money. By law, you've got forty-eight hours to withdraw your bid and get the money back."

"A whole forty-eight hours, huh?"

"Trust me," she says, getting to her feet. "It's plenty of time."

Right.

I turn to find myself nose to nose with my daughter. "Okay, Twink—if I do this, it's likely to mean I'm going to be very, very busy. So be honest, here…would you really be okay with that?"

She shrugs. "What else are you gonna do while I'm at school all day, huh? I think you should go for it. Hey…" One skinny little finger pokes at my shoulder. "Life is short, right?"

The ladies all crack up as I pull this strange creature I gave birth to into my arms. Then I look up through Starr's cloud of hair at Frances. "Forty-eight hours, you say?"

"Yep."

I sigh. "Okay. I'll think about it—"

But judging from the their reaction, I'm thinking nobody heard anything past *"I'll."*

I take a tour of the upstairs—the apartments are pretty typical over-the-shop types, but sunny and a nice size—and Frances assures me the building's in good shape, it was inspected a year ago and is in no danger of collapsing or anything. Reassuring, that. Afterwards, we all head back to Richmond Hill in Frances's Cadillac (told you she was doing well), dropping Dolly off at her place before taking the rest of us home. As we pull onto our block, she says, "I've got blank contracts at the house, I'll bring some by in a few, if that's okay," only then she mutters "shit" under her breath so only I can hear, since I'm riding shotgun.

"What's wrong?" I whisper.

"On your front steps."

I'm not sure what prompted *her* "shit," but I sure as hell know what prompts mine.

After all, there's only one reason Luke would be here.

chapter 27

Frances lets us out in front of our house, then backs up to pull into her garage. Starr lets out a squeal of glee and barrels into Luke's arms—I cannot tell you how many times she's asked these past couple of weeks when she was going to see him again. And I can tell, from the way he swings her up and holds on tight, burying his face in her hair, how much he's missed her, too. My throat constricts: no matter what's in that envelope I can now see clutched in his right hand, no matter what's happened between us, or why, none of that has anything to do with how much Starr loves him. And I can't—don't want to—believe Luke would let anything mess up how he feels about her, either. But then, I'm only the middleman, here. What do I know?

"Is this about what I think it's about?" Jen says in a low voice beside me.

"That would be my guess, yeah."

"Oh, boy."

Couldn't've said it better myself.

Luke sets Starr down and listens as she prattles on about the store Mama's gonna buy, until Jen takes her niece's hand and ushers her inside with promises of cookies. I half wish I could follow.

Especially when Luke's gaze swivels to me. "Mama's gonna buy a store?"

"Mama's *thinking* about *maybe* buying a store and *maybe* going into business. If I can fend off all the pushy broads in my life. Which includes your mother, by the way."

One side of his mouth twitches. "My mother? Pushy?" Then he sobers. "You know you should do this."

"I don't *know* anything. Except that just thinking about it makes me sick to my stomach. It's not like I can just go blithely into this without thinking about anybody else—"

"Jesus, El—when are you gonna stop being so damn scared?"

"Scared? Of what?"

"Of goin' after what you want."

My eyes burn, because maybe I didn't want to admit it, but Jen was right. My mother might have used Jen and me as an excuse not to pursue her career, but the fact was, she *was* scared of failing. And her fear was contagious, a fear I refused to acknowledge. Until now. "It's not that easy."

"I know that," he says softly. "But you gotta remember you got all these people behind you who're not gonna let you fall." I look away; he angles his head so I have to look at him again. "Right?"

I let out a sigh. "I guess."

"No guessin' about it. Look, all I'm saying is…whatever decision you make, make it because it's what you want to do. Not what you think you should do. Okay?"

After a moment, I nod. Then our gazes hang on to each other as we both remember why he's really here.

"Anyway," he says. "I was about to leave a note. But then you got here, so I guess I won't—"

"Luke, for God's sake, just tell me already."

His hand streaks through his hair, longer than it's been in ages. Then he looks at me…and shakes his head.

"N-no? You're not…?"

"Nope. I'm not." He hands me the envelope. "See for yourself. Hundred percent accuracy for exclusion, they say."

I sink onto the steps, staring at the report in my shaking hands, but not believing it. Then I start to laugh. The laugh of a lunatic.

"You know what this means? It means we've spent five years keeping a nonexistent secret. How screwed up is that?" He's sat down beside me, his hands linked between his knees. I look at him and say, "Why didn't we do this sooner, Luke? Why?"

"Beats me. Unless…"

"Unless?"

But he waves at the air, shaking his head. I decide I don't have the energy to pry out of him whatever he's thinking, so instead I glance again at the report, as if I expect to see something different this time. Of course, I don't. Which prompts me to say, "Well, at least you know you're off the hook now."

"What do you mean?"

"About Starr."

He frowns. "You can't be serious. You honestly think I'd turn my back on her just because of a stinkin' piece of paper? Ellie, I love that kid. I always have. And nothin's gonna change that."

"Then why haven't you been around to see her these past weeks? Dammit, Luke—things have *already* changed."

"No," he says, his eyes burning into mine. "I know it might have seemed that way, while Tina and I were trying to hash out some stuff, but I swear to you, Ellie—nothing's changed."

I bolt to my feet, muttering "Bullshit" as I storm up the stairs. Except he grabs my arm and pulls me back around.

"Christ—you think I'm still with Tina, don't you?"

"It doesn't matter what I think, it's none of my business—"

"Of course it's your business, you idiot. And I'm an idiot for assuming you knew what was going on."

"Luke, the last thing out of your mouth was how Tina wanted to get back together —"

"That's right," he says, letting go of my arm to hook his thumbs in his front pockets. "*She* wanted to get back together. Not me. I only agreed to go away with her so we could work out some stuff without everybody breathin' down our necks. But you thought that meant we'd patched things up."

"I didn't know what it meant. But I know Tina."

Oops.

One side of Luke's mouth hitches up. "Yeah. Me, too. But what you're forgetting is, I'm not the same guy I was five years ago. I'm a little better at spotting the traps these days. And if I can at all help it, I'm not gonna get caught." He hooks one foot on the bottom step, leaning against the railing. "I got friendship and concern and sympathy confused with love once, but damned if I'm gonna let that happen again. Believe me, El," he says, softly, "I will do everything in my power to avoid repeating my mistakes."

Not that he's saying anything I don't already know, but still. Hope's a stubborn little cuss. Especially the breed that lives inside me.

"Just answer me one thing," I say. "When you found out about the abortion…did that…influence your decision?"

He looks away, pushing out a breath before letting his gaze return to mine. "When Tina told me, I thought I'd die inside. I mean…for God's sake, El, it's not like I can just shove aside everything I've been raised to believe, you know? Especially…since it was my kid." His shoulders hitch under his T-shirt. "I felt like somebody'd torn my guts out. Even though, the weird thing is, I actually kinda understood why she did what she did, because she was right—I would've tried to talk her into having the baby. And that wouldn't've been fair to her. But to answer your question…no. It didn't influence my decision. That'd been made a long time ago. Not that I suppose Tina really believes that, but I can't help what she thinks." A wry smile pulls at his mouth. "Took me a long time to figure that out."

I sit back down on the step, not looking at him. "You don't hate me?"

He frowns slightly, but I don't have to explain any further. He knows exactly what I mean. After a second or two, he sits beside me again.

"I did, at first. I thought, Christ, why did I need to know this? But then I understood."

"Did you?" I grimace. "*Do* you?"

"Enough," he says, then gets quiet, staring out across the street at the flamingo. The bird's still doing his Uncle Sam impression, but at least he's standing up straight now. When Luke finally speaks again, his voice has gone so low, I can barely hear it. But I can feel the intensity of his words in every molecule of my being. "I still think sometimes there are good reasons for people to keep secrets from each other. But if that's *all* a relationship is based on, what's the point? I felt a lot more…betrayed because Tina didn't feel like she could be really open with me than I did because she'd had an abortion. That hurt, yeah, but the other…" He shakes his head. "That made me feel like shit. Especially since it wasn't like I couldn't tell something was wrong, anyway."

"And here I thought men were supposed to be oblivious to those sorts of things."

His eyes meet mine. Then he chuckles. "I'm not brain-dead, for chrisssake. Maybe I can't figure out *what's* wrong if somebody doesn't tell me, but I sure as hell can figure out *something's* wrong." Then something shifts in his eyes, and I get the strangest feeling he's trying to see inside my brain. "Just as I've always been able to tell when you're keeping something from me."

Heat roars up my neck and across my cheeks. *You bet your tush I'm keeping something from you. And nuns will streak through Central Park naked before I tell you what—*

"Ellie?"

My head jerks up. To see Alan. Who's pulled up in front of the house while Luke and I have been chatting. I glance at my watch and let out a yelp—I've totally spaced our date.

"Who's that?" Luke says as Alan gets out of the Lexus and beeps it locked.

"His name's…Alan," I say quietly, as he approaches the steps, smiling broadly. I hope to hell Luke doesn't think it weird that I'm leaving off Alan's last name, but there are only so many things I can deal with right now. Alan's dressed practically the same as Luke, in T-shirt and jeans, but I can't deny there's something more…posh about him. I'm thinking it's the way he moves, with this casual grace that makes him look more as if he belongs in a menswear ad than on a street in Queens. So how come I'm not feeling a ripple of anticipation or excitement or lust or something? "We, um, kinda have a date."

"Really?" Luke says. "You should've said something, I wouldn't've kept you."

I only have half a second to glance at Luke, but his expression isn't giving anything away. So I make brief introductions, holding my breath that nobody says anything to make this meeting any more awkward than it already is. But either Alan's forgotten Luke's name, or he's being discreet. As for Luke…

As for Luke, all he does is clamp a hand on my shoulder and say, "Gotta run. You have a good time, okay?" Then to Alan, "Nice meeting you," and he's gone.

And there go my emotions, trotting along right behind him like a flock of dumb sheep.

And dumb sheep aren't real good about coming back when you call.

"Seems like a decent enough chap," Alan says, then smiles at me. "Are you ready, then?"

Or, maybe if I just go off in another direction, the sheep will eventually realize they're wasting their time and come looking for me again.

One can hope.

I look up at Alan and smile. "Sure. Let me just go say bye to Starr and freshen up a bit."

Five minutes later, we're pulling away from the curb when I see Frances hustling out of her house with a folder full of papers. Which is when I remember she was coming over about the store.

And which is when I realize she could have come over anytime while Luke was here. But she didn't.

Hmmm.

"Did I interrupt something?" Alan asks as we pull into traffic. I nearly jump out of my skin.

"Interrupt something?"

His eyes veer to mine, a small smile playing around his mouth. "You got the results back, didn't you?"

Honest to God, my brain is like a sieve today. Talk to Luke, forget about Alan. Talk to Alan, forget why Luke came over to begin with. At this rate, I'm going to forget to put underwear on when I get up in the morning.

"Yeah, we did."

"And...?"

"Luke's not the father," I say softly, unable to wipe Luke's disappointed face from my brain. "Daniel is."

For a second or two, my words don't seem to register. Then Alan lets out a whoop and bangs his hand on the steering wheel. "A-*ha!* I *knew* it! I knew she was my niece from the moment I realized who you were!"

"It would appear so."

The man is grinning from ear to ear, as though I'd just announced she was *his* child. "But this is bloody marvelous, Ellie! I'm absolutely delighted."

"I can see that," I say, trying to muster at least a little reciprocal enthusiasm. But it ain't working.

"Ellie? Is anything wrong?"

I turn to face him, leaning heavily against the headrest. I suppose I should at least try to be diplomatic, but I'm too tired. "Other than the fact that I now have to figure out how, or if, to tell my daughter about her father? I mean, how the hell can I be objective about this? Or do I even want to? Your brother was a liar and a cheat, Alan. Kinda hard to couch those qualities in a flattering light."

Since the first part of that description fits me, too…all I can say is *Ouch.*

After a moment he says, "I can see your dilemma."

I sincerely doubt that. But I smile, a little, and say, "Thanks."

His eyes dart to mine, then back on the traffic. I must say, for a non-New Yorker, he gives the taxi drivers a pretty decent run for their money.

"But my guess is you're more upset that Luke's *not* the father, aren't you?"

I blink rapidly. "It sure would've made things easier."

"Would it?"

I sigh. "Okay, no, I suppose not. Not at first, anyway. But at least Luke and Starr are already bonded. He's always been there for her, and she's always been crazy about him. She would've been thrilled to find out he's her dad. Not that he's going to turn his back on her or anything now, but…" I shrug, fighting back tears. "It just would've been easier," I repeat softly.

We drive for a good couple of minutes before Alan says, "I'm going to say a few things that I'd actually planned on saving for later, after we'd gotten to know each other a little better. And after I knew for sure that Starr was my niece. But since I imagine I already know what your answer would be, I guess there's not much point in waiting."

Frowning, I turn to him, but he holds up one hand before I can open my mouth.

"Just hear me out. I mean, I suppose there's an off-chance I could be wrong—" his eyes meet mine for a brief moment, then he smiles "—but I doubt it. However, I believe people should be able to make decisions based on all available information, don't you? And I would think you'd want me to be completely honest with you."

"Well, yes, I suppose. But what—?"

"I was going to invite you and Starr to come live in London with me."

My jaw drops to my lap. "Are you out of your *mind?*"

He chuckles. "Oh, there's no doubt about that. But your reaction was even better than I expected."

"For God's sake, Alan—we barely know each other!"

"Which was why I hadn't planned on saying anything just yet. But I've always wanted kids, and I'd love to have Starr closer so I could get to know her better. And I'd love to have you closer so I could get to know you better, too. And I've talked to some people in the fashion business over there who are very interested in seeing what you've got. I don't think it would be difficult to find serious backing, if you're really interested in going out on your own."

He probably wonders why I've just burst into semihysterical laughter. But the last thing I expected when I got out of bed this morning was that, before dinnertime, I'd have, not one, but *two* offers to set me up in business. D'you think somebody's trying to tell me something?

"Alan. This is New York. I can start my own business right here, you know."

His eyes fix on mine, cool and silver and confident, just long enough to rattle me. "Believe it or not, Ellie, there's a whole world outside of New York."

I stare blankly at him for several seconds, then face front and stare blankly out the windshield, until something approaching coherent thought sifts through the shock. He's offering me a dream on a stick. Real backing, not just a bunch of women pooling a few thousand dollars to start up a line in an old storefront in Queens. The chance to live in London. And the attentions of the kind of man schleps like me just don't ever figure on having cross their path, you know? And my God, what an incredible opportunity it would be for Starr, right? And the best part is, I could work into all of it gradually, instead of being forced to make a life-altering decision in forty-eight hours.

"Ellie?"

I look over at him…and shake my head.

He just nods.

"One question," I say. "If you knew what my answer was likely to be, why'd you ask me anyway?"

"Because at least this way I *know*. As much as it stings, it's still far better than spending the rest of my life beating myself up because I didn't have the balls to find out." He reaches over and squeezes my hand. Just for a second. "Now you can tell me something. And I want you to think very carefully about your answer. Are you saying 'no' because you're afraid to take a chance?"

"No," I say, immediately and without reservation. "I'm saying 'no' because as tempting as your offer is, it's not what I want."

And with that, I can feel the last puny thread connecting me to whatever the hell I thought I needed to be connected *to* give way, sending me into a surprisingly exhilarating freefall.

"Do you believe in love at first sight, Ellie?" I hear through the whooshing in my ears as I spin and twirl, buoyed aloft by the currents of my own chutzpah.

"Yes," I whisper. Then I turn to him. "Do you?"

"I didn't think so, until I met you and Starr."

I half think of bringing up the less-than-inspiring kiss. But what would be the point? "Oh, God, Alan…I'm so sorry—"

"Don't be. As I said, I'd rather know where things stand for sure than wonder." He looks over at me. "Should I turn around?"

"Yes," I say, my heart beating so hard it hurts.

chapter 28

First things first. I track Frances down at her office and give her a check for five thousand bucks so she can make the offer. There's no guarantee this will even happen—if someone else bids more, I could lose out—but that's not the point. The point is, I'm ready to put my great big butt on the line and work myself half to death because I *will* die if I don't try. Because whether I live for another seventy years or another week, what's the point if I'm not living the life I want? And I vow that I can do this and still be a good mother, a mother my daughter can be proud of, a mother *I* can be proud of.

Then, after I've signed what seems like a thousand papers, I look at Frances, sitting across her desk from me, and announce, "I'm in love with your son."

Her head jerks up; her navy silk blouse ripples from her flinch. Then, slowly, a wide grin spreads across her jaw. "Are you sure?"

"Of course I'm sure—" I frown. "You mean, you don't mind?"

"Mind? Why the hell would I mind?"

"Because I'm an irreligious half-Jew who's never going to be anything but an irreligious half-Jew?"

Her brows crash together over her nose. "You think I only care about labels?"

"Well, I…"

"I'll tell you what you are, little girl. You're somebody who loved her grandfather and is doing a terrific job of raising her kid and who's always thought of other people before you thought of yourself. Maybe sometimes too much, but we can work on that," she adds with a crooked smile. "And you won't crush my son with your love. At least, I don't think you will."

I sit up straighter in my chair. "Not if I can help it."

"Then I don't see a problem here, do you?"

"But I thought you loved Tina?"

Her mouth purses; she frowns at the blotter on her desk for a couple of seconds before her gaze meets mine again. "I did. Still do. That doesn't mean I thought she should've been my daughter-in-law."

"You didn't approve of the marriage?"

"Not particularly. But one of the hardest things about being a mother is accepting that just because you give your kids life, that doesn't give you the right to live it for them. Or to force them to learn lessons they're not ready to learn." She sighs, and shakes her head. "My mother carped about every single choice I made, to the point that by the time she died, we were barely speaking. That's not the relationship I wanted with my kids. So maybe I wasn't all that hot on the idea of Luke marrying Tina. Maybe I could see she had problems I didn't think he was ready or able to deal with. And God knows there were times that I had to remove myself from the room so I wouldn't say something I shouldn't. But in the long run, I think I saved all

of us a lot of *agita*. And the boy is still talking to me, right?"
Then, grinning, she leans forward. "So…what's Luke got to
say about all this?"

"Actually…I haven't told him yet."

Her brows shoot up. "Then what the hell are you doing here?"

"Stalling?"

"You're afraid he doesn't return your feelings?"

The hairs stand up on the back of my neck. "I have no idea.
Do you?"

"Like I would tell you, even if I knew." She gets up and comes
around her desk, clapping her hands like an overly enthusiastic
P.E. teacher. "Come on, come on—what are you waiting for?"

I get up, only to discover my knees aren't working so hot.
There's so much more I want to say, want to ask her. But my
tongue feels swollen and stiff in my mouth as she hugs me, then
turns me around and gently pushes me out the door.

Aiyiyi. Whose idea was it to cut that last thread, anyway?

It's late enough that Luke should be home by now. And sure
enough, I see the Blazer sitting in the parking lot as I approach
his building. I park in one of the visitor's spaces, around the
corner from his entrance. If I lower my chin, I'll drown in the
sweat backed up in my cleavage.

If I don't hurl first.

With a wince, I peel my damp palms off the steering wheel,
open my car door, force first one foot, then the other, onto the
slightly squishy blacktop in the parking lot.

Okay. I'm out of the car.

Now I'm walking away from the car. Toward Luke's side of
the building. Muttering to myself. Mostly stuff like, "What's
the worst thing that can happen? He'll laugh in my face, I'll
be completely humiliated and never be able to go next door for
Sunday dinner again. Other than that…*Oh!*"

Preoccupied with my own fascinating conversation, I don't

notice Tina veering around the corner until our boobs practically collide.

"What the hell are you doing here?" we both shriek, except before I can reply, Tina says, "If you came to see Luke—" Like I'm here to take a stroll around the grounds, what? "—he's not there."

"His car's in the lot."

"Well, *he's not there,* what can I tell you?"

I cross my arms under my breasts. "So how come you're here?"

"None of your business." She pushes past me. "See ya."

"Teen, wait—"

"I've got nothin' to say to you, Ellie."

I totter to catch up with her. "C'mon, don't be like this—"

She whirls around. "Like *what?* Like poor, unstable Tina who needs to be handled with kid gloves?"

"Okay, honey, let's talk about this—"

"You wanna talk? Fine, I'll *talk.*" She gets right in my face, hands on hips, eyes glittering like ice. "You and your big ideas about bein' *honest,* all that shit about clearing the air. I told him the truth, like you said I should. So what does he do? Offers to pay for me to go into therapy."

Not that she needs it or anything.

"Teen, honey…" I try to touch her arm, but she slaps my hand away.

"All those years you let me think you were my best friend, that I could totally trust you, when here you slept with Luke behind my back. I mean, *Christ*—do you really expect me to just go, 'yeah, whatever,' like it doesn't matter?"

"Of course not! But Jesus, Teen—it was *one time.* One stupid, lousy, bombed-out-of-our-minds time that didn't mean anything, when you two weren't even together. Don't you see? There was nothing *to* tell. Especially since we knew how much it would hurt you—"

"That's right, let's not do anything to hurt poor little Tina, 'cause God knows she's too fragile to take it! God knows, Tina can't handle the *truth!*" She emphasizes the last word by shoving me in the shoulder with the heel of her hand.

"Hey—!"

"Let's do everything we can—" another shove "—to protect poor little Tina—" and another, making me stumble backwards "—from reality—"

"Teen, cut it out—"

"What kind of *friend* pulls that kind of shit, huh? I thought friends were supposed to stick together, to support each other?"

Heat flooding my face, I get right smack in hers. "What the *hell* do you think I've been doing all these years? Who got out of your way when you said you had a thing for Luke, huh? Who kept her trap shut about how she really felt, because I wouldn't have hurt you for the world?"

She rears back, her eyes wide. "So you *are* in love with Luke!"

"Oh for God's sake, Tina—I've been in love with Luke since the *first grade.*"

Nothing prepares me for the hot sting of her slap across my face.

But even less prepares me for my reaction.

With a roar, I lunge for her, sending us both down into a bed of impatiens. A *just watered* bed of impatiens.

Twenty-eight years old, four years at Richmond Hill High, and this is my first bona fide chick fight. Or would have been, had not a hand come out of nowhere and dragged me off Tina, hauling me to my feet before either of us could inflict serious damage.

"Jesus, you two!" Luke reaches out to heave Tina to her feet as well. She spits out an impatiens petal, I ponder whether I could be any more mortified. I decide not. "What the hell is going on?"

Tina looks at me. And spits out another petal.

I try to swallow the laugh, but nope. Out it pops, like some guy shot from a cannon.

And damn if Tina doesn't start laughing, too.

We fall into each other's arms, laughing so hard we end up back in the impatiens, hanging on to each other and spewing apologies and picking wet petals out of each other's hair, while Luke stands there muttering, "Women."

Eventually, our laughter subsides to occasional chuckles and lots of undereye-tissue-dabbing. Tina points a finger at me and says, "Don't go anywhere," then clambers to her feet, digging a large envelope out of her purse to hand to Luke.

As I hoist myself upright as well, I see his eyes shoot to her face.

"They're all signed," she says.

"Teen…" He sighs. "You didn't have to bring them."

"Yeah. I did. I needed…I just had to do this in person, y'know?" She grabs his arm, then lifts up to give him a kiss on the cheek. "And now I need you to get lost so Ellie and me can talk."

His brow creased, he looks at me. "Aren't you supposed to be on a date?"

I shrug. "It's over."

"Should I understand anything that's going on here?"

"No," Tina and I say in unison, although Tina adds, "Although you might not want to go far. Things might clear up yet."

Luke looks from one of us to the other. Then, shaking his head, he walks over to a full laundry basket a few feet away, which he hauls up onto his hip. "Well. I'll be up in my place, if, uh, anyone needs me?"

"Fine," we both say.

He stares at us for another second or so, then finally takes off.

I turn to Tina. "Okay. Care to tell me what that was all about?"

Tina crosses to a nearby bench and plops onto it, only to grimace. Wet butt, would be my guess. "You came along at a bad time, is all."

"I gathered that much." I sit beside her. "Are we supposed to hate each other now?"

"I don't know. Is that what we want?"

Slowly, I shake my head. "Not me. But I think you have more cause."

Her laugh is dry. "It's me I'm mad at, nitwit."

"Funny thing. It's my cheek that's stinging."

Tina looks at me, her mouth all screwed up. "I'm really sorry about that. Does it hurt?"

"Like hell. But I'll get over it. As long as you tell me what's *really* going on in your head."

Her inhaled breath expands her chest a full cup size. "Nobody got me into this mess but me, El. Yeah, I'm hurt you screwed Luke. And that you didn't tell me. But you're right—I've never exactly given anyone the impression I could handle the truth, have I? You wanna hear the kicker, though? I'd kinda figured somethin' had happened, because the two of you were acting really weird around each other for months. But as long as you guys didn't say anything, I could pretend I was just imagining it, right?"

I sink back against the bench. "Man. Maybe Luke could get us a group rate with that therapist."

Tina laughs, then twists around. "All I know is, it was wrong, the way I let you guys prop me up the way you did. At least for such a long time. And maybe talking to somebody without a personal stake in the outcome would help me sort through some of this, you know?"

A small smile pulls at my lips. "I am sorry about you and Luke."

"Yeah. I know. And when I leave here, I'm gonna go home and cry my eyes out. But him and me…" Her hair doesn't move when she shakes her head. A good sign—she must be feeling more like her old self if she's gelling her hair again. "It's not right. And it never really was. We don't want the same things."

"So what was all that about wanting him back?"

Another sigh. "Panic, I guess. It was scary as hell, being alone. I was just so used to having Luke around, y'know? Had nothing to do with us being right for each other. Or not." She smirks. "I was just balking at getting on with my life." Her eyes meet mine. "My own life. Without Luke."

I look out over the grounds. "You lied about the affair, didn't you?"

After a moment, she nods. "Yeah."

"Why?"

"Guess maybe that's something the shrink can help me figure out, huh?"

"Along with why you slapped me?"

Another laugh. "No, that one I can answer. Because I couldn't believe it took you so *fucking* long to admit how you felt about Luke. Because, you know, if you had, if you'd been up front from the beginning, maybe we could have avoided all of this crap."

I stare out over the half-flattened impatiens. "Maybe. Maybe not." I pause. "Starr's not his, by the way."

"Shit. I'm sorry."

She understands. That's nice. Whether or not it's enough to rebuild our friendship on a stronger, more legitimate foundation, though, I don't know. We'll just have to wait and see.

"Well." Tina gets up, yanking at the seat of her soggy shorts. "I'd better get goin'. You—" She looks behind her, in the direction of Luke's apartment, then back at me. "You be totally honest with him, you hear me?"

"Teen, I don't know…I mean, Jesus, knowing how you still feel—"

"Dammit!" She stamps her foot. "Quit worrying about *me!* Okay? I'm gonna be fine. In fact…"

"What?"

"Well, there's this guy at work, one of the managers?" Twin dots of color rise in her cheeks. "We've only been out for coffee a couple of times—" her eyes shoot to mine "—and God knows I'm not rushing into anything, not until I get my head on straight, but…" One shoulder hitches, accompanied by a half smile. "But he's really nice. And normal. And he's pushing me to go back to school, get my degree. And no, I'm not making it up, I swear."

Laughing, I get up and give her a hug. "You know I only want the best for you," I say into her hair, then lean back. "For all of us."

"Then you march your butt up there," she says, her brows drawn, "and you tell Luke the truth, and you fix this, once and for all. You got that?"

Our gazes mingle for several seconds, then I let out a shaky sigh. "Okay, I'll try—"

"Try, nothing, bitch. You do it." She gives me another hard, fast hug, then clomps off down the sidewalk.

"Teen?" I call after her.

She turns, obviously fighting to keep her emotions in check. Still, I can feel her anguish as if it were my own. Probably because, well, it is.

"You need to talk, you call me, okay?"

"Sure." Then she points in the general direction of Luke's apartment. "Go." Her hand drops. "And you be…everything to him I couldn't, okay?"

My vision blurs. But I get up, forcing my wobbly knees to support me as I take first one step, then another, toward my (don't hate me, I've got to say this) destiny. When I've made it all of ten feet or so, I look back.

But Tina's gone.

* * *

When I get off the elevator, Luke's standing in the open door to his apartment, one arm braced against the jamb.

I start. "How'd you know—"

"I've been jumping out in the hall every time the elevator opened. Scared poor old man Ciccone half to death." He frowns, backing up to let me inside. "Is Tina...is she okay?"

"She wants to be."

I feel Luke's hands on my shoulders, gently turning me to face him. I'm clutching my purse to my stomach to keep from throwing up.

"What about you?" he says.

"I...I..." I stop, giving him what I hope is a beseeching look.

But he shakes his head. "You want me to put words in your mouth, fuggedaboutit. I'm done playin' the safety net. So you got something to say, you just spit it out."

"Okay, fine. Well, see, it's like this. I mean, I guess, what's happened is, um, I haven't been totally honest with you."

Something flickers in his eyes. I decide to take that as encouragement.

"And, well, I thought there were good reasons why I had to keep some things to myself, like, oh, you being married to my best friend, and then you and Tina split so that wasn't an issue except it is still an issue, in a way, because the timing still seems all screwy, you know? Like it's too early or whatever, and then I thought, what if you're on the rebound or something and, well, here I am, convenient and all, and do I really want to be second choice? Then you said all that stuff about confusing friendship with love and how you'd never make the same mistake again, so what's the point of my even saying this..."

He's standing there, stony-faced, not giving me a clue. But there's no turning back now, is there?

"Dammit, Luke—I love you. I've always loved you. And not

in a best friend or like-a-brother kind of way, either, just so you can't possibly misinterpret what I'm saying. And if you can't handle that, I totally understand, so please don't feel bad for me or anything, but I just had to let you know——"

That's as far as I get before Luke takes my face in his hands and smushes his mouth on top of mine. And all I can say is, a millions little *yeses* have just burst from my heart and taken off like a bunch of hatching baby moths.

Okay, so maybe that's not exactly the most romantic image in the world. Deal with it. *Wordplay* isn't exactly a top priority at the moment. But damn, it's nice to finally get kissed by the right guy.

We break apart, panting slightly and looking at each other as if not quite sure what's next. Which is probably because we're not quite sure what's next.

Luke's hands are still framing my face, however, and his eyes are still holding mine captive. So far, so good.

"You're not second best," he says softly. "You never were."

"What?" I bring my hands up to smack his away from me. "Then why the hell didn't you say something, you idiot?"

Hands fly out, brows crash together. "I don't know! Why didn't *you?*"

"Because, birdbrain, I didn't think you were interested in me that way!"

"Well, guess what, lady? You were wrong."

We stare at each other for about half a second, then he yanks me into his arms. Where we kinda cling to each other. Like we'll fall over if either of us lets go. And this might sound really whacked, but I swear I can see Tina giving me a thumbs-up. Finally I mutter, "Is this scary?" into Luke's chest.

"That would be my take on it, yeah."

"But we shouldn't rush into anything, right?"

"Oh, yeah, I was thinkin' we should take it slow, too. You know, get to know each other first and all that shit."

Then he kisses me again. And I sorta blank out there for a second. When I open my eyes, he's grinning down at me. Wickedly. Somehow, I get the definite feeling he was lying about the taking-it-slow thing. I also get the definite feeling I don't have a huge problem with that. Except for the one currently pressing into my stomach.

"You remember our one time?" he says. "You know…in the shower?"

"Vaguely."

"See, that's *my* problem. I'm not real clear on what happened, either." He slips his hands underneath the hem of my shirt, teasing my skin. Everything that can get tight and tingly and wet, does. Oh, yeah—*taking it slow* just got crossed right off the list. "Was it as awful as I remember?"

"Worse."

"Yeah, I was afraid of that." Then he says, "I can do better."

Of course, faced with the reality of what's about to happen, my old buddy Caution butts in with, *"It's too soon….How do you know this isn't just about sex?….What if you do this and realize this is nothing more than a fantasy you've built up in your mind…?"*

Yeah, well, what if the world imploded tomorrow and I never got to feel this man inside me, ever again?

Shaddup, I say to Caution, even as I say, "Prove it," to Luke. Whilst unbuckling his belt buckle.

So he did.

Three times.

And if the world does implode tomorrow? I'm gonna go with a big old grin on my face.

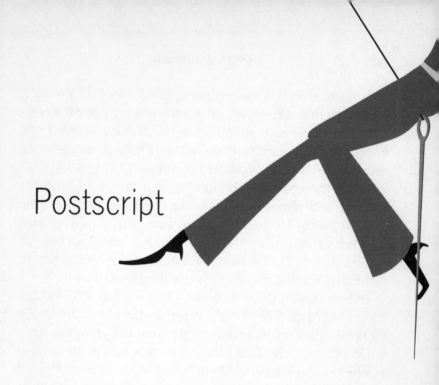

Postscript

Thanks to Tina, I already knew that Luke falls asleep after sex. And snores.

What I didn't know was that he's a cuddler. Which is nice, because I don't think most men are, and I am. So this alone makes him a prize. Of course, I may go deaf with the snoring in my ear, but all I really need is one good ear, right?

Do we have any idea where we go from here? Of course not. I'd like to think we'll get it right this time, but I'm a grown-up now. More or less. I know there are no guarantees.

I also know—now—that shoving the truth into some deep, dark hole in order not to hurt people rarely works. Because the truth, like a piece of glass, always manages to work itself to the surface. Still, human nature being what it is, people will always screw up, and hence always try to cover their asses by shoving the truth into a deep, dark hole. But…does that automatically make someone a bad person? Especially if the motives were, at least in the beginning, good ones? For instance, are the qualities I loved and admired about my grandfather totally erased because of choices he made long before I was born? I don't think so. Is what Luke and I have already doomed because of our past mistakes? I hope not.

Out of the roughly six billion people in the world, probably less than a dozen of them are perfect. And God knows, none of them live in Queens. So I guess all any of us can do is weigh a person's good qualities with their bad and see which ones tip the scale. And then remember that, at any given moment, somebody's doing exactly the same thing with us.

I know there will be those who will wonder why I chose Luke over Alan. (Who I fully intend to stay in touch with, by the way—I see no reason why Starr shouldn't get to know her uncle.) Or why I'm (God help me) starting up a clothing business in Queens instead of Manhattan. If at all. Frankly, I'm not sure, either. Except…this is what I want. This is what's right *for me.* It doesn't have to make sense to anybody else. And thank God (or whoever) that I think (hope?) I'm past needing to shove the truth—*my* truth—into that deep, dark hole.

A hand, firm and warm and gentle, starts stroking my ribs, inching toward my breast. A mouth, soft and hot and tickly, starts nibbling at my neck.

"You're awake," I say, giggling.

"And hungry."

"Chinese?"

Luke kisses me on the mouth, then on the forehead, before pushing himself out of bed. Ohmigod, you should see this butt. Then again, maybe not. I'm not in much of a sharing mood right now.

"I'm thinking," he says, zipping up his jeans, "we should go back and get the Twink. And your sister, if she wants to come along."

I melt. "You really mean that?"

I laugh as he lunges across the bed, pinning me between his arms. Hmm. I'm guessing wrestling will never be the same.

"Why not?" he says. "Unless you think we got something to hide?"

"Nope, not me."

Then his face goes all serious. "What do you want to tell the kid? About the test results?"

I don't even hesitate. "The truth."

He touches my cheek. "You sure?"

"Very."

"Scared?"

"Yeah," I say on a sigh.

"Hey. She gives you any lip, you tell her to take it up with me. 'Cause I've got no trouble telling her that her father was a rat bastard."

"And let you have all the fun? No way."

That gets a chuckle (nice), and another kiss (nicer), then he snatches my clothes off the floor and flings them at me. "So get dressed. Because I seriously need food."

"And I seriously need a shower first."

"Ah, hell—"

"Deal with it, bud," I say, doing the sheet-wrapping thing around me as I shuffle to his bathroom. Where I laugh out loud at the beard-burned, glowing, pudgy little chick grinning back at me from the medicine chest mirror.

The chick who's finally figured out the only truly unforgivable lies are the ones we tell ourselves.

Hey. No comments from the peanut gallery. After all, *finally's* a damn sight better than *never,* right?

You bet your ass it is.

Are you getting it
at least twice a month?

Here's how: Try RED DRESS INK books
on for size & receive two FREE gifts!

Bombshell
by Lynda Curnyn

As Seen on TV
by Sarah Mlynowski

YES! Send my two FREE books.
There's no risk and no purchase required—ever!

Please send me my two FREE books and bill me just 99¢ for shipping and handling. I may keep the books and return the shipping statement marked "cancel." If I do not cancel, about a month later I will receive 2 additional books at the low price of just $11.00 each in the U.S. or $13.56 each in Canada, a savings of over 15% off the cover price (plus 50¢ shipping and handling per book*). I understand that accepting the two free books places me under no obligation ever to buy any books. I can always return a shipment and cancel at any time. Even if I never buy another book from Red Dress Ink, the free books are mine to keep forever.

160 HDN D34M   360 HDN D34N

Name (PLEASE PRINT)

Address   Apt. #

City   State/Prov.   Zip/Postal Code

*Want to try another series? Call 1-800-873-8635
or order online at www.TryRDI.com/free.*

In the U.S. mail to: 3010 Walden Ave., P.O. Box 1867, Buffalo, NY 14240-1867
In Canada mail to: P.O. Box 609, Fort Erie, ON L2A 5X3

*Terms and prices subject to change without notice. Sales tax applicable in N.Y.
**Canadian residents will be charged applicable provincial taxes and GST.

All orders subject to approval. Offer limited to one per household.
® and ™ are trademarks owned and used by the trademark owner and/or its licensee.

© 2004 Harlequin Enterprises Ltd.

**RED
DRESS
INK**

The Last Year of Being Single

Sarah Tucker

**Just because he's perfect
doesn't mean he's Mr. Right....**

Torn between two men—her perfect-on-paper fiancé
and an intoxicating and flirty co-worker—twenty-
nine-year-old Sarah Giles writes a scandalously
honest diary of one life-changing year, and faces
the challenge of writing her own happy ending....